GOSSAMER WING

DELPHINE DRYDEN

B

BERKLEY SENSATION, NEW YORK

THE BERKLEY PUBLISHING GROUP
Published by the Penguin Group
Penguin Group (USA) LLC
375 Hudson Street, New York, New York 10014

USA • Canada • UK • Ireland • Australia • New Zealand • India • South Africa • China

penguin.com

A Penguin Random House Company

GOSSAMER WING

A Berkley Sensation Book / published by arrangement with the author

For information, address: The Berkley Publishing Group,
a division of Penguin Group (USA),
375 Hudson Street, New York, New York 10014.

ISBN: 978-0-425-26577-2

PUBLISHING HISTORY
Berkley Sensation mass-market edition / November 2013

PRINTED IN THE UNITED STATES OF AMERICA

10 9 8 7 6 5 4 3 2 1

Cover photos: *Couple* © Claude Marinesco; *Vintage Image of Eiffel Tower, Paris,
France* © Javarman/Shutterstock.
Cover design by Rita Frangie.
Interior text design by Kelly Lipovich.

GOSSAMER
WING

PROLOGUE

PARIS, FRANCE

Snow would complicate everything.

Jacques Martin kept an eye on the heavy clouds, but his primary focus remained on the hunt. The scrawny Dominion rat had left him with a knot the size of an egg on his head, and the sickest of headaches. He was keen to return the favor.

And he has my freedom in his hands.

The documents, all wrapped up and tidy in their leather pouch, that Martin had planned to present Dubois once he knew their agreement was at an end . . . the boy had them, and probably didn't even know their importance. Didn't know an agent—a brilliant agent, a beautiful woman, Martin's friend—had died for the information on those sheets. He'd taken them because they were there, because they might be worth something to his employers.

The cold raged through Martin's arm and raised a scorching chill below his elbow where metal met skin. He'd forgotten to oil the spring-clamp hand again this morning, and he'd left off the compression sleeve because of the itch. Never again. Already he felt the thing seizing up, become *less* instead of *more*, defeating its own purpose.

Martin ran through the streets of Paris, light and silent on his well-trained feet. Even with his enhanced ear he could barely make out his own footsteps, but he suspected the boy from the American colonies would not be so quiet or so fleet of foot. He'd looked like an analyst, a desk clerk, not a field agent. He could never have defeated Martin in a fair fight. He'd barely gotten away as it was, even with Martin's head still reeling from the first crack it had received.

Idiot, Martin chastised himself. His ears had been covered by a cap, again because the cold made the metal unbearable where it met skin. He hadn't heard the boy sneaking around the corner, had been so certain of his own security that he'd literally plowed into the fool. Then, caught off guard, he'd careened into the sharp brick corner of Dubois's building.

There it was, the sound he sought. A patter of rapid footsteps on a parallel street, the rough breath of a man near the end of his endurance, trying to be quiet as he pushed past his limit. The rat was fitter than Martin had thought, he had to give him that. They were a block apart, Martin calculated, but he could catch up to the boy on the Boulevard des Italiens, which was only a few paces away.

Martin paused at the intersection as the fool broke from the shadowed side street and darted across the broad boulevard, making straight down the block for the Opéra Garnier. Steam cars rattled by, not many of them at one in the morning but enough to make Martin proceed with more caution than the American had demonstrated.

"Paul Girard," the boy had introduced himself two days ago, in flawless unaccented French. He'd cornered Roland Dubois at the opera, as ambitious young men were wont to do on occasion. This young man had raised alarms in Jacques Martin's mind. His French was too smooth, too perfect. The cut of his costly clothing was off, a few years out of fashion. Most of all, Martin had been struck with an impression that the boy was both smarter than he presented himself to be, and lacking in the particular type of puffed up, self-important false confidence that invariably filled these up-and-coming industrialists.

With his enhanced ear covered by a prosthesis and his judgment still cloudy from the morphine he'd taken to manage the pain from his new implants, Martin had been far from alert. When Dubois dismissed his caution about the boy, he didn't pursue it. Dubois had been late for a rendezvous with his new mistress. Martin had been late for his next dose of morphine.

He felt vindicated now, in an ironic way, remembering the young man's startled curse when they collided.

"Bloody hell," the rat had hissed, revealing his true accent in that moment as clearly as if he'd hung a sign around his neck. It was always those little things, those unguarded seconds, that tripped one up. The American boy was still a baby spy, evidently. Martin would not enjoy killing him. But the baby spy had made a mistake in not killing Martin when he had the chance, and Martin would not make the same mistake.

Untimely traffic made crossing the boulevard impossible for several tens of seconds, and Martin cursed under his breath as the boy disappeared around the side of the Opéra. The brief rest refreshed him, however, and he sprinted after his quarry with new vigor once the street cleared.

This time he swung wide around the corner of the building, half expecting the boy to jump out at him. Instead Martin drew to a slow halt, staring at an empty plaza and the street beyond. Nothing. No boy, no cars, no sound from so much as a cat to disturb the night.

He'd lost him. He'd lost the documents.

Horror as cold as the metal biting at Martin's skin filled his mind as he contemplated what Dubois might do if he returned without those pages. Without proof of the device that could secure the martial future Dubois so fervently desired, a weapon of such breathtaking potential that it could change the course of this war . . . and all wars.

"A little insurance," Dubois had told him while he was still groggy from the anesthesia. "To make sure you do follow through on your promise to surrender the papers Simone stole from those English scientists, I had the good surgeon-engineer provide you with an additional implant." His piggy eyes had squinted in delight as he told Martin of the vial of poison planted in Martin's body, and the radiomagnetic trigger device that he, Roland Dubois, would carry with him until Martin had delivered on his end of their exchange.

Martin had gambled with the devil and lost, it seemed. He'd persuaded the engineering giant to provide a pair of implants his own employers refused him, enhancements he thought would make him the greatest spy the world had ever known. Without the documents, however—or perhaps even with them, Martin acknowledged—he was now bound forever to Dubois unless he wanted to die.

Martin did not want to die. He sent up a silent prayer to a God he wished he could still believe in, and like an answer to his prayer he heard a soft scuffle overhead.

The Dominion rat was scrambling up and over the lip of the roof, high atop the Palais Garnier. How he'd scaled the wall Martin couldn't begin to guess, unless the baby spy was an unparalleled second-story man.

Martin didn't linger to guess. He was no second-story man, because he didn't need to be. He could pick any lock ever made and was as silent as death. Within seconds he was inside the building, darting up the stairs that led to the roof. The Opéra was dark that night, but warmer than the outside air, and Martin felt almost hot by the time he topped the final stair and leaned, listening, on the door leading to the roof.

The scuffling sounds of feet on slate told him the boy was still up there and not close to the door. It was as good an opportunity as Martin would get. He swung the door open, silently praising the worker who must have recently oiled the hinges, and scanned the dark rooftop in front of the green glass dome. He saw nothing at first, then movement near the abutment on the opposite side from the wall the American had climbed.

The boy had evidently planned to go up and over, escaping on the opposite side of the building once Martin had given up the search. A decent strategy, Martin supposed, if it hadn't been for the implant that allowed Martin to hear him. That implant, and the metal throughout his forearm, were already chilling again as he crept across the roof toward his prey. Though it felt almost too cold for it now, snow started to fall, dusting all the surfaces. Martin slowed even further to minimize the risk of slipping. His head and arm started to throb all over in the bitter wind.

What the hell is the fool doing?

The boy's back was to Martin, his hands busy at the lip of the abutment, and Martin was still a few steps away when the American stepped up to the railing, turned, and leaped off the side of the Opéra. Martin saw a split second of utter shock as the boy registered his presence, then only blackness and snow where his face had been.

In the second it took for Martin to recover and spot the grappling hook and cord, the American had already made it to the top of the first tier of windows. Leaning over and shoving his coat sleeve up, Martin watched his enemy's progress as he fumbled with his implant, trying to recall by feel exactly where the forearm panel released to reveal a blade. The boy looked up in terror, seeing his death, and whispered, "Charlotte."

But he kept skimming down the wall.

Later Martin would blame the morphine, and perhaps the fear, for his stupidity. He was warned, after all. He had to snatch his fingers away from the icy metal once, because it was so cold it burned. Like a child, he popped one of those fingers into his mouth and sucked the end, warming it up. Then he reached down again and finally found the seam at the panel's edge near his wrist, pressing there firmly with a surge of triumph.

The triumph lasted only until he realized he couldn't pull

the finger away. It had frozen to the metal, like a tongue to a water pump handle. In his village, as a child, the boy who would later become Jacques Martin—*Coeur de Fer*, the notorious Iron Heart—had never been foolish enough to take that dare.

A few seconds' delay were all the false Paul Girard needed. Martin didn't bother to yank his finger away from the metal, though the prospect of the blood and pain was hardly enough to deter him. He simply saw no point. The Dominion rat was already gone, escaping into the night with one last look over his shoulder.

Martin didn't have enhanced vision, but he didn't need it to know what the boy's face must have looked like. Utter astonishment, incredulous relief.

That was exactly what Martin had felt when he'd first spied the pages of notes in his dead mentor's office, and realized what they meant to him. What they could do for him. Simone's parting gift, a piece of intelligence so valuable Martin could use it to strike a Faustian bargain.

Now they were gone, and his hope along with them.

ONE

✦❧✦

DEXTER HADN'T MINDED the commissions at first. A gauntlet-mounted riding rifle here, a stealthy rooftop periscope there. A dog automaton once, for a terminally ill child with allergies to the real thing.

But this . . . he looked at the leather harness in his hands, hefted the weight and swore at some length before his words regained a semblance of coherence.

"And you say he wants *more* rivets? Does he have any idea how much this monstrosity weighs already? The fool won't be able to walk half a mile before he buckles under the weight."

"Aye, sir. But the Marquis's son claims that Lord Ravensward has one that—how did he put it—is armored with rivets like a million brass nipples, gleaming in the sun. I merely quote, sir. The imagery itself was lost on me."

Dexter's sigh spoke nearly as many volumes as his curses

had. "If only they didn't travel in packs. They just incite each other to greater and greater excess."

The younger man snickered. Taking the harness back from his master, he slung it behind him and hooked his arms neatly through the shoulder straps. Then he broke into a curse of his own as the overdecorated strap continued its swing and caught his unsuspecting cheek a nasty blow.

Dexter clamped down on a grin. "Speaking of buckling, that one could probably do with some revision, Matthew. Perhaps three smaller straps, at intervals down the chest, rather than just the one? It would more evenly distribute all that weight."

"I agree, sir. May I take it off and begin on the changes prior to mounting and testing the firearm again? My ears are still ringing from the last time."

"My boy, as long as it's delivered on time and operational for the toff's house party, I really don't care what you do with it in the meantime. I trust you to get the job done."

"Thank you, sir."

Matthew sauntered off, the jangling buckles and creaking straps of the fowling harness making a merry din. Dexter shook his head, still baffled at the vagaries of fashion that so complicated his business at times, before returning his attention to a more interesting project.

An air helmet. He rarely touched the production of such a commonplace item these days, but he always handled Lady Moncrieffe's requests personally.

A monocular telescope was built into one eyepiece of the helmet, with controls that could be worked with the chin or mouth while leaving the hands free. Dexter had spent weeks of his own time on the thing, and frankly felt he had created a small masterpiece. The instrumentation was precise, the optical device providing clear views at a magnification of up to fifty times. All operable by the most subtle wags of the lady's noble jaw or nips of her no doubt aristocratically white and even teeth.

"In blue," her initial commission had specified. "Fleece-lined for warmth at a minimum increase to weight or drag. Overall weight must remain below fifteen hundred grams."

He had made the device per these specifications, which had come to him as usual in the lady's own elegant hand. It had been delivered to her just over a week ago.

That same flawless penmanship graced the note accompanying the rejected helmet when it arrived back at his workshop a few days later.

Dear Mr. Hardison,

The helmet you provided is satisfactory in its technical particulars. However, when I say it must be "blue" I mean it must be the color of a cloudless sky.

Sincerely,
Charlotte, Lady Moncrieffe

He looked at the helmet, which sat on a mesh-covered framework exactly matching the measurements of Lady Moncrieffe's head. The helmet leather was a peacock blue that had been the first stare of fashion this season, and at the time of its crafting Dexter thought it was at least a refreshing change from last year's craze for lilac and peony. It set off the brass nicely too. He'd heard the woman was very fair, and thought the bright blue might suit her.

But sky blue? He couldn't recall the last time he had received a custom order for anything in such a color. Dexter wondered if it was a particular favorite of the widow Moncrieffe, and it occurred to him that he had no real idea of her coloring other than "fair," though he knew practically every dimension of her body from the sundry devices he'd custom-built for her. Perhaps she simply looked good in sky blue.

"The color of a cloudless sky," she had written. For her airship helmet, which she used to see things from very far away while her hands were otherwise occupied.

Perhaps your Ladyship would care to review some

swatches—Dexter began, then put his pen back into its stand and crumpled the piece of notepaper. Retrieving a fresh page, he stared at it for a long moment pondering what he knew of Lady Moncrieffe.

In sum, it wasn't much more than any member of the public might know, despite four years of correspondence with the woman over a variety of topics, sometimes only tangentially related to the commissions she'd sent him. Dexter had always enjoyed those letters, but had never gone out of his way to meet the woman who wrote them lest his fanciful picture of her be marred by a less-than-stunning reality. It was a game he played with himself, picturing the Charlotte Moncrieffe of his imagination, engaging in feats of derring-do most unbecoming a well-bred widow. From their letters he sometimes glimpsed a sly wit, a hint of cheek, and though the Charlotte in his mind had never worn a particular face, she had developed a bit of a cockeyed smile. Even, on occasion, a coquettish dimple beside rosy lips, as she swashbuckled her way through his mental landscape.

Dexter laughed at himself every time he indulged in this fancy. He was no green boy, and he knew himself well enough to know it was probably best they never meet, as he would almost certainly be disappointed. The widows of his real-life acquaintance never derring-did much of anything, and he'd no real reason to think Lady Moncrieffe was the exception despite her penchant for odd contraptions. He was happier daydreaming on occasion about the mysterious woman with the intriguing commissions, content with only the few facts he'd learned through mutual associates.

What he did know for certain was that she was young, and had been widowed very early in her marriage some years prior. An oft-discussed tragic figure, Lady Moncrieffe still wore mourning for her husband and showed no interest in seeking another spouse. She lived on a vast estate not too far north of New York City, and was rarely seen at society events either in her own county or in the city itself.

Yet she had custom-ordered more than one weapon, an array of telescopic and sonic amplification devices, a small steam car and a velocimobile, and a set of equipment for use in mountaineering. And she apparently spent a certain amount of time on an airship, possibly at high altitudes given the need for added insulation. While riding that airship she required the means to view things over a mile away—things on the ground, in other words—while her hands were otherwise occupied.

The color of a cloudless sky.

Dexter realized Lady Moncrieffe was not being poetic, as he had first imagined. He should have known sooner, because she had never been poetic before. No, she literally wanted the helmet to be the color of the sky, and he suddenly suspected her reasons for that had nothing to do with fashion or whim. All Dexter's fancies about what the lady did with his inventions—the ideas he'd always told himself were too far-fetched to be anything but fiction—began to coalesce into one undeniable possibility. There were really only so many reasons a person would require the equipment Lady Moncrieffe had ordered over the years.

Dexter Chen Hardison did not like to do things halfway. To create something that would truly meet the lady's needs, he realized he had a need of his own: information.

The revelation made his return note much easier to write. Three words, in fact, sufficed.

My dear Lady Moncrieffe,

To what purpose?

Yrs, D. C. Hardison

By return mail the next day he received the answer he had already deduced, and it was even shorter than his own message.

Hardison—

Camouflage.

* * *

"PACKAGE JUST DELIVERED, ma'am."

"Thank you, Smits. Put it in my study, I'll open it after luncheon." Charlotte, Lady Moncrieffe, returned to her cold salmon and travel brochures, only to note that Smits yet stood his solemn, quiet ground at her shoulder.

"Yes?" she asked after waiting a moment to see if he would ever clear his throat to gain her attention.

"Beg pardon, m'lady, but the young gentleman who brought the package insists on delivering it personally. He says he's to report back to the makesmith on its suitability."

"Oh!" The smith had sent a boy along with her helmet? Charlotte wasn't sure whether this boded well or ill. "Well, take *him* to the study then, and offer him some refreshment. I'll be along shortly."

Smits vanished on his errand, leaving his mistress alone at the little round glass table in the solarium. Charlotte yearned to dash to the study as soon as he was away. Instead she gave it all of five minutes before rising gracefully from her meal and gliding along to the study as elegantly as if all society were watching her to learn how to behave.

The makesmith hadn't sent a boy, it transpired. He had sent a young gentleman, as Smits said. With a voice as refined as if he'd been sent off to spend his formative years at Eton, the young man greeted Charlotte and presented his box with a flourish. She was still trying to sort out where on Earth he must have come from when she pulled the contents of the box free from a layer of cotton wool, and finally beheld the result of her commission.

It was perfect.

The helmet was indeed the blue of a cloudless sky, and more specifically the very pale and almost pearly blue of the sky on a clear winter day. The layer of fleece that lined it had been tinted to complement the delicate hue.

The fittings astonished Charlotte almost to the point of breathlessness. She hadn't thought to request anything other than the usual brass or nickel. It had never occurred to her . . .

"What on earth has he done to the metal?" she gasped, running her fingers over the glassy-smooth matte surface.

The young man chuckled, touching the rim of the ocular with evident appreciation. "Everything he could think of, I suspect. He started by enameling the original brass. But that was apparently too glossy, and added too much weight."

Every piece of metal, from the ocular device and controls right down to the row of tiny buckles fastening down the back of the headpiece, were the same dull, pale gray blue. No extraneous pieces impeded the helmet's smooth lines, no decorative rivets or designs tooled into the leather. Only soft blue kid and cool, functional metal. Charlotte hefted the helmet, which seemed even lighter than the earlier model.

"This doesn't look enameled, and it's very light indeed."

"Yes ma'am," the young man agreed. "He tried a number of other processes before finally rebuilding the entire ocular frame from anodized aluminium. The matte texture took a few tries to accomplish, however. Still not sure how he did that and he isn't telling, but I know he swore at least one of our metallurgists to secrecy on pain of death."

The man's wink was cheeky but not offensive, and it looked naggingly familiar. But how could a young make-smith be familiar?

"I'm sorry, have we met, Mr. . . . ?"

"Pence, ma'am. Matthew Pence." He sketched a little bow scarcely less cheeky than his wink.

"Matthew—not Sir Paul Pence's boy?"

"The same."

"But I thought you were off at Oxford."

"I was. My parents certainly hoped I would return to the estate once I finished, ma'am, but I finally convinced them my time would be better spent right now working for Mr. Hardison."

It was not an entirely unprecedented move on Pence's part. More and more of the young aristocracy, second sons in particular, were turning to the new industrial trades. They didn't all need the money, necessarily, but all who hoped to prosper in the new century knew that industry would soon outstrip agriculture as the primary business of the American Dominions. Especially now that the war with France had officially ended, and the manufacturers could turn their attention away from battle machines to consumer goods once more.

Still, Pence's father had inherited and built on a fortune in the import-export line, and one might have expected his only son to study some polite subject at university then return to take over the family business.

"I'm . . . rather handy, you see," the young man offered in explanation of his aberration from the traditional path.

"Well, you're certainly in good company. I'm quite sure Baron Hardison's father never expected his son to become a makesmith either, but he seems to have done quite well in that vocation."

Matthew's mouth curled up at one corner. "He doesn't like us to use his title, ma'am."

"Of course. *Mister* Hardison. Excuse me, I had forgotten. You may convey my compliments to him, Mr. Pence. The helmet is exactly what I needed."

IN THE SKY, things were quiet. Cold, and sometimes uncomfortable, but blessedly quiet except for the intermittent rush of the gas feed and the occasional radio transmission.

When Charlotte had first seen the tiny dirigible called *Gossamer Wing*, she hadn't understood how it could possibly do all its inventor claimed. It looked more fantasy than machine.

Indeed, she thought as she made a minute adjustment to starboard and began the steep climb to cruising altitude, the miniature airship was her fantasy embodied, for all it was a technological marvel. One of her fantasies, at any rate.

A pity it must remain invisible to all but a few, and unknown to most. That was its purpose, however: high-altitude surveillance, nearly undetectable to the naked eye or even the average spyglass. That, and undetectable second-story work. Charlotte hoped to become the first field agent to use the vehicle in France, gathering information in an entirely new way, going where others could not. And then, assuming her superior in Le Havre approved the final mission, she might even use the *Gossamer Wing* to help prevent the French from developing a weapon that was almost guaranteed to bring war back to the globe.

Charlotte's ears clicked and she glanced at the altimeter, knowing she was near five thousand feet up even before the gauge confirmed it. Easing her angle of ascent, she smiled at the soft chime that marked another thousand feet of altitude above baseline. Her new inner ears were no less a wonder than the *Gossamer Wing*, and they allowed her to enjoy this part of her work in a way she'd never anticipated.

Silence. It was so rare, so precious. Even an empty house was never truly silent. There were always servants, guests, the nagging voice of one's own determined conscience. There was always the overwhelming absence, roaring at her by omission, reminding her the house she lived in had been meant for a family. That it was her husband's house, and he had died before she even learned to be a proper wife to him.

Reaching for the valve to her left, Charlotte cut the gas feed to the silken blimp and relaxed her legs within the rigging. Floating suspended, easy as a cloud, like a waking dream of effortless flight. The chill air swept through her, swept her clean, swept away all the doubts that gathered like so much dust while her feet were on the ground.

"*Shhhhh-ch* clear today but *shhhhhh-whoosh-ch-ch-ch* devil are you, Charlotte?"

She chuckled as she toggled the microphone switch. For all his many years of experience in the field, her father was still terrible at radio communications, always forgetting to hold the transmitter button down as he spoke.

"I'm directly over your house, sir. In fact"—she swiveled her jaw to the right, nudging the ocular control to zoom in on the ground below, raking her gaze over the scene until she found what she was looking for—"you're wearing that red cravat I like. Very dashing, but you have crumbs in your beard."

"Bloody *chhhhhh-shhhh*."

Her laugh overloaded the microphone, creating a moment of sharp feedback. Charlotte cursed and jerked her head at the sound, ruining her focus and causing her to bobble downward. The ringing vibration and sudden shift in position made her head and stomach swim for several moments, and she had to clench her teeth to keep her breakfast kippers from making an unwanted reappearance.

"Remember thou art mortal," she chided herself. An airship, particularly one as tiny and responsive as this one, was no place for tomfoolery.

"Godlike aspirations, my dear? Perhaps it's time you came down to earth."

That had come through loud and clear, at least.

"Presently. I'm still testing the controls on the new helmet. I need my mouth for that. I'll speak to you when I'm down." After toggling the radio off, she put the proof to her words by gripping the flat leather tab between her teeth and giving an experimental tug. A whirr sounded and a gray-violet filter snicked into place over the ocular's primary lens. The world jumped into sharp contrast below her. Another tug, and a glare filter darkened the view. Charlotte thought such a filter might be especially welcome when flying over water.

Whirr . . . snick. A moment's confusion resolved as she realized she was seeing a version of the world filtered to show only red.

Whirr . . . snick. Green, blue.

Clever.

She had been very specific with her requests in the past, and what she had received from the Makesmith Baron had been meticulous, beautifully crafted, and precisely what she had asked him to build.

But when he asked the purpose and she gave him no further guidance than "camouflage," he had given her all this. Options she hadn't even known existed, tools she would never have thought to ask for.

"I may never give him more than one word of direction

again," she mumbled to herself around the mouthful of leather. The movement of her jaw triggered the sensitive device, sending it clicking through several filter changes before it stopped. Disoriented, Charlotte clutched too hard at the airship's pitch control, skewing sharply downward several yards before she could correct. She very nearly lost her stomach's payload again. And again, she knew she had nobody but herself to blame.

Two

UPPER NEW YORK DOMINION

"It's finally ready, then."

Neville, Viscount Darmont, sounded more resigned than pleased at the news as he led the way inside the stately manor house.

"I believe so."

"You're resolved to do this, Charlotte? It's not too late for them to assign somebody else, you know."

She whirled on him, snapping her gloves against her thigh. "This is my project, Father. Mine." Then, more gently, "Do I ask for so much? I only want to serve the Crown as you do. As Reginald did. You of all people should never question my motivation."

"Oh, you hate the French, I've no doubt at all of that, and I won't say you've no cause." He rushed on when Charlotte opened her mouth to interrupt. "But I might well question your objectivity as well as your fitness for such a dangerous assignment. You have doubts of your own, or you wouldn't have gone behind my back from the start to volunteer your field services with the Agency. You knew I would object, and you knew why."

"You're my father, of course you object. It's dangerous. I didn't go behind your back, though. I merely waited until Lord Waverly had approved my participation and I had completed initial training before informing you of my plan to follow in your illustrious footsteps, sir."

The deliberately applied charm, the hint of a dimple at the end of her statement, was a rare glimpse at the impish Charlotte of the past. She knew it would distract and soften her father. He had always been helpless before the dimple.

"My dear, I would tell you that Reginald would have hated to see you risk yourself, but the truth is I'm sure he would have found you every bit as enthralling in this as he seemed to find you in all other things." They had reached her father's study, and he took his usual chair with more than his usual sigh of relief to be off his feet.

Enthralling? Reginald had always seemed so controlled, so determined and deliberate. *Enthralled* sounded like such an undisciplined, hapless state of being. Charlotte's skepticism must have shown, because her father smiled and shook his head as she seated herself opposite him. "I forget how short a time you really knew him as an adult. As his friend, I assure you he was more captivated by you than he ever let on."

Despite all the secrets their lives held, Charlotte and her father had never sought to conceal their thoughts and memories of her late husband, Darmont's protégé. She found it a relief to talk about Reginald openly, fondly. Most people were painfully delicate about it, though, including her mother who still treated her like a Tragic Young Widow.

"He did let on, in his own way. But thank you."

"There's a more pressing problem. Can you really spend weeks, perhaps months, effectively hiding how much you despise the French, even under this new Égalité government? You will tend to encounter a fair number of them in France."

"But Father," she said, dimpling again, *"J'adore Paris au printemps. Et Honfleur est tout a fait charmante!"*

"This isn't a game or a masquerade ball. Nor is it the office work you're accustomed to doing for the Agency. It could be *months*, Charlotte," he reminded her. He apparently had some selective immunity to her charm, or perhaps her demeanor was simply not as charming in French. "Yet another matter presses. In addition to recovering the documents and determining whether the French have started building their own device yet, Murcheson still wants a professional consultation on-site regarding some of the equipment at the new facility. He agrees with me that we can kill several birds with one stone by bringing in somebody from the outside, and Whitehall has approved a plan that will provide the perfect cover for you both."

Something about the way her father said "somebody from the outside" suggested to Charlotte that he had a particular somebody in mind. "What are the various birds, what is the plan and whom might this convenient new colleague be?"

"Hmm. Yes. Would you care for tea?" He reached for the bell pull before she could answer. "The birds are as follows: the consultation is necessary because a fresh pair of expert eyes might solve some of the lingering technical problems Murcheson's people have failed to conquer during this past year or more. Our own personnel are not without their talents, but they are only the ordinary sort of geniuses. They create what they are asked to create, quite brilliantly at times, but their vision is somewhat circumscribed. 'To a man with a hammer, everything is a nail,' that sort of thing."

Camouflage, thought Charlotte. To Hardison, one word had been more effective than a laundry list of specifications. He was not, it was clear, any ordinary sort of genius. "Go on."

"A makesmith could also perform any necessary on-the-spot modifications to the airship you might require. Someone from the outside has the added advantage of having no history with the Agency. One or two discreet visits from a social equal, conversations undertaken in private where there is no danger of eavesdroppers. It would be easy enough to approach him without anyone thinking a thing about it. Such a person would have no other record of a connection with our activities. Even if he fell under suspicion, there would simply be nothing for the French to discover, no matter how thoroughly they investigated."

"Assuming such a person would agree to work for you, of course. And have the time, means and inclination to leave his business and go haring off to France for weeks or possibly months."

"There is that, but that brings us to the plan. You're the widow of a baronet, and you've been quite famously in near seclusion for an unfashionably long mourning. Now, now," he waved off her protest, "we both know you've been far busier with your work than anyone knows, and the seclusion at your estate has made a very convenient cover for your absences during training. The fact remains, you're still known to people, and if we ship you off to France you will almost certainly be noticed there. You must have a plausible cover. Given the choice of your traveling companion, you must also comport with Whitehall's antiquated notions of propriety when it comes to female and male agents traveling together."

The twist to his mouth told Charlotte everything she needed to know. He hadn't been able to prevent her taking the assignment to become the first agent piloting a surveillance dirigible, nor had he been able to keep her from volunteering to use that dirigible to recover the lost weapon plans the British so desperately needed now that the French appeared to be gearing up for hostilities again—so he had engineered an obstacle, a challenge, to try to dissuade her. He expected her to cry off when she heard this new condition. He had invoked Whitehall—clever of him to refer to the faceless bureaucracy of the entire administrative wing of government, rather than blaming any individual Charlotte might try to make her case with—but she knew the real objection was his own. She also knew the officials in Philadelphia were far more puritanical than their counterparts in Whitehall. Still, it was a canny move on her father's part to point the finger of blame all the way across the Atlantic.

Her father underestimated her resolve. Whatever it was,

whatever she must do, Charlotte told herself she would accept it. Though she had never been a rebellious child, she was angry enough at her father's interference that she knew she would meet this challenge if for no other reason than to prove him wrong. And this mission was not only vital to the Crown, it was vital to Charlotte—a chance to literally follow in her late husband's footsteps and carry out the objective he'd never been able to complete.

"Traveling together?"

"That's the cover, you see. You and the consultant in question will pose as newlyweds, honeymooning in France."

"You want me to . . ." Despite her resolve, her jaw fell open for a moment as she saw the trap her father had led her into. A career was one thing, a reputation quite another, and her father knew as well as anyone how delicate the reputation of a widow could be.

The gleam of triumph in his eye gave him away. He thought he'd won, and his voice was almost jubilant as he continued. "The difficulty, of course, is that we can hardly faux marry you off to just anyone; it must be somebody plausible. Somebody who might conceivably have known you well enough socially to see you during your isolation and woo you out of your grief. Perhaps someone with whom you have already established a correspondence."

Charlotte kept her bitter smile to herself. "Someone . . . titled?"

Viscount Darmont might look genial and portly and getting on in years, but his amiable round face concealed a mind still sharp as a knife, and he knew his daughter did not tend toward idle speculation. "Indeed."

"I see. This is all beginning to sound a good deal more public than I had anticipated. And is this actually to be a faux marriage? Or is the Agency counting on a great deal more loyalty than that from myself and the titled gentleman in question?" She couldn't imagine that her superiors in either Philadelphia or Whitehall would risk the French discovering that the marriage of two such illustrious Americans was a sham. Not when such a discovery would mean unwanted scrutiny of their motives.

"You'd be allowed an annulment afterward. In the meantime, your mother would be thrilled. A baroness for a daughter." If Charlotte hadn't known him better, she might have missed the hint of smugness in his tone as he waited for her to demur. But she wouldn't. She couldn't. Not now. If this was what she must do . . .

"Goodness, and she had abandoned all hope of my ever marrying my way up in this world."

His smile faltered as he waited in vain for her to say more. "Charlotte, you can't mean to go through with such a scheme. Even for the sake of the Crown, it's too much to ask. There would have to be an actual wedding. You would have to share quarters on the ship, hotel rooms."

"Oh, but I do mean to go through with it, Father. It sounds like an excellent cover story, precisely because it's so implausible that anyone would go to such lengths. And as you say, we can have it annulled afterward. That will disappoint Mother, naturally, but it can't be helped."

For a long moment they locked gazes, fading steely slate eyes staring down ice-chip blue. Then the Viscount glanced toward the door as one of the upstairs maids opened it to make way for the tea cart automaton. A frippery, but Charlotte knew he ordered it when she was visiting because she had adored it as a child. The brass gleamed as bright now as it had then, a polish no mechanical means could ever accomplish quite as well as human hands wielding a soft rag and a simple compound of diatomaceous earth and naphtha. The gentle metallic clanking as the machine eased to a halt by her armchair was a sweet, soothing moment of auditory nostalgia.

She poured, but left her own tea cooling in the cup as she waited for her father to speak again.

"Political marriages are hardly uncommon even in these modern times," he offered at last, only the taut whiteness about his mouth revealing the extent of his dissatisfaction.

"I suppose I shouldn't be too shocked that you've outdone me at my own game. You have grown cold, Charlotte, these past five years. Perhaps pretending to like the French will be easy compared to pretending to be a happy young bride."

She ignored the insult. "I will do both, difficult or not. Will you be the one talking to him, then?"

She didn't pretend not to know the target of the Agency's plan. Her father's plan. It would have insulted them both. She was far too much like her father, Charlotte often thought, for all she was a physical copy of her mother, Lavinia.

"Yes. With your permission, I'll visit his workshop tomorrow and speak with him."

"My permission?" Her gaze flew around the room, landing on the frescoed ceiling, on the bookshelf, on the tea cart—anywhere but her father's face. She had no reasonable explanation for the embarrassment she could feel staining her face. "Isn't this a fine mess? The father asks his daughter's permission to go propose to a man she's never met?"

An interesting man. A man she had corresponded with for years, but with whom she had never truly *communicated* until that recent brief missive, jotted in a moment of frustration. Not another agent ordered on a mission, someone she could be polite and collegial with, but a person who would have his own unknowable motives for accepting such a dangerous charge from the Crown . . . if he did accept.

"Would you like to accompany me?" her father asked, as if the thought genuinely hadn't occurred to him until that moment. Perhaps it hadn't, as he'd so obviously expected her to reject the mission once the new condition was revealed. He'd been right to expect that. Any sane woman would have rejected it. "Or even go in my stead?"

"No." She hoped she didn't sound as abrupt as she felt. She wished she knew why her heart was racing. Charlotte lifted her teacup to her lips, finally taking a sip. "Tell him that the helmet is perfect."

"The new blue thingum with the outlandish eyepiece?"

She nodded, and then thought a moment before adding,

"Remember not to use his title. Apparently he doesn't like it."

DEXTER BELIEVED IN serendipity, believed in the importance and necessity of luck in his work. It was key to his sense of humility; he never took a moment of insight or an accidental discovery for granted. He worked hard, he reasoned through problems, he persevered, but sometimes it all came down to a combination of circumstances no one could control.

At times his delight in the serendipitous was tested, however, and his ability to accept the guiding role of Fate severely strained.

All Dexter could think of as he listened to Lord Darmont's proposal with dawning comprehension and disbelief, was that it was a short step from embracing one's fate to being Fortune's fool. If he wasn't careful, Fortune was just as apt to bugger him senseless and leave him for dead as she was to favor him. He wasn't stupid. He knew what a fickle bitch Fortune could be.

He wondered if Lady Moncrieffe might be an even worse one.

"I can't have understood you correctly, Lord Darmont," he said after hearing the man through the first time. "I mean to say, I do want to provide any service I can to the Crown and the Commonwealth, and I've no great love for the French. If it is within my power to help retrieve these plans and aid your colleagues in whatever it is they're constructing, naturally I will do what I can to assist. But—"

"It's the part where you participate in a not-quite-sham marriage to my daughter that has you stymied, eh?" For a wonder, the man sounded as though he were no more put out about the prospect than he might be about a troublesome argument between two of his tenants, or a horse that hadn't performed as well as expected at Saratoga. "Can't say I'm thrilled about it either, but she knows her own mind. She has her mission to perform and her own reasons for going through with it regardless of the additional conditions Whitehall has set."

"May I ask about her particular reasons?"

"I'm sure you may. Whether she answers you is no concern of mine."

"I see." He didn't quite, but Dexter got the impression Lord Darmont would not take well to being pushed on points he clearly wished to skirt.

"You made her a hat," the older gentleman said suddenly.

"Beg pardon?"

"Charlotte. You made her a funny sort of hat, for flying with that bubble of hers. She reports that it is perfect. Said she could see the crumbs in my beard from a mile in the sky. And she told me not to use your title, because you wouldn't like it."

Dexter fought an urge to punch at the air in jubilation. He had known, *known* she would like his modifications.

"Helmet, sir. It was a helmet. I'm very pleased it met her requirements adequately."

The portly Viscount was watching him with eyes that missed nothing. "She was very happy about that funny hat, Hardison. Happier, in fact, than I've seen her since her husband died. When you meet with her to discuss all this, as I suspect you will arrange to do as soon as I depart, you could do worse than to ask her about his death. Get it out of the way."

"I'll try to remember. Sir, it's my understanding that the Treaty of Calais was supposed to bring an end to this sort of activity. Haven't our agents been recalled from France? And theirs from England?"

Darmont shrugged. "I didn't take you for a naïve man, Hardison. Perhaps I was wrong."

"We still have spies in France."

"Yes," Darmont confirmed. "We still have spies in France. The French still have spies all over the Commonwealth, including the American Dominions. The old French government, the ousted post-royalist party who never wanted the treaty signed in the first place, have spies among the current French government, the Égalité types. Officially, of course, nobody in any of these governments knows a thing about all that. Nor do I. Officially."

"And the treaty?"

"Did the treaty make you start trusting the French overnight?"

While Dexter mulled this question over, Darmont stood and wandered over to the rear wall of Dexter's workroom, to the one frivolous element of design he had allowed himself when converting the room from a parlor to its current purpose. A portion of unplastered stone wall several feet wide was obscured by complex layers of pistons and gears, ranging in size from a few inches to a yard across. The cogs turned, the pistons drove here and there, the whole thing seemed nearly alive with purposeful motion. Its top and bottom workings disappeared into the floor below and ceiling above, suggesting it was clearly only part of some larger mechanism. To keep the dust off, the whole thing was secured under an improbably large pane of heavy glass.

"This is part of the original house, isn't it? The room, I mean, not . . . this thing here."

"Yes, sir. The first Baron built it shortly after the Colonial Uprising. His was one of the first Dominion titles." Those titles had secured land for a growing body of restless gentry in Britain, who were happy enough to swear new oaths of fealty to the Crown—and agree to forego the usual seats in the House of Lords, as they wouldn't be present to vote—in exchange for the prospect of nobility and wealth in the newly subdued American Dominions.

"I wonder what he would think of this, your ancestor?" Now Darmont was talking about the wall.

Dexter smiled, feeling much more at his ease discussing this than he had the surreal prospect of marrying Lady Moncrieffe in order to go help her spy on the French in violation of an international treaty. "I suspect he would be amused that I'd left it exposed, but I doubt he would mind. He did build it, after all. Or at least he started the process."

He enjoyed the Viscount's expression; the man was clearly startled. Dexter always enjoyed telling this tale.

"He was a suspicious old curmudgeon, you see, and after he was widowed at age fifty or so he married again to a much younger woman. She was very beautiful, and he was predictably jealous despite her being, by all accounts, the most virtuous creature ever born and quite in love with the old fool.

"He couldn't bear to be apart from her, and she did like to take a solitary ride every fine morning. It preyed on his nerves not to know where she went, but he dreaded the thought that she might catch him spying and think ill of him, or think he didn't trust her. So he rigged a sort of spy-glass on the roof. The stairs were hell on his rheumatism, though, so next he developed a periscope in order to watch her while remaining in his own study."

"I think I see the direction this will take," quipped the Viscount.

"These things never end well, do they?" Dexter agreed. "From there it became a fixation, and then an obsession. He couldn't see past the row of trees after she entered the lane from the south gate, but she would certainly question the removal of such a fine old row of elms. So he put a crude sensor in the gate, that tripped a bell if the gate was opened. The system grew in complexity, and he guarded his study as closely as Bluebeard guarded his wives' heads."

"We all know how that turned out. Can I assume this tale had an unhappy end?"

"Unhappy, possibly," Dexter allowed with a smile and a shrug, "but at least not grisly. He did get found out eventually, of course, and she was furious. Nevertheless, she went on to bear him five children that looked too much like him to doubt their parentage, so one can only assume some sort of treaty was arrived at."

"Based on the evidence of the children?"

"And on her journal. She was alternately horrified and flattered by his intensity."

"The first Baron Hardison was not a stable chap, I take it."

"Mad as a hatter, I suspect. But a dab hand with the gadgetry." Dexter took a moment to appreciate the wall of delicate machinery in front of him. "Of course his devices were mostly glorified trip wires and the like. Levers to pull at bells, essentially, with a few extra steps in between. But the second and third Barons added their own fillips, most notably the clockworks. All the clocks in the house are synchronized by this system here. It's still wound from a central location in the kitchens each morning. My grandfather added fans and thermostats. Centralized temperature control. I've contributed intrastructural communication devices. And this is a cross-section of the entire system. Remarkable, really."

"Your grandfather was the one who married Eliza Chen."

"Yes, sir." He couldn't help the note of pride that crept into his voice at the mention of his famous grandmother, who'd been a formidable political activist.

Lady Moncrieffe's father turned that oddly calculating gaze on him again. "And two generations later, her crusade for workers' rights and the destruction of the class system is honored posthumously by your habit of styling yourself *Mister* Hardison?"

Dexter stared back, suddenly feeling all the potential danger of this man. He heard, in Darmont's pointed questions, the equally sharp intelligence of his daughter. At least if her letters were any indication. He wondered again what she looked like, and vaguely hoped she took after her mother.

"I don't denounce my heritage, and I don't forego the use of my title out of any altruistic notions about the populace, Lord Darmont. One day I may take up the title and wield it for the public good if I can, but at the moment my business interests here and elsewhere aren't well-served by reminding people of my ancestry. You know it takes a great deal of money to maintain one's estate. The French and the Spanish buy all sorts of equipment from my workshops. They don't mind dealing with an American inventor, but I suspect they might be less sanguine about negotiating with the Makesmith Baron."

He threw the epithet out and waited for a response.

"But it's the Makesmith Baron who would make such a convenient husband for my daughter. You would need to use your title, foster the notion that you're a typical blithe aristocrat. Play the baron to Charlotte's baroness."

They both knew the truth of that. What other single man could fulfill all the necessary roles for this particular political ploy? Who else had the technical expertise to advise the Agency's engineers and work on the dirigible if necessary, the conveniently public disinterest in politics and the perfect credentials of gentility to marry the widow of a baronet, daughter to the eminently respectable Viscount Darmont?

Serendipity.

And Matthew, upon his return from delivering the "funny hat," had waxed rather lyrical regarding the physical charms of the widow Moncrieffe. He had met her a few times before, he said, but had clearly been too callow a youth at the time to appreciate the qualities of such a subtle blossom. He was no longer too callow, apparently. Dexter supposed the woman took after her mother, after all.

"Pocket Venus," Matthew had extolled. "Chilly as a winter day, and black isn't her color, but still. Fire under all that ice, you know? You forget she's tiny while you're talking to her, then all of a sudden it strikes you that you could break her in two if you weren't careful. Although . . ."

"Although?" Dexter had tried to pretend he wasn't interested in Pence's prurient gossip. He'd remained bent over his workbench, pencil in hand, sketching a design that wouldn't leave his mind's eye.

"She wouldn't break, I suspect. There's steel there." Hardly the thing to say in compliment to a delicate lady. But he said it with admiration.

Dexter hadn't risen to the bait. He hadn't asked for more detail about the potential charms of the interesting widow with her inexplicable need for esoteric devices. For *camouflaged* devices.

Now that he knew the reason for the camouflage, he had more difficulty concealing his desire to learn more, and to meet her face-to-face at last. She was intriguing, this Lady Moncrieffe, with her mourning turned to espionage and her father who was willing to pander her to him on a temporary basis if necessary. Not that her father seemed happy with the idea.

"Did you mean for her to be the inducement, sir?" Dexter asked him. He was politely horrified by the very notion, and mortified to have to ask, but he thought it best to have it out in the open either way. "I would have taken this on for Crown and country. Even if nothing comes of it, you can depend on my discretion. Title or no, I think my reputation and my family's honor are insurance enough of that."

"I *meant* for her to continue her safe, sedate work decoding documents for the Agency. Before that, I meant for her to marry my protégé Reginald and induce him into an early retirement from the field," the Viscount said gruffly, not meeting the younger man's eyes. "I also meant to have a grandchild or two to dandle on my knee by this time. Instead I have a daughter who rarely smiles, who wears black all the time and looks terrible in it and who wants to turn her work into some sort of clandestine suttee. If I could forbid her to work for the Agency, or even persuade her to give up this profession and look for a new husband in earnest, to build a happier life for herself, I would. As I can't, I will do my best to further her interests in the path she has chosen."

He smiled a resigned sort of smile, and Dexter saw the clean, aristocratic lines of his profile pulled into prominence for a moment. "I can't keep her safe. She's a grown woman, and I can hardly tell her not to do what I've admittedly done dozens of times. Not the marriage part, of course, I've only done that once, but the mission itself. This work is addictive, I warn you. Few escape it once they've begun."

"I'll take my chances on that, I suppose."

"The primary mission is Charlotte's, fetching this blue-print or whatsis that our man in Le Havre thinks may still be secreted somewhere in Paris. He'd like to rule it out, at least. I think it's a fool's errand and there's no chance the damn thing is still there after so many years. But we also need your expertise, Hardison. Badly. I think I can guarantee that once you learn what your part of the project is about—assuming you agree to the terms the Agency sets, of course—you will be so eager to work on it that the rest will fade into insignificance. It's the type of thing a man like you would never be able to resist. One day, it could make you very, very famous indeed."

"That part doesn't interest me," Dexter rushed to assure him.

"It is true nevertheless. The project is its own inducement, and if Murcheson is wrong and the French do have those documents, success only becomes more critical. There are other ways you could help too, unique tasks you could undertake that I think you would enjoy immensely once you set your hands to them. You won't get such an opportunity sitting at home. Charlotte is . . . a condition of the arrangement. You would be the perfect cover for one another. And as far as I'm concerned, that means her best chance of survival is with you."

Three

❧

UPPER NEW YORK DOMINION

EASY ENOUGH TO listen to a man discuss a proposed undertaking. It was an abstraction, a fancy, being asked to provide
assistance to the Crown in its clandestine efforts to conduct
espionage on the French despite the recent peace treaty
between the two nations. The offer of Darmont's daughter's
hand in marriage—however temporary—only lent an additional air of surrealism to the Viscount's words.

It was another thing entirely to stand in a beautifully
appointed solarium in the Upper New York Dominion,
awaiting the arrival of a woman to whom he might become
a sham spouse for a few months or even longer. Not to mention the woman who had fascinated him on paper for years.

The house itself had surprised him already. He was
expecting something as solid, staid, respectable as his own
stately residence. A manor house in the traditional style, or
perhaps even a small Italianate palace. Not this frosted layer
cake of a folly, with so many details on its façade he wasn't
sure which to smirk at first. The interior was at least more

subdued, if still somewhat more frivolous than expected. The solarium itself, with glass walls and ceiling panels bordered in intricate wrought-iron scrollwork frames, was the view from the inside of the wedding cake.

"*Mister* Hardison."

Lady Moncrieffe didn't match her house.

Not her voice, which was surprisingly low and sweet. Nor her severe, high-necked black jacket and jabot, or the tailored fawn breeches and high boots that suggested she'd recently come in from a ride.

And not her face, which was anything but a folly. She was quietly beautiful despite the unflattering black; the stark color served only to heighten the impact of her fair skin and hair. Skin like a white peach, Dexter noted with an instant, inappropriate desire to touch her cheek and see if it was as soft as it looked. Hair like a sweep of pale gold silk. And eyes . . .

Eyes that were icy blue, and staring him down rather coldly as he tried not to gape like a fish at the wholly unexpected vision before him.

"Lady Moncrieffe." He gave a short bow from the waist, to which she only nodded in return.

"And now, at least, we have established that we know one another's names."

He glanced back up, startled, to see a hint of humor flash behind her chilly mien. Only a moment, wry and sharp, gone before it could be pinned down. He thought he spied a dimple, but it vanished before he could be quite sure. Dexter had imagined that dimple, that spark of humor, so many times he felt a shock of recognition.

"It's a pleasure to meet you at last. I've enjoyed our correspondence these past few years. It should have occurred to me to make your acquaintance in person much sooner." Dexter clamped his mouth shut before he could say anything more. He feared he might blurt something all too revealing about his reaction to the lady's stunning looks, or that hint of something-or-other he could still feel from his head to his toes and points between. Particularly points between.

He didn't have to know her well to grasp that it would be a mistake to mention any of that at this point. He shouldn't even be thinking any of that.

"I always look forward to your letters. And your marvelous creations, naturally. Would you care to sit down, Mr. Hardison?"

He took the seat she indicated, hoping the delicate gilded chair didn't creak or simply give way under his weight. It held. Apparently, it was stronger than it looked. He tried to think of something to say, anything at all, but words failed him. Nothing in his life had prepared him for a scene in which he came to discuss an arranged marriage with a beautiful woman for the purpose of enabling them both to commit acts of international espionage.

"Your father visited me yesterday," he finally began. "He seemed slightly less uncomfortable than I believe us both to be at the moment."

She lifted an eyebrow at him as she sank gracefully into the chair opposite him. "He's cagey, I know that much. He wouldn't have wanted you to think him uncomfortable. Whether he was or not. He can't have been elated."

"I daresay not."

"I've ordered us some tea. Unless you'd prefer something stronger?"

"Bit too early in the day for anything stronger for me, but I thank you. Tea will suffice."

"What did he tell you? I don't mean about the specifics of the mission, I'm sure he told you only enough about that to get your curiosity raging. What did he tell you about this part of the arrangement, Mr. Hardison? About me?"

A stray cloud crossed the sun's path, filtering the light in the solarium down to a wintry gray. Without the sunbeams glancing around her head Lady Moncrieffe looked much more human, much less like an angel fallen to earth for the purpose of mourning. Her face, stripped of its poetic overlay for the moment, was all business. And her manner was very reminiscent of her father. On her, it was strikingly attractive. Dexter thought that on her, nearly anything would be strikingly attractive. Why hadn't he ever tried to meet her in person before?

"I asked him what your particular motivations were, and he told me I would have to ask you. Said I should ask you about your late husband, if I may be so blunt."

"Father's melodramatic at times. My late husband was killed by a French agent five years ago. Poisoned. The spy had been posing as a steward on the riverboat we were traveling on down to New Orleans. It was our honeymoon, Mr. Hardison," she explained. "We had been married for three days."

What on earth did one say to that?

"Why?"

"His guard was down. He was off duty, distracted. No doubt still a bit exhausted from the events of the wedding weekend. It was the perfect time, really."

"No, but why—"

"My husband was also with the Agency, Mr. Hardison. He was in Paris shortly before the Treaty of Calais was signed. Reginald recovered some information from a French agent, and he was attempting to get the intelligence back to his superiors. After the contretemps with the agent Reginald fled but managed to hide the packet, planning to return to the location later and retrieve it. Then the treaty was signed and our agents were officially recalled from France.

"Apparently the French thought Reginald had taken the information with him, or knew what it was at least, and they finally tracked him down. Or perhaps," she said as a footman entered the room with a laden tea tray, "this particular agent simply wanted retribution. That's always seemed more likely to me, as so much time had passed and they must have assumed Reginald had long since relayed the intelligence to Whitehall."

Espionage, retribution, death . . . and tea. Never let it be said that the American Dominions had strayed too far from their English roots. Dexter noted that the lady poured with the same exquisite manner as any blueblood in London.

"No sugar, no milk," he said, not waiting for the offer.

He suspected she cared little for empty pleasantries, despite her manners. "So it's your turn for vengeance now?"

She sipped at her tea, and his eyes were drawn to the perfect bow-shaped curve of her upper lip. Surprisingly full, those lips. She probably frowned in her mirror every morning, to see how pink and lush they were. So out of keeping with her somber garb, like a sweetheart bouquet bobbing atop a mourner's hat.

Having evidently approved the tea, Lady Moncrieffe placed the cup down carefully on its saucer before returning both to the table between them. "I was very fond of my husband, sir. But as I said, my father has a penchant for melodrama. I am in the Agency as he is, and I wish to do my duty for the Crown. I didn't trust the French before the treaty, and I do not trust them now. I have some rather special abilities that may allow me to be of service in France as Reginald once was, and I confess I hope this mission brings me some sense of completion. But one cannot avenge a death, not really. One can only try to honor the memory of the dead by furthering their life's work to the best of one's ability."

"I think most people have a less . . . *pronounced* sense of duty, madam."

"I don't think it vain to say that I am not most people, Mr. Hardison."

She wouldn't think it vain, no. She would think it the simple truth, and he couldn't argue with it.

"Perhaps if I explain some of the details of my mission," she added, "you'll understand better. None of the other agents can do what I can. I'm not being egotistical, merely pragmatic. It's the weight, you see."

"I beg your pardon?"

"The *weight*, Mr. Hardison. I weigh easily a third less than the next smallest agent in the Agency. So I am the only one who can take the *Gossamer Wing* to the necessary altitude to ensure covert surveillance. Because of this, I may also be the only one who can retrieve the item the Agency is looking for, without being spotted doing so. The Agency also needs information on a particular man, an industrialist and military contractor with good security measures. Rumors are he's looking to revive research on creating the same sort of weapon the British threatened to use, the one that ended the war. We *must* find out if those rumors are accurate, and whether he's secured plans to make such a device. The Agency can't get anyone close enough to him through conventional methods so they've decided to attempt an aerial mission as a last resort. France hasn't really embraced air travel yet, so neither the government agents nor any interested private parties are likely to be on the alert for dirigibles. We've tried with several other agents, but with anyone heavier the engine must work too hard. It's noisier then, you see. Useless for spying. But the *Gossamer Wing* is nearly silent for me."

"I see. And the *Gossamer Wing* would be?"

"My AIRSHIP, THE *Gossamer Wing*." She gestured with shy pride to the pile of closed trunks standing just inside the open door of the stable. Across the central corridor, a long dappled gray nose peered out at them with placid curiosity. The scents of well-tended horses and leather mingled with the earthier aroma of any stable, and sunlight danced through motes of dust around the unassuming trunks.

At last, feeling compelled to say something, Dexter nodded at the nearest of the three cases. "Impressive."

With a snort no lady should consider issuing, his companion hauled the case onto its side and flipped the latches open. "Here, help me with this, it'll go more quickly with two."

He helped Charlotte spread a lightweight tarpaulin on the dusty ground of the stable yard, then arrange a silk-covered blue pad and a confusing array of white leather straps. Beside this, from another case, came a rig he thought he recognized as a miniature version of a typical dirigible motor—but a version that looked more suited for a sugar egg than for any practical use. It was all frosted glass, enamel and silver, and so beautiful it took him a moment to see the sheer genius of the thing.

Camouflage. Of course. Once the propeller was in

motion, and with the rigging obscured by the pale sky-blue silk below it—kept carefully clean by the tarpaulin until it was safely in the air—the whole thing would be nearly invisible. Even the pedestrian little gas canister had a tidy silk and leather wrapper to disguise it from eyes below. The slightly pearly sheen to it all would bounce back enough light to minimize the appearance of a shadow on the underside of the rigging.

The pièce de résistance was the blimp itself, and Dexter couldn't help a gasp of delight as he helped Lady Moncrieffe free it from the last of the trunks.

"I've never seen anything like it. I knew there was a dirigible involved, of course, but I simply never imagined something like this. Is this . . . wood? Leather?" He felt at the seams and joints, the fragile-seeming skeleton he could feel within the opal-blue silk casing. Even his knowledgeable fingers had trouble identifying the light, sturdy substance that gave the thing structure and some shape before it was filled with gas or hot air.

"You're no ladies' man, are you, Mr. Hardison?"

She was staring him down, as cool as ever, but he somehow got the impression she was trying very hard not to laugh.

"A gentleman would never tell, madam."

"A gentleman wouldn't have to if he could identify corset boning when he runs his hands all over it."

"Ah!"

"Ah, indeed."

"That's brilliant!"

The whole thing was brilliant.

It was also clearly made for her, and her alone. He could see enough to know the little engine would be temperamental if overloaded, too noisy for its task, not nearly efficient enough on gas, and liable to run too hot for safety. Hence the necessity for strict weight limits on her helmet, as there must be on every garment she wore while piloting the tiny jewel of a craft.

"It's overcast today, and I'm not wearing proper clothing.

But since I'm in breeches, at least, I can still demonstrate for you if you'd like?"

She had already snapped the balloon's frame into place on the rigging, and pulled a trigger to ignite the little flame that would heat and expand it. It took only moments before the whole bullet-shaped structure, scarcely larger than a weather balloon, was filled with air and bobbing gently over their heads. Dexter felt lighter than air himself, struck with the unlikely prospect of seeing her fly the thing—like one of his daydreams come to life.

The mounting must be the most dangerous part. Lady Moncrieffe swung one leg into the harness, then kicked off hard and pulled at a handle simultaneously so that for a moment she seemed to be clinging sideways to the airship's underbelly as it rose swiftly. A single practiced hitch of her body lifted her fully into the cradle until only her head was visible.

Even though the sky was gray today, and even though he knew where the airship was, Hardison had trouble spotting it once she'd risen high enough. On a cloudless day, at full altitude, the illusion would be complete.

"How high does it go?" he shouted, not sure whether she could still hear him.

No immediate answer came, but the little blimp dropped to within a few dozen feet over him. He could see Lady Moncrieffe's face peeking down at him. A few stray blond curls whipped around her uncovered head, and her eyes appeared to be watering.

"Coming down."

Her words were nearly lost in the wind, but he stepped away from the tarp to give her plenty of landing room. That operation wasn't quite as smooth as her takeoff, as it appeared to involve some hovering, then a wriggle and leap from the airship with a tethering line firmly in hand. Precarious, but she did it capably, despite being quite obviously green around the gills.

"Fish for luncheon," she said tersely, not giving any other explanation as she hauled the ship down and shut off the gas and engine, letting it settle slowly down to the tarp and quickly pulling the canopy away from the propellor mechanism and gas nozzle. "I'm not a very good traveler."

"Ironic." And she intended to take a transatlantic ocean honeymoon? He suddenly wondered whether the price of sharing a cabin with her might not be entirely too high, if a five-minute airship ride made her this ill based only on the unfortunately timed consumption of a fish-based meal.

"Yes, isn't it? I have the Alvarez implants. They do help. Supposed to, anyway."

"Do you really? I've read about those. May I see?"

She shrugged. "I suppose. I don't typically let strange gentlemen peruse my inner ears, but as you're considering becoming my husband . . . and you're a makesmith."

He was already at her side, placing his fingers quite shamelessly on her head and tipping it to one side like a piece of delicate machinery. Alvarez implants weren't something a man got to see every day. Or any day, in his case. Fascinating.

"With these you shouldn't experience any nausea at all based on motion, you know."

"I know," she said wryly.

She held very, very still under his touch. He realized he had committed a huge breach of etiquette, but that pulling his hands away now would only draw more attention to it. Her skin felt like what it looked like. White peach. Every bit as soft as it appeared. Dexter willed himself not to sniff, to see if the smell matched the texture.

Business, he reminded himself. *It's business.*

He bent closer to peer into her ear; he could just spot the tiny gold mechanism glinting where it breached her eardrum.

"Do you have the retrieval hook with you?"

"Always," she assured him. Her voice sounded a bit breathy, a bit distant. "But Mr. Hardison, I'm not going to let you disassemble my inner ears in a stable yard. Potential engagement and prior correspondence notwithstanding, we hardly know each other."

That was her pulse, racing there under his thumb where it rested along the elegant curve of her jaw. She looked tiny, birdlike, compared to the scale of his hands. Dexter released her as gently as he had touched her, slowly, with a reluctance he couldn't quite define except that she felt lovely and soft and much more alive than he had expected. Not like an alabaster angel at all.

"Another time perhaps, my lady."

His bow was ironic, but his tone was as gentle as he could make it.

She didn't smell like peaches. She smelled like lemon verbena, and ever so slightly of tea.

CHARLOTTE WASN'T SURE what she had been expecting from the Makesmith Baron. But whatever it was, she knew it hadn't been . . . *this*. This big friendly bear of a man, with curious eyes and gentle paws, who looked like he might crush a teacup with two fingers, or break a chair by sitting on it.

He didn't fit into her world.

Oh, he was a gentleman. His ancestry was every bit as elevated as her own. He hadn't snapped the handle from the teacup, nor had he allowed his weight to pull so much as a squeak of complaint from the poor little chair in the solarium. He knew what he ought to say and do, whether or not he always chose to say and do it.

But he had made choices in his life that baffled her. He seemed so large, and easy, and . . . *free*.

His bulk was all muscle, she could tell, and mostly evident in his shoulders and the powerful muscles of his thighs that she could see when he knelt to help her with the airship. They stood out in sharp relief, despite the tasteful tailoring of his clothing. His hands had felt strong enough to twist her head from her neck in one swift go. But the way he touched her was so considerate, he might have been holding something as fragile as a robin's egg.

Charlotte was never one for poetics, and she wasn't inclined to begin now. More importantly, the man now knew a secret that might be vital to her own interest, no less than that of the Crown.

"You won't tell my father," she stated firmly. "About the implants not working as well as they might. They're modified to mark the altitude as well, they're necessary to my task. They might also be useful if I needed to pilot another sort of pressurized craft in the future. Submersibles, for instance."

"It's not a question of them not working as well as they might, it's a question of them not working at all, if you're still getting motion sickness."

"Usually only on the airship," she assured him. "And possibly at sea, but that remains to be seen. They've cured my motion sickness in steam cars entirely, and it used to be quite severe. I've consulted Dr. Alvarez and she's had the implants out and in again. It's her opinion that they're functioning properly and the real problem isn't with the equipment."

"She thinks it's all in your head?"

He was too quick, and she didn't like the way he'd smiled when he said it.

"My father can't know. The implants are another factor in the Crown's accepting me for this piece of work. If he got wind of this he would have word to Whitehall in a heartbeat."

The great bear of a smith was thinking, very obviously, while running his gentle, callused fingertips over the lower half of the dirigible's framework. Corset boning. She might have told him whalebone, and it would have been as accurate. Things seemed to slip out of her mouth around him. Charlotte had been far too long out of the society of men younger than her father, and this particular man was so very much to take in all at once. He seemed twice the size of Reginald. Familiar, unobtrusive, reserved Reginald who was dead, making any comparison suspect due to the passage of time and its effect on memory.

"So it's also about submersibles?"

It took her a moment to catch the drift of his thoughts. "Yes. In a sense. He hasn't told you about your part yet, has he?"

"The Viscount? No. We're set to meet tomorrow if I agree

to this, apparently he intends to make a formal presentation. But you know."

She nodded, unsure whether to tell him more than she already had. She knew she shouldn't, but she also knew he had worked on classified government projects before. He had also passed a rigorous security clearance before her father had ever approached him, and the particulars of the mission might be enough on their own to convince him to say yes. "Tomorrow when you meet with my father again, you must pretend never to have heard this. As I said, my part is straightforward. They need a packet retrieved, and they need more information on this man Dubois. It's just chance that I'm to be spying on him in the same general location where your skills might be welcome. There's a new military station, Mr. Hardison. A covert, submerged station with a tunnel leading from the shore, in the English Channel off the coast near Le Havre. The British government can use it as a base of operations for intelligence, and for practical matters like docking submersibles for repair, so they never have to be seen above water, even on the English side."

His eyes widened as he turned to her. Charlotte could almost see the thoughts churning frantically behind his forehead, trying to organize themselves amid the frenzy of excitement at the prospect she presented.

"It can't be done."

It was the sort of thing a man like him said for form, because it needed to be said to put it out of the way. She took a perverse enjoyment in contradicting him, even if she knew that he didn't really believe it. Even if he anticipated her words.

"Oh, but it already has, sir."

His decision was made then, if it hadn't been before.

"If it's dirigibles, submersibles and an undersea station, then I think it's obviously time we were married."

"Oh, Mr. Hardison, you'll make me blush. Will you pile the harness on the hammock section, please? It folds together more easily that way."

The *Gossamer Wing* was portable when stowed, but only

to a degree. It always seemed much larger going back into its cases than it had coming out. Charlotte tackled the blimp carapace, folding carefully to keep from putting undue pressure on the boning, and managed to keep the cursing under her breath as she wrestled it back into storage.

"The trunks weigh more than the rigging itself," Hardison scolded her. "You need lighter cases, perhaps something with flexible sides."

She looked at him over the soft mound of silk that puffed stubbornly out of the trunk she was attempting to close. The mini-dirigible's top half was as unstructured as any balloon, and as inconvenient to tame when deflated.

"Can I expect a prototype of this new luggage from your workshop within the week? I might decide it's quite convenient to be engaged to the Makesmith Baron."

"I assume it's a state secret, otherwise that would make a splendid wedding present."

So cheerful. So *easy*. His smile was dangerously contagious, and she found herself all too likely to make uncharacteristic quips in hopes of prompting more smiles from the man.

"A tasteful necklace or a new carriage would no doubt be more appropriate."

"Oh, I see. Do you need a new carriage? Perhaps a new steam car?"

"No," she admitted. "I hardly use the one you custommade for me three years ago. Motion sickness, you know. Besides, my driver is rather tall for it and my mother berates me when I drive myself."

"Pity. I could have made you a bang-up steam car. Even better than the last one. But I'm sure we'll come up with something."

DEXTER WAS SO preoccupied driving back to his estate that he nearly ran himself off the road twice. Finally he pulled over at a roadhouse, ordering a lager to soothe his nerves and ease his thoughts into some semblance of sense.

The good lady spy was no merry widow, but she had definitely piqued his interest. More than that, he admitted to himself. Of course he wanted her, but it was much more than just lust, which would have been simpler and easier to dismiss. Her letters had never conveyed her personality, only her keen intelligence and an occasional glimpse of wit. In person Dexter found her beautiful but fragile, a compelling blend of strength and delicacy. She was brittle, but he found her brittleness fascinating. He wanted to soothe her like a skittish horse, tame her to accept the things she had learned to fear, and he was more than old enough to know the source of that want was not located solely in his compassionate heart.

His thoughts on the woman were too complex, too instantly evolved, to signal anything other than a full-scale infatuation . . . but if so, it was infatuation with all the weight of unreasonable hope to lend it substance. Whether or not her father liked it, Charlotte, Lady Moncrieffe, was a significant inducement to him. She had a heady blend of physical and mental attractiveness that seemed custom-made to entice Dexter into taking foolish risks. And then there were the details of the mission itself to consider. The very pressing danger that the French might be on the brink of developing a weapon of devastating power. An undersea station, and some puzzle still to be solved there about which Charlotte hadn't yet learned the particulars. He could swear his fingers itched with eagerness to get his hands on the inner workings of such a structure.

By the time he finished his relaxing beverage and set off once more, Dexter was beginning to wonder why he had hesitated even a moment in agreeing to the proposal. He would write Lord Darmont his formal acceptance the moment he reached home.

Four

ACCOMPLISHING A BELIEVABLE sham marriage was a good deal more complicated than either Charlotte or Dexter had anticipated. Subterfuge usually was.

First there was a new wardrobe for Charlotte to acquire, completely free of black and pewter and the ghastly dull lavender that had never suited her. Then there were parties and outings to attend with Baron Hardison, so that the always inquisitive folk of high society would see them together and not view the coming engagement as sudden or in any way suspicious. Charlotte had expected to hate every moment of this plunge back into the social whirl, but somehow it all seemed easier with Hardison there. He was so open, so friendly, and as he rarely left her side she always had somebody to talk to. Somebody interesting to talk to, at that. Dexter seemed to enjoy her company, which Charlotte found flattering if a bit disconcerting. She felt strangely inclined to giggle and bat her eyes at him, and had to remind herself often that it was all for show.

Their timeline was necessarily shorter than most court-ships, given their need to sail to France as soon as practicable. A month or so into their dealings, there was a ball to attend, and a proposal to fake while there.

"It shouldn't be too difficult," Hardison reassured her, scanning the crowd briefly as they waltzed around the perimeter of the Vanderbilts' ballroom. "It's too cold for the garden to be very crowded tonight. We nip out for a few minutes, then we're back in. You'll be wearing a ring and a blush, I'll be looking unbearably smug, and the world will never know it isn't all as authentic as can be."

Charlotte nodded, her lips tight. She wanted to relax, to enjoy the night instead of just pretending to enjoy it. She had always loved dancing, and had had so few occasions to do so with Reginald.

This felt disloyal. While Reginald had certainly been a competent dancer—all properly raised gentlemen were competent dancers—the great clumsy bear who held her now had turned out to be head and shoulders above any man who'd ever ferried her around a dance floor. Figuratively and very nearly literally. Even in heeled slippers, Charlotte was short enough in comparison to Dexter that the top of her coiffure barely reached his shoulder. And the Baron, it transpired, was far more than a merely competent dancer. He could . . . *dance*.

He wasn't clumsy at all, she had learned, despite his size. His body was as careful, as deliberate and gentle in its movements, as his hands had been on her head. She could still recall that moment in the stable yard so clearly, even a month later—the odd stillness that had overtaken her when he touched her, the funny little twist in her stomach. She'd felt taken over, and she felt taken over again in the waltz tonight. Dexter's hand on her waist was as solid as a building, his firm grip on her gloved hand not painful but simply inexorable. He led, and she must follow. She didn't even think about the steps.

It was like floating, or flying. Like the *Gossamer Wing*, without the nausea.

For that reason, Charlotte could not feel at ease. Dreams rarely ended well for her, and she didn't trust herself when life felt too ethereal or pleasant. She tried to remind herself that people were never what they seemed, and this was all make-believe. But Dexter felt so real, so solid, from the deft grip of his hand on hers to the uncompromisingly hard muscle of his shoulder. Based on the dimensions she'd been able to glean thus far, Charlotte thought Dexter must have the approximate build of a Greek god as depicted in early marbles. Not one of the youths, but somebody fully ripened into manhood. Poseidon, possibly.

"Charlotte?"

The sound of her name drew her attention back to her partner, away from inappropriately specific thoughts of his body. She tipped her head back—and back, and back—to look up at him.

"Dexter."

They had been practicing, the better to lend an air of genuine affection to their engagement. *See*, her tone of voice told him, *I can say your first name with no hesitation at all, because I have taught myself to say it as part of my duty to the Crown.*

"Are you feeling quite well?"

She tried to think how to explain what she was feeling, but decided against it and went with a shrug instead.

"I'm not used to being back among so many people yet, I suppose."

"Steam car outings and salons aren't really adequate preparation for this, it's true," he sympathized. "I'd much rather be in my workshop. I've always hated these things."

His voice was mild, pleasant. He seemed to be enjoying himself well enough. Perhaps he was simply as good an actor as he was a dancer.

Charlotte allowed herself the luxury of a slightly longer look at her partner while he steered them around a tricky knot of fellow revelers. In the gleam of the gaslight, she could see the russet tint that softened the black of his hair and brows. Clean-shaven in the current fashion, hair neatly trimmed. The dark gold figured brocade of his waistcoat played up a golden hue she hadn't noticed before in his complexion. The Chen influence, she supposed, recalling Dexter's Chinese ancestry. His features were pure Hardison, however, elegant but just a bit boyish. It would have made an ideal face for a rake, had he chosen to wield it that way.

He didn't, of course. As far as she knew, he had never dallied indiscreetly, never played the cad, never so much as publicly sullied the reputation of the local barmaid her father had informed her was the occasional companion of the Baron's nights. The Viscount had had a man check on that sort of thing, apparently.

Dexter had given the young woman a generous settlement the day after Charlotte demonstrated her airship to him. That was before he had even spoken with the Viscount and given his official pledge of participation in the charade. He hadn't been seen in the barmaid's company since, her father had reported.

"It's time," Dexter whispered in her ear as the last few bars of the waltz drew the crowd to a halt. While the others applauded, Dexter led Charlotte quickly out to the terrace. As they descended the steps and headed for a secluded corner of the garden, she told herself that her shiver was only a result of the late April evening's gathering chill.

He pulled her to a halt around a corner formed by a boxwood hedge and an overflowing herbaceous border. A starlit fountain surrounded by low-growing white roses greeted them with charming sound and scent. There was a bench, of course, placed advantageously for courting couples. The Vanderbilts' townhouse was somewhat infamous for the convenience of its gardens when trysting was on the agenda.

"Shall I kneel?"

"Whatever for?" She looked back toward the house, to the relative safety of the lights and crowd, visible in twinkling glimpses through the spring foliage.

"Veracity," he said with a shrug. She could tell he was stung.

"I apologize."

"No, no. I didn't mean to be flippant. I know this can't be easy for you. I've never been married, much less . . . well. I shouldn't jest."

That hurt more, his being kind for the sake of her feelings. She couldn't allow that. "No, you're right. By all means, let's get into the spirit of the thing."

"Are you sure—"

"Quite sure, Mr. Hardison."

"Dexter," he reminded her.

Charlotte was glad for the night, for the cover of shadow in the secluded little lover's nook. Dexter had been so unfailingly kind, so courteous and thoughtful, these past few weeks. Ushering her into and out of steam cars, holding her chair, opening doors and fetching her drinks. Making painfully polite conversation with her mother and her mother's friends, always behaving as though he were eager to get back to her side.

He was the hero who had brought her out of mourning, the knight in friendly bear's armor who had won her from her dark castle of grief with his gentle, determined charm. For a novice, Hardison seemed brilliant at the long game.

Charlotte's mother had exclaimed with joy when Charlotte confessed to her—per the plan—that Dexter intended to propose at tonight's ball. And she had completely mistaken the reasons behind Charlotte's subsequent tears.

Charlotte had known Reginald for eight years, been courted by him for two of those years, and was married to him for fewer than seventy-two hours. Three nights. Theirs was a reserved but friendly courtship, and she had enjoyed his company in bed by that third night.

She had loved her husband, and welcomed his affections eagerly, if shyly. But she had never felt *this*. Charlotte had never felt a fraction of the huge, unnamable *thing* that overcame her when Hardison was anywhere in the vicinity. She had never breathed Reginald in, or felt his absence like the absence of some essential element in the air whenever he left her side. During their courtship, she had never missed Reginald like a limb when he went home for the day, or even when he went off to spend several months in Europa. Perhaps because she had known him so long, she had been unable to imagine that he might not return.

Reginald had never *loomed* the way Hardison—Dexter— loomed over her now without even trying, in a way that had absolutely nothing to do with the sheer physical magnitude of the man. Immense though he was, Charlotte couldn't lie to herself about the real reason he seemed so terribly real, so terribly *present* next to her in the dark.

She wanted him. She *lusted* for him, even though she knew she shouldn't.

It was new to her, such uncontrollable physical desire. And like all things she couldn't control, she distrusted it. She distrusted herself when she felt the pull of it, and she felt guilt beyond measure for never having felt this way about her actual husband. What had she been depriving Reginald of, by not responding this way to him? How had she deprived herself? Had Reginald known what they were missing? Surely he must have, men always seemed to know those sorts of things, no matter how new they were to the whole business. Had he cared? Whether she wanted to or not, Charlotte found *she* cared. Now, after the fact, when it was too late by five years. She cared very much.

It didn't matter. It couldn't. Her marriage to Hardison was to be a sham, a ploy, she reminded herself. His interest was in the technical novelty of his mission, and hers was in regaining the plans and helping ensure the French got no further in building their dreadful weapon, as she field-tested the stealth potential of the *Gossamer Wing*.

Here in the romantic dark, however, Dexter leaned over her as they sat side by side on the lover's bench . . . and it might have been real. For a moment, it seemed real.

For a moment, Charlotte decided, she might even let herself pretend.

HE'D THOUGHT HER an angel in the sunlight. Now, Dexter saw that he had been wrong.

Charlotte was a creature made for night gardens. She bloomed in the starlight and moonlight, opening like a sweetly scented white blossom under the indirect glow of the night sky. She was too subtle to need anything so blatant as sunlight in order to shine.

He wondered if she had chosen the color of the dress on purpose to tease him. Palest blue silk with an opalescent shimmer in the mesh overlay, the blue that melted into a cloudless sky, rendering her invisible on her airship. She was the opposite of invisible in the ballroom, wearing this blue. It matched her eyes, set off her hair . . . and the décolletage was inspired, more daring than a young unmarried woman was allowed. The prerogative of a young matron. Or a young widow who was finally out of mourning.

Dexter wanted to run his finger along the edge of the silk, push down the little extra rim of net that pretended at modesty to reveal another inch or so of peachy-soft skin. He scooted a few more inches away from her, lest he forget himself in the moonlight and give in to that temptation.

If he had been courting her in earnest the past month or so, he would have risked placing his lips just there at that moment, right on the soft rise below her clavicle. She was a widow after all, not a green girl. If he were a real suitor, he might well have dared far more than that by this time. Would she, he wondered, taste faintly of tea and lemon?

It was business, Dexter reminded himself. Charlotte had lost a husband, one she'd loved enough to want to avenge at the risk of her own life. She was no sophisticated companion to spend a night or two with and then leave after presenting a costly bauble. Nor was she an accommodating barmaid with a playfully liberal interpretation of morality and no illusions about his intentions toward her. She was a lady. And he, curse it, was a gentleman. According to the briefings he'd received from Darmont, aside from supporting Charlotte's mission, his interest in the matter was supposed to be confined to the undersea station and the need for seismic monitoring given the frequency of earthquakes in the English Channel.

If he were really to get into the spirit of the thing, he sighed to himself, then the delectable Charlotte, Lady Moncrieffe, would probably toss him on his arse. Petite she might be, but he knew she'd been well trained for her assignment and he had little doubt she could flip him onto the ground as easily as he flipped a hot cog out of a mold.

So he remained where he was, as far as possible from her on the tiny bench, feeling as though the weighty matter between them might shove him straight off his perch at any moment.

At that moment the universe, in its capricious whimsy, decided to intervene.

A gaggle of three chattering maidens and one married pseudo-chaperone came prancing along the path, and among their number was a young lady who had done everything in her power to gain the newly socially inclined Baron Hardison's attention that month. Never mind that the man was clearly attached to Lady Moncrieffe, and that rumor had them nearly engaged already. Either the girl herself or her mother was dead set on catching the elusive Baron's eye. There were not so many single, eligible young men this season that any of them could shake this sort of pursuit, except by engagement or marriage. Even a few broken engagements had been engineered as the Season neared its closing month and the young ladies grew more desperate. It was nearly May already; by June it would be too hot, and too late by far, to find husbands for all the wilting flowers.

The tittering group drew abreast of them with a fresh spate of murmurs, giggles and apologies when the trysting pair was spied. Then, bowing and glancing over their shoulders as they drifted away, the girls launched into an analysis that was not entirely as sotto voce as propriety demanded.

The phrases "On the outs," "So promising for *you*, Meggie," and "Ooh, could have driven a *steam car* between them" were not quite as hard for Dexter to hear as ". . . bit long in the tooth too, don't you think?"

Their voices echoed down the path until they were out of sight and the night's stillness settled again. Finally risking a glance over at Charlotte, Dexter saw that she had covered her face with one kid-gloved hand. Her shoulders were shaking gently and he rushed to clasp her free hand, to reassure her, to offer a handkerchief for her tears.

"You're never. Not in the least," he insisted in a furious whisper.

"Wh-what?" She lowered her hand at last and he saw she was not crying. She was laughing so hard her face was turning visibly red even in the moonlight.

"You're not long in the tooth," he explained, unsure what to make of her reaction.

"Steam car," she offered, waving a hand at the expanse of bench between them, then dissolved into another spate of helpless giggles.

He resisted manfully only a second or two, then joined her and laughed until his sides hurt, until the almost painful fit of mirth ebbed enough for them to speak again.

"Oh, lord. Was I ever that young and stupid?" she mused aloud, finally accepting the handkerchief from Dexter and dabbing her eyes with it.

"I doubt you were ever that desperate. So her name's Meggie. I kept forgetting . . ."

"You're no spring chicken either, you know. You're older than I am by a good five years."

"True. I'm practically doddering at thirty-two. Oh, heaven spare us, they're on their way back if I hear correctly."

"Give me the ring, we'll slip back inside before they spot us again."

"It's no good," he hissed, glimpsing the little group of walkers on the path directly opposite the bench from the fountain. In another few seconds they would see them again; sooner, if the faux lovebirds stood up and tried to abandon the bench. "I'm afraid there's only one thing for it."

"Indisputable proof of our affection?"

"If you're game."

"For Crown and country, Mr. Hardison?" Her smile was arch, but not at all unwilling. Dexter's stomach did a jig as he closed the distance between them and scooped her closer with an arm around her waist. No time for finesse. A moment before the gigglers rounded the fountain, he captured Charlotte's cheek in his other hand.

"Close your eyes and think of England," he whispered as he lowered his mouth to hers, and he caught another chuckle trying to escape from her parted lips.

Then there was heat, and breath, and the unparalleled thrill of feeling Charlotte begin to tremble as he swept his tongue deep inside her mouth. He was scarcely aware of the girlish giggles transforming to shocked squeals across the pathway, the horrified scuttling away of dainty maiden feet, as his hand dragged itself down of its own accord to tug at filmy net and expose more down-soft bosom, to cup that softness through its layer of confining silk and tease his thumb over the harder point that seemed to flare in instant response to his touch.

More, his body was insisting, and he probably ruined the arm of his jacket against the stone of the bench as he reached beneath Charlotte's legs to lift her into his lap, but Dexter didn't care. He didn't care about anything but *more*.

His hungry lips had blazed a trail down to her neckline and his hand had made a good deal of headway beneath Charlotte's petticoats and back up her leg when her alarmed gasp broke through the lust-fog.

"That girl's mother. *Dexter*. That girl is coming back with her mother!"

She drummed on his shoulder in a panic, and he released her and hurriedly smoothed her skirt back into place, then reached into his trouser pocket to snag the ring.

"Marry me?"

He didn't wait for an answer or bend to one knee, just shoved the ring toward her and grabbed her free hand to pull her off the bench and back toward the terrace.

"Certainly."

She caught up enough to loop her arm through his, and had the ring worked onto the appropriate finger by the time they passed the distressed girl and her mother who had clearly been working herself up to a fine outrage over the scandalous carryings-on in the garden.

"Lovely evening," Dexter said, tipping a nonexistent hat to the pair and picking up his pace, though Charlotte was forced to an unsightly scamper to keep up with him. She was quite out of breath when they reached the relative safety of the terrace.

The scampering was responsible for her flushed face and slight air of disarray, and the brightness of her eyes, of course. Not what had preceded the scampering. No, surely not. She couldn't possibly feel as flustered as he did, or as full of unsated arousal careening blindly about with nowhere to go.

"See? Our relationship is full of intrigue and danger already, Charlotte," he said, hoping he sounded more droll than hopelessly besotted.

Her look was definitely droll, if still a bit charmingly mussed. Her lips, he noticed despite himself, looked extremely freshly kissed and no mistaking it. He decided not to tell her.

"Nonsense. It's a highly respectable marriage of social convenience between a dull, long-in-the-tooth widow and an aging bachelor who's finally realized he needs a woman's touch to properly manage his ancestral estate. Nothing could be more ordinary. *Baron* Hardison."

But then she smiled, with those delightfully wicked lips. Like magic, two utterly charming dimples materialized on her cheeks.

How long, he was already beginning to wonder, might he be able to drag their mission out?

FIVE

CHARLOTTE'S MOTHER WOULD have preferred a wedding with all the considerable pomp and ceremony of her first. After all, she pointed out, the first marriage had hardly lasted very long at all, and even Charlotte's mourning had lasted longer than her engagement and marriage combined.

"A bit *too* long for good taste, these days, dear," she'd pointed out gently. "Although I know one can't hurry grief."

One can suborn grief entirely in the rush of learning to fly, and going through months of combat and strategy training, Charlotte refrained from saying. To her mother, she was a proper grieving widow. Just as her father was a proper gentleman who had never worked a day in his life.

Tell that to the French, who still spoke of him in furious hushed tones as *La Main de la Mort Silencieuse* . . . the Hand of Silent Death. Would she live long enough to earn her own melodramatic epithet, Charlotte wondered? It seemed a less romantic prospect lately, dying for her country. She rather thought she might prefer to live to fight another day. Her course was long settled, though. Looking to the distant future was pointless.

"The dove gray is pretty with your coloring, Charlotte. Unless you'd prefer blue? I know I won't talk you into pink. You're still young enough to get away with it, you know. It's quite fashionable this year."

"Peacock blue," Charlotte said, much to her mother's obvious surprise. "That's popular just now, isn't it?"

"Very."

"And it would flatter me, I think."

"Of course it would. Would you like me to arrange a visit from Madame Elaine?"

"I already have," she replied, running her fingers idly over the pearly, tailored lines of the silk dress laid out on the bed beside her.

She had come out of mourning so recently that her newly made clothes could easily serve as a trousseau. Of course she had ordered them with that in mind, although her mother didn't know that. There really wasn't much else to do before the wedding except plan the day and pack for the honeymoon. A widow's second wedding was far easier to orchestrate than a maiden socialite's first.

But she wouldn't deprive her mother of the pleasure of seeing her in a new gown, made especially for the occasion. Besides, Charlotte had to admit that the peacock-blue airship helmet had done amazing things for her eyes. She'd almost hated to send it back on that basis alone.

Not that it mattered whether her dress flattered her eyes on her wedding day. It wasn't to be a real marriage, and would last only as long as necessary to accomplish the vital mission it had been organized to facilitate. And there would be no further emergency occasions to pretend at passion while kissing her ersatz husband in moonlit gardens.

Charlotte told herself this in a very stern voice, as she had several times a day for the past week. Perhaps she was being less stern with herself than she thought, for her mother smiled at her in a knowing way as she passed by with another gown.

"I would have liked to see a longer engagement, but I think

perhaps you and the Baron are smart not to wait. People do like to talk."

"Pardon?"

"The Vanderbilt back gardens were notorious already, dear. No need to add to their notoriety. Even in the excitement of an engagement."

"Oh!"

She stared at her hands, not sure whether to laugh or cry from embarrassment. She should have nothing to be embarrassed about. Not only was she a widow—and she certainly wouldn't be the first widow to take a lover—she had in fact been doing only what was necessary to secure the public awareness of the affection between herself and her apparent fiancé. Their kiss had been a sort of state secret. Only rather less secret than public.

"In his lap, Charlotte? Really? And to hear Lady Elliot tell it, his hand was halfway up your skirt and he was close to ripping your dress off with his teeth."

"Mother!"

"I'm sure she exaggerated," her mother said, her calm voice soothing Charlotte's ruffled feathers as usual. "But I think soonest is probably best. So people won't talk."

About where the Makesmith Baron's hand had been. Or his teeth. She didn't explain to her mother that only one of those descriptions was at all exaggerated. He hadn't been using his teeth at all just then. Not on her dress, anyway.

"People should find more interesting ways to occupy their time than inventing scandals." Charlotte smoothed the dress out again and stood up, wandering over to her vanity and sitting down to fuss with her hair in the mirror. She allowed herself just a hint of smugness. "That little girl honestly thought she had a chance with Dexter, and her mother was foolish enough to encourage her. I imagine they were both having themselves a tantrum about being thwarted. Heaven only knows what the child thought she saw. And you know how these stories grow so quickly. They take on a life of their own."

Her mother's face appeared in the mirror over her shoulder, eyes narrowed. "*Charlotte*. You really did let him molest you in the garden, didn't you? I would never have expected that kind of coarseness from you. I do like Baron Hardison, but I'm not at all sure he's an appropriate match if he's going to encourage this sort of behavior."

Startled, Charlotte met the eyes that looked so much like her own and remembered that her father had married her mother for a reason. Lavinia Hardison put on a slightly vapid, vain façade, but she had never been stupid when it came to this sort of thing. She knew people far better than she let on, and Charlotte had a history of underestimating her mother to her cost.

"Dexter is the model of propriety, Mother."

Not quite denying, not quite confirming any illicit behavior that might or might not have been encouraged by either of them.

Her mother sighed, a long-suffering sort of sigh that Charlotte hadn't heard since before her marriage to Reginald.

"I must go. Please be careful, Charlotte. You know, I suspect I would be much less tolerant with you—or with *him*—if I weren't so pleased to see you happy again after all this time."

The embrace was swift, gardenia-scented, over before Charlotte could respond. Alone in her dressing room, she looked at her reflection again and tried to see what her mother saw. *Happiness.* But it was like a game of spot-the-difference with only one picture to look at. She couldn't see what was there now, that hadn't been before. She saw only herself, more or less the same as she had been for years. Charlotte thought mothers probably saw these sorts of things in their children, whether they were really there or not.

If she was happy, perhaps it was because she was finally about to attempt the work she had trained for, fulfill the purpose she had pledged herself to. For herself, and for Reginald's memory.

THE HAND OF Silent Death had fallen into his customary postprandial snooze in the library the next time Charlotte and Dexter had a chance to speak privately.

"He's worn himself out, poor thing," Charlotte whispered archly, leading Dexter from the room and down the hallway to the conservatory. "Father's quite exhausted from all his efforts to recruit you ever deeper into his network of intrigue."

Dexter chuckled, the low tone resonating in the marble-paved corridor despite their efforts to be quiet. "Why the assiduous chaperoning all of a sudden? I must not have ruined you thoroughly enough at the Vanderbilts', if your mother still believes there's hope for what remains of your good reputation."

"Oh, *please* don't make fun," Charlotte implored. "I know it's tedious to string her along like this. I don't like it any more than you do, but it's necessary. One day she'll understand."

Charlotte thought her mother already suspected something was afoot, in fact. But she'd held her peace thus far, and the amount of gossip she'd spread about the happy couple had done more to solidify their cover than Charlotte and Dexter could ever have done themselves, had they all the time and dimly lit garden benches in the world.

She closed the conservatory door behind them and ventured farther into the room, until they were shrouded by foliage from any prying maternal eyes.

"You're a grown woman and a widow. Doesn't she realize I could simply visit you at your own home any time I liked?"

"She thinks she has spies in the ranks of my household staff. Here, come and sit. We can talk for a few minutes at least before it's time for you to leave." Charlotte sat on a wrought-iron bench, scooting to the end to leave ample room for Dexter. She enjoyed their talks, but had felt awkward and nervous with him since the night of their engagement. Now she was determined to remedy that by proving to herself that she could be alone with him and keep her head on straight.

"Your staff are loyal to you and not her, I take it?"

"To the Crown," Charlotte corrected him. "Most of my staff are retired from government work. My late husband's family had a longstanding arrangement with Whitehall, which

I continue to honor, to provide work and homes for those agents in the Dominions who are unable to continue with field work, for whatever reason. The real wonder is that Mother never questions why so many of my domestics are sporting prosthetic limbs, or seem to do very little actual work. Most of the house is closed to visitors, of course. She'd be appalled to know it's because the staff are living in it."

"I suspect she knows more than you think," Dexter mused.

Charlotte tilted her head, meeting his gaze curiously. She agreed with him in principle, but thought it was impressive that Dexter had figured out the ruse so quickly. "What makes you say that?"

"She's not nearly as witless as she pretends to be. If she were, for one thing, your father wouldn't pay as much attention to her as he does. I think they understand one another perfectly."

"True. You're very astute about people."

"No." He shook his head, laughing. "She just reminds me of my mother, is all."

Charlotte couldn't help grinning back at him. "Oh, if that's all. You have my sympathies."

"Perhaps one day you'll be an equally devious mama." He leaned closer and gave her a conspiratorial wink.

"Oh. I . . . oh."

She sucked in a breath and tried to will her heart to stop its sudden mad thumping. Instead she caught a faint hint of Dexter's characteristic spicy scent, and felt close to swooning as her mind whipped back to that evening at the Vanderbilts'. Her body tingled as if his hands were still roaming over it, as the idea of babies led swiftly and inevitably to thoughts of baby making.

Charlotte knew a moment of relief tinged with vague regret when it became clear that Dexter mistook the reason for her reaction.

"I'm sorry, Charlotte. Terribly sorry. It was thoughtless of me to suggest . . . had you and Reginald planned a family?"

He took one of her hands in his, throwing Charlotte's

senses into deeper confusion. She had to swallow twice before she could answer. "We had discussed it, of course. We'd thought we'd like to wait a few years. But after that, at least two. We were both only children, you know. Both of us thought it would be wonderful to have a sibling."

"I'm fond of my brother and sister now, and I always imagine myself having three or four of my own one day, but I'm not sure I'd have agreed with you when we were all children. We fought like a pack of vicious little wolverines. I actually stabbed my brother in the back of the hand with a fork once, when he tried to beat me to the last pork chop."

"You didn't!"

"I did," he swore. "He has a scar to this day. In my defense, I was only five at the time and he was a very large eight, so he was usually the one doing the injuring."

Charlotte laughed despite herself. "I can't picture you doing such a thing. You seem so level-headed now."

"I was a horrible little boy," Dexter confided. "When I wasn't brawling, I was usually taking things apart to see how they worked, never mind that I had no idea how to reassemble them."

"Yet. You learned at some point, obviously."

"I learned a thing or two along the way. And stopped fighting. Or rather my brother did, when he stopped growing and I didn't. He's still a puny six-footer."

She could picture it, Dexter grinning down with smug good humor at an older, shorter brother who declined to fight him; it was easy to imagine, even though she hadn't met Dexter's family yet. That would come soon, of course, but Charlotte was trying not to think about it just yet. It daunted her, the idea of deceiving that many people. Dexter had reassured her, with his customary geniality, that they would welcome her with open arms, and he himself would be the one to handle any unpleasantness on that front after their mission—and "marriage"—ended.

It wasn't fair, Charlotte thought, that he should be handsome *and* personable *and* gallant. That she should yearn for his body even as she longed to talk to him about the mundane events of her day. In a way, that part was worse. She wanted to maintain a professional detachment, as she'd been trained to do. Dexter was a colleague, not a *friend*. In her experience, the two were mutually exclusive. It was best that way. Charlotte made herself recall a particularly grueling training session, a bivouac on some freezing mountainside in one of the northernmost Dominions. One of the other trainees had joked darkly about what they would do if the training exercise turned into a real survival test, if the snow continued to fall and they were unable to make their rendezvous to be transported back to the base camp.

"I vote we eat the young lady first," the whipcord-thin agent-in-training had said, smirking in her direction. His name was Adams, but they all called him Weasel because he looked like one. "She looks tender."

"And I'm chopped liver, am I?" the other female trainee, Beatrice, had countered. "Besides, ask McCormack there how far you'd get, trying to take down our Charlotte."

McCormack, cocooned up to the tip of his long nose in his sleeping bag, had snorted loudly at that. "She'd have your guts for garters, Weasel lad. No joy there. Not for eating or anything else."

Charlotte smiled fondly at the memory of her first mock combat skirmish with McCormack. He'd underestimated her. He'd learned never to do so again. Later that night he'd propositioned her outside the mess hall, and he'd learned never to do *that* again either. After that they got along quite well.

"Not for garters," she corrected McCormack in her most ladylike voice. "For supper. And not the guts, I'd start with the organ meat. Probably the heart, as it's the most nutritious. Even Weasel's."

She had meant every word of it.

She'd finished her field training well over a year ago. Weasel was a field agent now, last she'd heard. Beatrice and McCormack were both dead, along with another member of their squad, all killed in an exercise a few months after that chilly bivouac. An improperly placed piton had given way, three would-be agents whom Charlotte considered friends had plummeted to their icy deaths at the base of the cliff they'd been scaling, and Charlotte had learned why her father warned her not to view field training as a social occasion. Detachment in training was good practice for the job, he'd told her, because nobody ever knew in the morning who might be gone by evening.

It was a dangerous profession. Reginald's death was hardly an exception. If anything it was closer to the rule, though she hadn't known that when she'd married him. She'd been young enough to assume that he would live because he was hers, because she was not the sort of woman to whom terrible things like losing a husband happened.

Dexter, whose "training" consisted of a few extended briefings and a long weekend or two at a local armory, was meant to work primarily in the submerged station once in France, which should mean he was relatively safe. Otherwise, he would be even less likely than Reginald to make it back to New York in one piece.

He felt far too solid and alive next to her for Charlotte to believe for one minute he could die. His hands were warm on hers, his pulse steady and reassuringly strong where her fingertip rested lightly on his wrist.

"What are you thinking?" Dexter asked, his voice as soft and warm as the air in the conservatory.

That I'd like you to kiss me right now, and that I shouldn't be thinking it.

Charlotte cleared her throat. "I was thinking it's growing late."

She pulled her fingers free and stood more abruptly than she meant to. She was flustered, out of sorts, her body's lascivious impulses at war with both her heart and her head. Her heart said Dexter was dangerous because she was growing too fond of him, and it reminded her of Reginald. It wanted her to feel unfaithful, and reprimanded her when she didn't. Her head said she needed to focus on the job, not on the doomed dilettante who was only along to fiddle with equipment and be her cover story.

Everything from her belly down to the crux of her legs,

sadly, remained attuned to the big makesmith's every move, like a compass to magnetic north. When he stood, she made herself take a step back. There was an awkward moment, her pulling away just as he offered his arm. Charlotte covered it poorly by pretending to cough into her gloved fist, then walking briskly toward the door as though she hadn't noticed his gesture.

That night, back in the enormous house Reginald had left her, Charlotte sat at her dressing table contemplating a photograph of herself and Reginald at their wedding. He was seated, while Charlotte stood at his shoulder, resting one arm there. Just before the photographer told them to freeze, Reginald had lifted his hand to clasp hers. The moment was captured, as were the warmth in Reginald's eyes and the hint of dimples by Charlotte's mouth as she suppressed a laugh at something her new husband had just said.

She couldn't remember anymore what it was he'd said to her, and the loss of that memory was like a physical pain to Charlotte. Like another little piece of herself slipping away. In her darker moods, she admitted to herself that she kept the photograph there to remind her what her husband had looked like, because if she was being absolutely honest with herself, his face was slipping from her memory. She hadn't thought tonight was going to be one of those darker times, but apparently it was. She found herself deliberately trying to recall Reginald, his voice and face and touch, when she knew quite well it would do her no good.

Charlotte ran her fingers over the glass as she did every evening before bed. But this night, instead of pressing her fingers to her lips and then to the picture as usual, she pried the gilded frame open and slipped the photograph out to look at it more closely. It was warmer than glass, and softer to her touch, she found . . . but it was still just a face on paper. When she closed her eyes, she could see the photograph, but the man was gone.

This time she pressed her lips to the picture, dampening it with her breath and tears. The moisture made it tug against the glass when she put it back in the frame, but it didn't matter anymore. She carried it to the bed, where she opened the bottom drawer of the nightstand that she'd always thought of as Reginald's—even though they had never shared this bed—and placed the photo carefully inside.

Closing the drawer hurt less than she'd expected.

KISSES AT WEDDINGS were public and fleeting. In Charlotte's case, the kiss was also dulled by anticipatory champagne, applied in a liberal dose to numb her lips and calm the butterflies in her stomach prior to the event. Her lips weren't so deadened that she couldn't feel the heat of Dexter's breath and the gentle press of his mouth to hers, but she attributed the mild tingling afterward to nerves and alcohol, and not at all to the kiss itself or the whisper of a smile on the groom's striking face as he pulled away. For a moment they swayed toward each other, almost as though they might kiss again. The moment passed, but Dexter kept hold of Charlotte's hand, his fingers entwining with hers as he led her down the aisle while their families beamed.

It was a small affair, with only a few dozen friends and relatives, conducted in the village church in the afternoon and followed by a reception and dinner at Darmont Hall. No dancing, no fuss, because she had been a widow, after all, although now she was technically Lady Hardison and a baroness.

The great bear of a smith looked even larger when they were alone in his steam carriage afterward. It was perhaps an hour's drive to the hotel in the city where they would spend the night prior to embarking on the *Alberta* tomorrow morning. Their wedding had been timed with the Le Havre–bound ship's departure in mind.

It was a very roomy carriage. It held Charlotte, and all the luggage that wouldn't fit in the boot, and the huge Baron besides, with room left over. But it was very, very full of Baron by about ten silent minutes into the ride.

A gloomy, thoughtful Baron, Charlotte discovered, took up even more space. She had grown accustomed to his deep, gentle voice and the surprisingly witty banter that had sprung up between them. She had grown accustomed to his attention too, she realized, even though she was scarcely entitled to it. It was petty of her to miss it. Why should he dance attendance on her here, after all? There was nobody else to see them now.

"I think it was a successful event," she finally ventured when she could tolerate the quiet no longer. Her champagne had long since worn off, and the butterflies had resumed their ominous flapping beneath her ribcage.

"Yes."

Another few minutes passed, feeling like hours. Charlotte discovered she was wringing her hands, and she stripped her gloves off to give her something to do.

"Have you stayed at the Regent Arms before?" she asked.

Dexter frowned, shook his head and resumed staring out the window.

"I hear it's lovely."

"Of course it's lovely," he concurred.

"Well. Yes." Their set—Charlotte's former set, at least, and the set to which Hardison belonged by birth if not by choice—would not stay at hotels that were not lovely. Charlotte couldn't help the note of bitterness that crept into her voice when she added, "The time to rethink your choice would have been sometime before today."

This time he actually looked at her, as if noticing her in the vehicle for the first time, and Charlotte thought she would rather have held her tongue than bear that scrutiny.

"I'm not having second thoughts. But I admit I'm wondering how this is all going to proceed. The ship, everything. I've so little training for this sort of thing. And I'm worried about what will happen to my workshop in my absence. Whether they'll manage all right without me. I've never taken a holiday before."

His workshop. His life's work. She forgot so easily how important it was to him, how integral he was to its daily workings. He might be a baron, but he operated like an industrialist who'd learned the business from the ground up.

His decision to conduct his affairs that way was as unfamiliar to Charlotte as a poorly run hotel. His anxiety was just as foreign to her.

"Young Mr. Pence seems very competent."

"He is competent. He's also very young."

"Well . . ." She tried, and failed, to think of something comforting to say. "It will only be for a few months at most."

"I appointed him my heir, you know. In case I don't return. I thought . . ." His eyes returned to the window, which was lightening as they neared the city, with its eternal gaslights and numerous vehicles.

He was leaving his life's work behind, while she was traveling toward hers. Or so Charlotte fervently hoped. That there, in France, she would finally know the feeling of accomplishment, that sense of who she was, that had eluded her for so long.

She only had first to pretend to be a giddy young baroness bride for a few months, keep her dinner down long enough to fly her airship successfully over hostile French territory, determine the nature and extent of a potential plot to rekindle the war with a weapon that could destroy them all . . . and hope that her new husband managed to acquit himself well as a rich dilettante while solving a few unsolvable problems of aquatic engineering in the meantime.

Charlotte looked out the window, wondering whether something out there might calm her down or at least engage her interest, as it seemed to have engaged the Baron's. She saw the night, the increasing flow of traffic and the frenetic glare of the approaching city. And reflected in the glass, just visible from the corner of her eye, there was the profile of a man she hardly knew, but knew she must not want as she did.

The man with whom she would be sharing a stateroom on the ocean liner *Alberta* for the next two weeks, and a series of French hotel rooms for an as-yet-undetermined number of weeks following that.

Her husband.

Six

LE HAVRE, FRANCE, AND THE OCEAN LINER
ALBERTA, EN ROUTE FROM NEW YORK TO LE
HAVRE

MARTIN'S SHOULDER AND elbow always ached when it
rained. He watched the gathering clouds from the arched
window of Dubois's office, anticipating the drop in baro-
metric pressure that would soon make its presence known
as a slow, dense agony in those joints.

At least the new ceramic coating kept the arm from freezing in the winter now. The added weight might be hastening
the decay of his beleaguered joints and muscles, but he considered that a small price to pay. He did miss morphine on
days like this, though. He was no longer in government
service, so he was unlikely to be found out for using it, and
Dubois certainly paid him more than enough to afford it.
But Martin knew he couldn't take the risk of becoming
dependent on the stuff again.

"You'll take point," Dubois said. "Your usual team can
deal with the particulars, find out their itinerary and so forth.

This may mean it's time to increase the pressure on Murcheson. We can't afford his competition in this steamrail bid."

Glancing at his employer, Martin had to stifle a sneer. The man had once looked like the influential, powerful captain of industry he fancied himself. Now he had let himself go and it was even more apparent he was, at his core, a glutton and a slob. A dab of butter sullied his cravat, and now he was adding to the mess with a bar of chocolate. The meager sunlight glinted off the scalp that showed between his dyed strands of hair.

"What is the man's name again?" he asked.

"Hardison. The Makesmith Baron, this Dominion rat who makes the steam cars and the, the"—he gestured around his body and then pantomimed firing a weapon—"for the house parties."

"Fowling harness," Martin offered in English. Dubois waved an impatient hand at him.

"The honeymoon is a convenient excuse for him to join forces with Murcheson. I'm sure of this. Each can use the other to secure intercontinental trade. Combining resources would make them impossibly strong in the bidding process for the steamrail contract. It cannot be allowed. I *must* win the bid, Martin."

"*Oui.*"

It was always so with Dubois, always a drama about the dire necessity of quelling this or that competing business interest. Always about the money he wasn't earning, and rarely about the assets he already held. He had probably engaged in more intrigue in his private business dealings than he ever had during his brief youthful tenure in French intelligence. Even his outdated post-royalist political leanings were based on finding what he considered to be the easiest route to a greater profit margin—rekindling hostilities with the British, so he could resume his wartime practice of milking the French government for lucrative defense manufacturing contracts. He often bemoaned the fact that the French had never developed a doomsday device, something that might have kept the war going indefinitely, just so he could make more money. Dubois was the worst sort of privateer, with no political or moral compass to steer him from greed.

Others in France, of course, had more wide-ranging reasons to desire such a device—at least before the treaty, when it first became clear the British had developed one of their own. That was the weapon Martin had lost the stolen designs for, ensuring that the antitreaty elements in the old French government had no basis to argue against accepting the terms the British offered for ending the war. Fear of that device—lack of any way to counter it—was one of the prime reasons the French had agreed to sign the Treaty of Calais.

Those political motivations had long since ceased to be relevant, of course. These days, the men in power wanted nothing more than peaceful trade with Britain and its Dominions. Martin knew that, and always marveled that Dubois didn't seem to grasp it. Heaven forbid, Martin thought, the man should simply focus on moving forward, improving the quality of his shoddy merchandise and expanding his product lines. Dubois seemed mired in the past, and determined to find his way back to it and the success he'd once had. The man's imagination was as stunted as his body was corpulent. Even his greed was small-minded.

"One or the other of them can be removed, but I doubt even you could get away with eliminating both in such a short span of time. The Baron will be here in a few weeks, perhaps a month at the most, according to the gossip. So we monitor and control Hardison while we focus on neutralizing Murcheson."

"I'll need all you have on Hardison," Martin murmured, gliding over to the desk to view the newspaper column over Dubois's fat shoulder. The photograph at the top stopped him cold, hitting him like a blow to the gut.

"The woman . . ." he whispered.

"Charlotte, Lady Hardison. Née Moncrieffe. No, no, that was her first husband. Née Darmont. A young widow, it would seem. Hardison has exquisite taste, I must admit."

Martin agreed. He had seen the lady in person, and knew

the photograph scarcely did her justice. Five years hadn't taken much toll, and she still looked like a porcelain doll. Particularly beside the finely dressed brute who stood next to her in the picture.

"He's a monster, isn't he?" Martin remarked, to draw attention away from the bride. "I hope I'm not called upon to subdue him. He'd run me out of tranquilizers in no time at all."

"Just stay on him. Anticipate his movements, learn everything you can, be prepared for anything." Dubois's brow wrinkled. Martin thought he resembled a pug dog trying to work out how to chase its own tail. "Moncrieffe. Does that name sound familiar, Martin?"

The agent turned reluctant industrial spy shrugged, an elegant and quintessentially French motion. "I don't keep up with the names of the American pseudo-aristocracy, Monsieur Dubois. They are so numerous."

"True, true. Like the rats they are, eh?"

Dubois's plump hand had curled into his pocket instinctively when Martin moved toward the desk. He was fingering the button, Martin knew. Always ready to unleash the fabled poison if Martin stepped out of line. Dubois had never come to trust his captive espionage expert, and that was the one piece of intelligence Martin was willing to grant him. He was right not to trust Coeur de Fer.

Making a mental note to acquire his own copy of the newspaper, Martin bowed himself out of the office and slunk from the building. He would do as Dubois ordered, of course. But the presence of Reginald Moncrieffe's widow in France struck him as too unlikely to be coincidental. If it were, the coincidence must be nothing short of an act of Providence. Martin wasn't sure yet exactly what opportunity her visit might grant him, but he vowed to be ready for it, whatever it chanced to be.

It HAD BEEN a long few days, and Charlotte was beginning to feel her honeymoon must be some sort of awful penance—for what sins, she wasn't quite sure. Her ear implants worked brilliantly, except when they failed suddenly and dramatically, which had happened several times already since the trip began. Still, she'd been half expecting that, and at least Dexter had been forewarned. He pretended to ignore the disgusting consequences of the malfunctioning equipment, and dealt with the stewards who came to clean up.

Still, it was not entirely painful, cruising over a clear ocean, surrounded by luxury and waited on hand and foot. As working assignments went, occasional violent nausea notwithstanding, it was certainly a plum. Charlotte had assumed the biggest threat to her peace of mind on board the good ship *Alberta* would be the sleeping arrangements with Dexter. She was half right.

The difficulty was not that she had to share a bunk with a very large not-quite-husband. Dexter was more than obliging, and though he took up an inordinate amount of space in general, he left more than his fair share of bed free and clear for Charlotte by sleeping on his side at the far edge of the bunk, his back plastered to the wall behind. He insisted, moreover, that he was quite comfortable doing so and she shouldn't trouble herself to worry about him.

He didn't even snore.

Unfortunately, none of that helped the subtle dread that came over Charlotte when Dexter closed the bed-curtains for the night. She thought she was hiding her anxiety well, until the second evening of the voyage when Dexter sighed in the darkness and scrambled over her to unfasten the heavy protective drape. He crawled out of the berth to turn the lights back on.

"What?" he asked, clearly exasperated.

"What?"

"You haven't slept for two days, Charlotte. Not that I can tell, anyway. And you've been seasick as hell all day, so I'm sure you must need to rest. I'm doing my best not to keep you awake, but would you like me to try sleeping in the sitting room instead? Or perhaps I can ask the bursar if there's an empty stateroom."

"That would defeat the purpose of—"

"So would having you keel over from exhaustion." He put his hands on his hips, which drew Charlotte's attention to areas she'd been scrupulously trying to avoid noticing. He wore perfectly sensible, conservative, striped cotton pajamas, and Charlotte chided herself for imagining what he'd look like without them. "What is it? What do you need me to do?"

She bit her lip. She was weary to the bone, but it wasn't fair to Dexter to let him think it was his doing. "It isn't you. It's stupid, really. Only . . . I'm a little . . ."

Her eyes flicked to the thick, stiffened curtain, still half closed along the rail that hung from the ceiling. Dexter followed her gaze. "A little . . . afraid of damask? A bit terrified of slightly gaudy brocade? Constitutionally averse to the color oxblood? *Tell* me."

"Claustrophobic," she blurted, even as she smiled at his comic guesses. Saying it out loud felt surprisingly liberating. "I'm claustrophobic. There, are you happy? When that curtain is closed, I feel like I can't even breathe, much less sleep."

"Is that all? Why didn't you say something sooner?" He flicked off the light before he returned to the bed and tapped her legs, waiting for her to shift them out of the way before climbing back into his place by the wall. "Is this a recent development?"

"No, no. Ever since I was a little girl. It had improved for a while, then . . . then it got worse again. But the steward said we should close the curtains at night in case of swells, and loose objects flying, so—"

"I'm a light sleeper," he said breezily. "At least I normally am, when I haven't lain awake most of the previous night wondering why the hell the person in bed with me is *still* awake. I'll probably sleep like the dead tonight. But the weather's clear, so don't be concerned. Tomorrow we can go about securing loose objects. Henceforward, if any rough weather starts I'll be up in a flash and close the drape. In the meanwhile, leave the damn thing open and let's get some rest."

He was lying on top of the sheet and blanket, as he had the past few nights, while Charlotte snuggled beneath them.

When he flicked the counterpane over both of them, she thought sleepily that she should probably offer to find him an extra blanket.

Dexter sat up, rousing her from the drowsiness that had already started to weigh down her eyes. "Move over."

She slid out of his way once more, but he didn't vacate the bed this time, only leaned over her to push the curtain fully open on its track.

"Thank you," Charlotte whispered as Dexter flopped back down to the bunk and covered himself again.

"You're welcome."

After a few minutes of silence, time enough for Charlotte to grow drowsy again, Dexter murmured, "Please tell me Lord and Lady Darmont didn't lock you in a cupboard when you were naughty, or anything like that."

She snickered. "No, and neither did my nanny or governess. I've just always hated tight spaces. It improved for a time. For years I was able to talk myself out of it, but then . . ."

After a few moments of waiting, he prompted her. "Then?"

The sleepy humor was gone from her voice. "It all came back one day."

"I see." After another few moments, he added, "When I was a boy, I was afraid of dogs. Terrified, actually."

"Really? But you have dogs now, don't you? You've mentioned hunting with them."

"Oh yes," he confirmed, "I even have a few house dogs. I get along famously with them now. Big, small, doesn't matter. They seem to like me too."

"Hmm. What changed?"

He moved a bit, maneuvering onto his back and flexing his shoulders before lacing his fingers behind his neck. Charlotte could barely make out his profile in the gloom. Drowsiness was overtaking her again, and her eyes drooped despite her efforts to keep them open. She liked the sound of Dexter's friendly baritone in the darkened room. Charlotte wondered why it made a difference whether the curtain was open or closed when she could barely see her hand in front of her own face, but the air in the berth seemed clearer somehow with the drapes out of the way. She imagined she could feel a faint breeze across her face.

"When I was seven or eight, my mother brought home a dog one day. A half-grown homeless pup she'd found on her way back from visiting one of the villagers who was ill. The dog was a little terrier bitch, no higher than my knee. Fluffy little thing, once she was bathed and the knots combed out of her coat."

"Did this dog have a name?"

"Daisy," Dexter said. "Mother had already started calling her that on the ride home. The thing was, nobody could have ever been afraid of Daisy, she was too sweet and good-natured. A gentle spirit. I think she showed me what a dog *could* be, and after that I knew what to look for. Or maybe I just came to associate having a nice dog about with happy times at home."

"Mmm. I wish I could find a closet that had the same effect on me."

Dexter chuckled. "An anticlaustrophobia closet. I'll keep an eye out."

"If we find one," Charlotte pointed out, failing to stifle a yawn, "we could make a fortune. Excuse me." She was unclear on the etiquette of sharing a bed with a handsome but platonic colleague, but it seemed impolite to yawn quite so hugely in the middle of a conversation.

"Quite understandable. Time for us both to get some sleep. We have another long day of pretending to be blissful newlyweds ahead of us. Good night, Charlotte."

She thought she wished him good night back, but couldn't be sure the words made it out of her mouth before sleep exerted its will over her eyelids and dragged her down at last.

"LORD JOHNSON'S TARGET! Lord Johnson's target!"

"Pull!"

The trap launched off the deck above, striking a lazy

parabola that peaked somewhere over the ship's wake in time for the bullet to intersect it.

"Mark!"

Its twin, shot from the opposite side of the broad stern, seemed to come directly over Charlotte's head at a steep angle. She forced a little squeak and giggle out of herself as the fowling piece discharged, jerking Lord Johnson's shoulder back.

He had missed his shot, which she would have thought impossible given the lazy trajectory of the clay and the very fine make of the elaborate fowling harness Johnson was wearing.

The young Lord pushed the weapon, one adapted for the shorter-range clays, down along its track and off his arm. Then he made a great show of cursing and adjusting the trigger grip and stabilizing grip, all the while making pointed little remarks about the quality of Hardison's goods.

"Oh I know, isn't it *lovely*, Lord Johnson?" she twittered, batting her eyes and twirling her hat ribbons around her finger. "And so *shiny*!"

Dexter shot her a look and then stepped forward, clearing his throat.

"Johnson, if I may?"

With a few deft motions over the other man's harness, Dexter had reseated the shoulder pad and fastened the middle strap of the chest piece, which had apparently never been buckled. Perhaps because the abundance of decorative and very *shiny* rivets made it difficult to locate the actual buckles amid such a profusion of brass.

Not waiting for Johnson to reseat the weapon, Dexter nodded to the steward, who returned his nod and called out to the company, "Lord Hardison's target! Lord Hardison's target!"

"Pull."

A hit.

"Mark."

Another hit.

"Pull."

Hit.

"Mark."

Hit.

And so on, for the complete round, Dexter's voice as firm and controlled as his aim, Charlotte clapping like a giddy schoolgirl every few shots.

And aside from those holding the straps in place, Dexter's fowling harness was ostentatiously free from rivets. Charlotte knew he would have preferred simply using a gun. As would she, were she the one shooting, whether at clay or live targets. But they were masquerading as a fashionable young couple, and harnesses were the fashion.

These traps were filled with feathers that exploded in gay little puffs of color when they were hit. Charlotte looked for the feathers on the wind, but most of them were churned almost instantly into the wake of the huge cruise ship.

"Mr. Tanaka's target! Mr. Tanaka's target!"

That gentleman began his turn, faring somewhat better than Johnson, as Dexter shrugged out of his harness with a resigned expression. "He'll want to yammer about it for the next hour, mark my words."

"*Darling,*" Charlotte said a bit too loudly, warning Dexter with a nod that Johnson was headed their way, "You were *brilliant*, simply *brilliant*! You are going to teach me to use one of your splendid harnesses, aren't you? Remember, you promised. And when we get back home I want a robin's-egg blue one, with pretty gemstone rivets, exactly like my *very dear* friend Meggie's. But not paste! And one for riding to the hounds, as well. But in scarlet kid, to look well with my new riding habit." She giggled again, forcing the sound to the pitch and frequency that had seemed most distasteful to Lord Johnson on previous occasions. "Only that one wouldn't be for a *fowling piece* of course!" She tapped her folded fan smartly against Dexter's broad shoulder.

"Of course, my darling. Anything you like. I shall send a message to Pence to have him begin the work right away." He was almost as effusive as she, and sounded disgustingly besotted, but to no avail.

"Sorry, it didn't work," she whispered, and pretended tremendous interest in Mr. Tanaka's skill as the odious Lord Johnson ahem-hem-*hemmed* at Dexter's side.

"Johnson."

"The Hardison Harness not quite performing as expected this morning."

Dexter allowed a tiny, polite smile to bend his lips for the slightest second. "I have never referred to the style or the product as the 'Hardison Harness,' sir. But I'm sure if you try it again with the shoulder seated correctly and all the buckles, ah, buckled—"

"Quite. But you know—"

"I say, Hardison. Might want to look to your wife," another one of the waiting shooters suggested.

Charlotte had placed herself near the rail and was now leaning over it, pointing with dangerous enthusiasm at the wake in which she had just seen absolutely nothing unusual.

"*Darling*, a *porpoise*! I'm certain I saw a porpoise!" Hooking one foot under the lowest bar of the rail for safety, she let herself bend forward until anyone watching would surely think her set to pitch herself straight off the edge into the briny deep. "Look, over *there*!"

It had worked, she saw. In his need to rescue his obviously feather-brained wife from unintentional porpoise-motivated suicide, Dexter had ample cause to abandon all attention to Lord Johnson.

She could only hope that at least a few of the other passengers suspected she was not really as stupid as all that.

Then the boat hit a swell large enough to register despite the vessel's mass. Charlotte's body tilted and her stomach lurched, and she was suddenly incredibly grateful for the large, firm hands at her waist. And terribly, terribly sorry for the absolute mess she proceeded to make of the deck as she relived her breakfast in the most violent and graphic way imaginable.

Dexter muttered his thanks to the nobly silent, efficient stewards who swarmed to the spot and began to sand and swab before Charlotte had even quite finished retching. He tipped them handsomely, she noted with the one eye that seemed still able to open without causing her stomach to lurch again. Then he picked her up gingerly, without seeming to mind too much about the horrible state of her garments, and was almost all the way to their stateroom before giving in to the urge to say anything the least bit snide.

It wasn't snide at all, really, just, "And you didn't even have the fish."

Which was true, she hadn't.

DEXTER WAS EXPERIENCING difficulty keeping his rationalizations straight. He had explained his actions to himself at every step of the way, and at each juncture things had made a certain kind of sense.

His companion, his *wife*, had been unspeakably sullied by the products of her gastronomic upset. It only made sense to remove her clothing upon their return to the stateroom. He had called for the ship's surgeon, naturally, and that gentleman had arrived so quickly he encountered a baroness still clothed in her chemise and drawers, and wrapped in Dexter's dressing gown. She still had her stockings on, in fact. It was all quite modest.

Dexter declined the offer of a nurse to assist in bathing Lady Hardison and putting her to bed because, after all, he was supposed to be an ardent young husband on his honeymoon. It didn't make sense, viewed that way, to accept help from a nurse. Why would he require or want that?

So after the doctor had poured his restorative if highly narcotic tonic down Charlotte's throat and taken his leave, Dexter did what was necessary to see his young wife safely to bed. The dressing gown was removed—and sent out for cleaning—but it was clear the undergarments were also in need of removal. And once he had the giddy, woozy lady down to her stockings, it was also clear that actual bathing off was desperately needed.

He did that because it was necessary, keeping his sleepy wife wrapped in a blanket as much of the time as he could and carefully washing her off in sections. Charlotte was less than cooperative. She kept slumping to one side or the other in her chair as he sponged her off with a warm wet rag, or making giggling slurs on the shooting abilities of certain decidedly plump lordlings on the ship. Dexter wondered if he could get the doctor to prescribe some of that seasickness medication for his own use.

Then Charlotte raised a leg to the table and started to peel a stocking off, and Dexter was both chagrined and fascinated by the complete lack of modesty his overmedicated companion displayed. He could see things he had intended to studiously avoid seeing.

"You should put your leg down, Charlotte," he suggested in a hoarse voice he barely recognized as his own.

"Oh, Dexter." Her broad gesture swept the blanket free of her shoulders, revealing most of her bosom and taking with it the rest of the thinking portions of Dexter's brain. "You're bathing me off. That's so thoughtful, especially . . ."

After a moment, he prompted her. "Especially?"

"Especially what?" She blinked at him and smiled slowly. She looked barely able to keep her eyes open. "So kind. And so very, very . . ." She reached out to pat his cheek lightly, then lowered her hand and gave his shoulder a little pat as well. And then a shake. She was so small, it moved her more than it did him. She jiggled quite deliciously as she shook his shoulder, in fact. "So very *big*," she finally finished. "Like a lovely big *wall*. Or a bear. I do like your big, clever paws, *Mister* Hardison. Baron . . . thing."

She nodded off all at once, snoring in a way that was not dainty or charming at all, and with the most appalling breath . . . in only one stocking, her modesty hopelessly compromised by her foot still propped on the table's edge, and by the slipping blanket.

Dexter tortured himself by finishing Charlotte's bath before he slipped the clean night rail over her head and tucked her into the berth to sleep off the surgeon's remedy. The last thing he did, because he was a glutton for punishment he supposed, was reach under the fragile lawn gown to loosen her other gaiter. He rolled her stocking down her sleek thigh and trim calf until it popped off her foot in a silken ring.

Dexter forced himself to back away after that, wondering all the while if perhaps the good doctor was amenable to bribes.

WHEN CHARLOTTE WOKE up she was blessedly clean and dry. Her stomach was firmly in its proper place, no hint of queasiness. Her mouth tasted like the bottom of the Aegean stables pre-cleaning, but other than that she could hardly complain. Dexter offered her an iced soda water when her eyes were barely open, and she drank a tentative sip before she tried to sit up on the berth.

"No. You're staying right there. And you're telling me where the retrieval hook is."

"Retrieval hook?"

"For the Alvarez devices," he said with exaggerated patience. "In your ears."

"Oh, that retrieval hook. It isn't really a hook, did you know? It's a special sort of magnet with a—"

"Charlotte. For the better part of three days, I have been entertained with a parade of foodstuffs issuing from your person in very much the wrong direction. I have nearly run myself out of pocket money paying off the stewards, a team of whom seems to have been formed for the express purpose of following you around this ship with a sand pail and a mop." Well, she knew *that* was an exaggeration. He was not even close to running out of pocket money. "And I don't suppose I would find it quite so very annoying, and might feel a wee bit more sympathy, if it weren't for the fact that I know you to have a pair of medical devices worth more than that entire team of stewards makes in several years, implanted in your ears for the specific purpose of preventing motion sickness."

"No, they're really so I know where I am in the air. And

they work splendidly for that," she protested. "They chime and everything."

His jaw clenched. Charlotte could see a pair of muscles bulging along the chiseled line from his ears to his chin, and a matching set of muscles forming solid columns of contained impatience down the sides of his neck. "The extraction tool."

"All right," she agreed reluctantly. "But Dr. Alvarez had them out for me a few months after they first went in. And she said there was nothing wrong," she reminded him. She groaned as she tried to rise to a sitting position.

"Stay." He pressed her shoulder back into the pillow and glared until she stopped moving.

"In a little wooden case in my reticule. I'm supposed to keep it with me at all times."

"This reticule?" he said, pulling the small bag from the back of the doorknob to the sitting room area of their absurdly expensive stateroom. "The one you weren't carrying on deck today? The case was in here?"

"That's the one, yes. Don't be unkind, Dexter. It's not as though I've enjoyed casting my accounts all over the poor ship." Indeed, Charlotte felt somewhat ill-used in general for having to suffer vomiting *and* scolding.

"You had these put in when you first started training on the airship, yes?"

"Yes. For the altimeter chime modification, and there's also a port in the left one that can connect to a directional sonic amplificator built into the ship. Sometimes if the wind and geography are right I can pick up conversations on the ground from a few thousand feet up."

"Mmm. Remarkable."

He moved from the nearby chair to the edge of the berth, which sagged a little under his weight. Charlotte trembled as he leaned over her, turned her head to the side with three fingertips placed along her cheekbone, and deftly inserted the slender gold reed into her ear.

The click was wrenchingly loud, as always, and the

quarter-twist to loosen the implant from its shaft made Charlotte's hackles rise, as always. That moving *thing* felt horribly wrong inside her head. But that only lasted a second or so.

Once it was out, *everything* felt wrong—inside her head and otherwise. Without the equilibrium provided by having both implants functioning in tandem, Charlotte's sense of up and down fell into disarray. The loss of functional hearing from the temporarily disabled ear added its own disorientation, making it difficult to tell which direction sounds were coming from.

She hadn't even realized she was hyperventilating until she felt warm, heavy hands on her shoulders, rubbing in soothing strokes, and a rumbling voice from everywhere and nowhere reminding her to breathe *out*, not just in. She forced herself to relax, to open her eyes and focus on the nearest thing. Dexter's face.

"If I take out the other one," he said, exaggerating the movement of his lips to ensure she understood, "you'll be deaf but not nearly as dizzy."

She nodded, swallowed back her panic and presented her other ear. It was faster this time, the discomfort masked by the generally worked-up state she was already in.

And he was right. Though she could hear only echoing emptiness, like the sound of the ocean in a seashell, she could feel her body's own orientation to the world clearly again. She could even sit up, though she did so slowly.

Dexter was scribbling something on a notepad, and before she could peek over his shoulder, he turned to show it to her.

You might want to clean your teeth while I work.

He grinned and moved off to the sitting room, holding the implants carefully in one hand. She sighed, feeling irritated that the sound did not register in her own ears. And then, because she did desperately want to clean her teeth, she sighed again and swung herself out of the berth.

She was in her nightdress. And if her nose could be believed, she was quite thoroughly clean.

"How long have I been asleep?" she asked, hoping she wasn't too loud.

Not loud enough, apparently. He didn't move, and she aimed her second try directly at his big, impassive shoulders through the open connecting door.

"How long have I been asleep?"

He jumped and whirled, eyes wide.

Perhaps that one was a bit too loud.

He mouthed something. Charlotte read lips fairly well, having learned in the course of her unique job training. But perversely, she shrugged and made a puzzled face to see what Dexter would do.

He cocked that skeptical eyebrow at her, is what he did, and jotted on his notepad in a sharp hand that almost tore the paper.

4 hrs

"Four? Hours?" He couldn't be serious. She thought he'd said "a few" something. Perhaps her lip-reading was less accurate than she'd supposed. "*Four hours*? But when did I have a bath?"

More of a glare, this time, followed by another scribble.

Brush your teeth.

Charlotte put her hands on her hips and stood her ground. "Dexter! Did you change my clothes?"

He was securing one of the implants in a clamp under a magnifier, on the sitting room table he'd co-opted from the first day to house a number of vaguely scientific-looking devices, few of which Charlotte recognized. He didn't write anything down, didn't even turn his head to her this time, only nodded.

She tapped her foot. Opened her mouth to say something, then caught a whiff of her own breath and stormed over to the door to the lavatory, which the men all insisted on calling a *head*, just as the doors were all *hatches* on board the ship, and the beds were all *berths* or *bunks*. Tiresome.

After scrubbing her teeth thoroughly with a great quantity of tooth powder, Charlotte returned to her position in the center of the stateroom, feeling much better prepared to do battle.

Dexter was now hunched in intense concentration over the table, doing something intricate with what looked like a tiny pair of tweezers and a bottle of mineral spirit.

"Dexter," she said experimentally. Not loud enough. "Dexter!"

Perhaps a bit too loud again.

He looked around, querying with his eyes.

"Did *you* give me a bath?"

He smiled, a bit too broadly, and turned back to the table. Charlotte stamped her foot, feeling ridiculous and blaming him for it. She wanted her ears back. She remembered nothing of a bath, nothing of clothes being changed.

"Do you mean to say you saw me naked?"

He went still, head tilted to one side. For a moment she wondered if he would pretend not to have heard. Then he turned all the way around in the swivel chair, arms crossed over his chest. He was still smiling, an entirely different kind of smile now though. His dark eyes made a languorous circuit from her face to her ankles and back again, and he finished by meeting her eyes in what could only be a challenge. Then he swung the chair around to the table again and scribbled something longer on the notepad, then offered it over his shoulder without turning. She was forced to come closer if she wanted to take it from him and read it. While she did, he screwed the top back on the mineral spirit bottle and carefully replaced his tweezer-things in a little case with fitted velvet slots for holding various small tools.

The surgeon came by & gave you a tonic. You were charming after, & not sick at all. Obvs. had to burn clothes you were wearing. So I sponged you off and put you in a nightgown. You really don't remember, do you?

"No, I don't." She also wasn't sure she believed him.

He plucked the pad from her fingers and wrote on it again, letting her read over his shoulder.

I believe I have located and dealt with source of problem re: implants.

"No! That was five minutes. You can't have!"

He shrugged and picked one of the tiny gold and crystal tubes up with a clean cloth, gesturing to her right ear as he fitted the retrieval hook onto the end of the implant.

It went back in with the same uncanny twist, and a cacophony of noise attacked Charlotte's brain as her world lurched sharply out from under her.

A surface like a heated wall stopped her fall, and enormous reassuring hands steadied her, cradled her, as the wall rumbled in a comforting way.

"Sorry. I've got you. Left ear now, and you'll be better than ever. Be still."

She gripped the surface beneath her palms, braced her arms and tried not to move as a one of those warm, supportive hands moved into her hair, tucking the strands behind her ear and then cupping the back of her head to angle it just so.

There was a last sickening slide and the too-loud click as the implant latched itself into place, and then Charlotte's perspective restored itself.

She was sitting in Dexter's lap. Her legs dangled between his, her hands supported against the very solid thigh in front of her knees, and he was stroking one hand slowly up and down her back as he used the other to stow the tiny extraction tool safely in its specialized box.

"Don't you want to know what it was?" he asked, as if she were not sitting in her night rail in his lap, with her hands clenching his thigh.

"I suppose," she answered, exactly as if his hand were not lengthening its exploratory tour of her back to include a brief circular foray around her hip and buttock.

"Earwax."

If somebody had told her she would ever find the word *earwax* titillating, she would have laughed out loud. At the moment, however, it was not remotely amusing.

"Earwax?" Her mind engaged enough to register disbelief. "But the implants are sealed, and I clean the exposed surfaces daily with ethyl alcohol. Doctor Alvarez didn't mention anything about—"

"Not on the exterior, in one of the pressure valves. A tiny bead of it. It must have been overlooked during the initial installation. I suspect it originally adhered to the casing, then got dislodged enough to gum the works of the implant itself once it hardened. It was causing the valve to stick. But not, I think, every time. Mainly when the pressure tried to equalize while you were moving forward into a horizontal position." He demonstrated with his free hand, tipping it from the vertical, and Charlotte nodded as though this were profoundly helpful.

It made sense. The *Gossamer Wing* with its horizontal cradle. The deck chairs on the ship, so comfortable until she had attempted to roll over and sun her back. And the railing, beyond which there had been only fictional porpoises. She had been fine until she tipped that vital bit more forward, and that few inches and degrees of slant had made all the difference. And it might not have even occurred to the doctor to test the devices at that particular angle.

But the sense was hard to focus on, when his hand was making a much more leisurely round of her hip this circuit.

"But what I still don't understand," she said, focusing on the one thing that seemed foremost, "is why the ship feels like it's lurching? I mean if you removed the earwax, and the implants are working properly."

"That's easy." His hand tightened at her waist as one of those lurches threw them slightly off balance and the chair threatened to swivel into the table. "It's because the ship is lurching. We're heading into a patch of unfortunate weather."

Seven

⁂

DEXTER'S REASON STARTED to fail him when he held her head steady to reinsert the first implant. And he didn't even try to pretend to himself that his method of securing her for the insertion of the second was rooted in chivalry or even expedience.

He had wanted her in his lap, the better to touch her with his big, clever paws. He marveled at her delicacy, and at how very tiny her hands and limbs were compared to his own. How his fingers could span the width of her buttock from hipbone to tailbone. He knew that even very small women did not, in fact, break when a large man touched them. Or did other things with them.

The sorts of things men often did with their wives.

He had expected her to bolt once the implants were replaced. But she seemed incapable of moving, and he had long since used up his stores of self-restraint where Charlotte's body was concerned.

Even the weather seemed complicit in nudging them together, as the swell of the waves and the heaving of the boat urged Charlotte, who had less natural ballast, to cling to the nearest available heavy thing for security. And no heavy thing could be nearer than Dexter was to her at that moment.

"I need to stow my equipment," he remarked. Things were beginning to slide this way and that, and fetch up against the lip of the table. He caught a magnifying vise with one hand, but never removed the other from her posterior where it was now so comfortably settled. Nor did Charlotte seem inclined to shift herself from his thigh. He wondered if her paralysis was caused by desire, or perhaps more along the lines of what a rabbit felt when caught by the headlights of an oncoming steam car.

Then the boat did a new thing, not a lurch but a tilt, and both of them grabbed at the table as their world shifted to a sickening slant for what seemed like an eternity. Thunder cracked, and the gas lamps flickered ominously and then dimmed entirely until they were in almost total darkness. As the light faded, the ship seemed to slow to a halt, to an equilibrium, a balance that felt as tenuous as they both knew it must be. The very air was alive with terrified anticipation.

The ship went down the swell so quickly they nearly flew for a mad second or two, Charlotte's insubstantial weight almost leaving Dexter's lap altogether as he clung to the table's edge. An open case sailed slowly across the floor past his chair, and he began scooping his fragile, valuable equipment into it.

"Is it an emergency light?"

He glanced around, not sure what Charlotte was talking about, then realized he could actually see quite well given that the wall sconces and chandelier were still out.

"The doctor said the gas would be turned off if it got bad enough. And yes, he said—help!"

She leaned and snagged the case with her foot as it scooted back the other way, clutching at Dexter's shirt to keep from rolling off his knee onto the floor.

He deposited the last of his stray things in the small trunk and latched it firmly.

"I need to stow it under the berth with the other small baggage. We'll go before the next trip up. On three. One . . . two . . . three!"

As one they leaped through the dividing door and scrambled for the relative safety of the bunk, and Charlotte climbed up while Dexter opened the compartment below the platform and shoved the equipment case into it. He let gravity pull the door closed and carry him into the berth as the ship began its next descent.

Charlotte was already busy yanking at the heavy curtains, snapping them into place along the rails at the bottom of the bunk to guard against any remaining projectiles. When she had finished, she and Dexter were encased in a snug little cube of bed linens and tapestry, its dark softness punctuated only by a few leaks of the cold blue emergency lighting that seemed to emanate from a single bulb high in one corner of each cabin compartment.

"I think this may be my very last attempt at a honeymoon. They don't seem to work out well for me at all."

He laughed, caught off guard. "The first one was hardly the fault of the weather," he ventured, unsure how far to push a jesting mood in the face of such dark humor. Perhaps only she was entitled to find levity in the subject of honeymoons.

"On the contrary, it rained horribly on the first one. The alligators were interesting, however."

"I can't do much about the weather—well, I can't do anything at all about it, obviously—but I think I can promise you that our honeymoon will at least be free from alligators."

She shrugged, then gripped the wooden molding on either side of her as the ship began to pitch once more. She pressed herself even more firmly into the corner, but as best he could see in the limited light, she did not look terrified. He wondered if the claustrophobia was already closing in, but knew that if it was, his mentioning it would only make it worse.

"They weren't so bad, really," she assured him. "It's not as though they attacked the riverboat. They merely lurked. Alligators are experts at lurking."

"I can only imagine. I've never been to the South."

"It has a certain charm. The Spanish moss in the oak trees, that sort of thing. Very evocative. Although I'm not quite sure of what."

"Gothic decadence?" he suggested.

"Perhaps. There's a bit too much of the French feel down that way for me to ever truly relax and enjoy it. Though I didn't feel quite so fervently about that prior to my last visit there. My lord, I must thank you. I don't suppose I would survive this tempest if you hadn't repaired my implants. As it is, I must say I'm not feeling sick in the least."

My lord, is it now?

Dexter let a smile build slowly across his face, looking her firmly in the eye all the while and hoping she could see him. It didn't need much urging, that smile. He found he was enjoying himself despite the storm, despite the sheer unlikelihood of the whole situation.

In particular, he liked that the no-longer-ill and suitably clean Charlotte's night rail was practically transparent. And since it was slightly chilly now that the storm was raging outside and the gas was off, her good health was manifesting itself in the form of excellent circulation. Parts of her, parts he could see even in the dim of the berth, were practically burgeoning with suffusion. And delightfully crimped, although the lawn fabric wasn't quite transparent enough to reveal that detail. About that, he was making an educated guess.

Her nipples were the approximate size of small, wild raspberries. Not the overlarge farm-grown sort, with their blandly acceptable flavor. No, the little ones you almost overlook, the ones that grow in hidden places all on their own and taste like summertime in heaven.

Jerking his eyes away from Charlotte's breasts, Dexter tried to remember what they had just been talking about. He wasn't even sure when his eyes had drifted down.

But one glance told him that she had noted that drift quite clearly.

Curiously, she did not look angry or embarrassed. A little annoyed, perhaps. Exasperated. As if she now had a problem to deal with, and wasn't quite sure where to begin.

"I'm glad you're feeling better. Would you like a blanket?" Dexter offered.

She sat in my lap. She didn't move. Her hip felt designed to match the curve of my hand.

"You're sitting on the counterpane," she pointed out.

"Oh." He shifted enough for her to drag the quilted damask out from under him. She pulled it over her lap and arranged it around her waist and torso, high enough to cover her breasts.

"You were saying something about the emergency lights?"

"I was? Oh, yes. The surgeon mentioned they might come on. They run on battery cells, with a radio trigger. The gas lights are shut down in emergencies."

"I see. So we're to wait in near darkness until the all clear is sounded, I take it."

The creak and sway of the huge ship cut through her words and she nestled further down into her corner. Dexter propped himself carefully next to her at the side of the bunk and tried to think about anything but the groan of wood and metal and the pounding of the ocean against the vessel's frame. He surprised himself with his next words.

"I've spent worse nights."

IT WAS LIKE a fever dream, Charlotte thought. The little glimmers of icy light, the gathering womb-like warmth of the enclosed bunk. Perhaps she had not yet fully recovered from whatever euphoria the doctor's potion had brought on. If she had, she reasoned, the confines of the bunk would feel stifling to her, not comforting.

Dexter took up far more space than what was occupied by his physical form. The reality of him, the *presence* of him, might have suffocated her had it not felt so very much like pure oxygen. Heady and rich and elemental.

She had analyzed his scent, because Charlotte liked to analyze things, the better to place them into the tidy compartments of her mind. Dexter Hardison, Baron Hardison, was bay rum and peppermint, copper, a hint of sharp mineral spirit, and sometimes a little musk of perspiration as the day wore on. And also horse, although of course he had lost the horse component since boarding the ship.

None of which explained to her satisfaction why catching his scent made her knees go weak. Or why she had stayed so very much longer on his lap than was appropriate.

Except that it *was* appropriate in a sense, of course, because he was her husband. Not forever, but for now. Of all times, as the ship tossed them to and fro and screamed into the deluge, now seemed like a handy time to have such a thing as a husband. A bulwark, a helpmeet. Somebody to hold her throughout the storm. Somebody to sit beneath her on a bench, his hand slipping inside her garments as he plundered her mouth with kisses until she was breathless.

They hadn't discussed that night. Not so much as mentioned it. At times, she wondered if he had actually felt anything. Then she reminded herself that seated as she had been, she had felt more than enough of *him* to be assured that he was as moved as she was. Physically, at least. Even through all the layers of petticoat, she could feel that quite clearly.

Still, it was only a kiss. A ploy, a necessary bit of subterfuge. A practical measure. They were adults engaged in the business of espionage. All sorts of pretending went on in that business. And men reacted to women they didn't especially care for all the time.

He moved a little closer to her on the berth, and she pretended not to notice.

"Charlotte? Why did you regress just now, and call me 'my lord'?" His expression was in shadow where he sat, and she could not quite make out his tone.

"Regress?"

"You were doing so well. You must remember to call me Dexter. I am your husband, after all."

"Of course. Dexter. Thank you for reminding me."

"I think . . ." He turned his upper body a little more toward her, and she swallowed, wondering when her mouth had gone so dry. "I think it might be a good idea to practice these little displays of marital familiarity. The French are known for their amorous inclinations, you know. If anybody would be likely to ferret out the secret of our connection, it would be a Frenchman."

"I see. And what sort of 'practice' do you propose, Lord Har—"

"Dexter."

"Dexter."

"Charlotte. Must we pretend like this?"

Her heart hammered up into her throat. She didn't answer, and couldn't think. It was a small, small space, and he was filling it. Such a little step it seemed, to letting him fill *her*. Yet she knew it was no little step, and that she must not be quite in possession of her faculties if she was thinking that way.

After a moment of her silence, Dexter rose to all fours and crawled the scant distance left between them, until he was poised with his face a few inches from hers. His legs flanked hers, his hands rested on the quilt alongside her hips. Nowhere did he touch her, but she could feel him everywhere, all the same. She could smell him, his scent minus the horse, assaulting her awareness like an advance guard. His voice when he spoke again was lower, more intense. She wondered that she could hear it over the storm—or was that her own heart roaring so loud? Then she wondered she could hear anything else, as Dexter's voice was the only sound that registered.

"We both want this," he said. "We've both wanted this since that night at the ball. Even before that. I thought I could ignore it. God knows I tried, because I knew it was meant to be just business with you. But now I find myself trapped in a bed with you in the middle of a possibly lethal storm, and somehow the niceties of the situation seem to pale beside the overwhelming importance of being inside you at least once before we die at sea."

"We're not going to die at sea." She had intended to scoff, but managed only a hoarse little whisper instead. *Pathetic*.

"Probably not," he admitted. "The ship seems sound and I don't think the storm is all that bad. But the possibility certainly does lend weight to my position, and I'll confess I'm that desperate for you."

He didn't sound desperate. He sounded serious, and full of fierce need that he had been keeping under control too long. She swallowed and tried to think again. The effort was not meeting with success.

"Charlotte." A fraction of an inch closer every second. "If the storm hadn't interfered, I would have kissed you. And more. I could have taken you over that table. I think you would have let me."

She nodded, her eyes closing. Then she opened them again, trying to take it back, shaking her head violently. "No! I was only lightheaded from the implants coming out. I was about to—"

"Well now you're just lying," Dexter said flatly, "and I don't have to tolerate *that*."

He kissed her hard, because her attempt to dissemble had clearly made him impatient. If it had been softer, or he had approached more carefully, she might have had time and space to reconsider. With no time to think herself out of it, Charlotte just reacted and kissed back. And kissed, and kissed, until she wasn't sure if she could ever do anything else. As if kissing Dexter were now her sole purpose.

It felt so good to *feel*. She realized as she raised her arms to his neck that except for the night of their engagement and their fleeting kiss at the wedding, it had been years since she'd touched another person beyond a polite clasp about the shoulders or a handshake upon greeting. She had forgotten what an embrace felt like, what a man felt like. Reginald, however, had never felt quite this substantial in her arms.

Reginald had been considerate and kind. He had been

her very dear friend and he had wanted her in his bed, but not this desperately, not with this greedy urge to take and devour. Charlotte knew Dexter had that urge, because she had it herself and recognized it in him. It was something shared, created between them, and as ignoring it hadn't exorcised it, they could only try to exhaust it.

It was Dexter who broke away first, sighing and staring. He still cupped her face in one hand. Brushing his thumb down her cheek, he traced her lips and blinked a few times before finally speaking.

"I'm trying to remind myself that you were hardly married before you were widowed. Three nights. I know this isn't entirely new to you, but—"

"Behave as if it were." She already suspected it would be vastly different from her short time with Reginald, in any case. "You're new to me. This feels . . . new. Assume I know nothing. It won't be far from the truth."

He nodded and sat back on his heels, looking as though he were trying to solve a problem. Charlotte stared back, puzzled.

"Take off the gown."

A simple suggestion. An unprecedented suggestion. She blushed to her toes and tried to think of a suitable response to it. Dexter's eyes were dark, impossible to read in the inadequate light.

"You see?" Charlotte replied at last. "That's something new." Before she could make herself more anxious thinking it through, she reached for the hem of her night rail and tugged it up and over her head as quickly as she could. Like jumping into cold water all at once.

But this wasn't cold. It burned, the heat of his eyes on her body. Charlotte knelt with her hands wrapped in the quilt on either side of her knees, resisting the urge to cover herself. Braving the onslaught of his attention.

"This is new?" Dexter sounded baffled. "You never took off—"

"No. Never."

Reginald had treated her like a princess, or like his

dearest friend. But he had been shy, hardly more experienced than Charlotte, and he had never seen her bare breasts. He had never bent his head to lick her uncovered nipples, as Dexter did now.

The molten heat of his mouth was almost too much to bear, and it awakened nerves throughout her body in sympathetic response until she felt almost dizzy with vitality. By the time he returned his lips to hers, Charlotte wasn't sure whether it was the storm or her heart that raged so fiercely. She throbbed and ached, off-balance in a profound way. If she felt this horrible need for the first time now, what did that mean about who she was *before*? This felt like an expression of her very soul. So what had her soul been doing all this time?

Dexter picked her up as though she weighed nothing, scooped her down flat to the bed and covered her naked body with his still-clad one, never breaking their kiss. She felt something not completely new, the hard evidence of his masculinity pressing against her in a rough approximation of the act they would soon be performing. She thought of the pain, the blood of that first time, and the gingerly way Reginald had taken her on the second night. Apologetically, almost. If she hadn't known better, she might have thought him shy or even squeamish. But he had clearly enjoyed the act itself once he had initiated it, and been absurdly grateful afterward. Quite endearingly so.

There was no apology in Dexter's body, his lips, the broad shoulders that sheltered her, his hips pressing down in no uncertain terms to bring his erection firmly against her sex.

He seemed so practiced, so comfortable with his own body and with hers. He smoothed one big hand over her breast and rolled the nipple between his thumb and forefinger, chuckling when she gasped and arched up off the bed. When he kissed her neck, the sensitive skin behind her ear and the smooth muscle of her shoulder, Charlotte nearly wept with untapped desire.

She was almost angry at having never experienced this.

At having never even known of it. The married women with their subtle innuendos and ribald remarks had never suggested this madness of *wanting*. Perhaps it was just she herself who was mad.

If so, Dexter shared her insanity. He seemed hungry as a beast, eager as a boy. And so knowing. *Where did he learn this?* Charlotte had to wonder, even as she told herself she didn't want to know.

She didn't want to know how many other women had felt his lips suckling their breasts, his bear paw hands on their hips in a fond caress, or sliding—*oh!*—between their thighs and teasing a path upward until those big, callused fingers met petal-soft slickness.

On the third night of her first marriage, Charlotte had thrilled to hot lips over the silk covering her bosom and gentle fingers teasing into her, easing a path first. Exploring her slowly, and the shy joy on Reginald's face when she made those tentative motions against his hand was another thrill, one they had shared. It had been so sweet, and embarrassing and exciting all at once, learning each other like that. Working it all out together like a puzzle. She'd seen for the first time how a best friend could become something infinitely more precious, and she'd wanted to stay in that bunk with him forever. In a sense, of course, Reginald would be there forever. The memory tugged at her, wanting to distract, but was ultimately unable to withstand the power of the present.

"I'm almost afraid to ask," Dexter whispered, "did you . . . enjoy yourself, those few times?"

"I suppose so." She was thinking how very odd it was, to have a conversation with a man whose finger was sliding into one's vagina. Then she ceased thinking as his thumb brushed higher and set every nerve in her body alight.

"No," he said, and chuckled yet again. "I mean did he make you come? Have a climax," he clarified when she looked at him curiously.

There were feelings and memories, and then there were fairy tales. "Women don't have climaxes."

Laughter was wholly inappropriate to the situation, she thought. And these were no chuckles from Dexter but a deep, genuine belly laugh.

"I assure you they do," he said at last, wiping a tear against his shoulder.

"That's a myth, invented by whores to make men feel like gods," she replied, echoing the words she had overheard at a soiree, uttered among three married women who thought they were safe from eavesdroppers behind the cover of a large potted palm. She'd found it comforting to hear that, as she'd been worried she and Reginald hadn't had time to get to all the important things and an orgasm would definitely qualify as an important thing to have missed.

Dexter shook his head, bemused. He moved his hand on her sex again, causing an almost unsettling amount of pleasure. Charlotte had expected him to stroke there a few times, then enter her and proceed as usual. She wasn't sure what to make of this . . . playing for its own sake.

"I think I may well feel like a god when I make you come."

He sat up, hand still in her lap, and knelt between her legs. Charlotte felt exposed, revealed in more ways than physically. She didn't like not to know things. She didn't like to feel a fool. But she found it difficult to resist a challenge, and even more difficult to resist the idea of being touched by this imposing man in her bed. Such an unlikely husband.

"Nonsense." She already didn't believe herself.

"So you feel nothing when I do this? Or . . . this?" He described a circle with his thumb on that most sensitive knot of nerves, and smiled like sin incarnate when she moaned. "Then I don't suppose you'll be bothered in the slightest if I kiss you there?"

Suiting the action to the word, he dipped his head and went to work. Charlotte could tell, even in her feverish agony of arousal, that he was very familiar with the whole business. He never hesitated, he knew precisely where to put his tongue and lips and fingers, where to suck and nibble and lick and plunge. And he observed, Charlotte noticed. He adjusted constantly, responding to her reactions in an escalating series of moves and countermoves. A skilled negotiation of her pleasure. She knew, before she was even at the brink of the crisis, that she had never been more wrong about anything in her life than she had been about this.

Dexter lifted his mouth away when she was trembling, staring at a precipice of sensation, ready to fling herself over but not sure how to do it. At the loss of stimulation, Charlotte made a noise that was nearly a growl. He chuckled again, but not in a mean-spirited way. If anything, he sounded delighted for her.

"Please. Please, Dexter, don't . . . please do . . . I can't . . ." She couldn't find her words. They had all flown straight out of her head, and the only thing she could think of was *more*.

"But women don't climax," he reminded her.

She wanted to kill him. The smug bastard. But first she needed him to finish what he'd started. If he didn't, she thought she might die.

"Please!"

"Well, since you're begging."

It took her a moment to find it again, the keen edge of that bliss. And then he moved his lips and fingers again just so, and she found it and was sliced clean through by it, lost to everything as her body showed her what it could do.

Despite what she had told him, she had always had her suspicions that there was more to the whole thing than the first gentle, then frantic though not unpleasant prodding she had experienced with Reginald. But she had never imagined anything like this.

"Please," Charlotte whispered when she could form words again, as she watched him unbutton his trousers with frantic speed. She wasn't even sure what she was asking for. She felt an aching emptiness, and then Dexter filled it. Filled her, body and soul. He had to push himself into her a little at a time, letting her adjust. It didn't quite hurt, but it was unexpected. Different. Perhaps, she thought, each man really was a wholly new experience.

"So fucking tight," he said roughly, sounding not at all displeased. "*God*, Charlotte."

His coarse words, his tension, communicated with that heat low in her belly, firing it again. Like a magical creature, hard to dispel once summoned, her arousal hovered where her body met his. She didn't know what to do with it. This was nothing like those nights with Reginald, nothing at all. A different universe of experience. This would change everything. She felt it changing with every breath.

"Are you all right?"

He was still working deeper, languidly, and he raised himself to his elbows to look at her. Big hands framed her face, stroking her cheeks. Big shoulders blocked out her view of the dimly lit berth. Big body, splitting hers in two, so that she thought it should hurt and didn't know how it could feel good. More insanity.

"Am I all right?" She wasn't sure. Charlotte wasn't even sure who she was in that moment, much less how that stranger felt. "Dexter, I can't . . . I don't know how."

How to do this thing properly. Or how to speak, evidently.

He was driving the sense right out of her.

"You're thinking too hard," he reassured her. "Don't think. Just let your body tell you what to do, sweet."

Then he kissed her, which helped enormously. Soft and velvet, as gentle with his tongue as he was firm and determined between her legs. He finally hit her limit, somewhat before his own, and cursed softly against her lips.

"Move with me, Charlotte. Let me in. I'll make it good for you, I promise."

She believed him. She didn't think. She moved, raising her legs to wrap over his hips, arching her back to get closer, and letting him in. They sighed together, stealing each other's breath. The ship surged and so did they, until Charlotte's senses were completely overwhelmed with Dexter. When she came again, writhing closer still to the source of the pleasure, he laughed that same delighted laugh.

"I don't feel like a god," he murmured into her ear. "I

feel like I'm worshipping a goddess. Worshipping inside your body with mine."

She might have wept at that, she wasn't sure. It was too much. It did to her emotions what his touch had done to her body, changing the known universe in the blink of an eye.

When he followed her into bliss, finally collapsing exhausted and rolling her with him to keep them connected without crushing her, Charlotte clung to him like a barnacle. Unwilling to have it over, whatever this new thing was. But aware, somewhere in the back of her mind, that she had quite possibly made an error of such grave magnitude it could cost her everything.

EIGHT

DEXTER HAD LIED. He *had* felt like a god. Seeing Charlotte shatter, tasting her surrender, had been a moment so rare Dexter could not help but be anxious lest he never manage to repeat it. Being inside her was pleasure beyond comprehension. He had felt more than godlike.

He had felt *complete*.

Dexter had rather thought he was already complete. To find at this juncture that he had evidently been missing something so significant was extremely unsettling.

Charlotte unsettled him. Her determination, her attempts to be solemn and businesslike when she was alone with him. She was obviously set upon the idea of mourning her late husband forever, as if she were duty bound to do so and deserved nothing else. Dexter thought Charlotte perhaps saw herself as broken. Beyond repair. Dexter didn't think so. He wondered if she knew how much of her own clean, pure spirit shone through when she was acting out her little charade for the other passengers. Teasing and flirting and prancing about the ship as though she hadn't a thought in her head or a care in the world. She looked as though she were rediscovering what it meant to have fun.

Now she looked like a fallen woman, gorgeously debauched and sleeping the sleep of the exhausted unrighteous in his bed. A fallen, lascivious angel.

She was an angel who would be his only for a few precious weeks or months, if all went as expected in France. Then they would complete their masquerade with a genteel separation upon returning to America. At such time as either of them wanted to marry again in the future, there would be a discreet divorce or, if they could convince the court they qualified, an annulment.

For Crown and country, Dexter reminded himself. But here in the dark it was just the two of them, and Dexter found himself wishing the storm could go on indefinitely.

"But it's stopped," he realized.

"Mmm?" Charlotte nestled against his chest, eyes still closed.

"The storm has passed. Shh, go back to sleep."

She clung to him a moment, but he worked his way free of the tangled bedclothes and her enticing limbs to leave the berth. The gaslights, with their automatic pilots, were back on, and he turned them all down carefully while checking for damage about the cabin and ascertaining that it was still night.

After taking care of other needs he returned to the soft, warm cocoon of the bunk, and the woman still curled there with one hand tucked under her chin.

She was awake, and watching him.

"I don't suppose I could convince you it was a very bad idea, and we must never repeat it?"

Dexter grinned. "Never in a million years. Do you really not want to repeat it?"

Charlotte sat up, taking his breath away. She was still gloriously naked, and seemed to have overcome her shyness. Knowing her even a little Dexter suspected it was a brave front, a point of pride with her not to seem ashamed of herself or her actions. He admired that, and admired her. He already wanted her again.

"It doesn't matter whether I *want* it. Animals *want*. Human beings *reason*. I can forgive myself a momentary lapse, but I have a job to do and mustn't lose sight of my mission."

Which Dexter knew was absolutely true. But for at least the next week, it was a moot point and they both knew it.

He drew his legs in and pulled the curtain closed, not bothering to fasten it but hoping to recreate the earlier mood. Charlotte reached out and batted the curtain open again, seeming to relax a bit once her view of the cabin was restored. The storm had brought warmer air, it seemed, and the small enclosure was humid now. Dexter could feel the linen of his shirt sticking to his back. Funny, how little things could be magnified when one was aroused. As though all the nerves were suddenly operating at higher capacity.

"Human beings are animals," he reminded her, peeling the shirt off, "and though we can reason, we also have needs. We deny that part of our nature at our peril. People are also, I think, a bit like temperamental machines. We need to run at full speed sometimes, and stretch to our capacity. It clears the works, helps the settings keep their calibration. A steam car that's never throttled all the way up wears out faster than one that gets used at top speed on occasion, did you know that?"

"I am not a steam car, Lord Hardison."

Oh, but it was arch, her expression and the words she spoke. He felt a hint of something devilish and raw. Not only desire. She made him want to *play*.

"You're a very fine machine indeed, *Lady* Hardison. If you were my steam car, I'd run you at full throttle nightly."

She couldn't resist answering in kind, but her question was more pointed than he had expected.

"The sort of steam car you purchase outright? Or the kind you lease on holiday and return after a fortnight when the thrill of driving something new has worn off?"

He felt the smile play around his lips, a grace note of admiration rising above the symphony already filling his mind. "I suspect it would take a good deal longer than a fortnight."

She bit her lower lip, worrying it for a moment, and then repeated quietly, "I am *not* a steam car."

Mere hours earlier, he had asked her a question in much the same tone of voice. *Must we pretend*? They both wanted something more straightforward, apparently. The pretense had ended. Earlier it had seemed easier because lust was motivating them both. Reasoning her into doing it again, Dexter realized, would take more work.

"Give me this week," he suggested, not sure where the inspiration had come from. "While we're still on the ship. Once we're in France . . . we'll reevaluate."

Silence. Stillness. And then a small, quick nod, so subtle he almost missed it in the dark.

DEXTER HAD FOUND it easy enough before, if frustrating, to pretend he was a love-struck buffoon. He had enjoyed Charlotte's company, her quick mind and sly wit. It was especially amusing to see her fool people into thinking she was a blithe, vapid bit of society fluff.

Now he had a new element to contend with, something novel to him and quite unexpected. *Jealousy*. Dexter found himself following his young bride about the ship all day, bristling whenever she encountered another man who seemed to appreciate what he saw in her.

That was practically every man, of course. Even the ones who assumed her head was empty couldn't help but take the measure of her body with their eyes. She was tiny but perfect, a pocket Venus as Matthew Pence had once described her, and Dexter knew only too well the temptation presented by those dainty curves. A creature so delicate made any man feel larger and stronger, more protective. He had to constantly repress the urge to lift her, to carry her. If he could have, he would have stowed her in his pocket for safekeeping.

Days became insubstantial and too long, a purgatory of waiting for darkness. Nights were almost painfully real, fierce and sweet and desperate. He found Charlotte's passion astonishing, her occasional reticence a delightful challenge. He pushed, even as he knew she was still holding back some part of herself. He told himself each day that he would stop that night, talk with her, find the root of her fears and concerns so he could vanquish them.

But each night she was there in the berth. So vital, so much more present than anybody he had ever known. Though Dexter took, he knew Charlotte was taking too, using him to exorcise some personal demon of hers. How could he mind, when the process took him to Heaven again and again? But how could he ignore her obvious emotional pain? When he asked, she never would say what was wrong.

Later, we can sort it out later. We'll reevaluate after we get to Honfleur.

He didn't want to repair Charlotte, because she wasn't broken, even if she thought she was. He wanted to recondition her, body and soul, restoring ease and flexibility where stiffness and wear had taken over. If she were a steam car, or any other type of mechanism imaginable, he could have fixed her up by now and had her running like the finest Swiss clockwork. But with a person, Dexter didn't even know what tools to use.

It was a long week, but not nearly long enough. The charming, bubbly patter from Lady Hardison began to sound strained and forced to Dexter's ears by the last few days of the voyage. His own attempts at manly bonhomie were exhausting him, and only partly due to the lack of sleep. Nobody else seemed to notice anything amiss. Perhaps they assumed the newlyweds had overdone it, a safe enough assumption, especially given how sick Lady Hardison had been during the first half of the voyage.

They were in the bunk, overdoing it for perhaps the last time when the captain's voice on the intercom announced the French coast had been spotted. They would be landing in Le Havre in a few hours' time.

Charlotte startled at the announcement, looking for all the world like a deer about to bound away at the crackling of a twig. Dexter stroked her sides and haunches, shifting under her, settling her and reclaiming her attention.

"We still have time, love."

She nodded, but her fair hair was tumbling over her face. He smoothed it up out of the way to see her expression, then wished he hadn't. She looked raw, exposed. He didn't like to see her uncertain.

"We don't have much time," she corrected him, as though she felt duty bound to be the voice of restraint. "And when we get to Honfleur we won't have any. A week at the most, for you to evaluate things at the station and me to prove the *Gossamer Wing*'s suitability to Murcheson. We must be in Paris within nine days of our arrival here, if I'm to make this window of opportunity to try for the documents while there's no moon. Otherwise we'll be stuck in France another month at least before I can try again."

"So let's not waste this time." He waggled his eyebrows at her, relieved when she smiled. And then he gasped when she squeezed herself around him quite deliberately.

"I want to do something new," Charlotte said, shy but not quite whispering, "make the most of it."

With the limited amount of cognition available to him, Dexter ran through the past few nights in his mind. Mentally, he ticked off things they had already done, a surprisingly impressive list of accomplishments for such a short time. He realized he had quite thoroughly corrupted the girl.

Not a complete corruption, perhaps. Charlotte was still shy in front of him, and that was one area in which he hadn't pushed very hard. Now, seeing her so vulnerable, he was struck with a perverse desire to break her down even further. See just how far she would allow herself to be pushed . . . and perhaps create one last fond memory to tuck away in the album of his mind, depending on how things went in Honfleur. He tried not to think further ahead than that. He told himself it was just sex. Just sex with the most extraordinary women he'd ever met. Not lovemaking, and certainly not love, because that would never do. Charlotte would have none of that.

"Ride me," he ordered, pulling her hips into his.

"We've done this," she breathed, even as she complied.

"And touch yourself."

Her hips gave a little hitch, then kept moving. Her hair slipped forward again, hiding one eye. It swayed with each breath she took. After a moment, Dexter pulled one of her hands from his chest and put it where he wanted it, daring her with his eyes. Then, because he was anxious about what would happen once they disembarked, and because he felt like a petulant child about to be forced to give up a favorite new toy, he raised the stakes.

"You've never done that for yourself, have you?" He didn't expect an answer, but he knew she hadn't. She couldn't have, if she'd reached the age of twenty-seven still believing women couldn't have orgasms. "You wanted something new. This would be two new things in one go. Doing it in the first place, and also doing it in front of somebody else."

It was getting harder to control his urge to thrust, harder to resist the sweet pull of desire that swelled his cock and made him want to rush to a conclusion. But just as he had decided to let it go, decided she wasn't ready for that particular challenge, he saw her fingers start to move.

She was hesitant at first, finding the right spot. He ran one fingertip lightly over the back of her hand, feeling each tendon and muscle as she worked out the tempo and pressure. Her pace picked up as she grew more assured, as she found her own way down that path for the first time. It was coarse and fascinating, the storm of activity taking place at the spot where their bodies were joined. Dexter couldn't tear his eyes away, even though the sight made him ache for release.

Charlotte gasped, and Dexter looked up at her face as she began to tremble and clench around him. Her fingers flew, and their bodies collided again and again with noisy, wet enthusiasm that would have been enough by itself to send Dexter to oblivion. But the lewd sight of her pleasuring herself was nothing compared to the sight of her face, her eyes on his, the joy and embarrassment and need and relief. All shared in a single glance. She had never truly been naked before him, but she was now. She had pulled out her soul for him to see, and it was so beautiful it nearly blinded him.

He came hard, jerking up into her still-shaking body, shouting her name like a cry for help. Afterward, he had to pull away quickly so as not to compromise the sheath he wore. He had worn one every time after that first, mad night, and didn't mind it for her sake but for this one thing. He hated leaving her body so soon, particularly this time. He wanted to stay inside her until he hardened again, make love to her once more before the ship's docking forced them from the bunk.

He pulled out, but he wrapped his arms and legs around her and didn't let go until the hated voice of the captain on the intercom interrupted them for the last time.

Nine

❧❧

HONFLEUR AND LE HAVRE, FRANCE

Charlotte wanted to focus on her work. She wanted that very much. She had a list of coordinates to memorize then destroy, along with maps of Paris and Le Havre and a calendar full of notes about the phases of the moon. She had a dossier full of information about her target, Roland Dubois, all of which needed further study before she embarked on her first flight.

But after a night and half a day in Honfleur their contact still hadn't surfaced, and Charlotte felt no closer to accomplishing any of her goals than she had when she left New York. She was also frustrated and preoccupied by her body's obvious disgruntlement at being denied its newfound source of entertainment.

Their hotel suite was lavish, and Charlotte suspected Dexter was sleeping comfortably enough on one of the two overstuffed sofas in the sitting room. For all she knew, he was trotting out to find French whores every night to satisfy his obviously quite healthy libido. She only knew for certain he wasn't satisfying it with her anymore. He seemed content with the arrangement, but in her experience people were seldom what they seemed.

Why it bothered her so much to think Dexter was pretending to be content, Charlotte couldn't say. She said nothing instead, and the words on the pages before her swam and danced in an endless tedious whirl. Charlotte tried to keep her eyes on the work, on the ridiculous novel in whose margins she'd jotted the coordinates to study, rather than staring across the sidewalk café table at her temporary husband's sensual mouth.

"Lord Hardison?" A cultured voice, a British voice, startled Charlotte from her reverie. She looked up to see an older gentleman in a top hat nodding to Dexter. A wave of relief, flavored with excitement, swept over her. Dexter leaped to his feet, a broad smile on his face and his hand extended for a gentlemanly clasp.

Charlotte scanned their surroundings automatically as she stood, but saw no obvious eavesdroppers or onlookers. The rooftops across the street were clear, and there were only a few other patrons at the little café where she and Dexter sat lingering over brunch and enjoying the cool coastal breeze.

"I'm Rutherford Murcheson. Heard you were in town. Lad at the embassy said I might find you here."

Murcheson, Charlotte knew, ran one of the largest make-smith forges in Europa. He was an ideal business acquaintance for Dexter to make on this dual-purpose honeymoon. This also made him an ideal contact for Charlotte and Dexter, and the perfect covert spymaster for the Crown's agents in France.

"My wife, Charlotte."

She threw Dexter a warning glance for flubbing the introduction, but the older gentleman covered with a courtly bow over her hand. "*Baroness*, it is a great pleasure. I understand it's your first visit to Europa. Welcome to France."

She giggled, as that seemed an indelible part of her cover persona now, and bobbed a little curtsy. "Mr. Murcheson.

Oh, are you the Mr. Murcheson who makes those *lovely* curio boxes? How exciting! Dex, we must see if we can impose on Mr. Murcheson for a tour of his factory!"

The passwords *Europa* and *curio* having safely passed between them, they proceeded to make plans for a visit to the factory that very afternoon. Then they all shared fashionable coffee while the gentlemen talked smithing. Dexter was firm and businesslike, while Charlotte continued to speak in sentences that seemed to demand exclamatory punctuation. By the time they parted ways with Murcheson and she and Dexter returned to their suite, she was thoroughly sick of herself and her cheeks were aching from all the forced smiles.

"It really is like an optical illusion," Dexter remarked, loosening his cravat and shrugging his coat off onto the nearest sofa arm.

"I beg your pardon?" She sighed with relief as she removed her hat. One of the pins had been poorly placed, poking her with distressing frequency throughout the contact session.

"I know you're the same person. It looks like you, it's wearing the same clothing. But that insipid creature simply isn't you."

You seemed to like her well enough on the ship, Charlotte was tempted to say, but she knew there was a difference. On the ship she had come to feel almost childlike for a time, able to enjoy things freely. Playing the part had become a game, and not all her giddiness had been a pretense.

Now, however, the charade was in deadly earnest. Each giggle, each stupid question or eyelash-batting, had a purpose. To misdirect, to glean information from an unwitting source. She had to be, very deliberately and aggressively, the last person anybody would suspect of espionage. It was her job to be other than what she seemed.

"Of course it isn't me. That's the point," she snapped.

"She gives me a headache."

"Me too. But darling," she simpered, because the room might even now be under surveillance, "you know it's just because I get nervous around people." She shot him a warning look, which it took him a moment to process. When he did, he nodded with weary resignation and mouthed an apology. She shrugged it off.

"Would you like to come with me to see Mr. Murcheson's factory this afternoon, sweetheart? Perhaps there'll be a shop. You know how you love shops," he said with droll good humor, the perfect indulgent honeymoon husband.

She smirked. "Well dearest, a poor lonely widow has to find some way to spend her days." With an undignified flop, she slumped to the sofa opposite Dexter and let her head loll back. It was an unseasonably warm day in Honfleur, and the fans in the room only seemed to stir the air, not cool it. Charlotte had felt sticky since they'd reached the coast, even in the evenings when the temperature dropped.

"Her money too, I suppose. But lambkin, I know a number of widows who find other ways to spend their time. Fascinating ways, some of them."

She glared at him and whispered, "Lambkin?"

He shrugged, then grinned in a completely unrepentant way. His aggressive good cheer was almost grating.

"Volunteer work?" she guessed. "Charity balls?"

Dexter lifted an eyebrow, seeming to gauge the risk of his answer before speaking. "Yes, in fact I know several very accommodating widows who are well known for volunteering to work on balls, among other things. Perhaps not for charity, but certainly out of the goodness of their own hearts."

She held her stern face for only a few seconds before breaking. He laughed along with her, and she watched him with delight until she realized she was watching him with delight, at which point she quickly looked away. His next words caught her completely off guard.

"Charlotte, tell me more about Reginald."

Time froze for an instant, or perhaps it was only that her heart seemed to stop beating. Then it thudded in her ears, loud and insistent, as a rush of feeling came over her. It was something like terror, or panic. Charlotte couldn't name it, nor did she understand why it came upon her now. In broad daylight, in this peaceful setting, with a man she trusted.

"Why?"

"Because he was important to you." He was keeping his voice light on purpose, she thought, but she could hear the serious intent beneath that.

"What would you like to know?"

"Did you love him?"

She nodded. "Yes. Very much."

"What was he like?"

Might as well ask her what air was like, or water. It was there in the background and it was essential. You only noticed its importance when you no longer had it.

"He was quiet. I had known him since I was about fourteen, and the first time I saw him I thought 'There is the man I shall marry one day.' Reginald did not know this until much later, of course."

"Of course."

"He had come to see my father on some business matter. He can't have been more than eighteen or nineteen at the time himself. Still at university. He had started very young, though, so he was nearly finished at that point. My father's people had already tapped him. He was brilliant, you see. Do you know the, ah, nature of his particular work?"

Dexter paused and then nodded. "Yes. I'm familiar with it, although I don't understand it."

"Few people do." She tried to think of ways to describe Reginald, ways that didn't involve code-breaking or the Agency he gave his life to. "He was never good at people. Numbers and patterns, he had a passion for, and music. But people baffled him." She rose and wandered to the French doors that opened onto a narrow iron-railed balcony. The street, two stories below, was noisy and even hotter than the room. The balcony, however, offered a breeze and a splendid view of the harbor from one end. "Except for a few, and I was one of them. Even as a young girl, I could always talk to Reginald. It was inappropriate, I suppose, but I was always in the library and when Reginald visited the estate—which was fairly often, once he started working for my father—we would sit there together. Usually alone, which was the inappropriate part. We would talk about books and ciphers. Other things."

"His misanthropy?"

Charlotte smiled. "He wasn't really that way. He never could stop thinking, analyzing. I suppose I was just enough like him to understand. I even went into the same line of work, for a time, after all. Unlike him, however, I seem to be able to function in society without too much difficulty."

"It's an act, though."

"Yes. I much prefer being private." A gull cried overhead, sweeping through the air toward the estuary, and Charlotte longed to join it in flight.

Dexter frowned, stopping to choose his words. "You were willing to give that up, though. Privacy, I mean. When you married Reginald."

Letting her eyes track along the bright strand of the beach, Charlotte tried to think whether she had really even considered that factor when she married. She had been so young, only twenty-two, and she had barely known herself. Being with Reginald was hardly like being with another person at all.

It struck her, with a deep pang of honest regret, that if Reginald had lived she might well have grown quite miserable living with him. She would have suffered the most horrible loneliness of all, that of being with another person who isn't present in spirit. There was no way to explain the feeling to Dexter without sounding disloyal. Charlotte finally responded without really saying much at all.

"I was younger, and less set in my ways."

NONE OF THIS *is what it seems.* Martin avoided drawing conclusions too early in the game; he preferred to wait for the evidence to unfold. This, though, was an objective assessment he couldn't avoid. He reviewed the transcript of their conversation, still not sure he would believe these words if he hadn't chanced to hear them for himself.

It was she, the widow of his old enemy, as he had suspected. Martin supposed a younger version of himself might have experienced remorse while listening to her brave, loving reminiscence about the man he had poisoned.

Martin of the current day experienced only curiosity. His minions had reported the new baroness to be flighty, an overage ingénue of that tiresome American variety, as empty of thought as she was beautiful to look at. This profile comported with his perception of the Makesmith Baron as a man who would appreciate an ornamental wife, one who could entertain and charm his business associates and bear him attractive children.

The people he'd listened to in that hotel room didn't match their reports. The woman was no empty vessel, and the man no dilettante industrialist. Furthermore, Lady Hardison was evidently not just the widow but also the daughter of a spy. What might his superiors in French intelligence have made of that, Martin wondered? Viscount Darmont a spy all these years? It would have explained quite a few things. They would never know it now, and Martin supposed it wasn't important. The daughter was, however. He would bet his life she was following in her father's and dead husband's footsteps. He still wasn't sure what to make of the new husband.

Why had they come to France? Was it only to meet with Murcheson and scheme to undercut the steamrail bid, as Dubois suspected? Nothing to do with politics, except as it impacted on matters of business?

Impossible. If Martin had learned anything in his many years of working in the private sector for Companie Dubois, it was never to trust Dubois's assumptions about people and their motivations. Whatever professional assistance the American might need from Murcheson, Murcheson certainly didn't need the American to strengthen his own position. Yet he'd invited Hardison to tour his factory, and spent a cordial few hours away from his office just to chat with the man. Therefore, Hardison must have some other reason for being here, and so must his bride, who seemed unlikely to have chosen a honeymoon in France. Martin might work for Dubois now, and dwell on stifling competition and stealing trade secrets, but that didn't mean he'd forgotten every instinct of intelligence work. Industrial espionage wasn't so very far from spying for the government, after all. Trade secrets were trade secrets, no matter the business.

Martin handed the notebook back to the twitchy youngster monitoring the hotel room. "They travel to Paris soon. Have Claude find out where they plan to stay so we can prepare their room well in advance."

"*Oui,* monsieur," the boy said, practically jumping out of his chair in his eagerness to distance himself from the frightening Coeur de Fer.

Martin smiled. It was the sort of smile that might make the angels despair. He tapped the desk with one metal finger as he pondered the tasks before him.

"Why are you here, Lady Hardison?" he whispered, tracing the outline of a feminine profile on the wooden surface. "Who are you, when you're not pretending to be somebody else?"

THE FACTORY WAS a wonder. Murcheson billed it as such, "Murcheson's Modern Wonderworks."

"The finest craftsmen in Europa or the world, if you don't mind my saying so, Hardison."

Dexter let the remark pass. Charlotte could tell he was impressed, perhaps not so much with the quality of the work as with its sheer scale. Hundreds, maybe even thousands of journeymen and apprentices plied their trades on the factory floors of the large complex. Woodworkers and clockmakers toiled side by side with machinists and metallurgists, all focused on producing more goods for the newly expanded European trade.

Dexter kept his thoughts on all of it to himself for the most part, though he was quick to point out at least one item of interest.

"Look, sugarplum. They're assembling one of your curio boxes."

A team of aproned, goggled workers hunched over a broad table, one of hundreds spread out over the vast main factory floor. As one finished assembling an intricate system of tiny gears, another inserted the mechanism into the appropriate place within the unfinished wooden framework. The completed boxes would, when activated, spring open to reveal a unique collection of drawers, compartments, spinning display surfaces. Some played music. Most had secret storage areas. All were works of art as much as craft.

"Oh, you're right, sweetiekins! How charming they are already! Mr. Murcheson, will we see any of the finished boxes?"

"Of course, Lady Hardison," he assured her. He kept an admirably straight face, Charlotte thought, in the face of the escalating war of endearments. "I thought Lord Hardison might be interested in seeing the ironworks first."

They continued to another building, an enormous hangar of a structure, to see a great deal of molten metal. Charlotte could have done without that stop on the tour. Even staying on the platform near the entrance, far from the actual equipment, the heat in the forge was literally breathtaking. She tried to focus on the conversation between Murcheson and Dexter, but it quickly surpassed her comprehension when they began to discuss technical specifications and metallurgy. The reinforced leather and steel panels that turned her corset into stealthy armor hardly helped.

The spark-laden air was swimming in front of her by the time Dexter took her arm with a look of concern. "I think we should continue the tour and find something a bit cooler. The heat doesn't agree with the Baroness."

She leaned on his arm, grateful for the support, and reveled in the splash of cooler air once they left the demonic building.

"Time for the final stop on our review of the facilities, I think," Murcheson said cheerfully. He waved off the assistant who had been following him throughout their tour. "I won't need you, Tom. Just going to show them the warehouse and then back to my office. I believe I'll be a bit late tonight, would you be a good fellow and get a message to my wife?"

When the other man had scuttled away, Murcheson nodded to Charlotte and Dexter, who followed him quickly. They walked in the direction of the warehouse, but Murcheson took a sharp turn between two buildings before they arrived, and glanced all around before opening an unobtrusive door and ushering them into what appeared to be an unused storeroom. A few boxes stood against one wall, looking like losers in a fight against nesting rodents. Beside them, a chair missing one leg leaned in a corner. The grubby window let in barely enough light to make out even that much detail.

Along the wall opposite the door, Murcheson quickly located a panel that Charlotte hadn't even discerned in the faded gray woodwork. He pressed one hand there, opening a hidden doorway, and again ushered them through. The little space they entered was a gleaming brass frame with a floor of highly polished mahogany, and a bright lantern hanging from the ceiling. But the walls . . .

"Windows?" Charlotte stepped closer to the nearest wall and pressed her fingers to the surface, trying to peer past the glass into the darkness beyond, as Murcheson turned a key and they started to descend.

ATLANTIS STATION, BENEATH THE ENGLISH CHANNEL

DEXTER'S FIRST THOUGHT as he saw the rock walls sliding past was a single word that carried a great weight of concern.

"Chalk?" He couldn't keep a note of alarm out of his voice. If the station, or even this lift shaft, were built on one of the veins of chalk running across the channel floor, the last place he wanted to be was inside any of it. Chalk was notoriously unstable, and hardly suitable for building on or in.

Murcheson chuckled. "Directly adjacent, yes. But we're far enough inland here to be clear of it. Different lithosome, you know. This is clay."

"I see." Dexter had known their route to the submerged base would be unconventional. But he hadn't quite expected anything like *this*.

A million questions raced through his mind, nearly as quickly as the lift raced downward to its destination. By the time he could isolate one and begin to frame it they had arrived, coasting to a gentle landing. Dexter was amused when the lift control emitted a soft, pedestrian "ding" as the lift settled into place.

"Next leg of the trip," Murcheson said blithely, clearly enjoying his guests' reactions. "Hope you both have strong stomachs."

Charlotte grimaced at Dexter behind Murcheson's back as he led them down a tunnel carved in the native rock toward a sort of coach that resembled a giant teacup on wheels. It sat on the right-hand set of two pairs of tracks that extended down the dimly lit passage as far as the eye could see.

Dexter admired the beautiful joinery and the clever brass fittings of the vehicle as he handed Charlotte up and slid in next to her on the wide, padded velvet bench.

"Sit well back, and prepare for a bit of a lurch," Murcheson advised. Before he climbed into the coach himself, he cranked a handle on its side. On the third rotation, a motor turned over then purred to life, vibrating the vehicle slightly. It felt like a horse, eager to leave the gate. As he secured the crank and hoisted himself to the seat, Murcheson slapped another nearly invisible panel on the wall. All along the passage, tiny green-tinted lights flickered to life below the plain gas sconces. "And away we go!"

Slowly, at first. As the motor warmed up, their speed gradually increased. Dexter tried to ascertain the specific power source, craning his neck around the little semi-enclosed cabin. There was no evident steam, scarcely any exhaust.

"Do you want a hint, Lord Hardison?" Murcheson asked after a few minutes.

Dexter wanted to smack the smug expression right off Murcheson's face, but he wanted to know about the little tram's engine even more. They were tripping along at a nearly frightening pace now, the gray walls of the tunnel blurring and the lights appearing as mere streaks.

Finally curiosity won out over irritation. "How?"

"Modified Stirling engine."

"Too small," Dexter said instantly. "Not with a payload like this."

"Carbon-cooled cold reservoir. Increases the efficiency and allows us to reduce the size. We're also," he confessed, "on a gradual downhill slope. The ride back will be a bit slower, I'm afraid."

Dexter's fingers itched to open the tram's carapace and examine the engine, a closed system of what sounded like almost perfectly efficient heat exchange. He had seen similar devices, but if Murcheson's description was correct this would be more than incrementally better.

What other wonders awaited them at the end of the tunnel?

It wasn't long, twenty minutes or so, before they started to slow, then eased to a seamless stop at the far end of the track. The walls of the tunnel were every bit as undistinguished, cold and stony as they had been on the starting end. The door at one end of the vestibule they'd fetched up in was mahogany with brass fittings, highly polished but otherwise unremarkable.

Charlotte, like Dexter, surveyed the space all around as they disembarked, her sharp blue eyes detailing every element of the scene. Her cover persona was completely gone now, the agent showing through clearly in her every wary movement and expression. She was on high alert, strung tight as a bow.

A dangerous woman, his wife. It was the first time Dexter had considered that, the darker aspects of her training. Suddenly it struck him that this tiny gamine in pale periwinkle and lace could probably kill him a dozen different ways.

It did not lessen her appeal in the slightest.

The door led to a corridor, and Dexter got a general impression of more polished mahogany, more brass and steel, and black marble underfoot. It all felt new, almost unfinished it was so free from wear. At the end of the corridor was another substantial door, and Murcheson couldn't resist a dramatic, sweeping gesture as he opened it. "My lord, my lady . . . welcome to Atlantis Station!"

Dexter's jaw dropped, his mind shifting and recoiling at the attempt to make sense of what he was seeing.

Big.

"Our command center," Murcheson said proudly as he led them down a curving flight of steps to the walkway forming the perimeter of the room. "Dug into the bedrock. It's on an outcropping of clay, Mr. Hardison, not chalk. No worries there. The bulk of the construction was done in Brighton, then the pieces were assembled here a bit at a time. Air venting through a system that runs adjacent to the tunnel we just arrived by. Also controlled via a facility in one of my factory buildings, although the employees who maintain the system on that end believe they're working on a cooling device for some machinery at the factory.

"The ceiling, I admit, is almost pure folly. Still it's very impressive, wouldn't you say, Hardison?"

"Ceiling?" Dexter looked up some thirty or forty feet to see that the ceiling, which obviously rose above the bedrock and extended up through the channel floor, was a dome of steel and glass panels. Murky and dark at this depth, the ocean above still conveyed a sense of movement, of organic life and the transmission of filtered light from above.

"Amazing." Charlotte made no attempt to hide the fact she was flabbergasted. "I had seen reports, but I really had no idea."

The control station was teeming with dozens of men and

a few women, all obviously hard at work on tasks Dexter could not immediately identify. Their navy blue and white uniforms stood out in clean, sharp lines against the warm tones of the construction. As he watched, a youngish man separated from a group of conferring officers and joined them, taking the half-dozen steps from the main floor to the walkway in two graceful bounds.

"Mr. Murcheson, sir! And you must be Lord Hardison."

Introductions were made and then the young lieutenant— Phineas Smith-Grenville, whose relations in America happened to know Dexter's family quite well—led them around the room to the opposite end and another set of doors.

"Lady Hardison may find this of particular interest," he said as he ushered them through to yet another tunnel, this one leading to a twisting flight of stairs that seemed to be taking them back to the level of the ocean floor. Or above it, Dexter realized, as the monotony of the steel paneling was broken here by regularly spaced portholes.

They passed through another door and traveled back down a bit, to get to the chamber where a dainty submersible bobbed gently in a pool of water. It took Dexter a moment to deduce that the circular pool, which was level with the floor of the chamber but walled in by a low, broad metal parapet, was actually a docking bay. Behind the craft he could make out the faint outline of the tunnel mouth through which the submersible must travel to get into the water of the channel proper.

Charlotte studied the sub closely for a moment, and said, "It's . . . very small." Dexter wondered about her willingness to enter the thing, but she seemed charmed despite herself by its delicate beauty and began asking questions of the technician. She showed no inclination to continue on the tour. A quarter of an hour later, the lieutenant finally left her in the technician's care and continued along the passage to take Dexter to his own destination—a small interior room where two officers and three civilians sat arguing and puzzling over a workbench full of equipment and sketches.

Three of the four walls were covered with blackboards,

on which nearly every square inch of available space was taken up with equations and more hasty sketches. A bleary white underlayer of smeared chalk dust suggested that many, many erasures had taken place since the boards had last been cleaned. The men, even the officers, appeared blood-shot and slightly bedraggled, and all of them looked up like hunted animals when their workshop door opened to admit Dexter.

"Gentlemen," the polite young lieutenant began, "May I present Baron Hardison?"

When he got no reaction but a room full of blank stares, Dexter cleared his throat. "You may know me as Mr. Dexter Hardison."

And they were off.

"ALL WE KNOW of Dubois," Murcheson told Charlotte, gesturing to the thick portfolio he'd slid across the desk toward her. He'd come back to the submersible bay after seeing Dexter settled, and pulled Charlotte into his office for the briefing she'd been expecting since her arrival. "In addition to what you already have, of course. Three months ago, we intercepted some correspondence between Dubois and Maurice Gendreau, who's been in voluntary expatriation on St. Helena since the end of the war. It's almost laughably obvious that the letters are in code, though we haven't worked it out yet. They're far too bland and patently harmless to be real. Especially not given what we know of Gendreau's politics, and what we've long suspected about Dubois's."

Charlotte pulled a sheaf of letters from the file and flipped through them, taking a moment to establish the time frame and chronology of the missives. "Voluntary expatriation" was a nicer way to say "exile," she supposed, but it amounted to the same thing, and Gendreau certainly seemed unhappy in his exile. Dubois asked after Gendreau's health, Gendreau lamented his business prospects and intimated he was homesick for France—particularly the food and wine.

They seemed to be hinting around the possibility of a partnership, though the terms were very sketchy. Something to do with a steam car engine improvement Gendreau wanted funding to develop, and Dubois seeking assurances of exclusivity. It was all boring stuff indeed. Suspiciously so, as Murcheson said.

"The clincher is that the improvement he's discussing is a technical nonstarter, according to a few experts we've consulted. It was one of the first indications we had that something was afoot. Clearly a code phrase. You know who Gendreau is, I trust?"

Charlotte nodded. "I know who he was, at least. The old post-royalist French regime's pet scientist cum makesmith. The man who was deemed most likely to develop a large-scale weapon against the British."

"If he'd succeeded," Murcheson continued, "the war would have ended very differently. Or rather, it might well still be raging. If there were any people left on either side to wage it. And Gendreau's recently built a workshop on St. Helena to rival the one he left behind in France. We haven't been able to get inside yet, but it's not hard to guess what he's attempting to build there."

"But my notes indicate Dubois is now working with the current government intelligence agency in France. If he's working for the Égalité government, why is he contemplating going into business with Gendreau? Why would he foster such a risky connection?"

"We'd very much like to find out."

Noting the grim set of his mouth, Charlotte prodded a bit. "You have a theory, though?"

Murcheson shrugged. "There's always a theory, Lady Hardison. In this case, rumor has it that certain elements within the government are not as hostile to the old post-royalist viewpoint as they've made themselves out to be. Indeed, we've heard enough to be concerned that there's a significant faction of leaders here who would still be happy to see the treaty with Britain broken. They miss the unregulated freedom they used to enjoy, and they'd be more than happy to go back to essentially owning their workers even if it meant losing more of them to battle."

"They always did see the peasantry as fungible." The wealthy post-royalists were little better than the aristocracy they'd replaced, in that regard. In fact, most of them were just aristocrats with a thin veneer of republicanism; only the actual royal family had been formally deposed.

"Precisely. On the surface, Dubois seemed to have turned into a good little member of the more moderate Égalité-era elite, content to profit less but more steadily, in a country free from the uncertainties of war. We know he must be working with the current crop of spymasters, because he's in constant contact with several agents. We assumed he was still working as a contractor, making gadgetry and vehicles for them. That's a longstanding relationship, since before the treaty as far as we can make out. His personal secretary is a known active French field agent, and he has other positively identified former agents working on his security staff, so the arrangement isn't even particularly sub rosa."

"But if he's meeting with Gendreau," Charlotte surmised, "he's either playing Gendreau for the Égalité government, or playing the current government for the old regime."

Murcheson nodded. "And we need to find out which, because the last thing we want is for the post-royalists to regain their influence in government here . . . or for them to develop anything like the weapon Gendreau was working on before the war ended."

Ten

LE HAVRE AND HONFLEUR, FRANCE

THE AIR OVER Le Havre was nothing like the air over Upstate New York. Charlotte fancied it was uniquely French, this air. She had risen from a blanket of fog over the channel offshore from Honfleur, and within minutes she was soaring, feeling at home again despite the foreign sky. Her body eased into the familiar harness, her senses expanded with the use of her equipment, and all was well.

She was finally beginning it, the job she had trained for. Charlotte thought of Reginald, bent over a codex with his fine brow furrowed. She thought of him lying in their berth on the riverboat, gray and cold, so very obviously beyond the help of any doctor. She had distracted him, and he had died. Perhaps now she could begin putting that memory to rest, and her own guilty conscience at ease. But first, she had to jump through the hoops Murcheson had set her, and demonstrate her abilities with the stealth airship by gathering intelligence on Dubois here in Le Havre. Only once she'd done so would Murcheson approve her to embark on the main leg of her mission, over the rooftops of Paris.

Countering automatically against a buffeting wind, she took the *Gossamer Wing* higher still as she followed the terrain toward Le Havre. The city was of little interest to her, just the zone nearest the harbor, in which Murcheson had pinpointed the offices of Companie Dubois.

Only Murcheson's insistence had overcome Whitehall's reluctance to assign a female agent to an active field surveillance position, much less to the trickier job of retrieving the long-lost weapon plans. That had been Charlotte's good fortune. The geography of Companie Dubois's dockside buildings and some rather tight security measures had thus far thwarted all infiltration attempts from the ground. Charlotte, on the *Gossamer Wing*, wouldn't have to infiltrate. She would simply float and watch and listen, all while taking deep, refreshing breaths of fine French coastal air. If her efforts were successful, she might gain some critical information for the Agency; more importantly, she might help usher in an entirely new era of remote information-gathering.

The first day of her daring new assignment, however, was less exciting than disconcerting. Once aloft and in place over the appropriate building, she tuned her exquisitely precise equipment to the correct office, expecting to hear intrigue and see dastardly espionage in the making. Instead she overheard the infamous Roland Dubois planning to sneak his secretary away for the weekend. Then she turned away rather than watch him commit a lewd act with the secretary in question on his vast mahogany desk. If the young woman was indeed a French agent, Charlotte thought, she certainly seemed willing to give her all to foster an association between the French government and Companie Dubois.

Hoping to learn something else of interest, Charlotte shifted her directional microphone's focus to another room while she kept an occasional eye on the unseemly proceedings in Dubois's office. With her attention divided thus, she waited out Dubois while listening in on two other French businessmen argue about the outcome of a cricket match.

"Perhaps it was in code," Dexter suggested later as he helped her from the harness. To maintain the appearance of a honeymooning couple they were staying together as much as possible, dividing their time between Charlotte's test flights and Dexter's sessions with the engineering team in the station. Dexter had been put to work piloting the little dinghy that bore Charlotte from a secluded dock under Murcheson's guard to a point out in the harbor, a safe distance from shore, so she could launch the *Gossamer Wing* unseen. While he waited for her, he scribbled plans and fiddled with a pile of gadgets he'd appropriated from the team at Atlantis Station.

"The cricket conversation?" she asked, puzzled.

"No, I meant the sex."

Charlotte blushed. Dexter seemed less and less content with their platonic arrangement, and increasingly inclined to hint they might resume their shipboard relationship, but the risk of distraction was very real to Charlotte. She could not let emotion and physical urges cloud her judgment. It was a matter of life and death to her, and knowing Dexter didn't feel the same made her anxious. He should be as cautious as she; he risked them both by thinking he was safe to spend a single thought on dalliance.

"What are you doing with all this?" she changed the subject, waving in the direction of the equipment Dexter had brought along.

He followed her gesture with his gaze, then shrugged. "Contemplating possible improvements."

The second day, Charlotte risked a flight later in the morning. Though the weather had returned to the cool, overcast and intermittently rainy standard for the area, the *Gossamer Wing* still faded well into the sky.

"Minor success," she reported gleefully after touching back down beside the furled sail of the dinghy. "More cricket talk too. Perhaps it *is* code, he was talking about a British bowler. But Dubois was busy dictating a letter about an appointment with someone. The name was very familiar."

Gathering balloon silk with practiced motions as the

Gossamer Wing deflated, Dexter lifted an eyebrow at Charlotte. "The secretary was actually taking dictation? Sounds as though that young woman has *many* talents."

Charlotte coughed and avoided his eyes, unwilling to say more about what she had witnessed from her unseen vantage point in the sky. Voyeurism was all too easy with a large enough window and a strong enough lens. Though she hadn't intended to linger once it was clear the dictation was over, she had found herself compelled to watch.

She still felt aroused from what she'd seen, but she hardly wanted Dexter to know that. It was hard enough to watch him working in shirtsleeves on the tiny boat, his athletic body managing her dirigible and the dinghy's sail with captivating ease, without the added reminder of everything else that body could do.

"What, Charlotte?"

His question made her look up; his expression made her heart stop. Dexter's eyes had gone dark, heavy, a quality she had seen on the ship many times. How could he know what she'd been thinking? It was obvious he did, though. His expression screamed lascivious speculation.

"Nothing," Charlotte lied, returning to the task of stowing the little sugar-candy dirigible parts in their padded case. The tiny craft swayed on the water, making her task more difficult.

"You saw something else. Tell me."

Unwise, she chided herself, even as she spoke. "I saw the secretary demonstrate another skill. At least I assume she was skilled at it, since Dubois seemed highly appreciative. It was . . . not an activity of which I had been aware, though in retrospect it seems like an obvious possibility. You did it to me, after all." This last bit was sheer deviltry, a direct response to the glaze of lust over Dexter's eyes.

"Ah. So you would not be averse to trying this activity? Turnabout is fair play, and all that."

"You're treading on dangerous ground, Mr. Hardison."

But it was Charlotte who felt wobbly, unsure of her footing, when Dexter ignored her warning and kept pressing.

"Yet you led me here. You didn't have to tell me, but you did. You're curious to try it, aren't you, Charlotte? I think you liked what you saw."

"I think it's a wonder the French get any business done at all." Jerking the case down onto the floor of the boat and sitting a bit too firmly on the broad plank bench, Charlotte pointedly changed the subject. "Tomorrow afternoon, Dubois is going to be meeting with Maurice Gendreau."

It took a moment for the name to register with Dexter. Then his eyes widened. "Gendreau? The mad makesmith? He's supposed to be in exile on some island off the coast of Portugal."

"Then I hope he has access to a very fast boat, if he's to make it to that meeting on time."

"Does Murcheson know he's back in France?" Dexter asked, lashing the rudder in place then picking up what looked like a cross between a mechanical spider and a small toy steam car.

Charlotte shook her head. "I don't imagine so. He would have mentioned it, surely. He knew they were corresponding. He thinks Dubois is conspiring with Gendreau to build the post-royalists a weapon that will change the course of Franco–English relations."

"A doomsday device. These things always end up being about doomsday devices."

The very notion of such a device made Charlotte chuckle uneasily. "You shouldn't read sensationalist novels. They'll rot your brain," she scolded. "This is a serious business."

"And here I am playing with toys. At least they're more entertaining than doomsday devices. Here, watch." Dexter passed Charlotte one end of a slender, almost threadlike cable. "Hold that. Don't let go."

He clamped the miniature vehicle's crabbed "legs" closed around the cord. Then, holding the other end of the thread to form a gently descending arc between himself and Charlotte, he started the toy up and released it.

She held on and watched, fascinated, as the little car descended the cable toward her then reversed its course to return to Dexter's hand, seeming all the while to balance on the swaying cable like a tightrope artist. Dexter caught the mechanism, flicked a panel open, adjusted a knob and sent the car back toward Charlotte with scarcely a sound.

"Magic!" She held the gadget up, examining its workings, and found she couldn't lay it on its side even when she tried. It righted itself instantly every time.

"Gyroscopic stabilization," Dexter corrected her, "and some very nice clockwork Murcheson provided. It's a toy he makes at his factory."

"A toy, but you've improved it?"

Dexter grinned. "Not much point in having it go and come back, go and come back, up and down a vertical string. That grows dull quickly. Much more interesting if you can tell it exactly where you want it to stop and go, and make it follow a cable anywhere you can attach one, don't you think?"

"And carry a payload, perhaps? Silently?"

"You're quick. That room full of engineers back at Atlantis took ages to catch on to the possibilities. All they saw was a toy."

"Speaking of Atlantis, we need to get back. Murcheson will want to hear about this meeting with Gendreau. Whether or not it involves anything as dramatic as a doomsday device."

Dexter nodded and glanced at the sail, unlashing the rudder and sitting back down to direct the boat's rather lazy course. "We're heading in that general direction. I just thought it might be nice to travel at honeymoon speed. Good for our cover story."

A light drizzle had started. Charlotte pulled a tarpaulin from the equipment locker beneath her seat and tucked it over the packing cases, ensuring the *Gossamer Wing* didn't get too damp. It wasn't cold. In her snug, white leather flight suit, she wasn't bothered by the rain. Dexter, though not in waterproof gear, seemed unperturbed by the weather.

"Lovely day for a sail," she remarked, tipping her head back and letting the rain fall directly on her face.

She heard Dexter chuckle, the sound barely registering over the creak of the boat, the snap of the wind in the sail and the splash of water against the bow as they tacked. "Lovely," he agreed. "My sentiments exactly."

"MURCHESON IS UP to something," Dubois fretted.

Martin, with his face turned safely to the window, rolled his eyes. "What makes you think so?" he asked his employer, biting his tongue before he could add "*this* time."

"He's always up to something, of course. But now, just when we should have him in our sights, he disappears inside his factory for days on end with Hardison. He suspects something, Martin. You or your men, somebody must have been spotted tailing him."

After a moment of keen fear, Martin calmed himself. He knew none of his men had been spotted tailing Murcheson, for the simple reason that he had posted no men to watch Murcheson. Those who weren't watching Hardison were detailed to follow the Baroness, though Martin hardly planned to tell Dubois that. "He's simply courting Hardison," the former spy reassured his employer. "Murcheson and the Dominion baron share many obsessions. More important is the fact that no French officials have been seen entering the factory. There have been no meetings between the government and Murcheson or Hardison. The steamrail contract is still up for bid."

"So you say," Dubois grunted. "We should be keeping a closer eye on your former agency colleagues, Martin. Perhaps they are slipping in and out of the factory unnoticed by your team? Negotiating in secret on behalf of their turncoat masters? It wouldn't be the first time."

Those turncoats are the ruling party now, Martin thought. *And my former colleagues are already as close as you might wish.* Why, young Marguerite sat right outside Dubois's door each day, and a great deal closer than that on occasion, earning her keep on her back as Dubois's "secretaries" had always done and relaying everything she learned back to the Égalité spymasters who were her true employers. Martin had recognized the girl for what she was very early on. It amused him to think that the Égalité still thought Dubois merited that sort of attention. Dubois had no idea he was under such close surveillance. He had always had a blind spot when it came to female agents. *Even after Simone . . .*

"Monsieur Martin?"

The girl's soft voice startled Martin, who glanced away from the gray sky outside the window to see her bland, unremarkably pretty face just a few feet away. She was holding a cup of tea toward him, and he wondered how long she'd been standing there with it as he woolgathered.

"Thank you."

He took the cup and waited until Marguerite turned her back. Then he poured the tea into the soil of the large potted fern by the window, as he always did. He didn't trust the little agent not to poison him, to get him out of the way. Sometimes Martin wondered whether he was the one being spied upon, not Dubois. He wouldn't put it past his former employers to keep a watch on their not-so-lost lamb.

"Hardison isn't spending all his time meeting with Murcheson," Martin offered up, ready to give up a piece of his carefully hoarded knowledge if it meant a few days' respite from Dubois's sniping. "He's using one of Murcheson's boats, and leaving from a little-used dock near the factory. He and his new baroness have been spending quite a lot of time sailing on the harbor, it seems."

"In this weather? Why?"

"It's their honeymoon. Who knows why they're doing anything? Perhaps they simply enjoy fucking on boats in the rain. You know how odd Americans can be." Martin looked out the window again, noting that the rain had died down once more. A hint of blue peeked through the oppressive clouds here and there, and even the occasional beam of sunlight. He had always enjoyed the view of the harbor from this window, but today it seemed too exposed for some reason. Tiny hairs on Martin's back rose as he registered a growing sense that he was being watched by unseen eyes.

Marguerite. He turned to catch a glimpse of her face looking in his direction, barely visible through the open door between Dubois's office and the anteroom where the girl sat at her desk. She looked away instantly, but not before Martin saw the open curiosity, the sharp intelligence, the face she hid from them every day as she pretended to be a secretary with loose morals.

"I don't want you here when Gendreau arrives tomorrow," Dubois said, reclaiming Martin's attention. "He might recognize you, and that would make him uneasy. He's certain to suspect you're still working for the government, no matter how I reassure him. Never mind that nothing could be further from the truth, eh?"

"Why is he coming to see you here? It seems too public."

"He swears he's turning legitimate," Dubois replied with a snort. "He even traveled back to the country under his real name. He's already run through all the money he earned from skimming and bribes and side contracts during his years as a public servant. Now he wants a chance to do the same thing in private industry. He comes on bended knee, for all he pretends to be a powerful man. He claims to have a business partnership in mind, but he has little to offer. He's all but destitute, and the market for his more specialized trinkets is nonexistent where he is. My man in Portugal says he's spent all his remaining capital on a workshop, but it's useless to him at the moment. Gendreau was never more than a middling tinkerer himself, his real talent was in finding and hiring geniuses who lacked the common sense to realize he'd steal all the credit for their work. "

"I see," Martin nodded. His own contacts had already suggested as much. He had learned never to rely on Dubois's information alone. "Then why are *you* agreeing to see *him*?"

"He still knows people. I think this engine design of his is unpromising, but he may have made progress with other inventions during the war. And he still has some powerful friends who may be useful in encouraging the new steamrail minister to show preference to the local bidder."

"These friends of Gendreau's are the same people you

supported before the Treaty of Calais was signed? The ones who didn't want the treaty at all, and would be just as happy to see it violated? If those are Gendreau's friends he may be more dangerous than useful in the current political climate, monsieur."

Dubois's piggy little eyes narrowed even more as he glared at his pet spy. His fingers strayed as if instinctively to the jacket pocket where he kept the remote control that determined whether Martin lived or died. "I've warned you before, Martin, not to talk politics. I don't pay you to see eye to eye with me, I pay you to do what you're told."

He liked it, Martin knew, when he could throw Martin's Égalité loyalties back in his face. Dubois might act offended, but he enjoyed the fact that Martin despised everything he stood for. Not that Dubois stood for anything on principle; it was all self-interest with him, and always had been. Martin often wished he'd learned that about Dubois a bit sooner.

"My only concern is your safety, naturally," Martin demurred, pretending to ignore Dubois's smirk. "I'll be out of sight for the meeting, but never too far away."

THE AFTERNOON FLIGHT was riskier because of the sun's relative position in the sky, and Charlotte felt the tautness of her nerves as a vague discomfort in the harness, an over-awareness of her movements as she controlled the *Gossamer Wing*. She usually did it all without thinking, as though the airship were an extension of her body.

This is when mistakes happen, she told herself, and wished she could turn around instead of continuing to waft along an updraft leading north and east to the coast. But she had a job to do, so she focused her helmet optics on the now-familiar window below.

Her heart began to thump when she saw the profile and realized who was in that office, meeting with the philandering industrialist. It was indeed Maurice Gendreau. Murcheson's suspicions were confirmed.

Charlotte tweaked the little knob that fine-tuned her

sonic amplificator, and nudged the direction indicator slightly to focus in on the window.

She heard a snatch of French, a wave of interference from the glass, and then a clear stream of words as the onetime spy approached the window.

"Mother of—" A sudden gust stole the words from Charlotte's lips and she struggled to level the *Gossamer Wing* against the buffeting. The sound connection cut in and out, and she nudged her jaw to the right to zoom the ocular device in on the window. It was too far for her to even attempt lip-reading, however.

Determined to gather as much information as possible, Charlotte curled her fingers around the altitude control, pondering whether to risk getting closer. She knew the *Gossamer Wing* might be seen if she ventured too low, but the urge to learn more was nearly overwhelming. A catch like this would secure a future for the dirigible, and Charlotte, in the Agency.

Just as she began to pull the handle she caught a glimpse of something, a flash of light, on the rooftop of the office building. Jerking her hand away from the controls, she refocused from the window to the area the flash had come from.

Another flash hit her directly in the eyes. Banking sharply to change her angle, she thanked the heavens for Dexter's foresight in supplying the oculars with special photoreactive shielding against glare. Even with the shielding, she was all but blinded for a few moments.

Was it a piece of broken glass, or perhaps a skylight catching a stray sunbeam? When her dazzled eyes began to clear she wiggled her chin and perused the area once more, in time to see a tall, thin figure disappear behind the roof access door. He had something in his hand, a slender brass tube with a horribly familiar look to it.

"You don't know for certain it was a spyglass," Dexter reasoned for perhaps the third time since they had turned the boat back toward Honfleur.

"But we have to assume it was," she explained, also for

the third time, "because that's the worst-case scenario. And before you start in again, we *cannot* assume he was up there spying on a pretty clerk one block over. Or the handsome butcher's boy, or a rival shipping agent. The glass reflected off the sun that was roughly behind *me*. We have to assume he was looking for *me*. And that he found me."

"Fine," he capitulated. "What do we do next, if that's the case? Do you resign from the mission? Get on the next ship back to New York?"

Charlotte pressed her hands over her eyes, still suffering a headache from the harsh sunlight and harsher reflection. The glare off the water didn't help. "We tell Murcheson, and probably proceed as though nothing had happened until we know more. We'll also need to search the room thoroughly and if we find nothing, we assume the bugs are there but we simply haven't found them. And we remain alert."

"Are you all right, Charlotte?"

"Are you mad? Of course I'm not all right. Murcheson is sure to scratch my real mission now, if he doesn't send me home outright. Three days into my first real assignment and I've already been—"

"I meant your eyes. You look as though you have a headache." His voice was a little too level, too placid. Charlotte did not especially want to be appeased or pacified. She hated the idea that he was humoring her.

"I do, but I'll survive it."

"When we get back to Atlantis I'll ask Smith-Grenville to hunt down some headache powder."

"Dexter, the headache is the least of my worries. It should be the least of yours."

He frowned, flexing his fingers over the rudder of the little craft then gripping tightly enough for a moment that the wood creaked ominously. Then he relaxed and shrugged. "It's the only worry I can do anything about."

THEIR MEETING WITH Murcheson ran longer than usual that afternoon. They relayed the limited intelligence Charlotte had gathered—the fact of the meeting with Gendreau if not its substance—and Charlotte reluctantly added her concerns about the dark figure on the rooftop. Despite the furor over her possibly being spotted, Murcheson and the station head, Admiral Neeley, asked her to remain and discuss the prospect of a recruiting push for other female pilots, while Dexter joined his team in the bowels of the station.

When Charlotte finally left her meeting and found Dexter, he was embroiled in some fierce physics argument that couldn't be stopped midstream. She wandered back down to the submersible laboratory to wait for him, and spent a troubled hour attempting to convince herself that the minuscule craft wasn't really *that* small after all.

It was nearly sunset when they reemerged from the inconspicuous side door in the nondescript factory building. When Charlotte lifted a gloved hand to shield her eyes from the sudden unexpected glare, she realized the white kid was ruined with dark smudges of lubricant and inexplicable black scuff marks from handling the newly built equipment in the sub. She made a mental note to ask for some coveralls next time, and to remove her gloves before entering the vessel. She might as well outfit herself properly for the sub, since it seemed her tenure as an aerial surveillance expert was due to end abruptly; if she didn't quickly make herself indispensable in some alternative way she'd be shipped back to the Dominions before she knew it. Not that the submersible would have been her choice if she had any other alternative at all.

Coming out again into daylight was disorienting, like leaving a matinee and being startled to find it still light outside. When Dexter offered his arm she took it, stepping briskly to keep up with the men. Mr. Murcheson was back in his jovial factory-owner mode, and spouted a vast number of sales statistics that Charlotte ignored as they returned to the steam car.

"And finally, my dear Baroness, a gift. Something to charm you and perhaps inspire your husband to broaden the scope of his own work."

Through the open window of the car he handed her a curio box, an oddly heavy cube of carved teak with a delicate marquetry pattern of shaded woods and mother-of-pearl on each side. Brass gleamed at the corners, but there was no other hardware in evidence. Charlotte turned the box over and over, finally looking back up at Murcheson with a skeptically arched eyebrow.

"I thank you, sir." She wondered if the present was meant to soften a parting blow. Murcheson had declined to give her a definite yes or no on whether she would still be sent on her mission to retrieve the weapon plans.

"I'll be interested to learn how long it takes you to open it, my lady. And Hardison, I look forward to hearing what devious new uses you think up for it. We're already planning to outfit our surveillance teams with your modified cable crawlers."

He rapped smartly on the roof of the car, and the driver shifted from idle to get the vehicle rolling. Charlotte could see Murcheson waving, until the car turned back down the long drive that led away from the factory, back to the road to Honfleur.

"May I?"

Dexter pried the box from her hands without waiting for an answer. Charlotte chuckled at his obvious eagerness. "By all means. Tricksy, isn't he? I suspect the box is just for added veracity, since I've made such a fuss about them. Either that or he's deliberately trying to confuse me, just for sport."

"Mmm." His fingers, long and thick, were nevertheless dexterous; he handled the little trinket as delicately as an egg. Charlotte suppressed a shiver at the sight, and admonished herself for the inappropriate reaction.

Best to simply let it slide into the past. With her mission now literally and figuratively up in the air, Charlotte needed all the focus she could muster.

"Have you solved Murcheson's mechanical problem yet? I gather they expected you would have it all sorted out the first day you arrived."

"Their problem is not, strictly speaking, mechanical," Dexter muttered, his mind seeming more attentive to the problem in his hand than the one back at the submersible station. "It's geological."

She waited for him to clarify that, but he offered nothing, simply continued to examine and delicately prod the box. She was sorely tempted to demand it back.

Instead, she turned her mind to the submersible with which she'd just spent an afternoon further acquainting herself. The *Gilded Lily* was a little jewel-box of a vehicle, each part beautifully, even lovingly, constructed. An engine not unlike that of the tunnel tram gave it a surprisingly long range with very little noise. Built to echo the lean lines of a shark, it would slice through the water like a keen-edged blade.

It's precisely my cup of tea, she told herself sternly.

For all its wonders, however, Charlotte couldn't bring herself to enjoy piloting it. She could barely bring herself to contemplate getting in the thing again. Her mouth grew dry as she remembered the experiences of that afternoon.

When the technician had offered to take her for a short trip, she had been excited only until the hatch closed over their heads. From that moment on, she'd been nearly frantic to escape the close, suffocating atmosphere within the cabin of gleaming metal and reinforced glass. The water had seemed heavy and threatening, as though she could feel every bit of the pressure that weighed on the tiny craft. Minutes had passed like hours, and she had practically sobbed her relief when the *Gilded Lily* resurfaced in the docking bay and she could open the hatch and breathe again.

Charlotte was chagrined at how thoroughly fear had ruled her today. Her response made her all the more determined to give the sub another try and get the better of the dread.

"As good as your airship?"

"What?" She turned her head sharply, irritated at having her reverie interrupted. Dexter was staring at her, the curio box apparently no longer of interest.

"The submersible. Will it be as good as your airship? Get you out and away from the things of man? It might be a ready substitute, if Murcheson and his men decide the *Gossamer Wing* is too risky after today's incident. You could move from field-testing one to the other. Dubois's office is close enough to the water that you might not even have to change targets."

She couldn't quite tell if he was teasing her. His brown eyes were warm and kind, but then they usually were. The subtle crinkles at the corners were always there, whether he was joking or not, as if he'd spent too many hours squinting at tiny device parts. The corners of his mouth turned up too, sometimes with a wry curl but usually seeming predisposed to good humor. Now was one of the wry times.

Charlotte bit her lower lip against the impulse to place a kiss right there, at the slightly sarcastic corner of Dexter's mouth. Returning her gaze to his eyes, she found, did nothing to make her feel more in control. This was a small space and he filled it, as he had a propensity for doing. She could not have him filling her spaces this way.

"Not here," she said, nodding toward the front of the carriage. The car might be Murcheson's, the driver his employee, but that hardly meant he needed to hear everything they had to say. Their room too was almost certainly compromised. Dexter would have to search it for bugs before they slept that night.

"Later," he said in a voice that brooked no argument, "after dining, we'll walk through the town or on the beach, perhaps. We'll talk." Sitting back and contemplating the curio box once again, he let the curl of his lips develop into a full-fledged smirk. "After all, any newlywed couple on their honeymoon must spend a certain amount of time . . . dallying."

"We can talk," she agreed, trying for a frosty smile. "I'm not sure I approve of any public *dalliance*."

"Conversing into the wee hours, holding hands on a moonlight stroll. Sharing the occasional fond kiss. It's not as though I'm asking you to do what that secretary was doing, Charlotte. Unless you'd like to, of course."

His words were like a blow to the abdomen, pushing a

startled puff of air from her. The image of doing *that*, on her knees before him with her mouth and hands hard at work, forced itself into Charlotte's mind and raked the coals of desire she had struggled for days to keep banked. Instantly wet, breathless and trembling, she blinked the vision away and made herself frown as she replied.

"No, thank you."

"You're blushing," Dexter pointed out.

"The driver—"

"Probably can't hear us over the engine. Charlotte, we did agree to reevaluate . . ."

"*No.*" She threw all her intent into the word, and stared him down, never knowing where the strength to do it came from. After a long, long moment Dexter gave a shrug and a nod.

"Look."

She followed his gaze down to his hand, where sat a star-shaped wonder, its cunningly hinged lids now open to reveal numerous tiny compartments of varying dimensions. Midnight blue velvet lined the teak and brass. As she watched, Dexter closed and reopened one little lid with a fingertip, and a twinkling tune began to play.

"Like fairy bells," she whispered, not wanting to drown out the music with anything so coarse as a human voice.

"Mozart," Dexter said, nearly as low. "Serenade Number Ten."

"Yes, the 'Gran Partita.' I know. Shh."

They sat and listened until the song wound down, a surprisingly long time given how tiny the mechanism must be. After a pause to make sure it was over, Dexter passed his free hand over the opened box like a magician then presented the restored seamless cube to Charlotte with a polite nod of his head.

"Thank you," she said automatically. She knew he was expecting her to ask how to open it, and did not care to give him the satisfaction. She held its weight in her cupped fingers, letting the warmth of Dexter's hands transmit to hers through the wood. It felt good and solid to the touch, all that hardwood and brass. She suspected after she'd handled it awhile, the metal would leave its distinctive sharp smell on her hands. Right now, though, the only scent was of the fresh, clean wood and the oil and varnish it had been rubbed with.

It felt solid and smooth, Charlotte reflected, but it was so complex beneath the surface. And she didn't know how to open it.

With a sigh, she opened her reticule and dropped the box in, careless of the finish.

SHE'D NEVER KNOWN that earthquakes could be a problem in the English Channel. But evidently, as Dexter explained, it was a significant concern given the placement of the submersible station and the geological instability of the channel floor.

"They're worried about having enough warning to get the crew evacuated if there's a danger of being cut off. I know how to make a seismograph to detect vibrations, but I haven't a clue how to rig any sort of long-range sensor array that doesn't use some form of telegraphy."

"I thought you were planning to use the little spider-cars to help with that."

"I considered it," he sighed, "but they're not fast enough to be of much use, I'm afraid."

"Oh, I see. Well, why *can't* it use telegraphy? Or radio signals, like the emergency lamps on the ship?" Charlotte clenched her skirts more firmly in hand as they approached the surf. Her toes dug into the sand with each step, and despite the chilly damp numbing her feet, she found it an oddly luxuriant feeling. Sensual. She had never thought of anything as sensual before the voyage from New York, but now it seemed she was running into sensuality everywhere she went.

"No sound. No vibrations. It has something to do with this new device they're working on that they think the

French may be developing as well. To detect sound or motion underwater."

She nodded. She'd heard rumors. Indeed, she thought a gadget like that would be uniquely useful in her own line of work. She could hardly blame the French for wanting it. Nor could she blame the British military for trying to suss out the secret and beat them to building it.

"What do you know about Murcheson?" Dexter stopped to roll his trousers up before proceeding, and Charlotte lingered until he was finished.

"Not very much. I know his wife is French," she relayed. "But she's said to be above suspicion, on what basis I have no idea. She grew up in England. Gossip has it she's a great beauty, and they've a daughter about to debut who looks exactly like her. I don't suppose that was the sort of information you were interested in, however. Let's see . . . he was one of the first Englishmen to move his business across the channel following the treaty, as you probably know, and he's been by far the most successful. His contacts in the Égalité government range wide and deep. Right to the top."

"They've never found him out as an agent of the Crown?" He frowned, looking up at the moon as though studying it for an answer. "I'd think they would suspect him, at the very least. It seems so risky, having the tunnel extend from this side, and right from beneath his factory."

"Risky, yes. But I think it's brilliant precisely because it's so improbable. They may suspect him, but suspect something on that scale? And because he's building everything from curio boxes to steamrail coaches in his factories, any equipment would be so easy to bring in. He wouldn't even have had to disguise it. Even his own workers don't have to know what's going on. I mean look at the things you're doing to his toys, but the people who make them had no idea they'd end up as gadgetry for spies."

She paddled one foot at the wave that trickled toward them, slapping the top of the water with her toes as it swept over their feet. Moonlight and starlight glimmered on the water like so many metaphorical diamonds. It was hard not to be dazzled, and even harder to ignore the playful pull and slide of water and sand beneath her toes, but Charlotte reined herself in. Poetic thinking would not help her.

"They wouldn't be looking for an entrance on this side of the channel," Dexter continued her train of thought. "They can search on the English side until the cows come home and never find it, because it isn't there to find."

"Risky but brilliant," Charlotte repeated.

"Tomorrow you'll be taking the submersible out alone, I hear?"

She nodded. She was already convincing herself she could learn to enjoy it. A bubble, slipping between the waves, and she would be safe inside it. Safe and quiet and solitary. Exactly her sort of thing. She was practically giddy with anticipation. Giddiness often caused one's palms to sweat.

Dexter startled her when he spoke again. "You know you don't have to, Charlotte. It isn't an official part of your mission, is it? Murcheson hasn't reassigned you."

"Are you worried for me?" she asked with wry amusement. "I assure you I can manage the sub. It's no more dangerous than the *Gossamer Wing*, at least."

"But in the *Gossamer Wing*, you're not closed in. Genuine phobias can do strange things, cloud the mind, even when you think you're in control of your emotions."

She clenched her fists tightly, then made herself release the tension in her hands. "I don't have a genuine phobia. It's under control."

"I see."

He sounded indulgent, but also a little preoccupied, as though his mind had already moved on to some other topic. From the corner of her eye, Charlotte saw Dexter stop his slow ambling at the water line and frown down at his feet. She could see nothing unusual, only the sand and water flowing back and forth with the tide, over his feet and his ankles. The bottoms of his pants were damp despite being rolled, the cream-colored linen dark with moisture.

"What?"

He shook his head. "Nothing. Just . . . silica."

"Silica?"

"Mmm." He crouched and rubbed a bit of wet sand between his fingers, staring off across the water. "Tomorrow morning you'll try out the submersible again if you feel you must. But after that, since Murcheson has grounded the *Gossamer Wing* for daytime flight, I think it's time we moved along to Paris."

"To Paris? But we've only just arrived, we're supposed to have another three days here. Why do we need to go to Paris already?" She could sense a growing excitement and restlessness in him.

"Because it's only a few hours' steamrail ride from Paris to Metz or Nancy," he explained, standing and flicking the grains of sand from his fingers.

Charlotte suppressed a frustrated growl. "And what is in Metz or Nancy?"

Dexter grinned and started back toward the street with a swing in his stride, not waiting for her to follow as he called back over his shoulder.

"Glassmakers."

Eleven

ATLANTIS STATION, BENEATH THE ENGLISH CHANNEL

Dexter was anxious.

Charlotte should have been back fifteen minutes ago.

He stared at the self-contained docking tank, as if he could conjure the submersible back by sheer force of will. A dozen different scenarios played through his head, ranging from simple engine failure that might leave her stranded and unable to return, slowly suffocating to death, to an elaborate scene involving Charlotte taken captive by a rogue French agent who interrogated her using the most appalling torture methods imaginable. In between the two lay the all-too-realistic fear of her succumbing to panic from her claustrophobia and becoming disoriented, unable to pilot the sub back to safety.

He hadn't pressed because he hadn't the right. He wasn't really her husband, so he wasn't able to put his foot down. Nor was he quite a friend, because he hadn't known her long enough to get away with saying the things a friend might say. Now he was not even her lover.

He had been a fool. Such a fool. He thought he'd been giving her time to come to him on her own. Instead, he'd only wasted the time they could have been spending together.

"She was very eager to try it out, sir. Determined, I would say. She was a quick study learning the basics yesterday, and she has plenty of air and fuel. Probably just taking her time."

"She should be watching the time more closely than that," Dexter snapped.

"Yes, sir." The young midshipman manning the tank clearly knew when not to push a point.

"I'm sure she's fine," Dexter allowed gruffly. But by the time Charlotte's vessel broke the surface of the water some five minutes later, he was practically vibrating with a combination of fear and relief that translated into an unfocused rage when he finally saw her face.

"Dexter, you're here! I think you may have been right after all, are you amazed to hear me admit it? It was ghastly!" she nearly shouted, all decorum forgotten as she pushed the hatch up and muscled her way from the sub's cabin, visibly eager to abandon ship. "The longer you stay in the damn thing, the smaller it gets. Somehow being alone in there was even worse than having a copilot, but I refused to let myself panic and give up. It also took me a bit to get the hang of the controls," she admitted, leaping from the bobbing lip of the hatch to the pool's broad edge, "and then I decided to practice with the periscope, just to test my resolve I suppose, but *then*—"

Dexter snatched her from the ledge by the waist and hauled her down in front of him, barely letting her feet graze the ground before he spoke.

"Get out."

It took both Charlotte and the technician a moment to realize he was talking to the young man.

"Sir?"

"Get. Out." Low. Fierce. Not to be ignored.

The midshipman hesitated, his hands still on the rim of the hatch he had leaned over to close. Then, with an alacrity that might have been amusing in any other circumstance, he vacated the stony little chamber to leave them alone.

Charlotte was clearly far from pleased. "Dexter, what the hell do you think you're—"

He kissed her. Not because he wanted to silence her, or because he thought much could come of it, or to make any greater point about the future of their marriage. He felt big and clumsy, an ox without words to express what he could barely identify even to himself. And she was alive, and not being violated by a Frenchman.

Mine.

His lips forced hers open with no subtlety or seduction. It almost wasn't about sex, that kiss. Relief, yes. Possession, quite possibly. His arms folded her closer, wrapping around her at the shoulders and buttocks, lifting her higher. He ignored her effort to push him away, the tapping of her hand against his shoulder. She didn't tap him very hard, or very many times, before she seemed to resign herself and clasped her hands behind his neck.

By the time he let go, setting her on the floor and separating his mouth from hers abruptly, she was trembling nearly as badly as he was. Her mouth looked swollen, her cheeks were pink. The dark blue coverall she wore fit closely enough to reveal her ragged breathing. It revealed entirely too much, Dexter felt, as the trousers were tailored enough to show the curves of her ass and thighs to perfection.

He thought of the young midshipman watching her clamber in and out of the submersible, and had to dig his fingernails into his own palms to restrain himself from grabbing her and kissing her again.

Finally, into the shocked silence, he cleared his throat and said, "I expected you back a bit sooner."

After a few unsuccessful attempts to reply, Charlotte rallied a little. "I see."

He tried a smile, although it felt horribly forced and he suspected it was more of a rictus. "I'm pleased you're not dead. Why is there no radio on that blasted thing again?"

She laughed, but there seemed to be no pleasure in it. "You have a peculiar way of demonstrating that you're pleased about things, and there is no radio because silence is the key to stealth, remember?"

"Oh." He closed his eyes against the irritation in hers, and tried to slow his breath. So he didn't notice her approach, until he felt a touch tracking down the side of his face, soft as breath. He looked then, and saw that she was studying his face with the keen observation of a scientist watching a critical phase of an experiment.

When the fingertip passed over his lips, Charlotte's eyes changed. Darkened. She stared at his lips and then, so quickly he almost thought he might have imagined it, licked her own.

Without thinking, Dexter took her finger between his teeth. Not biting, not nipping. Just securing it there. He expected her to yank it away, and his heart flipped over in his chest when she didn't.

"You were concerned for me?"

He had to let go of her finger to answer. "Yes." Out of his mind with concern, not to put too fine a point on it. "And later, we *are* going to reevaluate."

"Going to . . . oh."

"Ahem."

The very pointed throat-clearing jolted them both, and they jumped away from each other, turning to face the interloper.

Mr. Murcheson and the station's captain were standing in the doorway, the former looking amused and the latter scowling.

"Pardon the interruption," Murcheson mugged. "Admiral Neeley is planning an evacuation drill this afternoon, and you'll want some time to pack and so forth if you're still planning to take the evening train to Paris. I believe it's time we were off. If you're quite through with everything you were involved in here, for the day?"

"Quite," Dexter assured him, rolling his eyes at the older man's wicked smile.

The young midshipman was standing in the corridor, looking abashed, and Dexter gave him a stiff nod in passing. He grasped Charlotte's hand firmly when they moved off down the hall, not letting her escape his side until she reminded him she still had to change back into her street clothes.

A STEAMRAIL COACH, BOUND FOR PARIS, FRANCE

"It was built for a larger person, that sub. It was the same when I used to try to drive my father's steam car," Charlotte grumbled, staring out at the passing scenic blur. The private steamrail coach was luxuriously fitted, but the ride was still tedious after the initial interest died off. They had already dined, then toured the saloon car and found nobody of interest there. There was not much to do, although Charlotte had spent a few minutes idly prodding at the curio box without any success. And now, with dusk falling, even the scenery was fading from view.

"You couldn't reach the pedals?"

She shot him a haughty glare. "It was not built to accommodate my unique specifications. Even though it was a relatively small car, because Father wanted my mother and me to learn to drive it, the controls weren't designed for a small person. It's almost as though the manufacturers can't really quite believe there are short people who might want to drive things. Sometimes it even happens when I'm having something custom-made. They have to do it over because they make it too big the first time even though I've *told* them . . ."

"Well, you are very tiny."

"You never did that," Charlotte pointed out. "All the things you've made for me, you never ignored the specifications like that."

Dexter smiled and shrugged. "I'm empirical. I confess I never really considered how very small a woman those measurements implied. I took the numbers at their face value. It's a weakness of mine."

The opposite of Reginald, Charlotte supposed. Reginald, who took no numbers at face value. To whom all symbols represented something other than the thing they first appeared to represent.

"Not a weakness. An inclination, rather."

"A tendency."

"Exactly. Mister Woolly Bear."

His eyebrow pricked up at the teasing tone. "Have you solved your puzzle box yet, dumpling?"

She gave him a little frown, a pretty pout of displeasure suitable for the Lady Hardison of shipboard life. Whether for the reminder about the box, or the implication that she was dumpling-shaped, she would never let Dexter know.

"I have not."

"Would you like me to show—"

"I would not, thank you, snookums. I'll get it."

"I'm sure you will, my little cinnamon scone. In the meantime, about that reevaluation?"

In the silence following his question, Charlotte heard the rhythmic clatter of the wheels on the rails, the huffing tension of the steam engine that propelled them, and the beating of his own heart. She felt turned to stone, her eyes trained obediently out the window and her expression giving nothing away. She waited long enough to speak that her response, when it finally came, seemed to take Dexter by surprise.

"What, precisely, do you propose?"

"Propose? I didn't really intend a formal negotiation, you know. I don't have *terms*."

Charlotte kept her eyes glued to the passing twilight view as though she could will herself into it. As though, if she concentrated hard enough, she might find herself outside the steamrail coach altogether and away from Dexter Hardison and the conversation he wanted to have with her.

It wasn't that she found the idea abhorrent, far from it. She found it pleasantly diverting in the extreme to consider resuming physical relations with the Makesmith Baron.

Whereas she had expected the time on the ship could be easily left behind, a fond memory fading like a dream, in reality she recalled every moment, every word. She could still feel him, his touch on her skin, inside her, wrapping her up and consuming her, as though they had just that instant tumbled out of bed. She thought she might go mad from remembering, and from wanting more. Or from the sense that she had somehow betrayed Reginald by enjoying it as much as she did.

The guilt was ridiculous, she reminded herself. The curiosity and attraction were normal. It was the timing she couldn't ignore, the horrendous happenstance that they should find this inexorable force drawing them closer together when they needed detachment the most. It was all she could do not to indulge in what-ifs. What if they had met sooner, what if their correspondence had led them to one another as she'd occasionally speculated it might?

Reevaluation. What was there to reevaluate? She wanted him, and she couldn't afford the complication of having him. That should make it simple. Her duty was to the mission, to Reginald's memory. Not to this maddeningly appealing giant who seemed born to bring her pleasure but had arrived too late.

But even now, as he shifted his long frame a little closer on the wide red velvet divan they shared, her body responded. She felt herself turning toward him, a flower opening to the heat and light of the sun.

"Perhaps we *need* terms," she suggested, finally abandoning the landscape to gaze on Dexter. Because she was tired, so tired of fighting this, and she didn't think she could resist any longer. The resistance was becoming as harmful a draw on her attention as the act itself would be. She wanted to unfurl. She missed the sun. But she needed a way to make it all right, to convince herself that it would not become a liability to them both. She needed limits, conditions. "If we are to do this—"

"Charlotte!"

Dexter leaned in, a smile already breaking, to take her hands in his.

"We mustn't make foolish promises we might regret later. No talk of when we return home." She saw a flicker, a hesitation in his smile, before he nodded. "The mission comes first. Always. No arguments, no discussion. We're here to do a job. This arrangement between us would be a convenience, nothing more. We must both assume it will end when the assignment does."

The smile was gone entirely now, which made Charlotte a little sad. It was such a handsome smile. If anything, Dexter looked a bit angry. She tried not to dwell on the fact that if he was angry, or hurt, she was the one who had made him so.

"A convenience. Just mutual physical gratification, then? No bothersome emotional entanglements, and afterward we go our separate ways with our respective itches nicely scratched? That's your proposal, Lady Hardison?"

She considered a moment, trying to decide whether he was sarcastic or in earnest. His jaw was flexed, suggesting his teeth were clenched, and his eyes looked steely. But he was clearly waiting for her response. Finally, Charlotte nodded.

Within a heartbeat, Dexter had her in his lap, his fingers already working at the pearl buttons down the front of her tidy emerald green traveling dress.

"Proposal accepted. Let's get right to it, shall we?" he growled, and Charlotte had no time to catch her breath before he stole it with a harsh kiss. When he finally released her, it was only to stand her up before him, where she stood with legs that were wobbling from more than the motion of the train.

He still looked angry and perhaps even hurt. But resigned to taking what she had offered, even if he wanted more.

"Take your dress off."

His own hands were at work on his trousers, tugging them loose and just low enough to free his erection. Charlotte glanced down and then had difficulty prying her eyes away from the sight of Dexter's cock springing up defiantly from his lap, from the nest of fabric there.

"Take it off," he repeated, "or I'll take it off, and I won't be careful about it."

"Oh." Charlotte's hands were trembling a bit as she picked up where he'd left off on her buttons, and she chided herself for reacting so strongly. It had been only a few days since the last time they'd done this, after all. But Dexter hadn't been so angry then, hadn't seemed so ready to take a bite out of her.

He's magnificent like this. I should anger him more often. She clamped down on the thought as soon as it popped up, but it was too late to unthink it. And it was patently true. He sat there all jutting manhood and rampant impatience, and she craved what she saw. Once the dress had dropped to the ground she started on her underthings, enjoying the flare of surprise and heat in Dexter's eyes as he watched her disrobe completely.

After the warmth of the day, it was cool in the darkening train car, and Charlotte felt her nipples puckering in the chill. She couldn't blame the rest of her reactions on something as simple as the temperature. The wetness at her core, the flush she could feel building, slowly and then in a heated wave when Dexter raised one hand and beckoned to her. She closed the distance between them in a few steps, sighing at the sense of rightness she felt when Dexter palmed her hip to bring her the final few inches.

He shifted his other hand, bringing it between her legs and sliding it up slowly, pulling a sigh from Charlotte as he finally connected with her sex. Like their first time, but so different too. He had made educated guesses with her body then, very good ones. But now he knew where to press, where to stroke. How to bring her to the very brink of ecstasy then let her dangle there while he teased and played with gleeful cruelty.

As her need grew, Charlotte grew more and more shameless, bracing a knee next to his lap to give him more access, leaning on his shoulders in hopes of luring his attention toward her breasts. He gave her that and more, but the more he gave the more she only wanted to feel him moving inside her.

When her pleading turned desperate Dexter finally gave in, tugging her into his lap and down onto him with a few brusque moves. Charlotte barely had a moment to adjust, to savor the delicious fullness, before Dexter was touching her again. First his hands on her thighs and rear, cajoling her into a rhythm. Then his fingers between her legs, moving in short, skillful strokes that served their purpose quickly.

Charlotte came in a sharp burst of pleasure that peaked far too soon and left her wanting more. But no sooner had her body stopped its convulsive clenching, than Dexter lifted her off again.

Shifting forward to the edge of the divan, he nodded at the floor in front of him.

"Go to your knees," he said. He didn't sound quite angry anymore. Charlotte heard a different sort of urgency there. She knelt, coming to eye level with Dexter's erection, uneasily aware of what he meant to do. Meant for *her* to do. Another new thing. Something she would never have dreamed of doing as recently as a few weeks ago, though she had certainly given it a great deal of thought over the past few days.

Charlotte couldn't take her eyes off Dexter's hand as he stroked himself in muscular, steady pulls. Then he angled his cock toward her and put a hand to the back of her head, firm and undeniable. A shiver ran through her as she licked her lips and set her mouth on him, still uncertain. His skin was soft under her lips, despite how hard he was underneath. When she kissed him, sucking a little as she did so, Dexter made a sound she liked very much. It emboldened her to try a lick, and her tongue encountered fluid, slick and salty, a unique concoction of their two distinct flavors. But when she would have lingered to taste it again, Dexter increased the pressure on the back of her head. He indicated in no uncertain terms that he wanted her to take him deeper into her mouth.

She tried it a little at a time, pulling away and then taking more in. His reactions thrilled her, each sigh and each flex of his powerful thighs encouraging her to take greater risks. Soon Dexter's fingers knotted in her hair, guiding her head the way he wanted, in a rhythm that Charlotte found almost as arousing to her as it seemed to be for Dexter.

Almost. She was writhing, frustrated, when he tensed and spoke in a guttural rasp.

"I want to finish in your mouth. I want you to swallow it."

Perhaps she wouldn't like it, she wasn't sure. But she felt powerful, and not inclined to back down from the challenge now. Charlotte hummed her approval, sensing the vibration would be one more form of stimulation. Dexter came silently, holding her in place as she swallowed around him.

When he started to soften, she pulled away to look at his face. He looked a bit shocked, though not displeased. After another moment or two, he tugged her up to his lap again and wrapped his arms around her.

"That was . . . I'm sorry, I shouldn't have asked that of you. It's just all I've been able to think about for days."

"You regret asking? Did I not do it well?" She hated not doing things well.

Dexter guffawed, the movement of his chest dislodging Charlotte's head from his shoulder. "Christ, Charlotte! You did it so well I can't even think straight. I can scarcely believe you're a beginner."

Snuggling back into place, she swung her legs to and fro and reflected. "I assure you I am. Perhaps it's a natural talent. Why shouldn't you have asked? As I pointed out the other day, you've done it to me." Her body, still tightly wound, grew even more tense at the memory. She fiddled with the buttons of his waistcoat, tracing the intricate brass filigree with a fingertip and trying to calm her mind.

"I meant the swallowing bit. I suppose I never thought of that as something a wife would do. Which is ridiculous, I realize. Why wouldn't a wife do that? But usually it's the sort of service one hears described as being performed by a mistress or a—well, you know."

"Yes, I know. Or a secretary. Men really talk about these things?" Charlotte was shocked. "Explicitly?"

Dexter shrugged, seeming untroubled. "Men are beasts, Charlotte. We talk about all sorts of appalling things. The nicest of us don't name names or discuss any characteristics that might give the lady's identity away. Which, perhaps, is why one rarely hears about wives in those conversations," he remarked, as though the idea had only dawned on him right then.

"Of course I'm not exactly a wife," Charlotte pointed out.

"True. Maybe I should look at it as taking a lover. A mistress. I like the idea of a mistress who sucks my cock and swallows what I give her. Do you also take dictation?"

She struck his chest in a firm slap, then kept her hand there to enjoy the feel of his laughter. "Personally, I like the idea of a lover who keeps a civil tongue in his head."

"I can think of better places for my tongue, love."

And he proceeded to demonstrate exactly what he meant.

Twelve

※

"Here we are. In *another* hotel."

"Dexter, I hardly think the staff at the Ritz would appreciate your referring to this as merely 'another hotel.'" Charlotte eyed the dresses in the wardrobe, assuring herself that they had been unpacked properly. "I do wish ladies' maids and valets were still the norm. Impractical for travel, I suppose, especially on this trip. But so useful."

"I don't think I'd like anybody knowing quite that much about the state of my undergarments. Present company excepted, of course."

Dexter was circling the room, fiddling with a device that Charlotte hadn't seen before. Flat, with wires and tiny ceramic bits soldered to it, and something that looked like a battery. He seemed to have an endless supply these little parts and wires, and was always busy making them into things.

"What's that?"

He held up a finger to his lips and shook his head, pro-

ceeding along the wall until he'd made a full circuit of
the bedroom. When he bent down to one of the nightstands,
he beckoned Charlotte closer and pointed under the rim of the
top, where the decorative molding formed a conveniently
darkened space.

Leaning over and squinting, Charlotte could just see
something under the edge, tucked behind the molding. It
was small and coppery, with a tiny silver filament protruding
some inches from it. When Dexter held his hand closer to
it, a minute propeller on his gadget began to spin in lazy
circles. The little copper thing was a bug.

He gave her a grim smile and kept going, finding two
more hidden bugs in the process. In the grandly appointed
sitting room, the cream and blue splendor hosted another
four of the little copper listening devices. Dexter frowned
up at the high ceiling, the chandelier he could not hope to
reach, the intricate crown molding.

"Pumpkin, we still haven't breakfasted. I think we should
go out for a bite to eat. And then, perhaps, for a nice long
walk."

"THE SUBMERSIBLE. WE talked about it on the train, Dexter!
We mentioned the mission. Dear god, what if—"

"Charlotte—"

"Perhaps while we were in the dining car, they could
have—"

"Charlotte! The coach was clean," Dexter said firmly.

"How could you know?" She glared up at him, filled with
sudden mortification. "Oh, Dexter. If they were listening,
that means they would have heard *everything.*"

"No. It was clean," he repeated, taking her arm and steering her around a dubious-looking puddle on the pavement.
"I couldn't sleep, after . . . anyway, I couldn't sleep. I built
the detector while you were resting. I tested it in the coach.
You see," he said wryly, "I do occasionally think about these
things."

Charlotte felt her shoulder relax a fraction. She allowed

her hand to curl over Dexter's arm, and forced herself to take a few slow, deep breaths.

"In Honfleur I think we were relatively careful in the hotel, particularly after your scare about the spyglass." Dexter continued. "Perhaps we're not utterly compromised."

She considered it with a moment of hope, but then dismissed it. "No. We can't take that chance. We have to assume they know. If not specifically why we're here, then at least that we're here for something other than tourism."

"*They* being the French equivalent of Whitehall?"

It seemed . . . off. Charlotte couldn't quite put her finger on why, but this didn't have the feel of government-sponsored intelligence to it. The lone figure with a spyglass on the roof of a private building, the exiled former makesmith-spy attending a daylight meeting in Dubois's company office below . . . even the bugs lacked the dull uniformity of government-issued gear. She felt her hackles rise and glanced around automatically, sweeping the crowd with her eyes and then smiling like any good tourist would at the panorama of humanity that was a Parisian sidewalk on the morning of a lovely summer's day.

"Let's see. If that was the Rue Saint-Honoré we passed back there, this must be the Rue de Rivoli coming up. There's sure to be a lovely little café or something looking out on the Tuileries. I'd knock my own mother over for a decent meal and a pot of tea right now. Let's go this way."

She tugged him along, determined to put some space between them and the Place Vendôme. Surely the whole of Paris couldn't be bugged. As Dexter had insisted on checking each item of their clothing, they could also be reasonably certain that any surveillance at the moment consisted only of somebody following them.

"Tea and a meal, my sweet little éclair? I thought the fashionable French stuck to coffee and pastries in the morning." Dexter was talking with one eye on the crowd, as well. Charlotte would have to remember to discuss subtlety with him. His vigilance was far too apparent.

"Oh, hang fashion. It was a long trip and I'm famished, my Adonis."

"Good one. I rather like that."

"You would."

Charlotte was actually running out of ridiculous endearments, a circumstance that annoyed her as Dexter seemed to have a constant supply. It was easier thinking up sugary nicknames for ladies, she thought. One could hardly call a man *honey muffin* or *cream puff*.

Resolving to spend some time later that evening thinking up more treacly soubriquets—perhaps in French, everything sounded like an endearment in French—she marched ahead, practically dragging Dexter in her wake.

She wanted to get to the restaurant before they discussed any more serious matters. It was past the usual breakfast hour, so it would be more unpredictable, and anybody who tried to finagle a seat near theirs would be easy to spot if there were few other patrons.

"Not outside?" Dexter asked, as they were taking their seats near the back of the bistro they finally selected.

Charlotte shook her head. "It's nice and quiet inside, I prefer it."

When the waiter departed to allow them time with the menu, Charlotte leaned over to speak quietly, turning her head away from the window as she did so. "Too many variables outside. Too many places to hide. And there's always the possibility of a lip reader."

"Really? That never even occurred to me."

"Or," she said, "there may be other surveillance devices in play. Long-range lenses, even directional microphones like the one on my airship. Being inside will make it harder for them to get a bead on us." An idea was trying to shape itself in the back of her mind, poking its way through. She couldn't quite catch hold of it, though.

"So no matter where we go, we're never really safe from observation. Is that what you're telling me?"

For a moment, Charlotte felt sorry for Dexter. For the

necessity that had gotten him involved in this. For the relative innocence he still held, that she herself had lost years ago. The underbelly of politics was an ugly thing, and those who never saw it were undoubtedly much happier for that particular ignorance.

"That's been the case since before we left New York, *mon cher.*"

A smile won through his somber expression for a moment, then faded as he contemplated the reality she had presented him.

"How do you bear it?"

"We'll learn together, I suppose."

They ordered food, and when the waiter was back out of range they covertly assessed the other customers and discussed what to do upon their arrival back at the hotel. Charlotte must play the flighty, adoring young bride again. Dexter must be the brash entrepreneur, bent on gaining all the business knowledge he could out of the trip, honeymoon or no, while still taking time to woo his pretty wife.

And they must steal away from the hotel, always, before talking about their plans for the day, or discussing anything about the mission.

"Tomorrow you're planning to visit Murcheson's factory in Gennevilliers, yes?"

Dexter nodded. "We're going to discuss the requisition process before I proceed to Nancy. He's gathering some glassmaking prospects for me as well."

Charlotte glanced around the room, allowing her gaze to linger for a moment on the elderly couple seated near the door. That pair and a trio of young matrons were the only other customers, and none of them looked in the least suspicious. But Charlotte had learned never to trust appearances. Very few people, if any, were what they seemed.

"You haven't mentioned what you plan to do, to keep yourself occupied while I'm there."

Turning back to Dexter, she gave him a simpering newly-wed smile, just in case. "That's right. I haven't." And then, god help her, she batted her eyelashes at him most shamefully.

She felt her heart skip a beat when his eyes flashed and narrowed, turning predatory as he leaned across the table toward her and captured one of her hands in his. And then that traitorous organ started to beat a furious tattoo as he stroked the inside of her wrist with his thumb, never dropping that carnivorous gaze.

"Perhaps I shall try to coax it out of you later. We won't be doing much talking at the hotel anyway, will we, my delectable little crème brûlée? I believe I'll enjoy having you for dessert, Charlotte."

She had been about to tell him her plans, having never really meant to keep the information from him, as her intention was merely to shop. Now she bit her tongue, wondering how he would coax it from her. Charlotte blushed, feeling the lurid pressure of delightful shame in her cheeks and down to her breast as the waiter approached, bearing food and tea.

Much as she wanted to give in to that feeling, wallow in it and in Dexter's attention . . . part of her kept scanning the room, the windows and the street beyond, wondering who else might be witness to their conversation.

THEY SPENT THE day as highly visible tourists. After dinner, Dexter had made good on his affectionate threats, and Charlotte seemed to let herself disappear into the role of giggling, besotted bride for a few hours. It was easy enough, and very little talk was required. They devoured one another and lay dozing afterward, limbs wound together and tangled in the luxurious sheets.

He felt her stirring first and tightened his arm around her, not yet ready to lose the feeling of warm, loose-limbed Charlotte snuggled against his side and chest.

"Mm. No, don't go."

"I'll be right back, silly." She pushed at his chest until he relinquished her, and for the next few moments he had the pleasure of watching her as she walked about the room, finding their various pieces of discarded clothing and draping it all neatly over the back of a chair. He was less pleased when she pulled a night rail from the wardrobe and disappeared into the bathroom.

He pouted when she emerged. "You're even more enticing with that thing on, you know," he lied. "All it does is make me fixate on what's underneath. You'd be better off without it."

She just smiled and turned the lights down completely, then slipped back into bed again. "I don't want to scandalize the maids in the morning. Poor things, they have enough to worry about."

"I'm sure they've seen it all before, and far worse," Dexter countered.

"Yes, but they haven't seen it from me. Nor shall they."

He grumbled a bit more, but his heart soared when she returned to the crook of his arm and nestled against him again.

"So tomorrow, my silly noodle, I must go pay a visit to Murcheson's local operation, northwest of the city. Oh, I know," he said, hoping he sounded as though he were quelling some gestured objection, "but it can't be helped. I really must see more of the small parts works. And also the direct sales outfit. He does a land-office business out of that factory, he claims. I could do with expanding that way, I think."

Charlotte gave a noisy sigh. "But Dex," she whined, "what am I to do all morning?"

"All day, poppet," he corrected her. "I don't think I'll return much before dinner."

She made another noise, conveying infinite exasperation without words. "Fine. But I think you're being beastly. It's our honeymoon, and all you care about is those nasty, overheated factories, and pages and pages of figures."

"Charlotte, nothing could be further from the truth. You know you come first with me. Haven't you noticed you always come first?"

He gave a little dig into her side and grinned when she squirmed and giggled at the double entendre. A real giggle, not the fake one she adopted for this sham persona. Funny how he could love the one and loathe the other.

"I plan to be quite put out with you, Dex," she replied a little breathlessly. "If you're going to the factory, then I shall take my revenge by spending the entire morning with the most expensive modiste in Paris. And I plan to order everything as a rush job, to drive up the price even more."

So that was her grand plan. If he hadn't known she would be spending her own money at it, he might have been concerned. Or perhaps not, as Charlotte's taste in clothing seemed nowhere near as extravagant as that of most fashionable ladies of Dexter's acquaintance. But she was certainly playing her part well.

"Kindly don't bankrupt us before we even return to the Dominions. If you're starving to death it won't matter how well dressed you are. Will you spend the entire day there?"

"Oh no," she reassured him. "Only the morning. Then I'll stroll about and sightsee, and in the afternoon I think I'll go to a museum or something like that. Perhaps a tour of important cultural sites."

"You must be prepared to describe it all to me at dinner, all right?"

"Of course, Dex. That is if I'm over being angry with you."

"I see. And is there no way I can appease you?"

"I doubt it."

"Well, what about . . ." He rolled toward her a bit and whispered a shocking suggestion in her ear, loving the way she tipped her head to accommodate him.

"That might work," she admitted. "Only one way to find out."

In the course of finding out, her gown came off again. And in the morning, though Charlotte was mortified, she found the maid who brought the breakfast tray and opened the curtains to be entirely adept at averting her eyes.

Thirteen

※⟡※

PARIS AND GENNEVILLIERS, FRANCE

CHARLOTTE FIRST NOTICED the man when she rang the bell at the modiste's small, tucked-away shop. He had just taken a seat outside the bistro next door. He was so tall and skeletally thin that his knees knocked the underside of the table when he folded himself into the chair, and she felt a wave of pity for him.

How hard that must be for him, she thought. *I should stop fussing about being so small.*

Then she promptly forgot about the odd-looking fellow as she was ushered into the shop and lost herself in the world of fabric and color and style. An heiress from the Dominions, a *baroness* no less, might as well have been a princess to the modiste and her eager assistants. Charlotte had intended to stay for an hour and spend a fixed and rather modest amount on some specific garments she'd been needing. Instead she left four hours later, having overspent her budget by at least several hundred percent, but secure in the knowledge that no woman in the New York Dominion would be better-dressed than she by the time the seamstresses had finished and delivered their masterpieces.

He was still there. She almost didn't notice this time, because his back was to her as she left the shop. When she walked past his table Charlotte noticed his hands, which held a newspaper in front of him. One of those hands, she realized with a start, was prosthetic. A glove—apparently dyed to match his skin—covered a structure that only peripherally resembled fingers and a thumb. His other hand held the paper gracefully, while the false hand rested like a cheap stage prop, holding the opposite edge of the page in a crude pincer grip.

Poor thing, Charlotte thought, a split second before she recognized the tall, lanky object of pity from earlier in the morning.

She forced herself to keep walking without a hitch, though her heart started to pound and a cold sweat broke out over her face.

At the corner she resisted the urge to turn and look behind her. It was a crowded street, in broad daylight; if he were to make a move, he would be unlikely to make it here.

A window display half a block down drew her to a bookstore, and she ducked inside to purchase a guidebook to the Louvre and an illustrated history of French fashions for her mother.

She didn't see him outside the window when she approached it to leave. Perhaps her imagination had been playing tricks on her. Paris and the attendant anxiety over her impending assignment must have prompted a memory of Reginald's lurid story—the only one of his stories that had ever been lurid—about his daring escape from the wraithlike, claw-handed agent with the curious metal device where one ear should have been.

Charlotte's mind lingered on Reginald, wondering what he'd thought of Paris. Despite her solid intention to hate the place, she had to admit the city was fascinating and often beautiful. Had Reginald's cover persona allowed him any time to sightsee, to marvel at Notre-Dame or wander through the Louvre? She'd never thought to ask, though she supposed in time she would have gotten around to it. If they'd *had* time. Mostly she'd been eager to hear his thrilling tale of intrigue, complete with horrific villain and the astonishing recovery of stolen plans for what appeared—at Reginald's single hurried glance—to be the infamous, mythical, war-ending British doomsday device.

Without realizing it, Charlotte had strolled all the way to the Boulevard des Italiens. She was about to pull out her map when she recognized the massive edifice standing almost directly across the street from her: The Palais Garnier, home of the Paris Opera.

MARTIN COULD ALMOST believe it was accidental. The woman showed no guile, no subterfuge, as she observed the Opéra from across the boulevard. Only curiosity, and a puzzled expression as though she were trying to solve a problem or recall some elusive memory.

She didn't plan to come here, his instinct told him. He listened to that instinct, and held back to watch her.

Dubois had ordered him to stick to Murcheson, and more recently to the Makesmith Baron, as though these men were some demons sent specifically to take down his empire. The more Dubois insisted, the more Martin became determined that the woman somehow posed the greater threat.

The American agent's face still haunted Martin's dreams on occasion, two aspects of the same man at very different stages of his life. The first, as the young agent saw his death approaching at breakneck speed but miraculously escaped it. The second, right before he lost all ability to control his speech, at the very moment he recognized that death had finally caught up with him.

Both times he had spoken the same, single word. "Charlotte."

Coeur de Fer had no nemesis. He was a legend to himself, a shadowy figure in the annals of international espionage.

But he did have a bit of an obsession with that boy from the Dominions.

"The only one who ever got away," he mused to himself, "though even he couldn't avoid me forever." Martin lost himself in the crowd as he followed Charlotte across the boulevard and up to the Palais Garnier. Despite his outlandish appearance, he was talented at fading into the background.

She was just in time to buy a ticket for the next tour. Martin almost laughed aloud. A tour of the building where her husband had almost met his grisly end. So be it.

Martin would buy no ticket. He already knew how to pick the locks at the Palais Garnier quite well.

Fifteen minutes later, when he finally accepted that she was not with the tour group, Martin saw it as another sign. The woman was an agent, clearly, he should have seen it from the start. Her story was too pat, her demeanor too glib, to explain her presence as a simple tourist in the country her husband and father had lived to defeat. Despite her earlier expression of befuddlement, her presence in the Palais Garnier couldn't be coincidental.

She was also still in the building, and he had a reasonable guess as to where she was heading. Just as he had once received a sign, Martin decided it was time for Lady Hardison to receive a sign. Or merely a scare, depending on her nerve and whether his guesses about her occupation and reasons for being here were correct. Sighing, he melted from the mezzanine and made for the service passageway to await her return.

"GLASS ISN'T MY area, to speak of. Can you be more specific? Are you interested in ceramics, resistor production, that sort of thing? Or specialized casings?"

"Neither, actually," Dexter told Murcheson's man Cormier. The rabbity, bespectacled Frenchman looked more like a clerk than the head of regional operations for a large manufacturer. Nevertheless, it was Cormier who ran things at the large Murcheson facility in Gennevilliers, and the various satellite facilities near Paris. Dexter could tell Murcheson held the man in the utmost respect, but he hadn't thought to ask before the meeting if the obviously local Cormier was privy to his employer's clandestine occupation. Murcheson's placid expression gave him no clue, so Dexter decided on circumspection. "It's a new application I'm developing. Trade secret, I'm afraid, but quite promising."

Cormier frowned, as well he might. "Not much to go on. But if you're heading to Nancy anyway, might try looking up young Arsenault. Late of the Lalique operation, has his own workshop now. He's known for innovation. If it's something new you're after, I suspect Arsenault's the one you ought to talk to."

Dexter noted the name, and thanked Cormier profusely as the man walked out to have his secretary fetch the address.

"I can have him send a message ahead, if you like?" Murcheson offered.

"No, no. I don't know when I'll be there, I want to keep things flexible." Dexter mostly wanted to keep from broadcasting any travel plans ahead of time. He was beginning to adopt the habit of caution, of suspicion. It gave him new insight into Charlotte's reserve. What must it have been like, only child to a notorious gentleman spy? Wanting to follow in his footsteps, just at the time it was becoming feasible for a woman to do so? She had been shaped by her father for this role, whether or not he'd intended to do it. Dexter knew a moment of fear that Charlotte might never be able to adapt to a calmer, less perilous life.

But the more time he spent with her, the more he grew convinced that he wanted such a life with Charlotte. Far from fading, his initial infatuation seemed to be deepening with each day that passed. She was not the fantasy woman he'd once envisioned, but he had long since ceased to day-dream about *that* Charlotte. The real Charlotte maddened him, challenged him, inflamed his passions and excited his intellect. But most of all he simply *liked* the lady so damn much it frightened him. He felt comfortable with her, and he had no idea why. She was nothing at all like the women he usually spent time with. Voluptuous, friendly, often tall and occasionally a bit too brassy for good taste. Good girls, all of them, but they were so many overblown roses, merrily shedding petals in every godless shade of red. And bless them, all of them, for he adored women like that. Especially in his bed.

Whereas Charlotte . . . Charlotte was a rosebud chiseled in diamond, dainty and crystalline and not nearly as fragile as she looked. But such sparks, such heat, if one could but look past the icy surface to see the flaring colors beneath. And when he was inside her . . .

Dexter crossed his legs, uncrossed them and crossed them the other way, clearing his throat nervously. He hoped his reaction to his own reverie was not as apparent as it felt. Chiding himself for regressing to schoolboy behavior, he forced his attention back to the factory plan that Murcheson was now describing to him.

"And here," the older man was saying, pointing to a dotted outline on the plat, "we intend to expand our research laboratory next year. More focus on battery efficiency. This will also free up much-needed space on the factory floor, once we've rebuilt."

"Impressive." Dexter traced over the closest factory wall on the floor plan, a double blue line bleeding a bit into the thin white vellum. "Not quite as impressive as Le Havre, of course. No offense to you, Monsieur Cormier," he said as the man returned to his seat, the secretary evidently duly informed.

"None taken, I'm sure."

"Your steam cars are built here prior to delivery, I gather?" Dexter asked, sensing that both men would be eager to continue discussing their operation.

He caught the first few words of Cormier's response, then lost the thread of meaning as his mind wandered forward to the afternoon's schedule. He wanted to be back at the hotel so he could greet Charlotte when she returned from her shopping and cultural tour of Paris. He wanted to know she had made it back safely. She had looked so small, so precious, when he left her that morning after breakfast. The unsatisfied urge to pick her up and carry her back into bed, strip her naked and spend hours making love to her, had been a physical ache in his body all day.

"But then elephants never have made very good chauffeurs, as they can't seem to learn their left from their right."

Dexter blinked and shook his head. "I'm sorry. Did you say *elephants*?"

"I wasn't sure you were listening." Cormier grinned at him, suddenly looking extremely French. Murcheson himself was doing a poor job of hiding a smirk. "This is your honeymoon, isn't it, Monsieur Hardison?"

"Yes, it is." It was *a* honeymoon of sorts, at least. The only one he'd ever had.

"What the devil are you doing here, then? Shouldn't you be with your bride?"

Shrugging, Dexter leaned back and tried to affect an air of indifference. He avoided Murcheson's gaze, not wanting to seem as though he was consulting the man for clues on how to feel about his honeymoon or his new wife. "She was at the modiste this morning, and this afternoon she'd planned to take in some cultural sights. I thought it was an ideal opportunity to occupy myself elsewhere."

Cormier gave him a long, pointed look. Somewhere in the middle of it, Dexter decided that the man must be in Murcheson's confidence, or Murcheson would have warned Dexter in advance. So more than likely he knew about the marriage, and that Dexter and Charlotte were conjoined only for purposes of espionage. But he spoke as he might to any young man who had been foolish enough to mix business and pleasure.

"Your mind isn't here, my boy, and I suspect I know where it is. I was a newlywed once myself, and I recognize the look on your face. I have a recommendation for you. Would you like to hear it?"

Dexter did look at Murcheson this time. The spymaster

merely lifted an eyebrow and shrugged at him. "The French, what can you do?"

Dexter turned back to Cormier and nodded, though he was baffled.

The older man smiled again. "Nobody ever really knows, before they wed, whether the marriage will be a good one or not. No matter what the original reason for the marriage, no matter the obstacles or benefits it might present, *any* marriage has as good a chance as any other, from all I've seen. What's more, we don't get to choose who captivates us. It simply happens, and denying it rarely works out well. And so my advice to you, Mr. Hardison, is that you go back to Paris and spend your honeymoon *with your wife*."

THOUGH THE PALAIS Garnier was in general magnificent, Charlotte had managed to see some of its least savory parts as she worked her way to the top of the building with only her sense of direction to guide her. Once she reached the final door, however, she was thwarted before reaching her rooftop goal.

Charlotte stared at the heavily fortified barrier in mounting frustration. She had managed to pick the lock on the door itself with little trouble, but the sturdy chain and padlock that further secured it were proving insurmountable. If she couldn't get to the roof this way, and Murcheson didn't allow her to use the *Gossamer Wing* as originally planned, Charlotte had little chance of finding out whether the documents Reginald had stashed away were still there, safe in their secret nook. Nor could she look out and see what he had seen that fateful night, and feel whatever tenuous connection with him the view might bring to her.

Charlotte knew she would have to give it up soon. If she didn't rejoin the tour group within another few minutes, she would almost certainly be missed. For all she knew, her absence had already been noted. Perhaps she'd been followed into the group. One of those portly, comfortable tourists could be the agent on her trail and not the skeletal man at all. Shuddering at the notion, she returned her attention to the lock for one last attempt.

The pins and tumblers defeated her efforts, and she finally gave up and retreated down the many flights of stairs until she found herself back in the hallway behind the cloakroom and toilets. She spotted the door to the lobby with a sigh of relief.

"Puis-je vous aider, madame?"

Charlotte jumped and whirled to find herself facing the man she'd seen outside the modiste's.

Time stopped for a moment while her brain registered details, as it had been trained to do. He was pale, and his unfashionably long dark hair was hanging down on one side, covering that ear and falling past his shoulder. He wore a black suit that only emphasized his lean height. When the clock of life commenced ticking again, Charlotte started backing toward the lobby door, toward safety. Relative safety, at least. Just a few yards more . . .

"Parlez-vous Francais? You require help?" he repeated in heavily accented English.

Where had he come from, and what had he seen?

"N-no. *Non, merci."* Charlotte donned her sweet, vapid mask, though it took even greater effort than usual with her heart racing as it was. "You gave me such a start, sir! *Parlez-vous Anglais?"*

"Oui, madame." The man gave a little bow from the waist then took a step toward her.

"Wonderful! I seem to have taken a wrong turn and lost my tour group. We were looking at the ceilings and I couldn't stop staring. Silly me, I never thought about it, but do you know that if you look up and turn around and around long enough, you'll grow quite dizzy? I nearly fell over!" She was still backing up as she prattled, stealing closer and closer to the door that opened onto the lobby. "Then, I went looking for . . . well, *you* know. Some water to splash on my face. But I must have gone through a wrong door somewhere because there were all these stairs and at one point I was on a catwalk over the stage! Can you imagine? It took me forever to find a way back down. Oh, does this go out to the front again? Splendid!"

She had the door open and was out in a trice without even checking to see that the coast was clear. She hoped she wouldn't be spotted by any theater employees, but was too frantic to escape the man to care about a scolding for leaving the tour group. When she glanced back, giving a last adorable little wave over her shoulder like an ill-timed reflex, the man in black was staring at her with such cold, soulless eyes that her step faltered for a moment. A stray sunbeam from the entrance glanced across his face, lighting the side with the hidden ear, and for an instant she saw a flash there through the curtain of hair, as of light reflecting against glass or polished metal.

Forcing a giddy grin onto her face, Charlotte turned and scampered back across the lobby and up the grand staircase to rejoin the group, feeling as though the hounds of hell might be at her heels. She would not allow herself to look back again.

"AT LEAST NOW I know who to be on the lookout for."

Charlotte didn't feel nearly as easy as she sounded regarding her brush with potential danger. And Dexter wasn't fooled, she suspected.

"You continued to stroll around even after you suspected you were being followed?" He spun around, incredulous, and stood in front of her with his arms crossed, looking stern and imposing, blocking her from taking another step.

Charlotte glanced around, hoping that anybody overhearing them would assume it was a marital spat and move along.

"More quietly, please. Yes I did, and I learned a great deal."

"How so?"

"For one thing," she pointed out, "we know he's more suspicious of me than of you. When we separated, he chose to follow me."

Dexter shrugged. "For all I know there was somebody

tailing me in Gennevilliers as well. I would be much less likely than you to pick up on something like that."

She shook her head. "I don't think so. At least if there was, it was just somebody sent after you for form. Furthermore, I believe I confirmed Murcheson's suspicion that Dubois is working with the French government."

Charlotte inclined her head toward the fountain that sparkled merrily in the streetlights a few dozen yards away along the walkway. Dexter followed her lead, and they found a bench beside it.

"The sound will help mask the conversation," she explained. "It's shadowy here too, which may give us a bit of cover if anybody is observing us."

"How can you know this is the French, and not just some lackey of Dubois's? You sound very certain. What do you know, that you haven't been telling me?"

She sighed, wishing she could resist the pull of her memories. She didn't want to believe her suspicions were true, wanted to think she was being melodramatic. But Charlotte had never been melodramatic, and she was fairly sure she knew who was tailing them.

"Reginald's last field mission before the treaty was here in Paris, as you know."

Dexter nodded and gestured for her to continue.

"He'd been following Roland Dubois as well, I gather, because at the time Whitehall thought they might be able to use him to get close to some French agent, a woman who'd apparently stolen some important laboratory notes from a scientist who was working for the British government. At any rate, that night I told you about, Reginald had an encounter with a French agent outside Dubois's office. He recognized the man as an enemy operative and managed to take a bundle of documents from him. Reginald only got a glimpse inside the bundle, but he thought they looked like the stolen lab notes. He ran off and escaped the agent by somehow making his way to the roof of the Palais Garnier then sliding down a line on the opposite side."

"How the devil did he get up—"

"I've no idea, and it doesn't matter. The point is, he'd hidden the packet up on the roof, in one of a number of secure caches that our men in France had constructed for leaving messages to one another. That's why he chose that particular building."

Dexter raised his eyebrows. "Reginald? It was Reginald himself who left the documents you're here to retrieve?"

"Yes. It was one of the reasons they assigned me. I'd worked with him, knew him, and might notice details others wouldn't. If he'd changed any of the equipment or codes used to work the pressure locks on the cache, with my background I'd be more likely to work out what new code he'd used. Nobody ever thought to ask him while there was still time, you see."

"I see."

"I should have told you. It didn't seem to matter."

Dexter didn't respond directly to that. "Did his foe see him stashing the documents?"

Charlotte shook her head. "Not as far as Reginald could tell, and that's why Murcheson hopes they're still there. Reginald's main memory after he'd secured the package was of turning to jump off the roof and seeing the man right behind him, hand outstretched. The wind was blowing, a snowstorm had started minutes before. Reginald said the man's hair had blown back from his face and he had nothing but some sort of metal device where one ear had been. And the hand that reached for him, that was metal too."

"Dear God."

"Reginald saw all this for a second, at the most, before he slipped down the cord and escaped, but the image was so stark it never left him. He never knew what kept the man from cutting the cord or prying the grappling hook from the abutment. His superiors identified the man from his report once he'd returned to England."

Dexter took her hand in his, and Charlotte was grateful for the warmth and for the contact. "From your description of the man you saw at the Opéra, It certainly sounds like the same agent."

"How many claw-handed agents with advanced auditory enhancements are there in French intelligence? I'd think it had to be the same man. The simplest explanation is almost always the right one, isn't that what they say?"

"*They* say a lot of things. And that's hardly simple, a spy who's half automaton, following the widow of an enemy agent he killed five years ago to the same building where he had a showdown against the man two years before that. But I'd hardly claim it was impossible either. So this man is still an active field operative?"

"No," Charlotte admitted. "Not if it's the same person. He hasn't officially been an agent for the French for years. Not since the treaty. They said he went rogue, though I always had my doubts. In any case, a few weeks before we were married, Reginald's superiors warned us that this former agent—Coeur de Fer they call him—appeared to be traveling to the Americas. Dubois was traveling there and Couer de Fer was posing as his bodyguard, but the Agency was concerned he might be tracking Reginald because of their history."

"Did he . . . wait, Reginald knew this man was coming?"

"We thought we'd taken every precaution. We had security at the wedding, we employed doubles to go on the honeymoon we'd originally planned, while we took a boat to New Orleans with tickets purchased under another name at the last minute. It didn't matter in the end. The man was obsessed, I think. He would have caught up with Reginald eventually, no matter what we'd done."

"It's been years, though," Dexter argued. "It may not be the same man after all. You never saw him yourself, correct? Besides, you were still hardly more than a girl when the treaty was signed. Why would he suspect you of anything now?"

"I don't know. But my showing up at the Palais Garnier can't have looked like coincidence to him. I need to speak with Murcheson about it. If this man has already made the connection between me and Reginald, and cares enough to pursue me now, the only thing he could be after is the one thing Reginald took from him. I can only assume it would be best for our side to recover those documents now, before he takes it in mind to look around the Opéra roof for old times' sake. I don't think we can afford to wait for the new moon."

For a moment Dexter said nothing at all but just sat, frowning thoughtfully. "But then again, perhaps it wasn't Coeur de Fer after all. Would an agent of that caliber, even a former one, make a mistake like that? Letting his cover slip, letting himself be seen by his mark? It seems like a pretty basic thing to slip up on."

"Oh, I don't think it was an accident," Charlotte said. "I think he wanted me to see. Wanted me to know that he was following me. To frighten me off, or see how I would react. He likes the cat and mouse game. He likes to taunt."

The basis of her knowledge swirled in her head, making her ill as it always did when she allowed herself to think about it. If she had only awakened, if she had heard the door, or if she and Reginald had stayed up to make love a second time—

"What is it?"

Dexter's arm was all the way around her waist now, Charlotte realized. It felt good and solid and safe. She couldn't let herself relax into it.

"It's difficult to talk about," she understated.

That warm, strong arm tightened around her, pulling her closer. "Do you want to know what I think?"

She looked up at him, curious. "All right."

"I think that man poisoned you too. Not like he did Reginald," Dexter assured her, "but with this memory, whatever it is. I see how it haunts you, Charlotte, and it festers like any slow poison. You need to purge it. Cast it up, have it drawn. Choose your metaphor. Either way you can't keep living with that foul rot inside your mind."

"You make it sound like gangrene."

After a long moment in which they stared at each other, Dexter chuckled and dropped his gaze. "Not the metaphor I intended."

"Don't they amputate for gangrene? This memory's in my head, Dexter. Precisely what are you suggesting?"

"I certainly don't advocate amputation of your pretty head. Forget the gangrene. Let's stick to man-made poisons, and go with a purge."

Charlotte was astonished to realize she was smiling, even in the face of this, the stuff of her nightmares. Dexter was like a wizard, waving a wand over her soul and making the impossible seem not only possible but essential.

Not easy, however. No magic could ever make it easy to let that story out. Charlotte had to steel her nerve and make a few false starts before she managed.

"I was asleep," she finally said, as though this simple fact disgusted her. "I don't remember hearing anyone enter our cabin, although the lock was forced. Later the doctor said I'd been given a light dose of chloroform, enough to keep me from waking while . . . to keep me from waking.

"Reginald had been given something before he was poisoned, something to paralyze him so he couldn't struggle. But I've researched the substance since, and although the forensic doctor didn't say so at the time, I know it wouldn't have rendered him unconscious, only unable to move or speak. And why would the killer go to the trouble of procuring that particular drug, if not to wake his victim up once he was helpless? To have him know what was happening? Reginald knew, and was unable to defend himself as that fiend shot the poison into him. And I never woke up," she whispered, because her throat was so tight the air could barely pass through it. "I was right next to him the whole time. I never saw him alive again. In the morning I found him next to me and tried . . . tried to wake him. Couldn't wake him."

"Stop."

"The curtains to the berth were closed and it was dark, so I leaned over to try to open them and felt . . . he was so still and cold. His arm, so cold under my hand. I couldn't breathe, couldn't think. I felt like we were in a coffin. I'd never seen a dead body before but I knew, even though I kept trying. I knew, I *knew*—"

"Charlotte, stop. Shh, shh. Stop now," Dexter whispered, pulling her head into his chest. She resisted for a moment then relaxed, slipping her arms around him and clinging with all her might. "I didn't mean to make you do this here, darling. I'm sorry. I wouldn't have for all the world. I didn't know."

"I'm going to cry, and I hate crying," she explained into Dexter's waistcoat.

He passed her a handkerchief then wrapped his arm around her again. "I'll pretend not to notice, then. I'll watch the fountain, and you just let me know when you're finished."

His humor and kindness broke the dam at last and Charlotte sobbed into his broad chest, no longer caring who saw, or that she was the one who had asked for no emotional entanglements.

She wasn't sure how long they sat like that, her weeping and Dexter pretending not to notice. He stroked her back and occasionally pressed a kiss to the top of her head, and it finally registered with Charlotte that they were in a public park where such a maudlin display was absolutely out of the question.

Too late. She didn't want to raise her head when the sobs finally hitched to a halt. It was all too embarrassing, and she had a horrible suspicion she'd ruined Dexter's nice burgundy moiré waistcoat. His handkerchief was irrecoverably sodden. She would have to remember to buy him some new ones.

Another kiss fell on her head, and the gentle stroking turned to a pat on the shoulder.

"Better?"

Dexter's voice rumbled in his chest, enticing her to stay. Reluctantly, she nodded and straightened up, trying not to meet his eyes.

He took her chin between his fingers and lifted it, procuring a second, clean handkerchief from parts unknown and wiping her face with it almost as though she were a child. To her astonishment, Dexter's cheeks bore evidence of tears as well.

"I didn't mean to make you cry too," she said.

"The wind caught the spray from the fountain and it wafted into my eyes," he replied dryly. "I really am sorry, my love. I never dreamed it was so—"

"No, don't apologize. I do feel better now. You were right. I needed a purge."

Dexter sniffled, then looked displeased with himself for doing so. "All right, then. Thank heavens it worked and we didn't have to resort to amputation after all."

"That would have been tragic. The modiste I saw this morning called in a milliner in the middle of our sartorial orgy. So in addition to a great deal of clothing I'm expecting a number of very frivolous hats to arrive in a week or so. I'll be needing my head for those."

"Tragedy averted," Dexter laughed. "You're wonderful."

She blinked a few times, not sure whether to reply or pretend she hadn't heard him correctly. "Thank you," she said at last.

"You're welcome." Dexter smiled, then looked away and changed the subject. "Does our newly identified villain have a name, by the way?"

Charlotte grimaced. "Jacques Martin. But as I said, they mostly call him Coeur de Fer. Iron Heart. I've no idea if it's literally true. I suspect not. They don't really make implants from iron, and he'd hardly be fit for spying with a mechanical heart. But the name still fits."

"This keeps getting better and better."

She laughed, Dexter's flippant remark breaking the chill that had overtaken her. "There is a very small bright side." She stood up and held a hand out, smiling at Dexter as he stood and laced his fingers through hers. She wondered at how easily they fit together, him so large and her so small. But there was a nearly audible click, a rightness in their joining, even when they did something as simple as holding hands. She pushed the notion down, forcing herself to focus on business.

"Even a minuscule bright side would be welcome about now," he said.

"Now that he knows that we know, I suppose we can sweep the room again and destroy all the bugs."

"Ah, true," he concurred. "I'll have to devise a way to check the chandeliers. Perhaps I can use one of the cable crawlers, and a tiny grappling hook. In the meantime, where would you like to dine, my lady?"

Anywhere you are.

"I hadn't given it any thought. Do you have a preference?"

Dexter pondered. "Someplace that serves simple, comfortable food I can pronounce, and where they demonstrate a healthy respect for the importance of decadent sweets after a meal."

Charlotte gave a happy sigh, then had to pretend she was only talking about the dinner plans when she crooned, "Perfect."

Fourteen

PARIS AND NANCY, FRANCE

MURCHESON'S MEN WERE able to confirm Charlotte's identification of Jacques Martin by the following afternoon, but there were still questions left unanswered about the precise nature of the relationship between Dubois, Coeur de Fer and the French intelligence agency.

"Obviously this means you can't risk going back to the Palais Garnier," Dexter said, to Charlotte's disgruntlement. "He knows we're here, he knows you're interested in that building. We have to assume he knows who you are, your connection to Reginald. He'll be on the lookout."

"On the contrary, it means I have to get to the roof of the Opéra soon, *tonight* if possible," Charlotte objected. "If Martin knows who I am, I've tipped our hand. We have to get to the documents before he finds his way back up there and ferrets them out for himself."

"I'm afraid I have to agree with your husband, Lady Hardison. Now is the worst possible time to try for them. You led Martin straight to the roof. He'll be waiting there to intercept you if you try again. If indeed the packet is still there at all, and he's not merely concerned with deducing your role in all this," Murcheson countered.

"No, I can't believe that. I also can't believe he revealed himself in that building by chance or whim. Those papers were important enough to kill Reginald over, even years after the war had ended," Charlotte insisted. "And apparently somebody remains interested enough to have Reginald's widow followed on general principle. Would they still be so interested if they'd already found the weapon plans? And if they haven't found them, that means there's still time to prevent it. I have to get there before Martin does."

Dexter cleared his throat. "Charlotte, what's the range of the *Gossamer Wing*?"

Charlotte blinked at the seeming non sequitur, then did some quick calculations in her head. "If there isn't much headwind, I can get between four and five hundred miles out of her. The fuel payload has to be small, of course. Weight is always the primary consideration, so that does limit the range. Why?"

"It's only a hundred seventy or eighty miles from Nancy back to Paris. An easy round trip without needing to refuel, as long as the weather holds clear."

"But we're supposed to be in Paris for several more days. I don't think we can wait that long."

"We could leave for Nancy tonight. We're frivolous wealthy folk on our honeymoon, we can change our plans without warning if we like."

She could tell that Dexter hadn't wanted to suggest the idea, that he'd felt compelled to do it. Out of some sense of duty to the mission, probably. But he didn't like the notion, it was clear from the look on his face. Still, he had proposed it, and it was probably the best plan available to them. After a moment or so, she nodded.

"Yes, it could work. If we go to Nancy now, right away, it will throw him off. He won't be looking for me at the Palais Garnier, and he may even follow us there to keep track of us, putting off a search of his own. If he follows us to Nancy, and I can get away to launch the *Wing* from there without being seen, I'd be able to return here tomorrow night and retrieve the package quite easily by simply landing on the roof. It would only be a few days to the new moon, so not too much risk of being spotted en route. The main factor would be the length of the trip, given that it's summer and the nights are short. I couldn't make it there and back in a single night and be sure of enough darkness for cover. I'd have to stay in Paris and return the following night."

Murcheson made a skeptical noise, but finally nodded. "I don't see a better way around it, not within a reasonable time frame. Hardison needs this trip to Nancy for glass anyway. Not much of a honeymoon, as far as your cover goes, but I suppose we must treat it as an opportunity. I'll arrange a safe place for you to hole up after you've retrieved the package, Lady Hardison."

Murcheson's Modern Wonderworks had a sizeable factory facility on the outskirts of Paris, more than large enough to successfully hide one small agent and one air balloon.

"There's only one other concern," Charlotte said, sighing sadly when the gentlemen both looked at her in curiosity. "When you grounded me, I'd hoped to avoid this, and I have to confess I was a little relieved because I hate to do it. But if I'm to be flying the *Gossamer Wing* at night, we're going to need an awful lot of black dye."

DEXTER STEPPED OVER a closed trunk and neatly avoided an open one to make his way into the bedroom of the suite. Although their hotel in Nancy was picturesquely housed in a Renaissance-era building, renovated stylishly with every modern convenience, the suite was not all that large. Currently, the little sitting room was more than fully occupied by a plethora of trunks, a pair of frazzled assistant modistes and his wife.

He thought perhaps Charlotte was subsuming her irritation at the besmirchment of the *Gossamer Wing* in this mania for fashion. Surely nothing short of temporary insanity explained the extreme concentration, the alternating frowns and giddiness, the second language she seemed to be speaking with the two young women. They were full of words like *bolero* and *bustlette*, and the room seemed full to bursting with all the new garments and fabrics they'd brought.

They had managed to turn what could have been a suspiciously unromantic side jaunt to Nancy into a chance for Dexter to shine as an indulgent husband. When Charlotte couldn't make her scheduled second fitting with the modistes in Paris, he'd simply paid the modistes to come to Nancy. Charlotte had made sure there was a certain amount of public fuss about all the trouble and expense. The ruse of their extravagant honeymoon was hardly jolted at all. The clothing gave Charlotte something to do while she waited, already a full day more than she'd expected, for the *Gossamer Wing* to be converted for night use. The dye and paint took longer than expected to dry, it seemed, and the wet silk was far too heavy. The wait was maddening.

"Dexter darling, don't forget you agreed to walk with me to the Parc de la Pépinière this afternoon. I want to see the roses. And there's supposed to be a charming pavilion."

He turned in the doorway, but Charlotte had already focused her attention back on the short, plum-colored brocade jacket one of the junior modistes was helping her into. Similar jackets in scarlet and midnight blue were laid out on the settee, awaiting their turns. It was a fraction of what she'd ordered, but the job could be rushed only so much. Half a dozen items or so had been produced, the rest to be delivered upon the couple's return to Paris.

"Of course, my sweet brioche," he said softly, and was rewarded by a swift and adorably dimpled smile from his wife.

His wife. Looking at her here, engaged in such an activity, seeing her smile, *wife* was suddenly all he could see. Dexter tried to regain a sense of distance, to recall the agent with whom he was meant to have only a pretense of marriage. Charlotte the professional spy, the once and future Lady Moncrieffe.

Instead, his unhelpful mind offered up the image of Charlotte the seductress, naked in his lap with her lips still ruddy from a shockingly intimate exercise. And then, even worse in a way, he recalled the way she had looked that very morning, when he had awakened early and spent far too long watching her sleep. She had one hand curled under her cheek, and he couldn't stop staring at her fingers—so very slender compared to his own—and the exquisite delicacy of the cheek pressed against them. Then she had opened her eyes and smiled at him, and he couldn't even name the feeling that had nearly overwhelmed him in that moment.

It was becoming harder and harder for Dexter to convince himself that he was merely scratching an itch. He knew himself too well to sustain the lie, and subterfuge was not his nature. His reactions were not those of a man motivated by lust or even something as innocent as friendship.

They were the reactions of a man falling hopelessly in love with the woman he had married.

SCANDALOUS THOUGH THE new fashion might be, Dexter decided he approved. Thoroughly.

Like many of the women they had seen strolling about since arriving in France, Charlotte was now clad in black breeches that left nothing to the imagination. The little red bolero jacket, in the finest Spanish style, was cut short enough to show off her tiny waist. Her midsection was made to appear even tinier with a wide satin sash that fit snugly in front and finished with a voluminous ruffled bow covering most of her rear end, with ribbons that trailed down almost to the back of her knees. The "bustlette," Dexter assumed. Although he thought it faintly ridiculous, he had to allow that it at least served the purpose of hiding Charlotte's remarkable derriere from public view.

Although her legs were more than enough to catch the eye of many a passing gentleman, he noticed. The snug black trousers disappeared into black riding boots, which were in turn gussied up with tall spatterdashes of some stiff, figured black and crimson fabric. Her hair was smoothed into a neat chignon beneath a small black top hat whose decorations of red and gold satin made it every bit as frivolous as she'd promised.

"I'm still not quite sure about this style of clothing. Are you preparing to fight a bull or ride to the hounds?"

Charlotte curled a hand around a lamppost and braced one booted foot at the base, swinging all the way around the pole and stopping when she faced him.

"Don't you like it? It's the only thing these days."

"I certainly don't dislike it," Dexter admitted, letting his eyes wander blatantly downward to linger on her legs. "You wear it well."

"I hope to start a trend when we return home. Trousers have been popular for ten years or so here in Europa, even in England, but it never caught on in the Dominions aside from riding breeches. We're too stuffy and provincial back home, I suppose. We settled for those hideous split skirts instead." She leaned back, hanging on to the pole for balance, and looked up at the whimsically gaudy gilded crown that topped the lamp. "Oh, I do love this city. I like how they've thrown all these gold swirls onto anything that stands still long enough."

"Arabesques, I think they call them."

It was true, the city of Nancy was delightfully ornamented, sporting gleaming gold statuary and colorful architectural fripperies in the most unexpected places. The park, once they located it, proved no less charming.

"It almost makes me wish I had a rose garden at Hardison House," Dexter said as they wandered between the carefully cultivated rows of blooming shrubs. The Parc de la Pépinière had started as a nursery, and was still a noted horticultural garden. The plants were almost obscenely healthy, so verdant and lush in the early summer air that they looked too good to believe.

"It probably wouldn't look this magnificent if you did

have one," Charlotte pointed out. "They take years to develop properly. But it is lovely to have fresh roses. Dexter, two of those trunks weren't clothing. They were from Murcheson. His people finished dying and painting the *Gossamer Wing*. He had it delivered along with the clothes."

Reality, cold and jarring, slapped Dexter back into the present, reminding him that he was no honeymooning lordling. He nodded stiffly and glanced around the nearly empty garden before answering. "I see."

"Murcheson's message said our friend has followed us to Nancy. The hotel seems clean, however, probably because the move was so sudden. He had his team make a sweep with some of your brilliant little bug detectors. We also have two men on surveillance duty outside the hotel. They say so far it seems our man is content just to keep watch, rather than making a move on the hotel itself."

"Or perhaps he's busy modifying his bugs to escape detection, before he bothers wasting any more of them." Dexter couldn't help but feel a moment's smugness at having hindered Coeur de Fer at least that small amount. "So when must you go?"

She brushed a fingertip over a bobbing pale pink rose, and then bent to smell the blossom. A peacock screamed from somewhere in the park, and Dexter had to strain to catch Charlotte's reply.

"Tonight."

CHARLOTTE WOULDN'T HAVE cared if Coeur de Fer had bugged every nook and cranny in the hotel suite. From the moment she'd read Murcheson's terse, coded missive, she had barely been able to think of anything but that evening and being alone with Dexter.

This was her mission, it was the sort of assignment she had trained for, planned for, even looked forward to in some ways. Night or day, the *Gossamer Wing* was designed for just such an occasion, and it had been entrusted to Charlotte only on the understanding that she could use it to go where other agents couldn't. What's more, she was getting an unexpected second chance to prove her usefulness with the craft, after her early disappointment at being spotted over Le Havre. She couldn't ignore the sense of rightness, of long-sought completion that followed when she thought of finishing this mission Reginald started all those years ago—not to mention preventing another war.

But now the idea that she might not survive plagued her as it never had. She hadn't considered herself suicidal before, but neither had she felt very strongly that she had anything to return to after completing her tasks in France. No matter what she'd told Dexter, she couldn't deny that on some level she had come to France to avenge Reginald. Vengeance was cold enough in the contemplation; once it was hers, she'd long acknowledged in her heart of hearts, she would have very little left to live for, no warmth to counter that icy satisfaction. A house that would never feel like her home. A profession that had already served its purpose. And an eternity of never quite trusting people to be what they seemed, because that capacity had been trained out of her.

Except. *Except.* Charlotte poked at her half-eaten dinner with a fork, and tried not to let Dexter catch her staring. She was hungry, but not for food and not even precisely for sex. Something else, something she couldn't or wouldn't define to herself in words, drove her that evening. Something about Dexter, who might be a temporary spy but who was otherwise, as far as she could tell, exactly what he seemed. She yearned for that, for something honest and wholehearted.

Tonight, she would have it. And if it turned out to be the last time, at least she would die with a fond memory.

Dexter met her eyes over the centerpiece, and the corners of his mouth and eyes tensed. Not quite a smile, not quite anything. But suddenly his attention was engaged, and Charlotte felt as naked as if he had stripped her down there in the middle of the hotel's elegantly appointed dining room. Resisting the temptation to look away until her blush subsided, she took action. She speared a piece of lamb and brought it to her mouth, removing it from the fork carefully and delicately with her teeth before licking a stray drop of sauce from her lip.

The muscles in Dexter's jaw flexed, and his eyes darkened perceptibly. Charlotte smiled as he gestured impatiently to the waiter without ever looking away from her.

A very fond memory.

THE DRESS CHARLOTTE had changed into for dinner was a delicate green. Dexter supposed the color had a special name, like *celadon* or *jade*, but mostly he just thought of it as *in the way*.

Charlotte had barely cleared the doorway of their suite before he was on her, propelling her forward into the room as he kicked blindly behind him to shut the door. She fetched up against the fat, rolled arm of the sofa and turned her head to stare at him over her shoulder.

"Dexter, what are you—"

"If you're going to look at me that way in public places, you're going to have to put up with the consequences."

He yanked her skirts up, bundling petticoats and all in his hands, and tossed them forward over her head. Her startled giggle was all the encouragement he needed to continue exactly as he'd begun. But if he'd needed more, he would have received it from the sight of her bedrawered backside, tipped up so invitingly as she bent over farther to rest her weight on the furniture.

"I was innocently eating my dinner," she insisted, though the muffling layers of silk and muslin were not enough to hide the coy, teasing note in her voice. Dexter reached under her to tug at the bow of the drawstring holding her drawers up, feeling a surge of more than triumph when the ribbon gave way.

"There was nothing innocent about the way you were eating your dinner, you wicked little quince tartlet." He yanked the loosened drawers down to Charlotte's ankles and drew his hands up the backs of her exposed thighs as he straightened up again.

"Quince tartlet? That one's plain silly," Charlotte protested.

"Shh. I'm busy admiring you. Don't distract me."

"That doesn't feel like admiration."

"If it's not, I don't know what is. You're wholly admirable, my love. Viewed from any angle." And despite her grumbling she was wholly ready for him, Dexter saw. She trembled when he teased a finger over her. When he ventured farther, she let out a soft, deep sigh.

It wasn't enough. He wanted moans. He wanted pleading, begging. And he decided he would have that from her before the night was out, even if it meant neither of them slept a wink. Dexter felt reckless, emboldened perhaps by the knowledge that Charlotte couldn't see him.

"Those trousers you were wearing today were hardly innocent either. You might as well have been wearing your underthings to walk around outside."

"They're comfortable," she argued. "And everybody's wearing them these days."

"They make me think of doing exactly what I'm doing now." He did a few more things to make the point more strongly.

"I rather like what you're doing now. Perhaps I should acquire more of them and wear them every day."

"They make every other man who sees you think the same thing. I don't like that."

Charlotte chuckled, the sound as velvety soft as sin. "Jealousy, Lord Hardison? Is that wise, do you think?"

"Bugger wisdom," he retorted, unfastening his trousers to give his viciously firm erection some breathing room and quickly sliding on the sheath he'd had the foresight to stow in his pocket earlier. Returning his hands to her rear end he gave her an affectionate squeeze, teasing with his thumbs. "Hmm. Speaking of buggery—"

"Not if we live a thousand years," Charlotte snapped.

Dexter laughed and obediently returned to the methods of sensual torture that seemed most effective in driving Charlotte mad with desire. "When we return to the Dominions, perhaps we can reevaluate."

She gasped at what he was doing with his fingers, but somehow Dexter knew it was his words and not his actions that prompted her to whisper, "Don't."

"Is it the idea of reevaluating that bothers you, or the notion that you might actually be alive long enough to worry about it?"

"We can't talk about what happens when we return. I can't."

"I'm going to," he said stubbornly. "For this one night. I don't care if it's unwise. I don't care if it's pretense on your part. It isn't on mine."

"Dexter . . ."

"You're my wife, Charlotte," he reminded her. "And tonight that's all I want. To make love to my wife. And imagine what it will be like in another few weeks when I'm making love to her in my bed at home."

She might have been crying. The shuddering breaths she took might have been caused by tears, not bliss, and Dexter knew it. But he sank into her anyway, no longer able to resist the temptation she presented. Her body welcomed him in with a shivering embrace, and if her groan ended on a sob he was too far gone to care. Or so he told himself.

He reached beneath her hips, hitching her closer, finding the place where his body slid into hers and using his fingers to give her the friction he knew she needed. She came in seconds, squeezing so tightly around him that he gasped. Struggling for strength, he rode her pleasure out but kept himself under control, not ready for it to be over.

When her trembling stopped at last, Charlotte pushed her head clear of the layers of skirt, but did not look back at him. He could see her fists clenched hard enough to whiten at the knuckles, peeking out from under the billows of silk and lace like meters of her tension.

"Your wife, you said," she reminded him in a whisper. She turned her head a little, and he could see the sheen of tears still dampening her cheek. "I want that too. For tonight, I mean," she said a bit too hastily, and Dexter felt a bolt of unreasonable hope shoot through him.

He leaned over her back, crushing her gown between them and pressing a kiss along her shoulder blade, feeling the movement of her muscles and bones through the silk.

"It doesn't have to be just for tonight. It can be for as many nights as you like."

"Not if I never come back."

"No, Charlotte."

"I never expected to, you know. Come back from this trip, I mean. I never planned for what I might do afterward, I was too busy getting to this point to think about that. Too many things can go wrong for me to hope for an afterward, anyway, and I've known that all along. If it happens, you rejoice, but you don't put your trust in it. That's part of the training. But I didn't think I would mind it this much when I came to it."

She was crying again and his heart broke a little. He felt responsible, as though by encouraging her to unburden herself to the point of tears the other day, he'd weakened Charlotte's defenses to her own emotions. Although he knew it was no way to help, he did the first thing available to him to try to take her mind off her pain; he moved again, easing into a rhythm, forging a connection the only way she seemed willing to allow.

Foolish, his mind insisted, *selfish*. But his body was so much more convincing. *Sweet*, it told him. *Mine, mine*. Soon all the words disappeared, melting into pleasure that mounted too rapidly to contain. When Dexter felt Charlotte tighten around him again, heard a cry that could not be mistaken for anything but pleasure, he pushed into her until he couldn't anymore and emptied himself like he was spilling out his very soul.

FIFTEEN

✦❦✦

"DON'T SLIP!"

Dexter would have rather found a private spot on level ground for launching the *Gossamer Wing* on its maiden night voyage, but the schedule simply didn't permit scouting for such a location. Once they'd recovered from their bout of amorous insanity, Charlotte had barely had time to change into more suitable clothing for her mission before it was full dark.

"Don't fall through the roof," Charlotte retorted in a whisper.

"Witty, my sweet meringue. Are you sure you remembered your canteen?"

"It's right here."

"Boot knife?"

"In my boot."

"Loaded pistol?"

"I have it, but I won't use it. I can't wear it on my thigh in the harness, and I'd never reach it in time in the shoulder holster with my jacket fastened."

Charlotte already had the larger, lighter of the two cases braced between the roof and a chimney. The back side of the building was dark, and Dexter's eyes were still adjusting. He wished he had looked longer at her in the light, back in the room.

"What do you need me to do?" he asked politely, wrestling the second case open and tugging out the rigging. Like the silk balloon, it had not been dyed black, but a very dark gray-blue judged by Murcheson's experts to be the best color for camouflage against the night sky. The color was certainly difficult to see here, on the darkened slate roof of the hotel. So was Charlotte, in her black jacket, breeches and boots— no decorative spats this time—with her bright hair tucked under her helmet, and smudged kohl masking the rest of her fair skin.

"Just hold that there," Charlotte replied, "I'll do the rest."

She was focused, brisk, accomplishing the setup of the *Gossamer Wing* far too quickly and efficiently for Dexter's taste.

"Take this. I made it for you. It weighs just under half a pound." He slipped a small, flat, black box from one of his coat pockets, and strapped it to the underside of the harness where it wouldn't interfere with Charlotte's movements. "It's a portable telegraphic transmitter. I have the receiver set up in the hotel room. I thought if you wanted to send a message once you were safely at Murcheson's factory . . ."

"So tiny." She ran her fingers over the smooth, painted metal box, but didn't take the time to open it.

"It had to be. You have your maps?" he inquired.

"You're worse than my father." She slapped at a pocket, and Dexter heard the soft crinkle of paper under her hand. "I have the maps. I have them memorized, though, so if all goes according to plan I shouldn't need them."

"Does anything ever go according to plan?" He handed her the harness, and she shook it out across the roof as quietly as she could, trying to keep the buckles from clinking as she let it down.

"There's a first time for everything. That's it, then, I

suppose. I can climb in while it's down flat like this if you'll hold the tether and the rigging. That way I won't have to risk jumping into it from this angle in the dark."

Dexter nodded, numbness beginning to creep through him. He knew this was the reason for her presence in France. He'd known that from the very start. But now, faced with the reality of her disappearing into the night, he finally allowed himself to acknowledge the danger. She was going after the hidden weapon plans, even knowing that the same man who had killed her husband over them might be waiting for her. If their trip to Nancy hadn't thrown Coeur de Fer off as they'd hoped, this might well be the last time Dexter saw Charlotte. Charlotte herself seemed to take that unthinkable outcome as a given. Except for those few brief, unguarded moments earlier, she always carried her fatalism like a shield. For the first time he comprehended why she might need to do so, why it was easier that way.

He wanted nothing more than to crush her in an embrace and keep her there, safe. He knew if she died he would never forgive himself for letting her go. It would make as much sense as Charlotte blaming herself for Reginald's death, but Dexter finally understood the origin of such notions. Loving her as he did, so furiously that it pained him, he should surely be able to keep her alive through sheer force of emotion. Sadly, as humans had been discovering since they first identified that emotion, love didn't work that way.

Charlotte's determined mask slipped again for a moment as she glanced out over the rooftops of Nancy. She looked miserable and frightened, and Dexter knew he needed to present a calm front. If he pretended confidence in her return, perhaps she would feel it too.

"Have a good trip," he said, resting his hands on her shoulders. "Be careful. I'll see you back here tomorrow night or very early the next morning." He kissed her briefly, resisting the urge to respond with more when she seemed poised to lean into it. Resisting too the urge to tell her how he felt. It would have been a relief to him, but only a burden to her.

After a moment Charlotte nodded and climbed into the

harness while Dexter held the rigging and started the infla-
tion process. In a few seconds, he was able to release the
balloon and let it bob upward, pulling Charlotte beneath it.

Dexter held the tether until the last possible moment.
Releasing his grip on that slim length of line was the hardest
thing he'd ever done in his life.

MARTIN HAD OPTED to travel to Nancy alone, and Dubois—
always interested in a chance to save money, and never able
to focus on more than one issue at a time—had allowed it.
Martin left his team in Paris, following a hunch that all was
not what it seemed with the latest change in the honeymooning pair's travel plans.

They spent too much time for his comfort in Murcheson's
factory, where Martin had been unable to place a mole. Nor
could he spare men to troll the harbor in hopes of spying
the Hardisons as they took sail from the factory slips. He
only knew Murcheson was up to far more than a plot to
outbid Dubois on a steamrail contract. So one of Martin's
men had remained in Le Havre to monitor comings and
goings at Murcheson's factory there, while another performed the same function at the Gennevilliers facility. A
third lookout was tasked with watching the Palais Garnier's
entrances, while a fourth man waited in reserve by the radio
communicator, in case Martin needed him.

Dubois was up to something as well, Martin could tell.
Something to do with Murcheson, something he was keeping from Martin, probably for no other reason than that he
could. This deception added a layer of complication and
worry for Martin in his own planning, and was another mark
in the long tally of Dubois's sins.

One day . . .

His fond imagining of Dubois's violent end was interrupted by movement in the window across the narrow street.
A sheer curtain shrouded the view of the Hardison's sitting
room, but Martin could make out their silhouettes, large
and petite forms moving about the room. They seemed to

be preparing to leave, as the Baron had hoisted what appeared to be a sizeable pair of suitcases or trunks under his oversized arms.

"What are you doing with those, brute?" Moving closer to the window, Martin all but pressed his nose against the glass, wishing once again that he'd been able to continue bugging their rooms. Once discovered, however, the bugs became pointless, and he wasn't one to waste equipment. He also found himself vaguely disgusted by their personal goings-on, he who had scarcely a memory of sex and no wish to revisit the issue.

Lady Hardison's silhouette looked wrong, Martin thought, but he couldn't quite put a finger on it. Smaller even than usual, and her movements seemed less graceful and flowing. Perhaps she was wearing the new trousers again, though they didn't seem popular as an evening style. In the trousers she looked like an androgyne to Martin, who cared even less about fashion than he did about sex, except as it informed him in his trade.

When the Hardisons closed the door behind them, Martin risked a moment with his eyes closed, then stole a swig of the brandy he kept in a flask close by. It would take them at least two minutes and twenty seconds to descend the stairs to the lobby, leave the key at the desk and exit, so he had that much time to collect his thoughts. When three minutes had passed, Martin wondered if they had taken the lift. At five minutes, he considered that the lift might have malfunctioned. He kept his eyes glued to the entrance for another five minutes before cursing under his breath.

They had obviously gone out of their room but not left the hotel. The place had only two entrances, both of which Martin could see from his vantage point. It was eleven o'clock. They had already dined at the bistro down the street and taken dessert in their suite, but now they had left their rooms again and taken luggage with them. Absconded, clearly, but how? And to where?

Perhaps they were still in the hotel. Martin had checked thoroughly, and he knew Nancy well. There were no other exits to the building. Only one door at the front courtyard, one side entrance the staff used, not even so much as a door leading to the—

Words his mother never taught him streamed from Martin's mouth as he jerked his gaze upward, scanning the roofline for any motion, any sign of activity. He was seconds from deciding that the peaked, pitched roof was not a likely prospect for any human activity, when something caught his eye.

Or rather, a *nothing* caught his eye. There was a dark spot, blanking out the stars in a flattened oval. As he watched, the oval rose over the rooftop and diminished against the night sky, a minuscule and fast-dwindling blue flame below it the only clue to its nature.

Through the spyglass he caught a glimpse, a shadowed shape, for a few heartbeats. He was warming up his radio transmitter even as the shadow vanished from his sight.

THE NIGHT WAS clear, for which Charlotte was grateful. She hated to think what rain might do to the sooty blue dye on the silk of her beloved airship. It was difficult to look at the *Gossamer Wing* in this tarnished incarnation. She had almost cried to see her beautiful helmet sullied so, but Dexter had promised her a new one soon.

He had kissed her exactly, *exactly* like a husband seeing a wife off on a weekend holiday.

Damn him.

She couldn't sustain any resentment, though. He was too kind, his recent forcefulness notwithstanding, and she could hardly deny his appeal at this point. She could, and did, wish she had met him years sooner. If she had, she wouldn't be here now. It seemed safe enough to accept that, now that it was too late for it to matter.

The balloon blocked out most of her view of the stars, but Charlotte could still make out enough to appreciate the beauty of the evening. A little too cool, perhaps, but she preferred that to having it be too hot. There was the tiniest sliver of a moon, not enough to give her away on the rooftop. She tried to shake the feeling of being rushed, of things happening more quickly than she could control, and forced herself to relax in the harness. The lights of Nancy dwindled beneath her as she left the smaller city behind and aimed toward Paris.

Hours later, chilled to the bone and struggling with fatigue, she spotted the grid of much brighter lights that marked her destination. Paris gleamed through the night. It beckoned her like a moth to flame, and she hoped the metaphor didn't imply similar disastrous consequences for her.

Sophisticated though the grand old city was, even Paris slept at three in the morning. Charlotte saw only a few passing vehicles in the street below as she lowered her craft to the blessedly flat roof in front of the green dome on the Palais Garnier. She trusted the brilliantly lit gilded statues on the façade to divert the attention of any onlookers from the tiny blue flame and blimp-shaped black spot against the sky.

The very ease of it made her nervous. She had expected some sort of difficulty to arise by now. For a good two minutes after freeing herself from the harness and tethering the airship, she crouched with a hand on her pistol butt, waiting for somebody to spring at her from some dark corner of the rooftop.

Nobody sprang, however. Once the slight panic had passed, Charlotte straightened up and headed for the base of the statue of Harmony.

She glanced around once more to be certain before reaching to the back of the main figure's robe where the hem nearly reached the pedestal. The gold-painted bronze fell in folds, and Charlotte said a silent prayer as she gripped a particular one of those folds as tightly as possible and pulled down on it with all her might.

At first there was nothing, no response, and her heart leaped to her throat before she heard a subtle click and felt the piece move under her hand just as Reginald had once described. Bronze squeaked against bronze, but the old mechanism still worked. The piece swung out and down, and she had only to twist it to the horizontal to reveal the little nook in which a switch waited. She flipped it before proceeding along the edge of the roof, counting stones in the low parapet.

First course, third from the corner, not the discolored brick but the one next to it. She pressed on it hard, twice to the top right corner of the stone, thrice to the lower left, once to the top left . . . and it sprang back against her fingers, swinging open with hardly a whisper. No changed codes, no tricks or traps with the mechanisms. The gears were a bit rusty, but a thick coating of grease had kept them functional.

And there it was. Small, innocuous, a nearly flat bundle of oiled leather secured with a strap. The buckle was green with slime, the leather mildewed, but other than that it was none the worse for its years in hiding.

A prickling on the back of her neck made Charlotte wheel around again, scanning the rooftop frantically. Nothing. Still, her heart was thumping again. The fear and the physical exhaustion were starting to overwhelm her. As quickly as she could, she restored the stone and the statue to rights and made sure she'd left no other trace of her visit behind.

The statue's brightly illuminated front meant the back was in deep shadow, so Charlotte knelt for a final check of her bearings, trusting that her pocket torch would not be spotted. Then, with her next destination firmly mapped in her mind, she swung her body into the harness, buckled in and released the mooring loop from the vent where she'd hooked it.

All that worry, and it was so easy in the end, she laughed at herself.

Her foot kicked off from the roof at the moment the access door slammed open and a dark-clad, stocking-capped man burst through with an evil-looking weapon in his hands. He cursed in a torrent of foul French as he ran toward Charlotte, one hand outstretched, barely missing her toe as she snatched it up into the harness.

As Charlotte frantically turned the gas higher to gain altitude, she realized the object in the man's hands wasn't a weapon. It was a bull cutter. The chain and padlock on the roof access door must have defeated him too.

Straight up she flew until her ears had chimed at her twice, until she could no longer make out the tiny figure or the roof he stood on. Still she waited for a shot to rip through her from out of the darkness, and she wondered if she would even have time to hear the bang before she fell.

The shot finally came, a slam of noise that followed over a full second after an impact against her hip sent her swaying in the airship's harness. Charlotte yelped and cruised higher still, waiting for pain to take the place of shock. It never did.

Fumbling with one hand, she reached for her hip and realized the bullet had buried itself in the box Dexter had secured to the rigging before she took off. The telegraph transmitter was no doubt ruined, but she herself was unharmed aside from the sharpening ache on her hipbone that presaged a bruise. As the knowledge that she'd escaped sank in, her heart quieted, but her body began to tremble as the massive influx of adrenaline seeped away.

He'd been . . . stupid. A stupid operative. Martin was in Nancy, he had probably seen her take off and surely notified his men here, yet this man hadn't managed in all the interim to reach the roof of the Palais Garnier. Who knew how much time he'd wasted attempting to pick his way through that lock, how much longer it had taken him to find the cutters after he'd abandoned the effort?

He must not be much of a second-story man, she thought, and laughed aloud with a sudden burst of ecstatic wonder at her escape by a hairsbreadth. The operative had waited too long to fire his weapon, and then he'd shot straight up into the night sky. He'd been lucky the bullet hadn't careened back down to hit him. Charlotte laughed again at the idea of the fellow standing there, staring up into the darkness, never expecting the bullet that felled him to be one from his own gun. She sobered quickly, however, thinking of how different the outcome might have been, had Coeur de Fer been the man set to catch her on that rooftop . . . or if the incompetent lackey's bullet had struck a few inches to either side.

No matter now. It was done. *Done*, she told herself, trying to generate more of that brief, giddy enthusiasm to sustain her for the last sprint of the night. She would land in the predetermined location on the roof of one of Murcheson's nearby factory buildings, and if all went according to plan she could review the documents with him on the spot. Perhaps after a meal and a shot of something stiff, for nerves.

Then she'd have a well-deserved rest, another midnight flight across the French countryside, and she would be back in Dexter's arms.

That prospect at last gave her some energy to go on with. Something to strive for. Half an hour later, her first glimpse of the factory's smokestacks gave her a true second wind as relief flooded through her. She tacked toward the landmark, calculating the distance as less than a mile.

She was more than close enough to be half-deafened by the blast that came from nowhere and everywhere, to be seared by the wave of heat that flooded the air in the wake of that horrifying sound.

Not from nowhere, Charlotte realized when her ears stopped ringing enough for her to gather her wits. *From the factory . . .*

It burned as she floated closer, unable to grasp what she was seeing. Huge gouts of flame soared into the sky from the ruined smokestack, nearly as high as she flew. She lingered too long, wasting precious fuel and darkness, until she could no longer lie to herself about the source or the cause of the explosion. Factories were dangerous places, but the coincidence of the timing was too great. Murcheson had been compromised, and she could only hope he'd had enough warning to escape the horrific act of sabotage.

Though Charlotte knew she was too far away to be burned, she trembled anyway to think of it. To think of all the people who might have been trapped in the explosion or the subsequent blaze that was even now beginning to spread to nearby rooftops.

Tears soaked her helmet lining by the time she turned her tiny craft north and began searching for another place to land and hide for the coming day.

"IT NOT ONLY can be done, it has been done. Not this application, precise, of course," Arsenault clarified, tapping on the sketch that Dexter had brought along. It showed a round or spherical central object, surrounded by eight slender radiating lines. At the end of each line was a symbol, and at one corner of the sketch was a key indicating that the symbol represented a lamp. "Medicinal? Medical, *oui*, they use the glass tube to bring the light." He gestured to his midsection. "*Içi*, here, inside the body. For the doctors to see when they do the operations."

He'd had to do something to occupy his time, and to maintain their cover. So, although Dexter wanted to remain on the roof, scanning the skies until Charlotte returned, he forced himself to attend to the business that had brought him to Nancy, and made an appointment with Arsenault, the man Cormier had recommended. He spent the morning trying not to think of her, trying to think of glass instead, with moderate success.

Slight language barrier aside, Dexter found he had little trouble communicating with the young French glassmaker. More than once already that morning, he'd found himself silently thanking Cormier for sending him to Arsenault for this project. Even through his concern about Charlotte, he could tell the dynamic young Frenchman understood what he needed and could create whatever the project required, even if Dexter himself wasn't quite sure what that was.

"What I've pictured, though, involves a much greater distance. Perhaps a mile or even more. And there is also a need for the system to be somewhat sturdy." At the young man's blank look, Dexter strained for another word. "Strong? Resistant?"

"*Oui, résistant,*" Arsenault said with a smile. "It is not a single glass tube, what you require. Many, together," he explained, bending to the page and rapidly sketching a cross-section of a bundle of tubes. "Inside a case, *comme une saucisse*. The only importance is the reflection of the light inside. And that you have not the loss of light over distance."

Dexter finally realized the man was comparing the design to a sausage. An external casing, holding all the gathered glass filaments inside and helping the light remain on the desired path without leaking out. "From a light source at one end, all the way to the other, even if the tubes are bent, correct?"

The young Frenchman nodded, his sandy hair flopping forward into his eyes. He tossed his head impatiently, looking even more like a schoolboy than he already had.

"And it must also be waterproof," Dexter said, presenting the final requirement.

Arsenault blinked a few times and then smiled. "Fresh water or salt water, *monsieur*?"

Dexter eyed him warily before answering. "Salt."

Suddenly the Frenchman looked nothing like a schoolboy; his eyes were all too knowing, his shrug all too mature. "Just as it is with *Monsieur* Murcheson. Always the salt water. The flooding, it must be terrible in Le Havre."

After another moment, Dexter gave a shrug of his own. "The high cost of maintaining our proximity to England and the shipping routes."

"One week," Arsenault said, tracing Dexter's sketch with his fingers. "If the distance is as you say, I can deliver your filaments to Le Havre in one week."

THE NEWS OF the factory explosion had reached Nancy by the midday post. Dexter, sleepless and out of sorts with worry already at the ominous silence of the telegraph receiver, had to read the headline three times before his rough mental translation finally sank in.

"Charlotte!" he blurted, drawing curious looks from the other patrons in the sidewalk café where he sat over luncheon.

Flustered, he coughed and pretended to take a sip of coffee while his mind roared in an agony of fear. The grainy photograph of the still-smoking factory stared up at him from the paper on the table.

She knew something like this would happen. Somehow, she knew, he kept thinking. And he thought of their parting—he so cavalier and straightforward, Charlotte so efficient and brave. He had pretended the danger was negligible, and he would regret that pretense for the rest of his life if anything had happened to her.

"I should have told her I loved her," he whispered at his coffee.

Now she might be gone, burned to ash, as if she'd never been. All he could do was wait for more news. Dexter thought the wait might kill him too.

Sixteen

❧✦☙

WET. SLIMY.

A slithery touch and the sharp smell of cut grass directly under her nose woke Charlotte from her fitful slumber. She opened her eyes and nearly screamed at the monster she saw before her, until her eyes and brain sorted themselves out and she realized it was only a cow.

It had seemed like a monster in part because she was viewing it upside-down, as she was lying on her back in an empty hay wagon and her head was slipping off the open end onto the sloping tailgate. And in part because it was very, very close; the cow had evidently mistaken Charlotte's sweaty, unwashed face for a salt lick.

In one swift move, Charlotte swung away from the cow and into a crouch on the bed of the wagon, scuttling backward to put even more distance between herself and the bovine creature.

The cow, unperturbed, began sampling the tufts of hay

caught between the rough planks of the wagon's side. Satisfied the beast meant her no harm, Charlotte looked around to assess her situation, wiping her horribly moist face on her sleeve as she did so. The assessment didn't take long.

She was in a field somewhere outside Paris, there were no nearby farm buildings, and a gently persistent reddish-brown cow was eyeing her with what Charlotte could only read as curiosity. When it lowed at her, she shushed it automatically.

From what she could see it was very early morning, as the sun was up but dew still dampened the shorn, trodden timothy grass of the field. The chronometer from the *Gossamer Wing*'s instrument panel confirmed this. Ravenous, aching from her flight and the few hours' dubious rest in the wagon, Charlotte pondered what to do next.

"Can't walk to the nearest town, can I, Bossie? Are French cows called Bossie? I'm hardly dressed for visiting a country village, but I don't think I can go a full day without eating either." She tipped her head to examine the cow's belly. "Hmm. I don't think I'm quite desperate enough to try my hand at milking a cow, however."

Bossie mooed again, and Charlotte heard a late-rising rooster crow as if in response. It was time for her to find cover, food or no food. With a last regretful look at the cow's udders, Charlotte tucked the leather harness of the *Gossamer Wing* under one arm, stuffed the voluminous midnight blue folds of the balloon under the other, and took firm hold of the gas rigging to keep it upright as she leaped from the wagon and started toward the nearest stand of trees.

THAT DAY, CHARLOTTE added theft to her list of dubious accomplishments.

It's only sort-of theft, she reassured herself as she wiped the black kohl from her face and neck with the clean cloth and butter she'd found in the farmhouse.

She'd left enough coin to pay for the cloth, butter and sprigged pale blue cotton dress many times over, right there on the table in the kitchen. Surely the farmer's wife wouldn't bemoan the missing items too long.

"I could hardly have walked up and asked somebody to sell me the things," Charlotte explained to Bossie, who had turned up at the side of the stream in the wood adjacent the hay field. "I was dressed like a cat burglar, after all."

She wondered if the cow was a runaway, or simply had the run of the place. A faded brand marked her as somebody's property, but she seemed to inhabit the wood and the field rather than a fenced pasture or a barn as Charlotte would have expected a cow to do.

The dress was a bit too long and a good deal too wide, but it was cool and wouldn't look suspicious if Charlotte ventured into the village she'd scouted a few miles away.

"My French may not be as good as Reginald's was," she told the cow when she'd cleaned herself up as much as she could, "but I think I can pass for a French milkmaid just this once. I just hope the farm wife doesn't see me and recognize her dress. Wish me luck, Bossie. I'm off to the village, and shall take no prisoners!"

The morning fog had long since burned off, but the day remained cool and pleasant. Perfect for walking, although Charlotte regretted the riding boots shortly into her journey.

For all her worry, she must have made a passable milkmaid. Nobody batted an eye in the tiny bakery when she bought a baguette, and the fruit seller in the market square winked at her and gave her two pears for the price of one. He also supplied a large cloth napkin that he cleverly folded and tied into a sort of carryall for her. She decided perhaps the French were not so bad after all, taken individually. Charlotte went on to secure a wedge of cheese and a bottle of cider before she decided she'd had enough of deceiving these gentle, unassuming and honest people.

She ate the first pear on the walk back to her spot by the creek. Bossie had wandered away again, leaving only deep hoof prints in the mud by the stream. An odd sort of wood sprite the cow made, but Charlotte still felt she'd been visited by a friendly spirit. She saved the second pear in case her bovine friend returned.

Half a baguette, a good deal of cheese and several swigs of surprisingly hard cider later, Charlotte felt like a new woman. The solitary walk, the charming little village, the sweet summery stillness of the wood, all seemed to fill her with an ease she hadn't known in years.

Things had not gone according to plan, it was true, but for the moment she was safe and fed, and she had at least retrieved the documents. She could do no more that day, and there was a strange peace in accepting that simple fact and this quiet stretch of time it afforded her.

Charlotte slept most of the afternoon away in the quiet glade. She had to laugh when Bossie—or perhaps another cow who resembled Bossie—woke her in exactly the same way as before. It was her own fault, probably, for using butter as face cream.

"Needs must, Bossie. I didn't have any other choice if I wanted to get away with a trip to town. Lucky for you, because I don't think you'd like my usual night cream one bit. Have a pear, woodland spirit."

The cow took the offering and ambled away, and Charlotte began to change clothes. It was sunset, and soon it would grow dark enough for her to fly.

MURCHESON'S MESSAGE REACHED Dexter in the late evening. A few short words, no specifics, enough for a shred of hope at best. No trace of a small dirigible or a small woman had been found on the factory grounds, the telegram implied. Nobody but one bystander injured, no other casualties known.

Dexter read it, repaired to the powder room and vomited, then returned to the sitting room to read it again. The flimsy paper had all but disintegrated in his hands by midnight, when Dexter finally gathered up a book, a blanket and a torch and left the room to take up his lonely vigil on the rooftop.

A few hours later, Charlotte nearly landed on Dexter's head when a gust of wind tugged the *Gossamer Wing* astray as she alit on the rooftop of the hotel and cut off the gas feed.

He didn't care. He wouldn't have cared if she had landed feet-first in his face and concussed him on the way down, so long as she returned. He opened his mouth to say he'd missed her, he couldn't live without her, he loved her. When she pulled her helmet off and he saw her grimy, weary face, however, all he could do was sweep her into his arms. Words weren't enough, so he didn't waste them.

After a time, Charlotte removed her face from where she had pressed it into his shirt. "Harness needs to come off."

Dexter realized the *Gossamer Wing* was still attached to her, sagging slowly behind her as it cooled. Charlotte held up the rigging with one hand, clinging to Dexter's coat with the other.

With quick, efficient motions he set the fuel assembly down away from the spent balloon, unbuckled the harness at Charlotte's shoulders and feet, and simply lifted her out of the thing.

"I'll come back for it," he said when she pointed over his shoulder. He was halfway to the window that would lead them back inside, back to their suite, where he could bathe and feed and cosset her until she was in the right frame of mind to hear his declarations of devotion.

"Somebody could find it," she murmured, sounding half asleep already.

"I don't give a rat's arse."

"Hmm. That's sweet." Her head settled onto his shoulder, and Dexter's heart soared as his mind churned out a simple refrain.

She's alive. She's alive. My Charlotte is alive.

MARTIN COULDN'T KILL Philippe, although the thought did cross his mind. He was out of the business of indiscriminate killing now, the Dominion rat had been his last. Now he took only the lives Dubois ordered taken; he would only take a life to save his own.

Martin sent orders for Claude and Jean-Louis to beat Philippe thoroughly, put the fear of death into him and advise him to leave the country and make a life for himself elsewhere.

"Perhaps he should consider apprenticing with a locksmith," Claude retorted.

Martin chuckled, keeping the transmission switched off so Claude wouldn't hear his mirth; he had a reputation to uphold. He had recovered fully by the time he thumbed the switch back to the open position.

"Advise him as you see fit, my amusing friend. As long as you advise him to be gone before I return to Paris."

Get to the rooftop. Had that been such an unreasonable request? The others had managed it at their respective locations, but hours after Martin gave the order, Philippe had only just made it to the roof of the Palais Garnier. He was right on time to see the quarry escape with the documents, and the fool had only attempted a shot at the balloon after it lifted off and was nearly out of range. Philippe's had been the only rooftop that mattered, and if anger and frustration were sufficient justification for murder then Martin would be halfway to Paris by now.

Instead he was still alone in Nancy, entering the glamorous old hotel through the service entrance. He hoped to strike it lucky rifling through the Hardisons' suite for the bundle of documents while they dallied over brunch in a café down the street. For once, he might be able to use Dubois's pathetically outdated perspective to his own advantage; if he brought the documents to Dubois—even after all these years—the industrialist might finally grant Martin the freedom he'd all but given up hope of attaining.

Depending on luck, rummaging through rooms like a two-bit burglar looking for a poor man's life savings under a mattress. Sickening. Next, Martin supposed, he would be flipping coins to decide which mark to follow. He, who had been one of the finest agents in France during the war. Who prided himself on leaving nothing to chance.

Martin was dressed as a courier, carrying a large package and a clipboard and wearing the most apathetic expression in his repertoire. Nobody stopped him, though he passed a kitchen full of chefs, a room-service waiter and at least three chambermaids on his way in.

The rooms were fairly small and the Hardisons were tidy, so Martin thought he could do the job quickly and perhaps leave things looking as he'd found them, always his preference.

As it happened, however, not even that much effort was required. Two things happened at once. Martin spotted his long-lost leather pouch, in plain view on the console table in the sitting room. He also heard the squeaky wheel of the housekeeping cart in the hallway, not directly outside the suite he stood in but perhaps only a few doors away.

He could find a way to hide from the maid—a difficult prospect in rooms so small—and complete his search afterward, or he could snatch what he'd come for and walk away without risk of being spotted in the suite.

With a moue of distaste at the moldy patina on the leather, Martin slipped the pouch into his shirt. He hoisted his box again and set his false ear to the door. Even with the prosthetic on, his implant gave him more acute hearing than any unenhanced ear. He could mark the progress of the cart by the squeaks, and the progress of the maid by the soft knock and the sound of an opening door.

When he was sure she was safely in the next room and the corridor was clear, Martin moved. It was out, down and away with his prize, his only concern that it had been too easy.

THE PACKET OF loose papers Charlotte had retrieved crawled with scribbled notes and hasty sketches. There were also a panoply of scattered letters, numerals and mathematical symbols, but Charlotte insisted it wasn't actually a cypher and Dexter was not inclined to argue. His attention was torn at best anyway—between the paper scattered across the broad table in the restaurant's private dining room, Charlotte and Murcheson's discussion of what was on those documents and his own vivid memories of the previous night.

. He had run a bath and mustered up what food he could for Charlotte, assuming she would fall asleep immediately afterward. After a few bites of a sandwich and two cups of tea, however, she astonished him by dragging him into bed for a bout of fierce, celebratory lovemaking. Sated, exhausted, she finally collapsed into a deep slumber with her head still snuggled against his shoulder.

Dexter's body still tingled from the manic intensity of the interlude, but what kept his mind returning to it was the memory of Charlotte's weight against his chest and the utter trust and relief on her face as she drifted off. He knew her expression had mirrored his own. Relief and humble gratitude, because having her back in his arms was nothing short of miraculous.

With Herculean effort Dexter focused on the present, on the task at hand. He'd expected that finding the plans intact would be the end of Charlotte's mission, and Murcheson confirmed that her work in France was officially done, but it seemed the documents had only raised a host of new questions. Or rather, old questions that Reginald's truncated tour of duty had left unanswered. While it wasn't Charlotte's job to answer them, Murcheson was willing to listen to her perspective on the possible chain of custody of the packet she'd recovered. Even with the notes recovered, the question of how the documents wound up in Dubois's hands to begin with was still critical. Only by knowing who'd held the notes, and when, could Murcheson be certain none of the parties had obtained a copy at any point along that chain.

"You've said the French claimed that Martin went rogue *after* the treaty, so you assumed he was really still working for the Égalité, retrieving the documents from Dubois, when he tangled with Reginald," Dexter said, breaking several

minutes' silence. "But I wonder, what if he was really working for Dubois and the post-royalists all along? Perhaps
Martin was just then bringing the documents *to* Dubois's
office, when Reginald encountered him. That would still
leave the question of where Martin obtained the packet, of
course."

Murcheson's usually implacable demeanor slipped as
Dexter's suggestion registered. Dexter could almost see the
thoughts working themselves out on the man's face, as a
spark of possibility caught, took hold, lit him with excitement. "We never put it together that way before, but then I
don't think anyone really considered the importance of
Couer de Fer's history in all this until Charlotte saw him in
the Palais Garnier. The fellows who identified Jacques Martin, Dubois's security expert, as a former Égalité agent, only
saw the connection Martin once had with the French and
knew he'd left their service under something of a cloud.
They still assumed he was aligned with the Agency in some
way in his new capacity, and lumped him together with the
other known agents in Dubois's employ."

Charlotte sat up straighter. "But if Martin was a post-
royalist all along, wouldn't that mean Dubois still is as well?
The French would have to have known that. What if the
agents at his company aren't there to liaise with the government, but to keep an eye on Dubois and possibly on Martin
as well?"

Murcheson tapped his nose. "But at the time, seven years
ago, they didn't suspect Martin was working for the other
side. It all falls into place then. He could have taken those
documents directly from Égalité's HQ. From his colleague
Simone Vernier, the French agent who acquired them from
the laboratory in Cambridge."

"Simone Vernier? The same agent who pretended to be
Dubois's mistress?" Charlotte asked.

Murcheson nodded. "The same. It was hardly a pretense,
however. The French take a much more liberal line with
these things than we do, and he wouldn't have kept her as
a mistress if she hadn't, well . . . played the part with

conviction. She died in his bed, after all. Vernier made many a noble sacrifice for her country."

"Like his current secretary," Dexter offered, stifling a grin when Charlotte glared at him. "Another woman who positively drips with nobility and patriotism."

"Here now," Murcheson huffed.

"Apologies. Especially as this new information suggests the young woman in question may indeed be using her wiles to spy on Dubois for her country, just as Vernier did, rather than using them to ensure she keeps an easy job as liaison between Dubois and the Égalité. It seems they still trust him about as well as we do. Charlotte, may I see those notes?" Dexter gestured, and Charlotte shuffled together the sheaf of papers, handing the stack to him as Murcheson cleared his throat ostentatiously and continued talking.

"This could narrow things down considerably. If Martin acquired the notes directly from Vernier, and hadn't yet delivered them to Dubois when Reginald intercepted them, that means Dubois couldn't have made a copy. And we're already fairly certain the French government never had time to do so. By the time Reginald was sent to Paris, the French were already beginning to panic and the government here was in turmoil. They'd got wind of the invention that this team at Cambridge were allegedly perfecting—not an invention, really, but a formula for an explosive. One so powerful that a lump no larger than your fist could have wiped a city the size of Paris off the map."

Dexter's mouth dropped open. "It really is a doomsday device! See, I told you, Charlotte."

"I'm sure that's an overstatement."

"Not much of one," Dexter said quietly, staring at the pages in front of him in disbelief now that he had enough context to know what he was seeing. Even though chemistry wasn't his area of expertise, Dexter knew enough to tell that if the substance described in the notes were actually concocted, and one could keep it stable enough to transport it, it might indeed flatten a city with a single explosion. He could feel the blood drain from his face as he envisioned the scenario. A fist-sized lump wouldn't do it, but a steam car full of the stuff most certainly could. "It's one of those formulas that's frighteningly simple. I have no idea why this hasn't been done already. You're right to worry that the French might have a copy of these papers. It's a terrifying prospect."

"It was a lucky bluff, in the end. As far as I know, our chaps never could stabilize the substance in large enough quantities to use it in any meaningful way," Murcheson explained. "We assumed that the French had been working with these notes for years but had experienced the same difficulty, hence their continued willingness to abide by the treaty. It seemed as though they thought *we'd* deduced the secret of how to use the stuff without blowing ourselves to kingdom come, but they still hadn't. That was a source of great relief, of course, as after these notes were stolen we'd feared the worst. And once we heard that Gendreau was being courted by a former arms manufacturer who was once a prominent post-royalist sympathizer, well . . . it seemed certain there was a plan to revive this research. That, my friend, would have been a terrifying prospect indeed. With help from Dubois's network of factories and freight transport, the post-royalists could have blown us all to smithereens with that information, French and English alike.

"But if these notes truly went straight from a French agent's hands up to the top of the Opéra and stayed there for seven years, this can't have been what Gendreau was called in to work on. Begs the question of what he and Dubois are really up to, if it isn't this. Good heavens, and I suppose the French still think we really do have a dooms . . . well, an ultimate weapon."

Charlotte rested her chin on her clasped hands, staring across the table at the far wall, for long enough that Dexter grew uncomfortable waiting for her to say something.

"*Doomsday substance* doesn't have quite the same ring to it," he remarked.

"My chemistry knowledge is sketchy," Charlotte admitted, "but from the looks of those notes it's more a sort of doomsday putty. If they're not working on that, though, perhaps Dubois and Gendreau haven't been writing in code at all."

Murcheson frowned. "Either way, you've done your part well, Lady Hardison. And if Martin isn't reporting to the French, he hasn't told them about *Gossamer Wing*. So perhaps the dirigible program has a future in the Agency after all. Something for you to look forward to working on, after you return to the Dominions."

CHARLOTTE TRAILED HER fingers over the demilune console that stood by the door of their suite, tapping the gilded wood with a sense of unease.

"Dexter, did you move the pouch the documents were in?"

He peeked around the frame of the bedroom door. "I don't even want to touch the pouch the documents were in, my sweet. Perhaps the maid moved it. Or took it to the incinerator, if we're lucky. Are you sure you left it there?"

Charlotte was struck by the cheerful domesticity of Dexter's response, of the whole moment: the fretful wife who knows she wasn't the one to move a thing, the indulgent husband who knows the odds are he'll have to apologize later when it transpires the wife was correct after all about whatever it was. For some reason she didn't want to examine too closely, a surge of joyful tears pricked at her eyes and clenched her throat.

The happiness faded as Charlotte cast her mind back to that morning, when they had left the suite not planning to return until after the debriefing with Murcheson.

"That's right, you wouldn't touch it. Remember, I asked if we should bring it, or just take the papers? We were standing right here by the door, you had just picked up your room key from this table."

"I said if you brought that thing you could sit at a separate table with it." Dexter crossed the room to stand next to her, rolling his shirtsleeves up to his elbows as he walked. "You're right, it was right there when we left."

Charlotte struggled to focus on the problem of the

missing pouch. Dexter had shed his cravat, jacket and waist-coat in the bedroom, and his white linen shirt clung to his chest and shoulders in a highly flattering way.

"If we don't find it this afternoon," she suggested, "we can ask the concierge about it when we go to dinner."

"We should let Murcheson know. I'll also rig something at the door to let us know from now on if anyone's been into the room." He headed for the bedroom again, doubtless to begin creating a device for that purpose from spare parts in his trunk.

Charlotte sighed and decided to put the issue aside. She thought it more urgent to loosen her corset, put her feet up and enjoy a cup of tea while she read the Paris newspaper she'd picked up in the lobby downstairs. She was still recovering from the strain of her long flight, and her body demanded more rest than she'd given it.

The newspaper, sadly, had other plans for her.

"Bloody hell!"

Dexter dashed in from the other room. "What happened? Are you all right?"

"Yes! No. Damn. Look at this!" She held up the paper to let him see the headline below the fold on the front page. Not a top story, but not exactly buried either.

"I only know about half those words," Dexter admitted. His French had never been strong, and he'd been sticking to the English papers.

"Mysterious floating black object in the night sky," Charlotte explained, skimming down the column then flipping a few pages into the paper to read the continuation. "Seen in multiple places by 'anonymous witnesses.' In Nancy, Paris and three villages in between, only one of which I think I actually flew over. This is a plant. Somebody wanted to ground the *Gossamer Wing* for good. Oh, that's just spiteful!"

"Do you think Murcheson will really call the whole dirigible program off?"

"In a heartbeat," Charlotte confirmed. "Not worth the risk. Damn!" She threw the paper down on the floor and sat on the divan, frustrated that her corset kept her from flinging herself down in a more dramatic way. "Can you get this bloody straightjacket off me? I can't rail and moan properly with it on."

"Language, darling." Dexter smirked as he slid into place next to her and turned her shoulders so he could get at the fastenings to her gown. "If you wanted me to undress you, you had only to ask."

"I'll keep that in mind," she assured him, heaving a sigh of relief as Dexter finished with the dress and began loosening her corset strings.

"You don't need these things."

"I like pretty clothes," Charlotte said with a shrug. "Corsets are part of the price one pays for that. It's not nearly as bad as it used to be. My mother used to require two maids every morning to help her tight-lace. At least I can dress myself."

"Not in this dress," he pointed out. "I had to fasten it for you."

"I ordered it without thinking," she admitted. "I just liked the style. Usually I'm more careful about my choices, but this time I was blinded by fashion."

"Lucky for you I was here to serve as ladies' maid. Otherwise you'd have had to roam the streets of Paris in your undergarments. Not that I'd have objected, as long as nobody else looked at you."

Charlotte shivered as Dexter tugged her chemise up past her shoulders then ran his fingers down her back, one on each long muscle framing her spine. "Most of my corsets are designed in the new style, they fasten in the front. I have other dresses. You're hardly indispensable to my toilette."

He laughed, the sound like a warm velvet touch against her skin. "Careful, sugar plum, or I'll get in a snit and refuse to tighten you back up. You'll be left naked."

"Nonsense. I'll just ring the concierge and have a maid sent up once I've woken from my nap."

"These marks won't have faded by then, I suspect." He traced the impressions left by the formfitting garment, pulling a contented hum from Charlotte. "I prefer your skin in the morning, when the only lines are the ones the sheets have left there in the night."

"You're assuming I've slept without a nightgown, I take it."

Dexter pressed a kiss to her shoulder, letting his lips linger there as his hands began to wander. "In my imagination, you *always* sleep without a nightgown."

After dinner later that evening the concierge assured them that the housekeeping staff had not moved, or indeed seen, a leather pouch of any sort in the suite.

Seventeen

PARIS, FRANCE

CHARLOTTE HESITATED A long few moments at the curb when the taxi deposited her and Dexter in front of the brilliantly lit Palais Garnier.

It was their first night back in Paris, after an uneventful few more days spent in Nancy for the sake of their cover. Murcheson had secured tickets, and Charlotte wanted very much to see the spectacle of the famous opera in action, all lights and music and glamorous crowd. She was very tired of the building that housed it, however. Looking at it, she was struck with a pang of homesickness for New York City, its familiar theater district, the soaring façade of Trinity Church.

Paris had its own beauty, but it didn't feel quite real to Charlotte somehow. She felt unreal in general, stranded in a limbo of inactivity, caught in the same haze of sunlit faux-honeymoon days and sex-crazed nights that had characterized the voyage to France. She still couldn't quite believe her mission was over. None of it had sunk in yet. Although she knew she would have to work it out at some point, she had no idea what came next. The future was even more daunting than the prospect of entering the opera house again.

"Did you know they wanted to turn the Palais Garnier into a museum, decades ago?" she asked Dexter, halting just outside the periphery of the gathering crowd. "Somebody proposed a new building for the opera, more modern. Instead they renovated this one. I'm glad they did. It's a beautiful structure."

Dexter waited at her side, seeming sensitive to her reluctance. "What happened to the new building?"

"They couldn't raise the funds," Charlotte murmured, lifting her gaze to the roofline where the golden statues seemed to shine with a light of their own in the brilliant electric illumination. "There was a war on, after all."

"We could return to the hotel," Dexter offered. "Leave a message for Murcheson and go back? The Ritz is almost like a second home to me now."

She smiled. "We'll stay for at least the first half. I don't know why I'm being so silly. I did get away."

"By the skin of your teeth, from what you said."

"I suppose I'm just still wary. I keep telling myself my work in France is done, and yours doesn't put us in nearly as much danger. But some part of me is still on alert. Perhaps by the time I'm back home, my nerves will have finally settled down."

He pulled her hand more firmly over his arm and led her into the glittering gilded foyer.

Charlotte relaxed within a few minutes. It was different with people crowding the rooms, movement on the stairs, lights everywhere sparkling over gowns and headdresses and jewels. Merely standing in the midst of it all provided a rich and heady visual feast, the people and paintings all so ornate and colorful the eye could scarcely find a spot to rest.

The grand box in which Murcheson was already seated was a respite from the crowd and noise, allowing an overview of it all without the overwhelming business. Such, mused Charlotte, was the privilege of the privileged—to have access to every luxury, but suffer only as much excess as one cared to tolerate.

"Sit and have a drink," Murcheson advised them as soon as they entered. He snapped at a page who stood by with a tray of champagne, then shooed the lad out once Charlotte and Dexter had each taken a glass.

"I have my industrialist hat on tonight, I'm afraid. What do you know about the French steamrail project?" he asked bluntly once they were alone.

Charlotte shrugged, at a loss, but Dexter leaned forward with a frown. "I know they want to expand it vastly over the next several years. I also know you're most likely bidding for it, and I wish I were in a position to compete. The contract will mean years of steady revenue."

"Yes, the sweet low-interest milk of the government teat," Murcheson confirmed. "Of course, as France is only late to the game of large manufacture—excepting war machines, naturally—most of their people are at a disadvantage. Their late entry into the global steam-car market hasn't profited them enough to retool for anything larger and more lucrative. So the contract will almost certainly go to a foreign bidder . . ."

"Except?" Dexter supplied.

"Precisely," Murcheson nodded. "Except . . . our friend Dubois. I just found out he's preparing a bid that would undercut me substantially if my information is correct. However, his bid is almost completely unrealistic because it's based on equipment and facilities he does not yet possess. Even that could be remedied, if he could afford them, but it seems he can't. Not remotely."

"How badly off is he?"

"All but bankrupt. If it weren't for his political connections he'd be in debtor's prison right now, I suspect. He *must* win this bid to survive."

The house lights dimmed and the crowd rustled to a hush.

The orchestra finished tuning up and swung into the overture.

"Perhaps that's why he's bold enough to meet with Gendreau at his own office in the middle of the day," Charlotte whispered as the curtains drew back. *Norma* had never been her favorite opera, and she was far more interested in what Murcheson had to say. "Desperation. Maybe that's what Gendreau is really doing back here; he has some secret new invention Dubois thinks will make him money. But if I may, I had a question about something we discussed yesterday?"

Dexter agreeably sat back, letting the two of them whisper in front of him. Charlotte almost jumped as his hand skimmed over her back, which was bare in the sweeping plum-colored satin gown she'd chosen.

It was another husbandly gesture, that delicate touch— proprietary and deliberately flouting propriety just because he could. Charlotte willed herself to ignore it.

"I'm not a huge fan of Bellini myself," Murcheson confessed. "What was your question?"

"Well, I thought perhaps by focusing on Dubois and Gendreau and Coeur de Fer, we're coming at things from the wrong angle. Tell me more about Simone Vernier."

"That could be a long story. First let me remind you that officially, there is no 'we' here, Lady Hardison. But in an informal capacity, let's see . . . as far as we know, Vernier slipped into Dubois's confidence by pretending to be a double agent. She made no secret of the fact she was a spy, but had convinced him she was secretly working for the postroyalists against the ruling Égalité faction. He'd been working both sides himself, courting the current regime but still making money selling weapons to the ousted party on the side."

"That was why the Égalité were watching him?"

"We can only assume so. But shortly before the treaty was signed, Vernier traveled to Cambridge in the guise of a well-known Swiss chemist. While she was there, she managed to purloin the formula for the explosive. The researchers were all quite charmed by her, from what I hear. Never suspected a thing. Apparently before she became a spy, she'd been a chemical engineer, which was probably why the French sent her after the documents. She knew their language."

"Would you like to change seats with me, sugarplum?"

Charlotte glanced at Dexter, startled. "Oh! Oh, that's very kind. Yes, thank you, I believe I would."

She was surprised that Dexter was so interested in the opera, but quickly forgot in her curiosity about the documents and the conversation with Murcheson.

"You said Vernier hadn't shared the notes with anyone in the French government. How can you be sure of that?"

Murcheson shrugged. "She wouldn't have had time. By the time she returned to France, it seems Dubois had found her out. He killed her within a few hours of her return, if the reports are accurate. Drugged her, then stuffed a pillow over her face. Ignominious way to go. Dubois was charged, but evidently managed to buy his way out of a guilty verdict."

"That's monstrous. Especially if—was she really Dubois's mistress in . . . in practice?" Charlotte asked, glad for the dark that hid her blush.

"Oh, yes. He wasn't quite as revolting in those days, of course. Since the war he's degenerated. His appearance finally starting to reflect his habits, I suppose."

"Now he's monstrous inside and out," Charlotte concurred. "Vernier must have been fanatically devoted to her country, to make such a sacrifice. It hardly seems right that she died for it. Even if it was the French she was loyal to."

"Even then?" Murcheson teased. "Are you growing fond of the French, Baroness?"

"I've grown exceedingly fond of their food and wine, sir."

"Ah, understandable."

"I confess I'm disappointed. I thought perhaps I'd come up with a new direction of enquiry, but apparently—"

Dexter tapped Charlotte's arm, getting her attention and handing her the opera glasses he'd been using for the duration of her conversation. He pointed not to the stage, however, but to the first box just above it on the opposite side of the theater.

"Look who's here."

She looked through the device, puzzled, and fiddled with the focus knobs until the image popped up, sharp and clear, and she saw the man's face: it was Roland Dubois.

THE CRUSH AT the interval wasn't any bother to Dexter, but he could tell it was no joy for Charlotte. She nearly disappeared in the crowd several times before he latched onto her hand firmly and instructed her to walk behind him.

Thus aligned, they beat a path to the other side of the lobby where special opera programs and books of historical interest about the Palais Garnier were sold.

Charlotte excused herself and dashed for the doors that led to the necessary—after making a quip about it being lucky she already knew where they were—while Dexter and Murcheson kept a wary eye on the crowd.

"Monsieur Murcheson," an oily voice intruded.

Just as Murcheson had suggested he might, Dubois had found them. Murcheson believed he would push for a meeting with Dexter, ostensibly in hopes of luring his business interest away from Murcheson. The real reason, Murcheson predicted, could be far more sinister. As Coeur de Fer had been working for Dubois and had clearly identified Charlotte as a person of interest, Dubois must know Dexter and Charlotte were in possession of the recovered plans. He might even suspect that Dexter's role was in some way related to the doomsday substance. Dexter and Charlotte would both be at risk as long as Dubois thought they knew something about the explosive, and the increased scrutiny from Dubois might impede Dexter's ability to accomplish all he still needed to in Le Havre.

"Dubois," Murcheson deigned to answer, his tone suddenly dripping with aristocratic hauteur. Dexter was quite impressed with the transformation. "Allow me to introduce

Baron Hardison. Lord Hardison, Roland Dubois. M'sieur Dubois makes steam cars and so forth."

Dexter accepted the handshake Dubois offered, suppressing a grimace at the soft clamminess of that hand.

"The Makesmith Baron," Dubois drawled. He said it like it was an insult, a title of shame, but Dexter only nodded. "Here to strike a deal with my adversary?"

"I'm on my honeymoon, actually," Dexter corrected him, unable to resist adopting a hint of Murcheson's disdain.

"So I've heard. Congratulations. When will you be returning to the American Dominions, then?"

Another insult, with the clear implication that Dubois hoped it was soon. Dexter ignored the hand Murcheson placed on his arm in warning. He was a businessman, after all. He had dealt with men like Dubois too many times before, and he wouldn't let himself be drawn.

"We're fortunate enough to be at our leisure here, with no particular deadline for our return. The climate is quite pleasant, and I gather Lady Hardison has a great deal of shopping still to do. Apparently there are substantial qualitative differences between the shopping opportunities in Paris and those in New York."

Dubois's smarmy smile made Dexter glad for Murcheson's restraining hand. Something about the man made him want to cuff him sharply on the side of the head.

"We must meet then, during your long stay. Discuss business? I believe we may have some mutual acquaintances. Other than Monsieur Murcheson, of course."

"Ah. Well, no promises, old chap. My schedule is already rather full and after all, it is my honeymoon." Dexter tried as hard as he could to inject the suggestion that even to ask had been wildly inappropriate of Dubois; he suspected he didn't do it nearly as well as Murcheson could have, however. Perhaps he had just spent too long working to shed that aristocratic demeanor. Or perhaps he just wasn't cut out for spying.

Charlotte, however, obviously was. Her headache-inducing persona was firmly back in place as she reattached herself to his arm like a limpet. Murcheson had advised her to appear as harmless and as brainless as she possibly could to divert any suspicion Dubois might have about her real purpose for visiting France, on the off chance Coeur de Fer hadn't already spoiled that angle for her.

"Dexter," she pouted, "you're not talking *business* at the *opera*, are you? Oh, hello there."

"My wife, Lady Hardison. Monsieur Dubois," said Dexter.

"*Enchanté*, madame."

Instead of taking Charlotte's hand in the polite lady's version of a handshake she was obviously offering, Dubois pulled her gloved fingers to his lips and kissed them as though he relished the act.

Charlotte's other hand dug into Dexter's arm like a claw, but her facial expression never flickered.

"Ooo, how *continental*!" she simpered at Dubois. "So *charming*!"

"Your husband says you are enjoying Paris. Perhaps he and I can meet one day while you are occupied in enriching the city's coffers, *non*?"

"Oh!" Charlotte cried with a giggle at the end, "*No*, actually! Isn't that funny, you said *non* meaning *doesn't that sound nice*, but my response *actually was no*! It's our honeymoon, you see. I'm afraid he couldn't *possibly*. I simply can't spare him!"

"Well, it wouldn't have to be a long meeting, cupcake," Dexter said thoughtfully, just to watch her at work a little longer.

Somehow, Charlotte managed to keep smiling and simpering as she began flaying him with tiny verbal knives. "You've taken such a great many meetings with Mr. Murcheson already, *darling*. One might almost think you weren't on your honeymoon at all. Isn't that *so silly*? If you spend too much time on all *your* business I'm liable to forget it's our honeymoon *too*, and then where will we be?"

Certainly not in the same bed, she somehow managed to imply. Her eyelashes seemed to have grown half an inch or so, expressly for the purpose of batting. Had he been a henpecked husband in truth, Dexter thought he might be in serious trouble. "Of course, darling, but as we're in Europa anyway and the opportunity to meet with—"

"Ah!" Charlotte said, a dainty little cry of distress. Her fingers pressed to her temple in a tasteful display of genteel agony.

"Lady Hardison, are you quite well?" Murcheson asked, leaning in like a considerate grandfather.

"Oh dear. I'm terribly sorry. I'm suddenly feeling *quite* overcome!"

"Darling, perhaps we should return to the hotel."

"Yes, that's exactly what we ought to do," Charlotte agreed. She pressed the back of her hand to her forehead, as though she might faint at any minute.

Dexter caught a lapse on Murcheson's part; the man couldn't help but roll his eyes at the swooning bride. For his part he was struck by the utter absurdity, all of them standing there pretending they didn't know what the others were about. It was not just theatre, it was farce. Suddenly he was sick to death of the whole ridiculous thing.

"You must take my car," Murcheson offered. "Plenty of time in the second act for my driver to see you home and return for me."

"Oh, how very kind," Charlotte said, drooping picturesquely against Dexter's arm.

"Do you think that wise?" Dubois said suddenly. Dexter looked at him sharply. He seemed unduly agitated, and was hiding it badly; his face was decidedly pale and damp. "Should we not summon a doctor here for the lady if she is ill?"

"Nonsense." Dexter put an arm around Charlotte's waist, taking shameless advantage of the feigned illness to press her inappropriately close. His interest in her, at least, was genuine. And the sooner they were back at the hotel, the better. "A bit of fresh air and quiet, a few minutes out of the crush and the lady will be right as rain. Won't you, my love?"

"If you think so, husband," Charlotte answered with a breathless earnestness. "You *always* know best."

Murcheson suffered a sudden coughing fit, and Dexter sneezed in a way that strongly resembled a stifled snort of laughter.

The chimes sounded the approaching end of the interval, drawing the crowd back into the house. With a last frantic glare at Murcheson and Dexter, Dubois departed reluctantly to return to his seat as the two men half-carried Charlotte out the door.

"Overdoing it a tad at the end, don't you think, my fruit-bedecked meringue?" Dexter teased Charlotte once the coast was clear.

"Shameless," Murcheson agreed, hailing his driver from the middle of the rank of waiting steam cars.

"It was either that or slap him. Didn't something about that man just make you want to strike him?" Charlotte asked.

Dexter nodded. "Yes, but to do it I would have had to touch him, and he's such a slimy toad I decided it wasn't worth it."

"You can come out of the shadows, Martin. Here, sit."

As Dubois swept past him, Martin stepped forward from the darkest corner of the booth, eyeing the theater warily before taking the seat Dubois indicated. In general he avoided theaters, the boxes particularly. He hated the feeling of sitting at the edge of a precipice, exposed and trapped at the same time. Anyone in the audience could lift a weapon and fire before he even noticed the threat. Anyone could slink into the box from the hallway behind and end him with a silent garrote. And then there were the fires. Theaters were deathtraps.

"I nearly lost an agent," Martin said without preamble. "He'd been set to watch on the roof of Murcheson's Gennevilliers factory. He suffered severe burns and a broken leg, and barely managed to avoid being identified by his rescuers. Some warning might have been helpful."

Dubois shrugged. "He lived, I take it. If he hadn't, he certainly wouldn't have been the first peasant in history to die in service."

Gritting his teeth, Martin swore an oath to himself that one day Dubois would die in lingering agony.

"This is a man in your employ. A good man."

"No," Dubois contradicted him. "He is a man in *your* employ, and his goodness doesn't concern me. Don't think I'm unaware you have your own agenda, Martin. Why would you ever think I'd let your agenda interfere with mine?" When Martin remained silent, Dubois shook his head, for all the world like a father disappointed in a child who has failed to learn a simple lesson. "Jacques, Jacques. Are you still so naïve? You're Coeur de Fer, are you not? Where is the iron, my friend? Did you learn nothing from Simone's death? I'll eliminate anybody who stands in my way, even a person I care for. It's as simple as that. I know my priorities. And don't try to claim you're any different. You've done the same in your time."

Never a person I've cared for, Martin thought. But then he'd never found out a mistress of several years' duration was a government agent gathering potentially ruinous information on him, preparing to have him exiled or shot for a traitor. Perhaps he would've done the same after all. He would never know. When the documents had come into his life, all else of importance had left it, including all the people he'd once cared for.

At least I have my pouch back. Empty and ready for use. Perhaps a cobbler could recondition the leather.

"Simone cared for me too, you know." Dubois went on. "That was her weakness. It blinded her, and after all those years she let her guard down. Just once, but that was all I needed. She really shouldn't have been foolish enough to fall asleep in my bed. Though the first stupidity was drinking wine I'd poured out of her sight. She made it very easy, in the end."

Martin didn't need to hear it. He knew how Simone had died, knew the cretinous malignancy beside him had suffocated her in his own bed, then paid a doctor to testify that the death had been from natural causes. Simone's downfall was legend in French intelligence.

Dubois was right, however. She had been foolish to visit him while exhausted from her jaunt to England, and even more so to drink his wine. As foolish as Martin had been to think that his deal with Dubois could ever end well. And now that he'd lost the documents to the British—for the second and final time—the deal would never end until either Dubois or Martin was dead.

Martin thought that considered in those terms, the choice became very clear to him. The plan of action practically sprang to mind full-formed. All he needed to do was choose a time and place to implement it.

"She never did care for you, Dubois," Martin said softly but firmly. "She thought you were scum, and a pig in bed."

He didn't know why he'd said it. So careful, he was usually so very careful. But Dubois normally steered clear of this topic too, knowing that Simone had meant something to Martin, even if he wasn't sure what she'd meant.

Dubois's tone was jovial, though. Perhaps he had finally forgotten what a danger Martin could still be when pressed. He seemed to assume the old dog had lost his fangs. "You think I didn't know my own woman? She was a whore for me, whatever else she was."

Martin permitted himself a smile as he turned to the dismissive Dubois, letting his imagination run for a second or two. There was a beauty in the extremity of death, sometimes, a poetic quality to the last expression on a victim's face as the breath left the body. Martin suspected even Dubois might display that sort of beauty at the very end. "Believe what you will."

"You're tiresome this evening, Martin, and the second act is beginning soon. Go find a whore of your own or something, leave me to my amusement. Your little errand boy will heal in time, and Murcheson needed to be hit hard. I'm only disappointed the bastard wasn't there as I'd hoped. Still, there's time. Other plans are already afoot." He frowned, tenting his fingers over his ample midsection. "This very evening, in fact. Perhaps they are going a little awry, but I think the outcome might be just as useful in the end."

Dubois's plans, Martin thought, usually did go awry. But his own would not.

THE DRIVE FROM the Opéra to the Ritz was a short one, even in traffic. But they had barely turned onto the Rue de la Paix when Dexter leaned forward, tapping the glass that separated the driver and passenger sections of the steam car.

"Do you hear that?"

The driver slid the window panel open and spared a glance back before returning his eyes to the busy street ahead. "Sir?"

"The boiler. Do you hear it? The pitch is wrong, and it sounds . . . dull."

"Sir? I don't hear anything different than usual. Shall I pull over? We're only a few blocks from the hotel."

"What is it?" Charlotte asked, looking on her way toward being irritated.

"I'm not sure," Dexter admitted. "But I'm familiar with this model of engine and it just sounds *off*."

She frowned at him for a moment then leaned forward, clasping the frame of the communicating window with one hand for balance while she addressed the driver. "Let's pull over, just to be on the safe side."

Dexter apologized to the driver and to Charlotte, but he was relieved when the car rattled to a halt at the nearest stretch of empty curb.

"It's probably nothing," he said to Charlotte as he handed her down and led her to stand under the awning of the closest storefront. "But I'd like to have a look. Come over here and wait with Lady Hardison, if you would," he instructed the driver, who nodded and shut the engine off before he leaped down, swinging the door closed behind him.

His foot touched the pavement just as a *whoof* of pressure

and superheated steam blew the bonnet from the car. The explosion swept the driver straight into Dexter and Charlotte as the sound ripped the night apart. Dexter threw himself between Charlotte and the steam car, but the unfortunate driver floundered into the gray stone wall of the nearest storefront. One half of the bonnet flew straight into the large display window next to them, and as his ears stopped ringing from the blast, Dexter heard a brassy alarm bell jangling from inside the store.

"Charlotte!" He rolled off her, patting her frantically all over. "Are you all right? Darling, are you hurt?"

"I've been better," she admitted. "Dear god, you're heavy. Are you all right?"

"I'm fine. I think."

Charlotte was already crawling past him to get to the driver, who seemed to have knocked himself unconscious when he was flung face-first into the wall. He'd crumpled to a heap below the shattered display window, but as they watched he groaned and pushed himself to a seated position.

Then he saw the remains of the car and began cursing in French that Dexter didn't understand and Charlotte pretended not to understand. Dexter saw the shock on her face as she looked from the driver to the car, which was burning white-hot. A scrape high on Charlotte's cheekbone started to bleed, one drop seeping out and finding its way down her cheek. Her elaborate coiffure listed to one side, the ribbons and pins yanked out of place by the fall; the hair was starting to slide free one soft, golden curl at a time. She was beautiful, and she was simply the thing he held most precious in life. It suddenly all seemed very clear to him.

"You saved us all." Charlotte returned her attention to Dexter, running her hands down his chest, reassuring herself he was unhurt. "If you hadn't heard that something was wrong—"

"I love you."

She blinked, hesitated, then stared into his eyes intently

as though she were searching for the truth written on his soul. A long moment, saturated with potential, passed between them before she spoke again.

"Your pupils are equal, it doesn't seem to be a concussion. We should have a doctor examine your head, just the same."

She stood up gracefully, all at once, backing away from the heat of the burning steam car and brushing herself off as if her satin opera gloves were any sort of use against the devastation the explosion had wrought. The skirt of her gown was torn, and splinters of glass sparkled on her cloak.

"Mr. Murcheson's steam car has blown out the window of Cartier's," she remarked, nodding toward the broken display pane. "I wonder who pays for the damage in cases like this?"

The subject, it seemed, was officially changed.

Dexter rose more slowly, making a few passes over his clothing with his hands then giving it all up as a loss. Sirens were already nearing, and the gathering crowd pressed closer as the fire began to die down. The seats of the ill-fated vehicle didn't burn nearly as hot as the engine had.

Looking behind him, Dexter offered a hand to the still-muttering driver, who took it and wobbled to his feet.

"What caused it, monsieur?" he asked Dexter, as if by predicting the explosion, his passenger had proved himself an oracle of the first order.

"That remains to be seen," Dexter said, though he had his suspicions. To Charlotte, he murmured, "There's nothing wrong with my head."

He felt irritated, cross with himself and Charlotte, and he knew that was a ridiculous emotional response to having just had a steam car explode and nearly kill three people. Later, he expected, he would need a great deal of liquor and suffer many nightmares before he was rid of the trauma. For the moment, though, it simply hadn't hit him yet. It was all too unreal. His mind was apparently only capable of dealing with one minor detail at a time, and it had chosen to concern itself with Charlotte's less-than-ideal reaction to his unplanned declaration.

Dexter felt nominally better when Charlotte tipped her head back to study his face, lifting a hand to brush the hair back from his forehead and whispering, "I know there's nothing wrong with your head, my delicious slice of coconut cream pie."

"That one needs work," he said automatically, feeling a glimmer of giddy happiness even less appropriate to the situation than being irked.

"It was the best I could do on the spur of the moment," she replied, nestling into the crook of his arm as the first wave of police arrived on the scene.

Eighteen

❧

"No. It's absolutely out of the question!" Dexter insisted.

Charlotte clenched her fists, wanting to strike out at something and vibrating with the effort to restrain herself. *How* dare *he*?

"Out of the question for whom, precisely?"

"This has gone well beyond any reasonable expectation of danger you might have encountered *flying about* in a *balloon*." Dexter's face had turned fierce and hard. Charlotte thought his jaw looked as tightly bunched as her fists, and made a mental note not to punch him there if she decided she simply couldn't hold herself back. She'd be more likely to hurt her hand than his face.

"You do realize it was a spy balloon? And that I was using it to gather vital documents and conduct covert surveillance on potentially deadly enemies? I understood you were aware of all that."

Dexter dug his fingers through his hair, gripping it so

tightly Charlotte was surprised he didn't pull out two handfuls. "Charlotte, be reasonable!"

"I am being reasonable," she said, forcing herself to calm down. The situation called for education, not rage. "I'm being a very reasonable agent of the Crown, still on an assignment. That's why we're here. Besides, stowing me at the embassy for safekeeping would be pointless. We're not in any more danger today than we were yesterday, Dexter. We weren't the targets."

"I'm sorry? We nearly got blown to bits."

"In *Murcheson*'s steam car. A steam car nobody expected us to be in," she reminded him.

"It would have been easy for somebody to—"

"No. The driver was only away from the vehicle for fifteen minutes during the middle of the first act. He left it to pick up some tobacco for Mr. Murcheson, as he'd been instructed to do, and when he returned he didn't notice anything amiss. Whatever was done to the steam car was done very quickly while he was gone. Well before Murcheson volunteered his car to take us back here. That implies advance planning. So unless you suspect Murcheson or his driver of plotting our demise . . ."

Dexter shook his head and sat on the end of the bed with a grunt. "Damn. I feel like I've been run over by a tractor."

"Me too. You should try a warm bath. I left some Epsom salts for you."

"That won't help my ears to stop ringing, I suppose?"

"Only time will help that, I'm afraid."

She bent over and untwisted the rough huckaback towel from her hair, letting the damp strands fall where they would as she stood back up. Dexter was watching her with nothing like the keen interest she had come to expect, and the change upset Charlotte more than she cared to admit.

"I want you to be safe," he said gently. "I won't apologize for it anymore."

"I understand that. I do. It's just that . . . well, who do you think you are?" It took Charlotte a second to register the hurt on Dexter's face, and realize how she'd phrased herself. "No, no, I don't mean it like that. I meant . . . in all this. What's your role in all this, as you see it? Who do you think you are?"

She watched him think it through, discarding the first answer he bit back, deciding how to phrase it in some more acceptable way than "your husband." Finally he shook his head, unable or unwilling to put any other words to it.

Charlotte approached him, speaking as gently as she could. The impulse to lash out had been replaced by an aching compassion; she could see Dexter was suffering, and she hated to know she was the cause of it. He'd said he loved her. She couldn't allow him to keep thinking along those lines. "You came here to do a job. I came here to do a job. The rest . . . is compelling, I grant you, but it doesn't mean I can forget the mission, even if I've accomplished my main task. I've tried more than once to make that clear, though I know I haven't done very well at following my own terms. I've let you muddy the waters, and I've muddied them myself. Still, the fact remains, I don't report to you," she concluded, "I report to Murcheson. To Whitehall."

Dexter reached out to coax her closer, then leaned his cheek against her stomach, hands resting on her hips for a moment before sliding around to clasp her waist. After a moment, unable to help herself, she started stroking his hair. The soft, straight strands fell through her fingers in a soothing flow, an interesting contrast to the prickle of whiskers she could feel through the linen of her night rail.

"This is why *they* advise against this sort of entanglement, I'm sure," she murmured.

Dexter chuckled, the vibration and the heat of his breath warming her skin. "*They* never like any of the really enjoyable things. I don't know why we all keep listening to *them*, anyway."

"We didn't listen, and look where we are."

"I can think of worse places to be." He gave her a squeeze. "Charlotte, when all this is over, I—"

"Don't," she warned him, tapping him on the head

sharply a few times with one fingertip before she resumed carding his hair in slow, smooth sweeps. "Don't."

THE FLASK OF brandy was empty by lunchtime, and the bottle too. Martin tipped one then the other into his glass, idly watching the last lonely drops creep down the side of the tumbler to pool in the bottom. Most of it evaporated on the way back to the rim when he tried to eke a final swig from the dregs.

Empty, empty, empty. The flask. The bottle. The disgusting leather pouch. Martin tried to make himself throw it away, but he couldn't do it. He'd had it for years, that little pouch. He couldn't even remember its original purpose now, but he had used it to stow loose papers as a schoolboy. He'd strung a rope under the flap and slung it over his shoulder when he worked as a bicycle courier for a few short, miserable months in his sixteenth year.

Years later he still had it, and it had been the first thing to hand when he thought to run to Simone's office at the agency after learning of her death. Before anybody else thought to do it. An instinct he had thanked the heavens for at the time, and cursed shortly thereafter and ever since.

"You are a metaphor for my entire life," he said, raising the empty glass to the pouch. It sat on his table silently, refusing to respond to his toast. "A promising start. Then one wrong turn and the next seven years wasted. Unable to serve any useful purpose, stuck in the dark to molder and rot. By the time you're free once more, it's far too late for you. You contain no secrets, have no more power, no more teeth with which to bite. Empty and hideous. You're fit only to discard."

You're boring a leather pouch with drunken philosophy, imbecile. Martin transferred the tumbler to his right hand, pulling a lever near his wrist. His more-than-fingers began to tighten, squeezing inexorably closer until, with a pop, the glass shattered, sending shards to the ground.

Martin didn't bother to sweep up the pieces. The landlady

could take care of the mess. He'd never been particularly fond of her anyway.

"Time to pay a final call on Monsieur Dubois," Martin said to the flat, which was too small and mean to echo in reply. "Today I call his bluff, or I die. But either way it will be the same to him."

CHARLOTTE HAD DECIDED to lend more credence to her cover and spend the morning shopping again while Dexter reviewed his plans for the work at Atlantis Station. Even with two agents assigned to cover her she was jumpy and uneasy, prone to glancing over her shoulder, then checking to make sure her guards were still in place.

Tittering with salespersons and bargaining poorly in atrocious French took all her energy, and by noon she was more than ready to find Dexter and repair to some quiet bistro where they could pretend to be a honeymooning couple in love.

When she walked into the suite, however, Dexter was packing his trunks.

"The glass is ready. Arsenault just sent a wire. It's being delivered to Le Havre, so I'll need to start work there tomorrow. We can stay in the same hotel we used before, in Honfleur."

"We've barely settled into the suite here," she sighed.

"With the documents recovered, there's no reason to linger in Paris." Dexter placed a pair of shoes neatly into a drawer-like compartment within one trunk, securing it closed with a snap. "You could always remain here, you know. For a few more days at least, assuming Murcheson doesn't have anything pressing for you to do in Le Havre. I'll need a week or so for the installation, and God knows Honfleur won't offer you nearly as much diversion as Paris during that time."

Charlotte tossed her reticule on the bed and started to remove her gloves, trying to account for the queasy fluttering in her stomach. "Are you asking me to stay here while you go on?"

He abandoned the pretense of interest in packing and sat on the bed, picking up the yellow silk purse and toying with the strings. "I'm giving you the freedom to choose whichever option seems best to you."

She wanted to resent him for laying the decision on her shoulders. He was trying so hard to do the right thing, though, that she couldn't bear him a grudge for it.

"If I were a stronger person I would stay, for both our sakes."

"If I were a stronger person I would carry you to the embassy kicking and screaming and make them lock you in a room until it's time to put you on the next ship to New York." He sounded as though he had given the idea serious thought.

She thought of his possessive anger in the submersible bay, the fierce way he'd taken charge on the train after she'd frustrated him by setting her terms. Not to mention that long-ago fork jabbed into his brother's hand over a chop. Perhaps that was his usual response to being thwarted in matters of the mind or heart, to settle the matter through brute force and determination. That, to him, was strength. It had probably served him quite well over the years, and Charlotte was suspicious at his suddenly adopting a less direct approach.

"You mean you're *not* going to club me over the head and drag me off to your cave?"

"Do you want me to?" He smiled wryly. "We both know I'm capable of it. And have essentially done so a few times already. Charlotte, you do know I'm not normally so—oh, never mind, of course you don't know. That's the trouble."

For some reason his humor angered her, where his anger hadn't. "There's so much trouble here, I don't know where to begin. You're right, I don't know you. I hardly even know *myself* anymore, since we started this . . . this—"

"Affair."

"Affair?" She threw her gloves on the bed and crossed her arms over her chest, feeling a need to shield herself. "I don't have *affairs*."

An affair was something temporary, sordid, the business of unhappy wives and jaded widows. Rakehells and faithless husbands had affairs.

What happened to "I love you"? Charlotte grimaced at her own hypocrisy.

"What would you call it, then," he challenged, "since you're determined to end it when we get back to New York? It isn't a marriage, Charlotte, no matter what people may think. You and I know better."

"I ought to end it here and now."

His jaw was tight again, his eyes an icy wasteland. "If you were a stronger person, perhaps you would."

Her eyes narrowed. "I'm feeling a sudden surge of strength. Consider our *affair* at an end, Lord Hardison."

"Mister Hardison, if you please." For a moment they stared at each other in a silent contest of wills, then Dexter spoke again. "Charlotte, I don't want to do this. Not this way."

Charlotte looked away, biting the inside of her cheek to keep from crying. "What do you mean?"

"I mean we were friends before, and we can be friends still." He rose and offered his hands. Charlotte reluctantly unfolded her arms and let him pull her into the circle of his embrace, slowly relaxing against him as he held her. "Whatever happens, and even if it was all a product of the excitement of the mission, we both know it meant more than just an affair. At least it did to me."

Charlotte slipped her arms around Dexter's waist, burying her face in his warm, broad chest for a blissful moment before forcing herself to pull away. She patted his shoulder and nodded. "I know. We're both just tired, I suspect. It will be so good to get home."

"Soon," he said in agreement.

"I'll come to Honfleur," she decided, "because you're being gracious. I'm sure Murcheson can find something for me to do while you're working on your . . . what did you call it again? Multi-seismical Phototonic—"

"Multi-hyalchordate Phototransphorinating Seismograph."

"While you're working on that. Besides, we can hardly make things more complicated at this point, anyway." She moved to the wardrobe, sighing at the prospect of packing it all up yet again.

MARGUERITE, THE VASTLY skilled secretary, flashed Martin a stern look when he entered the vestibule outside Dubois's office.

"He is occupied, monsieur."

"He usually is. Yet I see you at your desk now, so I assume he must at least be fully clothed." He bypassed the two uncomfortable chairs set out for guests, and sat instead on the corner of Marguerite's desk.

"Why do you do it?" the woman asked after a few minutes of painful silence.

"Do what, *ma petite*?"

She sneered at the endearment, as if Martin needed reminding that his gaunt face and ruined ear were offputting. "Work for him. How did you come to do that, from what you were doing before?"

"I sold my soul," he said without hesitation. "It wasn't worth it, regrettably." For the first time he scrutinized the woman carefully, noting her delicate features and intelligent brown eyes. He hadn't paid attention before, and he should have. The way she looked back at him gave her away; she was daring him to guess her secret, and far too confident that he never would. Spying was apparently no longer as subtle a game as it had been during the war.

Marguerite could have used some lessons from Simone Vernier, Martin thought. Or even from the lovely Charlotte, Lady Hardison. She thought the skills she employed on her knees were enough, no doubt.

"Is Gendreau in there with him?"

The girl just raised her eyebrows at him. Sighing, Martin leaned a little closer to her, propping himself on one arm and speaking softly so as not to be overheard by anyone who happened to wander in. "Marguerite, I need you to take a message to your employers after I leave Dubois's office later, can you do that for me?"

"Monsieur? You'll be with Dubois, would you not just tell him—"

"Your *real* employers. Listen closely. They were right to suspect him all along. Their mistake has always been in assuming he had a higher motive than greed. Had I brought Dubois the information Simone Vernier gathered seven years ago, he would have happily used it to plunge the country into another decade or more of war, just to turn an easier profit. Simone was right to keep it from him, and I'm thankful I was thwarted in my attempt to undo her effort. What I do today, I do for Simone, to honor her sacrifice. You understand?"

The girl's eyes had widened, but she said nothing, which Martin thought to her credit.

"Murcheson's factory, and the steam car that exploded on the Rue de la Paix last night, both were also the work of Dubois. Not in the service of his country, or anything so lofty. Just filthy lucre, as was ever the case with him." The voices from within the office grew louder, and the doorknob rattled. Just before the door opened, Martin bent even closer to Marguerite's shocked face and whispered, "You will thank me after this day, mademoiselle. You'll never have to suck Dubois's cock again."

"In that case, go with God, m'sieur," she said quickly, dropping her gaze as Dubois and Gendreau emerged.

"If so," Martin said, "it will be the first time in many years."

"Martin," Dubois grunted once Gendreau had gone. He was clearly not pleased to see his dour henchman. "I was about to give some dictation."

"I won't be long," Martin promised, proceeding into the office. Dubois followed, slamming the door behind them.

Now that the moment had arrived, Martin found himself unsure how to proceed. His planning, conducted in an alcoholic daze, had left much to be desired.

"What is it?" Dubois snapped. He crossed to his desk and sat in his large leather chair as though assuming a throne.

"Gendreau should exercise more caution. He's not even bothering with a disguise now."

"His exile has been formally lifted," Dubois reported. "People have short memories, and Gendreau has a great deal of influence. He's planning to find backers among his friends for our steamrail project, and he has a design for a more efficient engine that would be cheaper to produce."

"And will he actually succeed in raising money or improving the engines, do you think?"

"What do you want, Martin?" Dubois was fingering the button in his pocket, and Martin smiled. "I don't have time to make chitchat with you."

"Very well, monsieur, I shall put my cards on the table. And now, so shall you. I am calling your bluff."

"Bluff? I don't recall making any bluffs."

"No? It occurred to me that I've been of great use to you these seven years, but I've also learned a great deal about you. One of the things I've learned is that you are far from subtle. Also you are a poor judge of character."

Dubois's lip curled. "I judged yours well enough."

Martin nodded, conceding the point. "You saw that I was afraid to die. That I wanted to become something more than I was. A man willing to undergo such pain to improve himself is unlikely to give it up easily. I also had hope, of course, that one day I might regain the leverage I needed to free myself."

"Have you lost your hope, Martin? Is Coeur de Fer rusting away?" Dubois taunted.

"I no longer have hope, it's true. More importantly, though, I no longer have anything to lose. Perhaps I'm wrong, but if I am it doesn't really matter to me anymore."

"Wrong about what?" Dubois sat back in his chair, arms crossed over his chest, one hand clutching the trigger device.

"Poison is a subtle man's weapon, monsieur. And as I said, you are not a subtle man. You're not a man who restrains his impulses. I believe if you had really possessed the means to kill me all these years I'd be long dead by now."

A horrible smile transformed Dubois's plump, bland face into a mask of demonic delight. "Oh, Martin. How wrong you are. I watched the doctor install the vial of poison myself. Did you really think to challenge me? I have nothing to fear from you. This little display changes nothing, *nothing* between us except providing me entertainment."

"As I said," Martin replied, an unearthly calm stealing over him as he slipped his coat off, draping it over one of the chairs in front of Dubois's desk, "it doesn't matter either way whether I'm right or wrong."

"No, it doesn't," Dubois assured him. "You are right about one thing, I am impulsive at times. Several years ago in a fit of pique I destroyed the formula for the antidote that had been sitting in my safe for so long. It gave me no little satisfaction, I must say."

It was almost a numbness, the peace Martin felt. His only recourse lay before him, clear in his mind. He slid the switch in his forearm from one position to another, circled the desk matter-of-factly and placed his mechanical hand around Dubois's neck before the man could even raise a protest.

"Wha—" the man squeaked before the pressure on his throat stopped the air. His fingers fumbled frantically at his lap and he flipped the wire guard off the button on his controller and pressed it repeatedly, stabbing at it as Martin simply held his neck and watched.

"I don't feel anything," Martin informed him. "No click. No burning or pain. Seven years is a long time, Dubois, do you think your mechanism is rusty?"

Kicking and thrashing, his eyes starting to bulge, Dubois slapped the device flat onto Martin's chest and pounded his meaty fist against it. He dropped the thing with a clatter when Martin raised his hand to flip the forearm switch yet again, triggering the springs that clamped his claw down to a tight, irregular cylinder of diameter much smaller than the throat of a portly man.

I should have made it last longer, he thought as Dubois's twitching slowed to a halt. Blood washed from the ruined neck over Martin's hand, and he let it die down to a trickle before he released the clamps and stepped away.

The deadly calm was fading, a faint twinge of nausea rising in its place. Martin used a handkerchief to wipe the worst of the blood from the smooth surfaces of his arm before putting his coat back on and stepping out into the vestibule.

Marguerite glanced at his hand, then quickly away. "I'm going out to have a smoke in the park with one of the other secretaries. I'll be gone about fifteen minutes."

Martin nodded, and the girl rushed away, leaving him to exit the building unobserved.

His mind whirled, flooding with possibilities for his next step. He had done it, he was free, but what now? It occurred to Martin that part of him never believed Dubois was bluffing. Some shred of doubt always remained, keeping him from planning too far ahead lest he suffer more disappointment.

The weather seemed to have changed while he was inside, Martin noted as he stepped out into the open air. In the morning it had been quite cool and mild, but now he felt overheated. A sweat had broken out on his face. He strolled away from the building, hands hidden deep in his coat pockets, trying to ignore the sensation of dread that had taken root in his chest.

A surgeon-engineer, he thought. *Just in case, I should find one. A surgeon-engineer, or else a very good makesmith.*

Nineteen

✦❧

CHARLOTTE WANDERED THE cobbled lanes of Honfleur, charmed by the picturesque town's transformation. She and Dexter had returned just in time for a festival, it seemed.

"Is it really almost Whit Sunday?" Dexter had asked as they stared, bemused, at the colorful gauze and flower garlands festooning an ancient archway near a prominent church. "It doesn't seem like Easter was that long ago."

"A lot has happened since then," Charlotte pointed out.

She had far too much time over the next several days to consider all that had happened. After another half-hearted attempt at conquering her fear of the claustrophobic submersible, she admitted defeat and returned to championing various uses of the *Gossamer Wing* to anyone who would listen. Two days later, Murcheson kindly suggested she might benefit from some fresh air and relaxation, and Charlotte reluctantly left the station and returned to Honfleur.

More than anything else that had happened, the increasing awareness that her whole mission had been precipitated by a series of lies and misunderstandings depressed Charlotte. None of it had been true, all the way back to the British bluff about having a working doomsday device. True, it had won them the war. But the treaty, the peace, all she had done in France, even Reginald's death, all of it was premised on falsehoods. Real people, people who thought they were doing the right thing, had died over this information but it had all been a game of grown-up make-believe.

Around and around her thoughts raced, and when they weren't chasing after Dubois and the bomb that never was and all that implied, they were circling her relationship with Dexter. She reviewed each encounter, all her words, until she was so tired of thinking about it all she felt like screaming.

Dexter crept into the suite for a few hours each night, trying not wake her as he collapsed on the sitting room sofa, exhausted. By breakfast he would be gone, back at the station, his mind fully occupied with his . . . photo-phoroseismochorinator.

"Multi-hyalchordate Phototransphorinating Seismograph," Dexter repeated patiently when she asked him about his progress on one of the rare occasions she encountered him long enough to converse. "*Hardison's* Multi-hyalchordate Phototransphorinating Seismograph. And it's going quite well, thank you. We've finished laying the glass cables and calibrating the mercury triggers to respond to any minute seismic activity. Now it's just a matter of making sure the central sensors light up when they're supposed to."

She felt redundant. Murcheson refused to let her take the *Gossamer Wing* up anymore, and in any case it was ruined for daytime flight by the dye. COULD MYSTERY BALLOON BE THE WORLD'S SMALLEST MANNED DIRIGIBLE? asked the newspapers.

There had been no further hint of threat from Coeur de Fer or Dubois. Murcheson had sequestered himself in the station. He had been unable to pin the steam-car attack on Dubois as yet, but firmly believed Dubois was responsible.

He considered the attempt proof that Dubois knew of his role with the Agency, and wanted him out of the way to facilitate whatever nefarious political move he and Gendreau had planned. Charlotte simply didn't believe Dubois had ever taken any action on behalf of a greater ideal than his own profit margin, but she had no hard evidence to support her feeling in the matter. She thought Dubois had tried to kill Murcheson, and nearly killed her and Dexter instead, over business, and resented it because that was a circumstance she had never signed on for.

Murcheson discounted her opinion on the matter out of hand, and his refusal to even consider it wearied Charlotte at first. Finally she pushed past the point of disillusionment and into a kind of fatal humor at the absurdity of it all, at Murcheson's insistence that his trouble was the Crown's trouble. She liked him, respected him still, but Charlotte finally accepted that the life-and-death make-believe hadn't ended with the war, and would probably never end. It was the only way people like her father and Murcheson knew how to operate. They would keep this secret war going forever.

Charlotte realized, then and there, that it didn't necessarily have to be *her* secret war. Not anymore. She had a choice.

She had a future in which to make it. And for the first time in years, that future rose up before her as an opportunity, rather than a duty.

To her surprise, once she'd had this epiphany, Charlotte found herself beginning to enjoy the town and the enforced relaxation.

Sipping bitter Turkish coffee and enjoying the salty afternoon breeze off the estuary, Charlotte sat outside an old half-timbered building and watched the meticulously detailed model boats bob along the water. A choir was singing traditional French sea shanties somewhere nearby, and families wandered past on their way home from the festival, exhausted children carrying buckets of shrimp they'd spent the day catching.

Holiday, she finally realized. *I'm on holiday.*

Her last holiday had been her first honeymoon, so she forgave herself for not recognizing it sooner. This was nothing like that trip, or even like her voyage to France with Dexter, all tension and anticipation. This reminded her more of her unplanned day in the countryside, when her soul seemed to calm once she resigned herself to the fact she had nothing to do but wait. She had done all she could.

Charlotte saw the delivery boy bringing the evening paper to the newsstand down the street and abandoned her table only long enough to buy one and return. She flipped it open, and her jaw dropped as she translated the headline. The mystery airship had been forgotten, shoved aside by a more newsworthy story:

ROLAND DUBOIS MURDERED! the paper blared. WEALTHY INDUSTRIALIST STRANGLED BY MYSTERIOUS ASSAILANT IN BRUTAL DAYLIGHT ATTACK.

The police, it seemed, had named no suspects yet. Charlotte suspected immediately who the murderer was, but thought it unlikely the police would ever apprehend him unless French intelligence willed it so. Perhaps she and Dexter had been wrong and Coeur de Fer had never stopped working for the Égalité French, after all. Or perhaps, after years serving the execrable Dubois, he had undergone a change of heart and done away with the villain.

So that was it. Whether Murcheson was right or not, whether Dubois had been plotting with Gendreau to build a doomsday device and take over France or not, it didn't matter anymore. Either way, Charlotte accepted, her part in the intrigue was over.

MARTIN'S HEAD THROBBED in time with his heartbeats. The fever that had plagued him on and off for days seemed to have taken permanent hold now. Even when chills overtook him and sweat poured from his face he could feel the heat, only banked, never extinguished, always ready to return even hotter than before.

Still, it could be an infection. It could be something

treatable, removable. He'd been nearly as sick at least twice before as his body reacted to the metals and other foreign substances attached to it during the implant process. He was lucky, he knew, that the arm had lasted as long as it had, that it hadn't rotted off entirely as often happened with such extensive implants after a few years. Martin's body seemed uniquely amenable to the grafting, but even he had suffered from it on occasion.

The fever is making you stupid, he warned himself. He was still determined to follow through with his recent decision. A surgeon-engineer could take the arm off, but a highly skilled makesmith might be able to locate the poison vial within the workings. Failing that, a makesmith could still perform an amputation if he had to. Without the arm, the poison vial would be no danger, the infection would heal. So Martin's overheated brain insisted, ignoring the quiet voice that said the vial might be anywhere in his body, even inside his skull with the ear implant . . . or the poison might have spread too far to stop it now, no matter where the vial was.

No, it must be the arm. Take the poison out, even if it meant taking the whole arm off, and the world would be right again. His nightmare could actually end. Dubois was dead, and the secretary's delay in "finding" the body had been sufficient to help Martin escape detection. He could be free. He could even make a life.

You're already dead, that maddening little voice whispered, but Martin doggedly continued down the corridor of the hotel, leaning on the maid's cart for support as he pushed it before him. The maid would never miss it, because he had made sure to take it at a time when the housekeeping rounds were well over for the day.

A convenient corner in the hallway would provide him all the cover he needed to await the Makesmith Baron's return, because the man was obviously no agent and would never think to scan the entire hall before approaching his room. Martin had been watching him come and go from Murcheson's factory for three solid days now, and knew

Hardison would also be tired and off guard when he returned from whatever he was doing there. Martin no longer even cared what that was.

He would take Hardison to the place he'd prepared, convince him to remove the arm, and then kill him. One final life taken, to save Martin's own. It would be simple, and Martin reassured himself he would be up to it despite his weakened state, as long as Hardison obliged by being tired and inattentive at the crucial moment.

DEXTER RUBBED HIS eyes, leaning against the back of the lift gratefully as it rose. The attendant smiled politely then ignored him as usual. Dexter was glad for any silence that didn't result from a room full of people waiting for his next instruction.

The project was thrilling, captivating, but after four . . . *five?* . . . days of nearly nonstop work, he was too drained to continue without a decent night's sleep and a large, uninterrupted meal.

He wondered, as he stepped from the lift, whether Charlotte would be in the suite, and whether she would be glad to see him so early in the evening.

Relatively early, he amended. It was almost nine o'clock, but perhaps they might still have time to share dessert. Dexter tried not to think beyond that but he was tired, not dead. He hadn't really intended to neglect her entirely these past few days, but his work at the station simply hadn't allowed him the time to see Charlotte or talk with her, much less attempt anything more intimate. When their paths did cross for a few minutes they were increasingly polite with one another, and he could feel the wedge slipping between them as though it were a physical object.

He had made such a mess of things with Charlotte, but they would be returning to the Dominions soon. Her work for Murcheson seemed to have concluded. The danger was over. Perhaps it was time to broach a discussion of the future, even if she had rebuffed his previous attempts? Even if it wasn't time for that, he still wanted her. That much hadn't changed, and he wasn't above attempting to take advantage of the situation during their last few days in France.

Dexter had to laugh at his own presumption as he fumbled for his key. He was so sleepy already he could barely keep his eyes open to find his way to the room; he'd probably be lucky to make it through dinner, never mind an attempt at seduction.

The maid's cart squeaked behind Dexter and he sped up his search so he could clear the corridor and let her by. He patted his pockets one at a time until he finally located the key. As he lifted it from his pocket in triumph something pricked the back of his neck, making him flinch and slap at the sting.

His last thought as he crumpled over, falling into the cart that seemed to have positioned itself to catch him, was to wonder why he hadn't just knocked on the door so Charlotte could let him in.

THE CLOCK ON the sitting room mantel stood at two minutes to nine. Charlotte sighed in irritation at the noise in the hallway, the squeaking of the cart and the clumsy thumping as the housekeeper fussed with her equipment. After a moment the wheels squeaked away, however, presumably making toward the end of the hall where a corner and an alcove hid the entrance to the service lift.

Nine o'clock.

Charlotte tried to focus on the horrid novel she was reading while she waited for Dexter's return, but something bothered her into looking at the clock once more.

It's nine o'clock.

The maids don't service the rooms at nine o'cl—

She ran to the door, yanking it open to an empty hallway. A few steps away and around the corner, she saw the service lift was already in use. No maid or cart was visible anywhere in the corridor.

Charlotte dashed back to the suite, missing the hint of

brass on the colorful oriental runner. Her bare toe struck something, however, and she looked down as the object skittered into the baseboard with a tiny metallic *chink*.

A key. Their room key. *Dexter's* room key.

"Dexter!"

She ran for the window to signal Murcheson's men, blood rushing in her ears even louder than the ocean.

MARTIN CRANKED THE window down, his need for fresh air trumping his fear of a passerby overhearing a sound from his unwilling passenger.

"I knew you would tax my supply of tranquilizers," he said hoarsely.

Dexter grunted through the gag, and Martin felt the steam car jolt as the large American tried to kick his way out of his bonds.

"I'm very good at knots, my friend. Try all you like. Brute force is not going to help you here."

Another series of grunts. It sounded as though the rat was attempting to scold him around the gag.

Martin chuckled, feeling better than he had in days. He felt purposeful, in control, even hopeful.

Febrile euphoria.

Whatever the reason, he appreciated the respite from heat and pain and despair. He had fully convinced himself, in the days since Dubois's death, that he was not in fact ready to die. Feeling so close to death was unsettling.

Martin's imagination ran over the events of Dubois's last moments, lingering on the way the man's stubby fingers had pushed the button on his triggering device over and over. *Nothing happened.*

The blare of a horn made him jerk his head up, and he yanked the wheel to correct the steam car's course across the narrow bridge. He had been inches from sliding into oncoming traffic.

A whimper from behind him assured him that his passenger had noticed the lapse in attention as well.

"Sorry, my friend. I am not as well as I might be. But you can help me with that, and soon I will be better than ever."

"Can't you make this thing go any faster?"

Charlotte clutched the seat in front of her, urging the driver to push his own limits as well as those of the steam car. Bad enough they were not following Dexter and his abductor, they didn't need to drag their feet not doing it.

"You'll report here," Murcheson had ordered when Charlotte and the two agents outside the hotel notified him. He'd stated in no uncertain terms that only one of the agents was to follow Coeur de Fer, while the other was to bring Charlotte directly to Atlantis Station for further instructions.

Charlotte knew a team was already being assembled, and that the trailing agent would radio Murcheson with whatever information he could. She still would have rather gone after Dexter herself, instead of arriving in the second wave.

The agent watching the front entrance of the hotel had seen Charlotte's frantic signal with a hand torch at the window, and met her in the lobby as she reached the bottom of the stairs, practically flying down the last flight. They joined the agent in the rear of the building just in time to see Coeur de Fer drive away, traveling around the corner from a side street in a steam car.

The second agent hadn't paid attention to the unattractive maid with the laundry cart, naturally. He hadn't seen Coeur de Fer put Dexter into the steam car, but the key and the abandoned cart suggested an abduction. The radio was fired up and Murcheson contacted as the first agent lit out in pursuit of Jacques Martin.

Charlotte had thrown off her dressing gown and pulled on the most practical garments she could find in a hurry, a pair of the new breeches in a soft fawn, some short walking boots, a simple linen shirt cut like a man's and the white leather jacket she'd once worn to pilot the *Gossamer Wing*. She'd neglected a hat, and her hair was still in the long braid she wore it in for sleeping.

"You look like a rebellious young girl," Murcheson said in surprised disapproval when he saw her attire. Perhaps, Charlotte later reflected, that sentiment was behind his ordering her to proceed to the station instead of joining the agents who were already mustering near the factory.

"I can take the *Gossamer Wing* to those coordinates and be there before—"

"And be seen by every security guard or late-working longshoreman from here to the estuary? You'll stay at the station, where I can at least ensure you'll be safe, and you won't present Coeur de Fer with an additional target."

"Where I'll be out of the way, you mean," Charlotte snapped, feeling very much the part of the thwarted youth. She didn't care. She was frantic, her heart pounding, desperate to do *anything* to get to Dexter. Nothing else mattered, and the need was so paramount it crowded out all other thoughts in her mind.

I have to get to him . . .

Murcheson scowled at her, and she lifted a hand to her forehead, pressing against the temptation to cry. She knew it wouldn't help her case if she did, but a voice in her head was screaming for action.

It can't end this way, I was stupid, so stupid . . .

"I have to do *something*."

"You're far too emotionally invested to be objective in this matter, Lady Hardison."

Charlotte didn't attempt to deny it. An idea had started to form in her mind. She closed her mouth and listened in brooding silence as Murcheson briefed his men; then she allowed herself to be escorted down to the tram and into the station with no further protest.

Admiral Neeley barely noticed her arrival, more concerned with an ongoing training exercise than with one off-duty agent at loose ends. He noticed her departure from the bridge still less, and nobody batted an eye at the sight of Lady Hardison making her way down to the miniature submersible's docking bay. She'd spent so much time there already, after all.

Charlotte felt bad about tricking the young technician, but it had to be done. She milked him for the status of the fuel tank, a last few bits of information regarding the navigation system, and then she asked him very sweetly if he could possibly find her a decent cup of tea. It was cruel; she knew the boy was smitten, and she took advantage of him even though she knew he would surely be reprimanded for dereliction of duty. But she needed that submersible. She waited two minutes after he left the lab, then ducked into the *Gilded Lily* and took the little craft down and out into the dark, murky waters of the channel.

Her plan had solidified once she heard the report of where Coeur de Fer had taken Dexter. The agents traveling overland were at a decided disadvantage, Charlotte had realized during the debriefing. They were in steam cars, which ran far slower on average than the speeds the sub was capable of in calm waters. They had to travel on the convoluted byways of the quays of Le Havre, and they were beginning from the Murcheson factory well north of town. From the station, though it was farther away, Charlotte could steer the submersible in nearly a straight line to the dock and the hulk of a decommissioned cargo freighter that Martin was evidently using as a base. What's more, she could use the sub's specialized listening devices to pinpoint their location on the freighter. She might even hear something that could help them take Martin without risking Dexter's life.

The main challenge, as Charlotte saw it, would be maintaining her sanity in the claustrophobic confines of the tiny submersible long enough to get to the docked ship where Jacques Martin was holding Dexter hostage. Once she survived that, she reasoned, the rest of the rescue would seem easy in comparison.

Twenty

❦

LE HAVRE, FRANCE

Icy water splashed over Dexter's head, waking him with
shock, and he blew the salty, stinging stuff from his mouth
and nose as he tried to get his bearings.

His stomach lurched and he choked back vomit, struggling to breathe, panic setting in as he began to remember
his circumstances.

"Bastard!" he sputtered, finally realizing he was no longer gagged and could speak again. Coeur de Fer was standing a few yards away from him, an empty tin bucket next to
his leg. "Where's Charlotte? What have you done with her?"
Dexter rocked back and forth on the chair to which he was
bound, accomplishing nothing but nearly falling over.

The question seemed to surprise his captor. "I have done
nothing with her, monsieur. Have you misplaced her?"

"What?"

They stared at each other, both confused now. Coeur de
Fer finally broke the silence by coughing weakly. He shook
his head and repeated, "I have done nothing with Lady

Hardison, monsieur. I took only you. She will come to no harm, as long as you agree to assist me."

What the hell would you want with me? Dexter couldn't help but think. Despite recent events, he knew he was no spy. Unless Jacques Martin was interested in recent technological advances in seismology, or desperately required a specialized weapon harness or custom-made machinery, Dexter didn't know what he could possibly do for the man. He feared what Martin might ask, knowing that his probable inability to provide whatever it was would most likely result in his death. Everybody knew that was how it worked: when the deranged killer no longer had need of you, he killed you. Usually not in a quick, merciful way.

"Are you after the documents?" It was the only thing Dexter could think of.

"Do you have them?"

"No."

The former spy shrugged. "I suppose it was worth asking."

Dexter looked at Coeur de Fer more closely, noting for the first time that he seemed not so much deranged as exhausted, like a man at the end of a badly frayed rope.

"What did you want them for?" he asked, figuring that if he was to die, at least he might clear some things up first. "Were you already working for Dubois before the treaty?"

Martin slumped back, letting the wall support his shoulders. "In all this time, Whitehall really never worked it out? Moncrieffe's death was even more pointless than I supposed, if so. I wasn't working for Dubois back then, monsieur, I was using the plans to pay him. For these."

He waved his mechanical hand, then used one artificial "finger" to tap the shiny device that replaced his ear. Dexter winced at the unnatural clinking sound.

"Not for the post-royalists? Not . . . not for a return to the old French regime?"

Coeur gave an odd, humorless chuckle. "No. I'm not especially political. If anything, I lean Égalité."

"But you're working for Dubois now."

"No," Coeur de Fer corrected him. "I have been working for myself for days now. Dubois went too far. I may be a monster, but I do have some limits. I put Dubois down like the dog he was. France is better for his absence. Perhaps I'm a patriot after all."

Dexter knew he was just forestalling the inevitable, but he didn't want to ask Martin the reason for his abduction. Once he asked, it was just a short step from Martin realizing Dexter was no use to him. But the man seemed willing enough to converse, even if Dexter was having some trouble following Coeur de Fer's train of thought. He wondered if Charlotte had noted his tardiness. Perhaps she would contact Murcheson if she grew concerned; then they would discover he was missing. *If I can just keep him talking long enough . . .*

"How did Dubois go too far?" The second after he asked, Dexter thought perhaps he should have first said something more conciliatory, like taking issue with Martin's description of himself as a monster. Fortunately, the monster in question seemed to take Dexter's query in stride.

"He was growing nearly as bad as he was during the war, killing indiscriminately to accomplish his goals. In war, this is one thing. In business, it is quite another. He was very put out that none of his attempts on Murcheson succeeded, you know. I thought it was . . . unseemly."

"The factory. And the steam car!" Dexter brightened. "It really was all targeted at Murcheson because of his business, then. Charlotte was right."

"You sound relieved."

"It wasn't you, then?"

"No," Martin confirmed. "Those were both Dubois. I learned about them only after the fact. He would have been just as happy to rid himself of you, however, with the steam car. And I would have gladly killed Lady Hardison to get those plans. Don't feel too relieved."

CHARLOTTE HAD ENSURED the fuel was topped off, but she hadn't asked whether the air supply was adequate. The oxygen meter read as near full, but Charlotte was convinced it must be broken because the air in the minuscule cabin was growing more stale and stifling by the minute.

"Almost there," she encouraged the little craft and herself, consciously loosening her death grip on the steering assembly.

The red proximity light flashed, and Charlotte made out a great black mass looming close in the dark water. The breakwater. She slipped between the seawalls, breathing a shallow sigh of relief as the water calmed all around the *Gilded Lily*. A cargo ship was heading out of port, and she navigated downward to avoid it until her little craft was nearly skimming the sandy floor of the harbor. The ship passed over and out as she traveled under and in, toward the slip where a lone agent waited for backup while a killer threatened the love of her life.

Charlotte stuffed that thought deep down into the recesses of her mind, focusing every scrap of her attention on slow, careful breathing and the navigation instruments before her.

A few minutes later—though it felt like hours—Charlotte steered past a trio of docked freighters and around another breakwater into a smaller, less traveled channel. It was also shallower, and with her hands already shaking on the controls it was all she could do to keep the craft level and avoid any unexpected obstacles. Only the knowledge that she was almost at her destination kept her from breaching the surface and throwing the submersible's hatch up to gasp for air.

There it is. She double-checked all the instruments and her map against the coordinates and topographical sketches she'd jotted down during the briefing, while Murcheson's attention was elsewhere. The decrepit freighter, destined for the slag heap soon, didn't merit a slot at Dubois's primary docks. It was moored by itself in this less convenient byway, and it made the perfect hideout for Coeur de Fer.

As she neared the old ship, Charlotte considered what to do next. Slipping her craft beneath the freighter, she observed the layout of the dock before maneuvering to one end of it and coming closer to the surface. Despite the risk of being seen, she raised the periscope and surveyed the dock and the freight yard beyond, hoping for something to confirm she was in the right place.

Right there. The periscope, more sensitive than the human eye, picked up the outline of a man crouching between two shipping containers. Charlotte fiddled with the focus and gave her eyes a moment to make sense of the dark scene; after a short time, she was able to make out more details. A pair of binoculars aimed at the ship, a portable radio communicator slung over the man's shoulder on a broad strap.

As she watched, he took a tiny spider-car from a pouch, then whipped a weighted cable around his head like bolas, finally letting it fly in an arc toward the ship. A moment later, he sent the car zipping up the line. Charlotte assumed it carried a beacon or transmitter of some kind.

The memory of Dexter showing her the gadget's prototype made her throat tighten, and Charlotte had to force her mind back to the dilemma at hand. Lowering the periscope, she spent a minute trying to visualize the interior plan of a cargo ship before tilting her sub down again and swinging underneath the massive hull.

"All right, Jacques Martin. If I were an insane former spy bent on wrongdoing, where on this thing would I hide my prisoner?"

After picking a possible location more or less at random, Charlotte set out to recall how to operate the sub's listening system. The trick was to place the "ear" in such a way that it attached to the hull silently—a matter of the proper finesse with the controls for the automatonic arm on which the microphone was attached—and then used the hull itself as a sort of speaker, channeling sound from within the vessel.

Charlotte had watched the technician demonstrate the controls for the listening device's extension arm, but it was harder than it looked. At first she couldn't get the arm moving at all, then she found herself confused about up and down, and ended up shooting the thing straight out and into the hull.

She winced and waited, praying that the acoustic padding on the ear's exterior kept it from clanging when it struck the ship.

A minute went by, then two, and when nothing happened she gingerly took the controls and tried again.

This time she managed to position the arm properly and bring the ear to lie flat against the hull as the technician had shown her, but the telephonic earpiece inside the ship remained silent but for a few creaking noises.

Charlotte tried tweaking the volume and sensitivity controls, but all she accomplished was half-deafening herself with the same echoing creaks.

Another spot, then. She retracted the arm and turned back to the sub's instrument panel. Her hands trembled and she had to put her head down on the steering rig for a moment while a wave of dizzy fear swept over her. She was hyperventilating again, she realized, and forced herself to control her breathing until the tingling, numb lightheadedness passed and she could once again handle the controls.

Time was passing, and Dexter was inside that ship somewhere with a madman, and so far she had been no help at all.

MARTIN HAD PLANNED to beat Hardison first, to assert his dominance and apply a healthy dose of pain and fear. It was a crude method of establishing control, and not his first choice, but he knew he was on a short timetable.

When it came time, however, he was mortified to realize he was far too weak to do the thing at all, much less do it properly. And Hardison was a brute, a big village blacksmith of a man, not an effete aristocrat; he would take more than the standard beating, unless Martin missed his guess. A few taps wouldn't affect him at all.

The last of the tranquilizer was wearing off too, Martin could tell. Hardison's questions were growing more pointed and he was alert, scanning his surroundings when he thought Martin wasn't looking. He'd given up his earlier effort to force his way out of the knots, but from the slight movements of his arms Martin deduced he was still working at his bonds as he spoke.

The knots would hold, Martin wasn't concerned about that. But Hardison was dangerous, even lashed to a chair. Martin needed leverage, which he didn't have.

"What do you want with me?" the man finally asked.

"Once we get to our destination," Martin said, making a show of checking his watch, "I'll be taking you to a medical facility where my men will supervise as you do some maintenance on my arm. We should arrive in a few hours."

I'll use my last dose of tranquilizer on you, move you to the cargo bay where the operating theater is set up and hope Claude and Jean-Louis show up when they're supposed to.

"Maintenance?" Hardison sounded skeptical. "Implants are hardly my specialty. I'm not a surgeon-engineer."

"This will be simple," Martin assured him. "Merely removing something that never should have been there in the first place. Nothing integral to the function of the arm."

Perhaps he really can do it. Take the poison vial out but leave the arm in place.

"You're ill," said his prisoner bluntly. "Too ill to take anesthetic."

Martin clenched his teeth. The man was no doctor, how would he know? "It's an infection. A reaction to the implants. Not uncommon."

"Your face, your hand . . . they're bright pink, you know. The skin on your palm is peeling. You're in a constant sweat, and you can barely stand. In the past few minutes you seem to have started struggling for air," Hardison pointed out. "Your speech is beginning to slur. This is no infection, nor is it a reaction to the implants. I think we both know what this is, and that there's nothing I can do to stop it."

The man seemed to realize only after the fact what a risk he'd taken, detailing the situation to Martin that way. His chin came up, belligerent, daring his captor to take issue with what he'd said.

Martin looked down at his hand, turning it over and examining the palm where, just as Hardison said, skin was peeling off in flakes and translucent white curls. He was dying by inches, disintegrating one very thin layer at a time.

"We both know what this is? Suppose you tell me, monsieur."

He knew what he would hear before the Makesmith Baron spoke.

"Poison. Mercuric cyanide, if I had to guess. I saw a chemical metallurgist die of it once, although in his case it took months. All from a single accidental drop on his skin. The symptoms were the same, however, and they're quite distinctive. I'm . . . I'm sorry for you."

He was sorry, Martin could tell. Naïve though the sentiment seemed, it made a difference. Martin hadn't believed Dubois, hadn't even quite believed himself. He believed Dexter Hardison, though, about both the poison and the sympathy.

It really is over.

"This was more than just a drop, I suspect," he said softly, with a wry smile.

THE NEXT ATTEMPT to place the listening ear had gone more smoothly than the first, but Charlotte still heard nothing when she bent to the earpiece. It made the sound of the ocean, nothing more.

"Damn it!"

The craving to pilot the sub upward again, crack the surface and swing the hatch up, was almost too great to resist. The cabin seemed so small she could barely move inside it now. The atmosphere was thick and heavy with fear. Her fingertips tingled constantly, buzzing with tension from her taut shoulders and her ongoing struggle to keep from hyperventilating into unconsciousness. Her head was throbbing, stomach churning, and Charlotte thought if she ever escaped the submersible she would never, never allow herself to be put into such a tiny enclosure again. She would live on her front lawn, if need be, weather and elements be damned.

Closing her eyes, she tried to imagine herself on the *Gossamer Wing*. Soaring through open air, the whole world below like a picture from a storybook, a chill but bracing breeze on her face.

Soon, she promised herself. *Dexter first.*

She would make one more attempt. One more try at finding them, getting a read on the situation, anything she could learn to tell the agents speeding to Dexter's rescue, to make it safer for him when they went in.

Really, she just wanted to reassure herself that he was alive.

Charlotte piloted the craft down the length of the ship and stopped midway before turning and cranking the handle to maneuver the extendable arm out once more.

Thinking about it less, and barely looking at the viewfinder, she had better luck. The ear pressed flat against the hull and sealed itself there on the first attempt, and a startled laugh bubbled up as Charlotte leaned down and twisted the earpiece toward her ear.

"If I'd known it was that easy I would have just tried doing it blind from the start," she muttered to herself. Then she stopped breathing as she heard a voice from the earpiece.

"Even if I could remove it, there's no antidote for . . ."

Dexter!

The connection was feeble, and Charlotte turned the volume higher once more, straining to catch as much as she could; she didn't dare risk attempting another placement of the listening device.

"Was in a vault in his office. He claimed to have destroyed it."

That was Coeur de Fer's voice, she supposed. He spoke remarkably clear English.

"He was lying," Dexter replied. "There's no known antidote

for mercuric cyanide. It kills some fast, some more slowly, depending on the victim and the dosage. But either way it's death, and not a very nice one. Taking the arm off now wouldn't do a thing to help."

"I should have known. He never did have any honor."

"Look, I know this ship isn't really moving, there's no engine vibration. We could just go ashore right now. If you went to a hospital they might be able to make you more comfortable," Dexter suggested.

Coeur de Fer chuckled. "Good effort, my friend, but I think not. I do not care to spend my last few days—"

"Hours," corrected Dexter.

"Or even my last few hours—in a jail cell as a murderer and a traitor."

"Understandable. Are you going to kill me?"

Charlotte gasped to hear Dexter's direct question. *Don't put ideas into his head*, she thought.

"Probably not," the dying spy conceded. "I don't think I have the strength. You can tell my story after I'm gone, I think."

"What version would you like me to tell?" Dexter inquired, his dry humor coming through even over the earpiece in the submersible. Charlotte smiled, touching a finger to the device. He wasn't even attempting to trick his kidnapper, to plead or lie or wheedle his way out, she thought with a hint of pride. He was just . . . being Dexter.

"One that finally gives Simone Vernier the recognition she deserves, and that casts Dubois as the fiend of the piece."

"From what I gather that wouldn't be too difficult. I'd only have to tell the truth, then, wouldn't I?"

She was astonished. *A joke*. There he was, being held captive on a derelict freighter in a remote by-water by a rogue agent who very likely planned to murder him, and Dexter was making *jokes* with the man. Amazing.

Martin didn't seem to mind. "It was all just about money to him, you know? Dubois. He claimed to care about France, about pushing the British out. But that was never the true reason. He just wanted to make the war go on, so his contract would go on too and he would make more money. Always more. That's why he wanted to kill Murcheson, to eliminate his competition for the steamrail project. He didn't do it for any noble cause, not for France; he did it for himself. He made a traitor of me too, which saddens me. I would not have had my life end in this disloyalty."

After a pause, Dexter spoke again. "Perhaps it doesn't have to. I think we might be able to reach an agreement."

TWENTY-ONE

❧❧

LE HAVRE, FRANCE

CHARLOTTE FINALLY LIFTED the hatch to the submersible to find a row of pistols pointed at her from the dock.

"Lady Hardison?" one of the men asked, clearly in shock.

The weapons wavered then lowered as she clambered from the sub to the dock with the help of the agent who had recognized her first.

"You need to get back, ma'am. If you take cover behind one of the shipping crates, that should—"

"Put your weapons away," she demanded. "I don't need to take cover. I think they're about to come out."

"Lady Hardison," another of the agents said, "our priority is to take down Jacques Martin. We need to take that ship. We'll do everything we can to avoid collateral harm, but you really must—"

"No, I mustn't," Charlotte insisted, alarmed. "I heard Dexter and Martin talking. Dexter is in no danger from him right now, but that could change if Coeur de Fer is threatened by a bunch of hotheaded idiots waving guns in his face."

"I don't think you're aware of all the circumstances, my lady."

"I don't think you're aware of the danger your career is in with this agency if my father learns that his son-in-law negotiated himself out of a hostage situation only to be killed by friendly fire."

Charlotte knew Murcheson had remained at his factory, in an attempt to preserve his cover should it be intact after the events of the past few days. She found herself longing for the man's presence, even if he had been a bit paternalistic earlier, because he would at least have listened to her. She had no assurance these men would. They had all put their guns away, but it seemed obvious they were only moments away from deploying them again to go after their quarry.

"Please," she begged. "Don't storm the ship. Give Dexter just a little more time. Just . . . just ten minutes. If he doesn't come out with Coeur de Fer by then, you can go in and do your worst."

"We have our orders, ma'am." He stepped toward Charlotte, reaching for her arm. She backed away nimbly, drawing her pistol from its holster on her thigh.

"I don't give a damn what your orders are, I know what I heard and I won't let any of you risk my husband's life." The men stood stunned, hands halted on the way back to their own weapons. She'd drawn too quickly for them to respond in time, however. Clearly they hadn't been expecting anything like this from Charlotte. She wondered briefly if it was her size, her gender or the situation that had put them off guard.

"Lady Hardison," the agent in charge said slowly, "put your weapon down. You don't want to do this." He sounded as though he were trying to placate a child.

Charlotte backed another few steps away and fixed the group with a glare. "You're making a grave error to think I won't shoot. Do you really think I value any of your lives more highly than my husband's? You there!" she snapped at the agent standing farthest from her, "hands where I can see them. All of you, hands up. If anybody else tries reaching for a pistol, he'll be shot for his trouble. I won't kill you but I will incapacitate you if I have to."

The agent moved his hand away from the holster and raised his arms. The others followed suit, looking miserable and baffled about what to do next.

Charlotte kept the gun trained on the lead agent and pulled out her pocket chronometer. "Ten minutes. That's all I asked for, that's reasonable, and if he doesn't come out by then we'll . . . reevaluate."

"Three minutes," offered the agent.

She shook her head. "You're still not taking me seriously, are you? I don't want to have to shoot you, but I will not let you board that ship, sir. Don't try my patience. You're in no position to negotiate."

"Murcheson will see you hanged if you're wrong, Lady Hardison."

"My father is more frightening than Murcheson, trust me."

The noise of a hatch creaking open alerted Charlotte even before the agents' amazed glances did, and she had to resist the urge to turn her head to see whether it was Dexter or Martin standing on the deck of the ship.

"I'm all right. I'm coming down," Dexter called out. "Please don't shoot."

As the wave of relief struck her, Charlotte's hand began to tremble. She forced herself to breathe steadily and stay focused on the agents in front of her as Dexter spoke again.

"Mr. Martin is coming with me," he told them. "Please, ah, don't shoot him either. I've given him my word he won't be hurt. Charlotte, what's going on down there?"

"Have you been harmed, Lord Hardison?" the lead agent called. His hand twitched down as though he were thinking of reaching for his gun, then snapped back up again when Charlotte made a warning noise.

"No, not really," Dexter said. "Have you?"

With a feeble smile, Charlotte replied, "I haven't shot anyone yet. These gentlemen are rather set on killing Mr. Martin, though. Shall I keep them from doing that?"

"I suppose so. We're coming down, but this gangplank will take me a moment. I'll have to do it myself, Monsieur Martin is in no shape to help," Dexter explained as he started turning the giant crank to extend and lower the gangplank to the dock. From the corner of her eye, Charlotte could see the mechanism working.

Then there was a moment of silence, and she backed up even more to put the gangplank between herself and the agents, so she could see Dexter. He stood at the top with an arm braced around his slender, pale, black-suited companion.

"All right. Don't shoot," Dexter warned them again, though the agents made no move toward their weapons. "He's dying already, anyway, so there would really be no point."

Dying? Charlotte watched them descend, the sight confirming Dexter's words. Martin was obviously sick unto death, his breath a rasping wheeze, his legs barely able to support his trembling body. As they approached the circle of watery light provided by the dock's single lamp, Charlotte could see that Coeur de Fer was flushed an unnatural pink, and drenched with sweat.

"Dear God. You can lower your weapon now, Lady Hardison," the agent in charge said as Dexter stopped by a piling and lowered Martin to sit on the rough stump. "Your husband is right, there would be no point to shooting this man. He's done for. Stand down, gentlemen."

Charlotte considered him for a moment, then cocked her pistol back and flicked the safety on before tucking it back into its holster. She turned to Dexter, who was still bending over the crumpled husk of a man he'd half-carried off the ship.

"He has a story to tell," he explained, straightening to look at the agents and Charlotte.

Coeur de Fer nodded, then took a breath and began. "Seven years ago, I sold my soul . . ."

THE AGENTS HAD gathered around Coeur de Fer, straining to hear his voice, one of them writing it all down in a notebook he'd procured from somewhere. From time to time in the narrative, one or another of them would exclaim as another years-old mystery was resolved.

Murder and sabotage, callous cruelty and greed. If half what Martin said were true, Dubois was a monster indeed, even worse than the sort Murcheson had suspected him of being. And Coeur de Fer had been his creature, trapped into service by his own ambition and poor choices.

"Simone Vernier probably had all the information she needed to have Dubois strung up. If she had only lived long enough to report . . ." The British agent's voice trailed off as he considered what might have happened had Dubois received the justice he'd deserved back then, when he really had been committing deliberate treason, actively conspiring against the ruling faction of the French government in hopes of derailing the treaty process.

"Ah, but if she had, she would have probably also gotten those notes to our superiors, and if that had happened the French might never have come to the negotiating table with the British," Martin countered. "Who ever knows about these things? That was one of Dubois's mistakes, thinking he could predict the outcome of such complicated plans."

An ambulance siren sounded in the distance, approaching rapidly. Martin reached out, clutching Dexter's forearm. "My mother is Marie-Terese Imbert. She lives in Bayeux. See that she gets my remains, at least the metal. I am worth far more dead than alive, and I should like to be some good to her after all these years."

"I will," Dexter assured him.

A fit of coughing and retching overwhelmed Martin, and he could barely speak by the time he regained what little breath was left to him.

"I was Jean-Michel Imbert once," he whispered. He swayed on his post, and Dexter leaned in to support him again. "My greatest regret was letting my mother think I had died. But I couldn't let her know what I had become."

Dexter thought of his own mother, several years widowed but nevertheless peaceful and happy, and extravagantly proud of her son. She had cried at his wedding. That had been *his* great regret, lying to his mother about Charlotte and the marriage, but he'd known she would forgive him after the fact and be proud of him for serving the Crown so selflessly. He was struck by how fortunate he was, and how ridiculous it was that he took his luck for granted most of the time.

"Perhaps you'll last long enough to talk to her yourself," he comforted Martin, but the other man shook his head.

"Thank you, my friend," he whispered. Dexter could barely hear him. "You've rid me of the poison after all."

As the attendants swarmed down from the ambulance and muscled the nearly dead Jacques Martin into a gurney, Dexter stepped away and walked toward Charlotte. She stood several yards from the frantically active scene, staring at Martin. Dexter couldn't read her expression, but she was so beautiful it made his breath catch in his throat.

Her hair fell over her shoulder in a loose plait, stray curls catching the rays of the cheap floodlight in a halo around her head. The white jacket she wore was fastened up tight against the chill. She wore holsters on both thighs, a pistol in one and a wicked knife in the other, and on the whole she gave the appearance of a dangerous but angelic child. A fierce guardian spirit. A creature of myth.

Too good to be true, he told himself. *Too good to be true for me.*

"You forgive him, and I can't," she greeted him. She didn't sound angry, just puzzled and exhausted.

Dexter stopped short a few feet away from her. "What makes you say I forgive him?" He wasn't so sure, himself, that he'd forgiven anything. The man had nearly killed them both, by his own hand or by proxy. He'd chased them, and then drugged and kidnapped Dexter. Charlotte had lost her husband to the man. It would take a great deal to forgive all that.

"Maybe not forgive. But you pity him. I was so frightened when I realized he'd taken you, but all the time you felt for him. I still see a monster."

"Dubois was the monster. Martin did terrible things," Dexter said, "but in his own mind he didn't have much choice."

"We always have a choice."

After an awkward silence, Dexter cleared his throat. "This wasn't quite the greeting I expected. And not the one I'd planned. Thank you for coming to my rescue, Charlotte."

Charlotte shook her head. "No. I just kept the agents from rushing in. You rescued yourself. You were so reasonable in there. So . . . kind."

"Why don't I feel complimented?"

Dexter was irked, in fact. He was tired, very tired. He wanted a substantial kiss and a great deal of coddling, and instead Charlotte seemed too stunned at his forgiving nature, too awed by his supposed *kindness* to provide those things.

"I'm sorry. You should feel complimented. I'm . . ." She blinked back tears, shaking her head sharply then flinging herself at him in a ferocious embrace. "I'm just so glad you're not dead!"

"That's better," Dexter chuckled into her neck.

"What?"

"Nothing."

He wrapped his arms around her, dipping down and picking her up by the waist for a few seconds. Amazed, as always, by how light she was. He set her down gently and framed her face with his hands, wiping a tear away with one thumb.

"I just realized, you came all the way here in the submersible, didn't you? I can't believe you did that for me. That was very brave of you."

Charlotte nodded. "Murcheson may be less than pleased, though."

"You did it without his permission?" Dexter asked, taken aback.

She blushed as she confessed, "I did it against his express orders to stay at the station."

Dexter frowned. "My knight in shining armor. But you took too great a risk holding the agents off like that. They had their orders to follow. You can't go drawing weapons on your own side, Charlotte. Murcheson will be even less pleased about that than about the sub."

"Sir? Ma'am? We're heading back to the station. We'll need you to come with us."

Dexter ignored the agent who'd spoken, and indulged in another few seconds of staring at Charlotte. She licked her lips and offered a tentative smile, and Dexter couldn't help himself. He bent and kissed her as chastely as he could manage, then pulled away long before he wanted to and nodded at the waiting agent.

"I'll meet you there, I suppose," Charlotte said. "I'll have to take the sub back to base."

"It's already on its way there, Lady Hardison," the agent told her, as he set off for the waiting steam car, clearly expecting them to follow. "I sent Jensen with it. Boss's orders."

"Oh. I see," she responded, and shot a guilty glance at Dexter. "I'm already in disgrace, I suppose."

He took her hand in his. "Not if I have anything to say about it."

THE AMBULANCE SPED toward the hospital, steam engine roaring and the stoker working constantly to keep the fuel and water levels steady. Jean-Michel Imbert had just enough consciousness left to wonder why they bothered to hurry. The poison had nearly finished its work inside him, he could tell. He would be surprised to survive the trip.

At least I die as myself, he thought. *At least Dubois died first.*

He hoped that Hardison would hold to his word and see that his mother got his body. Between the arm and the ear, he was probably carrying close to a pound of gold around inside himself; as the least reactive metal, it was the standard for lining implants, and his were top-of-the-line models.

I always loved you, Simone. He wondered if he would see her in heaven, some special section set aside for people like them who had done terrible things in the service of a greater good.

"Simone," he whispered.

"Shh," the attendant sitting next to him said. "Save your strength, monsieur."

"For what?" Jean-Michel wondered. He thought he said it aloud, but the medic didn't respond so perhaps not.

For what, indeed? When it came to the moment of truth, it seemed, dying was really quite easy. Painful, yes, but it required no action on his part. He could struggle or he could give in, but he would die either way.

Jean-Michel decided he had struggled quite enough; it was finally time to give in.

TWENTY-TWO

HONFLEUR AND LE HAVRE, FRANCE

TO CHARLOTTE'S DISMAY, once she and Dexter finished their debriefing and returned to Honfleur things seemed to go back to exactly the way they had been.

Dexter slept for half the day then returned to the station, eager to finish the work on his seismograph. Charlotte went to the station as well, where she received an official suspension from duty for her unauthorized use of the submersible and for interfering with the other agents. The paperwork made no mention of her pulling a weapon on them, a small concession to the fact that her argument for not storming the freighter had proven accurate. Murcheson strongly implied she was lucky to get off so lightly, however, and that her interests might best be served by resigning her position as a field agent upon her return to the Dominions.

"I'm better at desk work anyway," she admitted.

"It was bad luck about the airship," Murcheson offered, though it was cold comfort. Charlotte missed her dirigible keenly. Martin—Imbert—had admitted to tipping off the press about it. "Perhaps the Agency will be willing to try again in another few years."

"Will you tell me something?" she asked Murcheson before she left Atlantis Station for the last time. "It's about Reginald."

"Anything I can, my dear."

"When Dexter asked about that night Reginald took the documents, you said something about Reginald going up the *side* of the Opéra. I was just curious what you meant? Was there scaffolding there at the time? If there was, why didn't Martin—Imbert, I mean—just follow him up? It must have taken much longer to pick the locks and use the stairs inside."

Murcheson shook his head. "No, Reginald scaled the side, like a monkey. You know how acrobatic he was. The boy left everybody in the dust during training whenever the job was to climb a wall or scramble up a rope."

"I'm sorry?" Charlotte felt like she'd been caught in the wrong conversation. "I was talking about Reginald. My late husband."

"Yes. Moncrieffe. Skinny chap, tall, very fit, spectacles, good at maths? Moncrieffe."

"But . . . but Reginald hated sport. He wasn't remotely athletic. We used to laugh about that, about how in school he never played for the teams, he always—"

"Oh, dear. No, of course he wouldn't have, would he? They wouldn't let him. He was usually a good many years younger than the other boys in his form, as quickly as he went through."

Charlotte nodded. "That makes sense." Something still struck her as strange about it, though.

Murcheson reached over and took one of her hands, patting it kindly. "I forget how young you both were. My dear, I have a question for you. Do *you* like sport?"

"No," Charlotte said immediately. "I enjoy riding but on the whole I've never been a fan. Particularly of anything involving teams."

"Yes, I see. And Reginald knew of this, I suppose?"

She considered it for a moment. Had he known? He must have. She had never held back her opinion on the matter. Far from it, in fact—there might have been a certain amount of open scorn. "I think he must have."

"I think it's possible he wasn't so much averse to athletics, then, as keen to share *your* aversion. He did like to impress you, you know. But when you weren't looking, he was a demon on the cricket pitch for the interagency team. And the lad could scale a sheer wall like a lemur on cocaine."

She smiled at the image, even as her heart ached to learn this new thing about Reginald, too late for it to do any good.

"He should have just told me," she sighed. "It's not as though I would have minded. Why would he be so dishonest?"

Murcheson patted her hand again, seeming to cast about for the right words. "He was young and in love," he finally said, "and desperate to marry you. He was hardly the first man to lose his head under those circumstances and do stupid things in an effort to present himself in the best possible light. You shouldn't think ill of him for it."

Charlotte nodded, but her mind was already elsewhere. On Dexter, his calm and steady voice in the bowels of the rusty freighter, saving his own life simply by being himself.

She might have discussed this with Dexter, but he had sent her a terse message to the effect that he would be remaining at the station for the duration of his work there. Charlotte took to walking the quaint streets of Honfleur and second-guessing all her own choices of the past several years until she thought she'd go mad with the knowledge that she had let a vital moment pass her by. She'd been too overwhelmed by the events of that night on the dock to simply state her mind to Dexter, and having failed to do it at once she had lost her nerve and her opportunity.

The newspapers were diverting for a time, as they were full of the scintillating tale of the heroic agent who sacrificed everything to reveal a traitor to France. True to the promise he'd made the dying man, Dexter had convinced Murcheson and the somewhat bewildered head of French intelligence that Martin's death could be a public relations opportunity for them both. The official story was that Coeur de Fer, really Jean-Michel Imbert, had spent seven years in deep cover to expose Dubois. He had done it, the papers claimed, for the love of France and the love of Simone Vernier, the notorious femme fatale who had died in pursuit of the truth about Dubois and his involvement in an attempt to prolong the war.

Charlotte liked the story. Enough of it was true that she forgave the French government their hyperbole in reclaiming Coeur de Fer's achievement for their own. Whitehall too had conspired in the story to cast Dubois in the worst possible light. He became the violent extremist they had always suspected him of being, seeking the steamrail contract only as a stepping stone to effect greater, unspecified evils against the state. Imbert had stopped him just in time to avert calamity. There were strong hints that Dubois had been seeking out mad engineers to build him a doomsday device of his own; this was treated as de facto proof of his desire for world domination and general malfeasance. Of Gendreau, the papers said nothing. The man himself had returned to St. Helena, his exile reinstated.

Charlotte knew this whole approach was more about political convenience than anything else; the current powers wanted to discredit not only Dubois but the politicians and old government officials he'd been aligned with—the faction that had fallen from power shortly before the treaty was signed. Still, that version of events lent a romanticism to Imbert's deeds, and perhaps because of the propaganda she found herself able to forgive him just a little for his actions toward her, Dexter and Murcheson.

More cold comfort. Charlotte was tired of France. She no longer hated the French, but she longed to be back home, hearing the comfortably familiar accents of the Dominions. The prospect of Reginald's big, empty house was less alluring. It had never felt like home to her. She had felt more at home with Dexter, even those last few fraught days before his abduction, than she had ever been in the house her late husband had left to her.

She and Reginald had never shared that house, never even stood in it together. Their first time there would have been when they returned from their honeymoon, ready to start their married life together. That day had never come, and Charlotte thought she'd been suspended ever since, unable to move forward. But the only one holding her back was herself.

I just want to go home. But how?

IT WAS FINISHED. The last cable had been laid and tested, the technicians thoroughly trained and vetted. They had even been favored with a live test in the form of a slight tremor from the fault along the chalk lithosome to the east, and the system had worked beautifully. The switch was triggered, the silent beam of light shot from the remote sensor back along the glass cable to the station, and the alarm had gone up, just as Dexter had envisioned. The station crew had evacuated safely, and Dexter had been hailed by one and by all.

The next day, as Dexter made his final adjustments, Murcheson handed him a pair of tickets for a fast clipper ship departing Le Havre for New York in the morning.

"There's really no reason to stay any longer," Murcheson told him. "Your work is done here, and Lady Hardison will need to report to the Agency offices in New York soon to discuss reassignment. This won't be as comfortable as a luxury liner but it'll get you home in half the time."

"What will happen to her?" Dexter still thought Murcheson might have turned a blind eye to Charlotte's escapades if he'd wanted to. None of his arguments on her behalf seemed to carry any weight, however. Dexter suspected Lord Darmont's hand in having her sent down from field work.

"I think they have some decoding for her to do," Murcheson replied. "The same sort of thing she was doing before. She's quite good at it."

Dexter nodded. "I'm sure she is."

I just don't know that she ever liked it much, he thought. It had been an interest she shared with Reginald. They had often worked together, she'd mentioned, but she'd begun pressing for field work shortly after his death. She liked to *do* things. Fly dirigibles and test her nerve in subs and dance around lampposts while wearing trousers. Charlotte strode around Paris and cased opera houses, braved wild cows and shopped like a demon even in provincial French villages.

It broke his heart to think of her withering away in a dusty office, nose pressed to a stack of encrypted pages. Never flying again.

Dexter knew he should be racing for the hotel to let Charlotte know about the tickets so she could pack. He wasn't sure why he was dragging his feet.

Letdown, probably. He wanted to be home again—his head was full of ideas for when he got back to his workshop—but he felt like he still had things left to do in France.

The marriage ends when the mission ends. Dexter put his tools away in their cases and the cases into the trunks, his hands moving automatically as his mind poked and prodded at the dilemma.

She'd sent him a message at the station, asking after his health, reminding him that he was welcome at the hotel if he needed to sleep. Dexter had stayed away, even as he'd cursed himself for doing it. He avoided her because he didn't want to discuss the end of things, didn't want to do or say something and realize, "this is the last time."

The same wish for avoidance spurred Dexter's irritation when he opened the door to his berth on the fast clipper only to discover the tiny space crowded with Charlotte's trunks in addition to his own. Unlike the cruise ship, the clipper featured Spartan accommodations even in first class. With all the luggage, there was barely enough room to walk from the hatch to the bunk.

Blast.

He wondered if he'd be able to find a steward and sort out

the mess before the ship embarked. The citrusy scent of Charlotte's perfume already wafted about the cabin, and Dexter was damned if he'd spend the next several days steeping in that fragrance. It was already hard enough to forget their last time together—the night of the steam car explosion in Paris—without having a constant olfactory reminder of the woman to whom he would shortly no longer be married.

Damn. Damn!

"Damn!" he repeated aloud.

"Language, sweetiekins."

DEXTER SIGHED AS he turned around to face her. "Your bags were put in my berth by mistake. I was just going to find a steward to move them. Which cabin are you in?"

Charlotte steadied herself against the force of his glare. She saw this flash of honest irritation as an improvement over not seeing him at all. Avoiding her hadn't seemed like him at all. Anything was better than Dexter not being himself.

"I'm in this one."

"You're in—no, this is mine. Oh, never mind. Let's both go. The bursar can sort it out."

"No. There's nothing to sort out. We're *both* in this one."

"Bloody hell."

She pressed forward, forcing him to back up, and closed the hatch behind her. "You've been avoiding me for days. This will give us a chance to talk."

With no room to maneuver, Dexter gave up and sat on the bunk. "You arranged this? On *purpose*?"

"You sound horrified. That's not entirely flattering." She threw her hat atop the nearest trunk and pulled her gloves off in relief. It was another unusually warm day in Le Havre, and Charlotte was eager for the ship to cast off so she could enjoy the cool ocean breeze.

Her reticule still hung on her wrist, and before she set it aside she pulled Murcheson's curio box from it, presenting it to Dexter atop her palm. He took it and turned it around in his fingers, not saying anything.

Charlotte swallowed nervously, unsure how to proceed.

Best to just jump in, start talking and something will come to me, she decided at last. "I'm no good at those things, and you are. Will you show me how to open it?"

Dexter raised his eyebrows. "Just like that? You're through trying?"

"It's not my strength," she shrugged. "I don't really care about how it's done, I just like the result. Show me, please?"

Dexter turned the ornate little cube over once more and pointed to an inlaid starburst pattern on one face. "You see this? The circle around the star? Look here, there's a seam."

Charlotte bent to scrutinize the wooden box, tracing a fingertip where he indicated. She couldn't see it but she could feel it, an indentation slightly greater than that of the inlay itself.

"You take two fingers and press, then twist," Dexter demonstrated, "and it opens."

The curio box fanned out into its star-like pattern on his hand; he started the music and handed the box over to Charlotte.

It seemed so easy now that she knew the trick. "I wasn't even close," she admitted, "I never would have thought to try that. Have you worked out some secret spy use for it yet?"

"No. I like it just as it is."

They listened to the Mozart for a few measures, then Dexter cupped a hand over the box and closed it up again to silence it, setting it aside on the railed shelf over the bunk.

"So this is our last hurrah?"

Charlotte ignored his question and asked one of her own. "Do you know what I think I'll do when we get back home?" She continued once Dexter had shaken his head. "I think I'm going to quit the Agency and try my hand at being a dauntless society matron who embraces charitable causes and spends a great deal of time and effort cultivating roses that win awards in local flower shows."

"I see."

"I'm tired, is the thing. Tired of pretending to be one thing and secretly being another. Tired of never knowing where people stand on anything. All this pretense, it's exhausting after a while. I don't know how my mother's managed it all these years."

Dexter was starting to eye her as if she'd sprouted a horn in her forehead or an extra nose, but Charlotte pressed forward, though even she wasn't quite sure where she was headed.

"My mother has pretended all her life not to know what my father's profession is. And he's always pretended to be a silly stuffed shirt peer who simply travels a great deal. It's ridiculous. She knows, why pretend? I've never understood it.

"Even Reginald, telling me he hated sport when in reality he was apparently a gifted lemur. I mean acrobat. He even lied about being good at cricket, all because he thought that was what *I* wanted in a man. Because *I* didn't like those things."

Dexter coughed into his hand. "Reginald was a lemur?"

"No, no. He just . . . I praised him for his mind, but I would have loved the rest too. I would have even cheered him on. I could have been *that* wife to him, that wife who tolerates a lot of talk about googlies and innings. But I never had the chance, because he never showed me all of who he was."

"All right. I agree, that does sound silly. I'm still not clear on why your bags are here."

He shifted his weight forward as if to stand, and Charlotte panicked. She put a hand on each of his shoulders and pressed back, tipping herself halfway into his lap in the effort to keep him from leaving.

"I'm doing a terrible job of explaining," she said. Then she kissed him, leaning into it until, like a switch flipping on, he started kissing her back.

Kissing felt right, kissing made sense, and when Dexter pulled her down to the bed and rolled her under him that made even more sense. Touching him again was like a cool drink of water after a long, hot day; it restored some parched part of her spirit.

"You always show people all of who you are," Charlotte said when they came up for air and lay panting, staring at one another. "Except this past week, you've been avoiding me and I haven't known what you were thinking, and I've hated it."

"You said you didn't want to talk about what happened when we got home," he reminded her. "I couldn't face you when that was *all* I wanted to talk about."

"I was wrong," Charlotte admitted. "I was stupid. I want the other Dexter back, the one who fixes my ears, and cares whether I come back when I'm expected, and holds me in the dark and makes me *want* to feel things for the first time in years." Saying it aloud took a weight from her heart.

He grinned and brushed his lips against hers. "It really was also that I was just so busy. The whole team was. It was quite an undertaking, getting the whole system installed in such a short time. I'll probably have to return within the next year or so to make adjustments and take some readings. Particularly if I want to duplicate it elsewhere."

"I'll try harder to remember the name. Hardison's Multi-hypercordal Photophosphorescent—no, I've got it wrong again, I can tell by the look on your face."

Dexter bit his lip, then said the name again for her. "Multi-hyalchordate Phototransphorinating Seismograph."

"I do know the seismograph part," she assured him. "If I can ever get that far."

"You won't need to. The men have already given it another name, and I suspect that's the one that will stick." He sounded resigned, but not too upset about it.

"What do they call it?"

Dexter sighed. "The Glass Octopus." She snickered before she could help it, and he shook his head with a mock frown. "For shame, Charlotte. If people could only be bothered to remember their Greek and Latin roots . . ."

"You are like a balm to my soul," she murmured at him, stroking a hand up his cheek then feathering her fingers through his forelock. Dexter closed his eyes for a moment, leaning into the caress. Free from his gaze, Charlotte felt brave enough to take her final leap.

"I love you," she whispered, "and I want to keep being your wife. I want to go home with you and clutter up your bedroom with negligees and dancing slippers and frivolous hats."

Dexter opened his eyes and Charlotte quickly pressed two fingers over his lips before he could interrupt. Then she closed *her* eyes, because the look on his face was too much to take without bursting into tears, and if she did that she'd never finish.

"I want to plant an outrageous rose garden, since you said you didn't have one. With benches for trysting. I also want to have your children, but no more than three at the most. I want you to make me a new dirigible, in pretty colors, because I want people to see it this time, I intend to start a new craze for them. I want to do something useful, but not this anymore. Not being a spy. I'm not sure what, exactly. And as a shorter-term goal, I'd like to spend the trip home in this bunk with you, making love day and night until the crew becomes concerned for our safety and we're both sore in places we didn't know existed."

She punctuated the end of her speech with a huff of air, expelling the rest of her nervous energy, then dared a peek up at Dexter. He was propped on his elbows, looking down at her, blinking in amazement.

She blinked back at him. The silence grew until she couldn't take it anymore.

"Well?" she risked.

"I prefer to keep my bedroom tidy," Dexter said solemnly. Charlotte's heart soared.

"The frivolous hats are not negotiable," she insisted, ignoring the break in her tear-stricken voice. "I shall require them if I'm to be a fashionable young matron."

"Oh. Then perhaps I could design a special revolving hat stand. Or better still," he posited, warming to the idea, "outfit an entire room as a wardrobe, with cranks and levers to move the shelves about, and—"

"Dexter."

"I love you, Charlotte."

"I love you," she said again. "What a lucky thing we happened to marry one another."

Kissing ensued, but after a few seconds Dexter lifted his head and nuzzled the tip of her nose with his own, looking delighted.

"Mrs. Hardison."

Charlotte grinned. "*Lady* Hardison, if you please."

"Good heavens. I've created a baroness."

"You have indeed. Now whatever shall you do with her?"

Charlotte hardly needed to ask. She already knew Dexter had a limitless supply of ideas.

THE OLD MEN sitting in the front row presented Eliza Hardison with a uniform front of disapproval as she took her place at the lectern. She was accustomed to this, and told herself she didn't care. Every time, she told herself this. One day she might come to believe it.

"Ladies and gentlemen," she said firmly, then paused as if to wait for the smattering of polite applause that had greeted each previous speaker.

From out on the street, noises drifted in to fill the silence. A rumbling steam lorry, the honk of a horn. Somewhere in the back rows, a man cleared his throat.

"Ladies and gentlemen of the Society, thank you for this opportunity. Today I present for the first time my recent findings on the underpinnings of certain tenacious mythologies in the lower-class working culture, and the very real limiting effects those mythologies can have on behavior and the perception of available alternatives, with a final consideration of who might benefit from—"

It wasn't a throat-clearing. It was a snort, contemptuous and disruptive. This time, snickers of thinly veiled laughter radiated from the noise like rings in a pool, finally lapping up against the front row in a wave of raised eyebrows and frowns.

"With a final consideration of who might benefit most from what may at first appear to be a harmless superstition." She stared into the back of the lecture hall, waiting for further indirect commentary, then continued when she felt the audience growing restive. "Even in San Francisco, workers who disappear are said to 'go west,' never to return. While some argue that the fanciful term originated from tenant farmers abandoning their home lords' lands to become independent pioneers in the early days of the Dominions along the Atlantic Coast, the geographic inconsistency of the term's use along the Pacific suggests that it is purely metaphorical, a subconscious invocation of the great unknown . . ."

She spoke at length, clear and loud, projecting her voice to the back of the hall as she'd trained herself to do. At only twenty-three and fresh from university, Eliza was the youngest member of the Society for the Study and Improvement of Workplace Reform. She knew she couldn't afford to appear frivolous, not even for a moment.

Even now, as she neared the end of her speech and congratulated herself, she noted the mood of the crowd was still tenuous, liable to shift either way. There was some interest, some skepticism. The few old crones in the audience eyed her with the usual suspicion, looking for flightiness. Half the men in the front row were asleep. Of the remaining half, most looked bored, but several wore sour expressions that boded ill for the question-and-answer portion of her presentation.

Two were leering at her. Always the same two. She ignored them and gave her papers a neat tap on the podium to indicate she was finished. "Thank you. At this time I would be pleased to entertain your questions."

There was the usual scuffling, hemming and hawing, a few hands raised tentatively in the air then lowered just as quickly. Eliza was already preparing to leave. They never bothered with questions. Not for her. They only allowed her to speak because she was Eliza Chen's granddaughter, but she would continue until she had won her own place in the Society's esteem. Or perhaps, she thought some days, she would form her own damn reform society.

"Miss Chen!"

A murmur ran through the crowd, and the whisper of wool against upholstered seats as every head turned to the back of the house. A man stood in the next-to-last row, leaning on a cane in a somewhat dandified pose. His bright golden boutonniere caught the light, gleaming against his wine-colored jacket.

"It is Miss Hardison," Eliza reminded him. "Did you have a question for me, sir?"

Even across the many rows of seats, Eliza could see the man's smirk. His entire posture conveyed condescension. Instinctively, she braced herself.

"For the Society at large, rather. I came here today expecting to learn information beneficial to my business, from like-minded gentlemen with experience in industry. Instead, I apparently stumbled onto some sort of recital for children. To whom do I apply for a refund?"

The crowd's outburst ranged from horrified gasps to outright giggling, and Eliza could feel her control of the room slipping away as though it were palpable, a rope being yanked from her hands while she scrambled for purchase on treacherous ice.

"I say! I say! Order!" One of the senior members, the Duke of Trenton and Drexel, pounded his walking stick on the floor repeatedly, to no avail. "Order!"

"Did you have a question about the topic of my presentation, sir?" She lifted her voice, straining to be heard over the uproar. It was difficult to unclench her teeth enough to speak. The temptation to hurl insults was almost overwhelming.

The man chuckled, leaning to one of his companions to share something, then straightening and raising one indolent hand for silence. The crowd granted it, and Eliza knew with a sick certainty that she had lost any hope of salvaging the situation. Whoever he was, he had the audience now, and she could be no more than the punchline of whatever horrific joke he had planned.

"Tell the truth, Miss Hardison. You didn't do any research. You just had your nursemaid tell you some bedtimes stories, didn't you?" Over the laughter, he called out, "Do be careful on the way home, miss. You wouldn't want the bad men to get you and go west forever!"

The tide had turned for good. Anything she might say could only make things worse, and the only thing she could salvage was enough poise to make a dignified exit. With shaking hands, Eliza gathered her notes and made her way offstage, fumbling for a moment to find the gap in the velvet curtains. Her eyes were full of unshed tears, anger and mortification vying for control. She had bitten the inside of her cheek so hard she tasted blood.

When the hand curved around her elbow, she jerked away, ready to fight.

"Easy. Easy there, Miss Hardison. Stand down, it's only me."

She blinked rapidly, clearing her sight enough to recognize the man beside her. "Mr. Larken."

The mild-mannered elderly gentleman had been in charge of lecture arrangements since the Society's beginnings. He gave her an encouraging smile and, to her fierce gratitude, said nothing of her heckler.

"This way, please."

Eliza let him lead her swiftly from the wings and out a side door of the lecture hall. The noise and smell of the street rose up to greet them, harsh and acrid despite the cool spring air.

"What are we doing out here?" Eliza tried to catch the heavy door but it latched behind her before she could reach it. "Who *was* that man? I'd planned to have him ejected."

"His Grace asked me to make sure there was no trouble. To see you made it outside the building without further . . . harassment."

Of course. The Duke of Trenton and Drexel was a powerful patron to the Society, but shunned any hint of controversy like the plague. Larken hadn't been sent to secure her safe departure, but her quiet one. No public ejection of the heckler, no formal complaints. Bad enough the press would report the incident itself, no need to add ruffled feathers on top of that. She could almost hear the Duke's pompous, lugubrious voice speaking the words.

An ornate steam carriage pulled up before them on the cross-street, hissing and creaking to a halt. As she and Larken rounded the corner, Eliza realized it was one in a long line snaking down the street. She glanced at the lecture hall's doorway, half a block away. Her presentation had been the last of the day, and the attendees were starting to emerge.

"This is perfectly ridiculous. Are you going to let me back into the hall at some point? I've left my satchel and scarf inside, along with my driving things."

"Oh. By all means, miss. My apologies."

Eliza stopped again, just yards away from the entrance, when the next group issued from the door with her persecutor at their head. Sunlight caught his glistening boutonniere much as the light in the hall had, this time forcing Eliza to squint against the reflected glare. His companions wore similar fripperies, all in the latest style. No simple rosebuds, but elaborately enameled and jewel-encrusted flora limned in gold or platinum, often with tiny mechanisms that opened the petals of the "blossom" at the flick of a switch to reveal a secret compartment, or offered up a flame suitable for lighting a pipe.

"Do you know him?" she asked Larken. "The one with the gilded pansy whatsit in his lapel."

"I don't, Miss Hardison. He was the guest of one of the less regular members, and the name escapes me at the moment."

No name had escaped Larken's memory since his birth, Eliza was fairly certain.

"You're not planning to accost him, are you, miss?" the gentle old fellow asked in a quavering voice.

Eliza hadn't moved from her spot to the side of the entrance, nor did she intend to until the man left. Eliza might petition to have him tossed out on his ear, but she was no ill-bred harpy or impetuous child to fling harsh words on the open street. Much as she might wish to. Instead she bit the much-abused inside of her cheek once again, forcing back the many unladylike sentiments she longed to hurl at the heckler's sleek top-hat-covered head. The man's dull brown, silver-streaked hair was long, clubbed back with a black velvet ribbon, and she noted uncharitably that the rakish style did not flatter his narrow, unremarkable features. It was too much for him, like his flashy suit and flashier jewelry, almost as though he were all costume, no content.

"Of course not, Mr. Larken. That would be begging for trouble, and I assure you I want none."

The man and his cohorts entered their ornate carriage, and Eliza breathed a little easier as the threat of confrontation passed. But just as the heckler turned to take his seat, his eyes lit on Eliza through the open carriage window, and his look of icy calculation chilled her to the bone.

He did not look at all like the flippant dandy who'd ruined her presentation, and possibly her professional reputation to boot, with his boorish humor. In that unguarded moment, swift but unmistakable, his gaze had revealed both intelligence and malevolent speculation. Eliza wasn't sure which she found more troublesome.

THE LATCH ON the boiler's cover was stuck, and Eliza knew she was about to spoil a glove getting it open. She didn't care, as long as she made it to her cousin's party in time to wish him a happy birthday. That, at least, might end her day on a positive note. Nearly anything would be better than her experience at the lecture.

The India rubber gasket sucked at the lid, keeping it closed, resisting her tug. When it finally popped open, a spray of superheated droplets caught Eliza's forearm above the kid glove, prompting a curse she would never have uttered if she hadn't been alone.

Though she was standing in a relatively safe zone, Eliza

still felt her hair and dress wilt in the steam. She waved the hand with the stained, crumpled glove to disperse the vapor, and peered at the inner boiler casing and cooling tank gauge in dismay.

"Bloody hell!"

A gently cleared throat startled her and she jumped back from the velocimobile. A fresh puff of steam clouded the face of the intruder for a moment.

"Pardon. Can I be of any assistance?"

The voice was smooth, pleasant. The gloved hand that waved the steam away this time was elegant, the glove itself expensive and pristine. And the face . . .

"You."

"Oh! Eliza, I had no idea you were back from school. Welcome home."

With a sigh, Eliza stepped back toward the velocimobile and faced the interloper over the hot boiler.

"Matthew, an unexpected pleasure. May I assume you're also on your way to my cousin's party?" She tucked the offending glove behind her back and hoped the rest of her appearance wasn't too unkempt. She'd paid little thought to her appearance when she changed out of her lecture suit. The snug driving helmet kept her plaited hair in place, and her lightweight coat and split skirt were sorely wrinkled and coated with road dust. She would have to do, she supposed. It was only Matthew, after all; he was used to seeing her streaked with engine grease, although it had certainly been awhile since he'd seen her at all. Nearly four years, she realized with a start.

"Indeed I am. Are you having trouble with your boiler? I know a little about engines, as you know, I might be able to help—"

"No!" Eliza bit her tongue and smiled sweetly. "No, thank you, you mustn't trouble yourself. Please, proceed to the party. I have matters well in hand. I know more than a little about engines, as you may recall."

Hubris, her hindbrain warned. *That never ends well.* Eliza ignored the warning. She could handle things quite well alone. After that morning's set-down at the lecture hall, the last thing she wanted was the company of a man who assumed her less than competent merely because she was younger and female.

If Eliza'd had a big brother, Matthew would have given him a run for his money when she was growing up. He had never let her tag along when it came to working on the truly exciting projects. He found her interest in delicate clockwork devices charming and appropriate for a young lady, but not so her interest in things like locomotive engines and velocimobiles. And he always, always pointed out that she could lose a finger in the machinery, as if the mere prospect of such a hazard should be enough to dissuade any properly brought-up girl. As if he were not himself at the same risk. But if you didn't take that risk, how could you find out what made the thing *go*?

The early afternoon sun shone through the dark bronze of Matthew Pence's hair, lending him a halo that Eliza couldn't help but view as ironic.

"I'll put myself at your disposal," he insisted. She didn't remember him as being so obnoxiously chivalrous. "Consider me your minion. With two of us working, surely you'll be able to repair your vehicle more quickly?"

"It's just overheated," she explained. "Or nearly so. It ran close to dry but I caught it in time. There's really nothing to do but wait for it to cool enough to add more water. My own fault, I'm afraid, I've been stopping frequently to take photographs and letting the engine idle too long. This one builds up steam quickly, which is convenient, but it needs close minding because it's so small."

And it needed a thorough tune-up, something she hadn't been able to accomplish often enough while attending college. Poughkeepsie hadn't been much of a town for motoring, though had she needed to render a whale for blubber she would have been in the perfect place.

The young man leaned his weight onto one foot, settling into a pose common among fashionable toffs of the day. It irritated Eliza, who knew it was just an affectation he adopted out in public, for polite society. A pretense that he was still a son of privilege rather than a machinery-loving apostate. He had always been good at blending in, though, becoming part of the prevalent social scenery. In some ways she envied him that skill. "Photographs? Flora or fauna?"

"Workers who claim their lost loved ones have 'gone west,' never to return again," she told him, daring him with her eyes to take her up on this topic. "I photograph them holding portraits of the missing. I was also conducting interviews and gathering anecdotal data. I've noticed some interesting correlations."

Matthew raised an eyebrow, but didn't take the bait as he once might have. Back in the days when she had run into him frequently at Dexter Hardison's factory, Pence would have been the first to chide Eliza for taking such a risk, haring off on her own and talking to strangers.

Now it seemed he had lost some of that interest in her welfare, or perhaps simply developed more circumspection about stating it. In fact, Eliza thought, he seemed a bit distracted in general. Perhaps it was the problem of the engine. It was clear he still itched to get his fingers on it.

He wore a metal flower on his chest, a sleek, stylized, closed lily bud in some silver brushed metal. It was far more understated than her heckler's had been, but it reminded her of the man all the same. She wondered if Pence knew him.

"Hardison House is only twenty or so miles from here," Matthew pointed out. "I'd be more than happy to give you a lift, so you can make the party sooner. It wouldn't do to cross Charlotte by being late. She's inclined to be touchy these days."

"I suspect she has good reason."

Eliza thought she'd be touchy too if she were as tiny as Charlotte, Lady Hardison, but carrying the undoubtedly huge child of a man the size of her cousin Dexter. Because she was nearly as small as Charlotte, the very idea daunted Eliza. She had recently vowed only to look at slight, slender men as spousal prospects should she ever decide to marry. Preferably men with smallish heads and narrow shoulders.

Pence's shoulders were rather broad, like most makesmiths', despite his fashionable slimness. It made her even more irked at him, though she knew she was being unreasonable because of the incident at the lecture. She couldn't help it; she resented those effortlessly capable-looking shoulders.

"I'll be fine," Eliza said firmly. "I don't require help, but I thank you for the offer." She procured a large bottle of water from under the seat of the vehicle, then used a funnel to add a slow trickle of liquid to the cooling unit. "In fact, you should start off again now or I'll beat you to the party."

In Pence's smug chuckle, Eliza heard the first hint of the younger version she remembered. "Not likely. You never could have before."

"Really? A dare? Would you care to wager on that? I'm more than old enough to gamble now, lest you be concerned for my morals." She was already tightening the fittings, closing up the boiler and securing the latch. A bet would make the last few miles to Dexter's party fly by.

Sadly, Pence declined to make it as interesting as he could have. "Certainly, Miss Hardison. If I win—and I don't mind saying I intend to—I'll claim the first waltz of the evening from you once the dancing starts."

"I . . . oh, fine then. Fair enough." Eliza was not inclined to waltz with anyone, least of all with Matthew Pence. But she didn't plan to lose, so it seemed a safe enough stake. No need to tell her competition about the Leyden jar battery cleverly concealed beneath the velocimobile's seat, and the boost its charge would give to her starting speed until the boiler reached full steam. "If I win, I'll claim fifty pounds and when my book is published you'll put an endorsement in the *Times*. Quarter-page at least."

The terms took him aback, it was clear, but he covered nicely. "All right. May I ask what this book is about? A novel, perhaps? I didn't know you had writing aspirations, those must be new."

With a final yank to the boiler cover's handle, Eliza cranked the engine until it kicked into life, then stalked back to the velocimobile's seat where she stowed the half-empty water jug and funnel before she strapped herself in. "It's a monograph on worker–landowner negotiation inequities and the impact of subliminal psychological manipulation by authority figures on common laborers."

Grinning at Pence's look of dismayed astonishment, she released the handbrake and engaged the gears simultaneously, triggering the start capacitor.

"Ready, steady, go, Matthew!" she called back to him, as he belatedly ran for his steam car.

*First in an all-new series where
seductive danger and steampunk adventure abound
in the gritty world of the Iron Seas.*

FROM *NEW YORK TIMES* BESTSELLING AUTHOR

MELJEAN BROOK

The

A

After freeing F

Trahaearn has

Detective Inspe

gerous world to

intends to mak

NEW ORIGINAL BONUS NOVELLA AVAILABLE

IN THE MASS MARKET VERSION!

facebook.com/ProjectParanormalBooks
penguin.com